Praise for *The Apocalypse of Elena Mendoza*

★ "Provocative and moving . . .
A thoughtful story about choice and destiny."
—*Publishers Weekly,* starred review

★ "Hutchinson artfully blends the realistic and the surreal. . . .
An entirely original take on apocalyptic fiction."
—*School Library Journal,* starred review

Praise for *At the Edge of the Universe*

★ "An earthy, existential coming-of-age gem."
—*Kirkus Reviews,* starred review

## Praise for *We Are the Ants*

★ "Bitterly funny, with a ray of hope amid bleakness."
—*Kirkus Reviews,* starred review

"A beautiful, masterfully told story by someone
who is at the top of his craft."
—*Lambda Literary*

★ "Shaun David Hutchinson's bracingly smart and unusual
YA novel blends existential despair with exploding planets."
—*Shelf Awareness,* starred review

## Praise for *The Past and Other Things That Should Stay Buried*

"A fearless and brutal look at friendships and the emotional
autopsies we all do when they die. Like a real relationship, you
will laugh, rage, and mourn its loss when it's over. If you haven't
been reading Hutchinson, this is a brilliant place to start."
—Justina Ireland,
*New York Times* bestselling author of *Dread Nation*

"Simultaneously hilarious and moving, weird and wonderful.
Have you been looking for a zombie book that will make you
laugh and cry? Look no further than this one, by one of
young adult literature's sharpest talents."
—Jeff Zentner,
William C. Morris Award–winning
author of *The Serpent King*

ALSO BY SHAUN DAVID HUTCHINSON

*Brave Face: A Memoir*

*The Past and Other Things That Should Stay Buried*

*Feral Youth*

*At the Edge of the Universe*

*We Are the Ants*

*Violent Ends*

*The Five Stages of Andrew Brawley*

*fml*

*The Deathday Letter*

# THE
# APOCALYPSE
## OF
# ELENA
# MENDOZA

## SHAUN DAVID HUTCHINSON

**SIMON PULSE**

NEW YORK  LONDON  TORONTO  SYDNEY  NEW DELHI

SIMON PULSE

An imprint of Simon & Schuster Children's Publishing Division

1230 Avenue of the Americas, New York, New York 10020

First Simon Pulse paperback edition May 2019

Text copyright © 2018 by Shaun David Hutchinson

Cover illustration copyright © 2019 by Jon Contino

Also available in a Simon Pulse hardcover edition.

All rights reserved, including the right of reproduction in whole or in part in any form.

SIMON PULSE and colophon are registered trademarks of Simon & Schuster, Inc.

For information about special discounts for bulk purchases, please contact Simon & Schuster Special Sales at 1-866-506-1949 or business@simonandschuster.com.

The Simon & Schuster Speakers Bureau can bring authors to your live event. For more information or to book an event contact the Simon & Schuster Speakers Bureau at 1-866-248-3049 or visit our website at www.simonspeakers.com.

Cover designed by Sarah Creech

Interior designed by Nina Simoneaux

The text of this book was set in Adobe Garamond.

Manufactured in the United States of America

2 4 6 8 10 9 7 5 3 1

The Library of Congress has catalogued the hardcover edition as follows:

Names: Hutchinson, Shaun David, author.

Title: The apocalypse of Elena Mendoza / by Shaun David Hutchinson.

Description: First Simon Pulse hardcover edition. | New York : Simon Pulse, 2018. |

Summary: Elena, the first scientifically confirmed virgin birth, acquires the ability to heal by touch at age sixteen, the same year that people start disappearing in beams of light, causing her to wonder if she is bringing about the Apocalypse.

Identifiers: LCCN 2017020322 (print) | LCCN 2017037003 (eBook) |

ISBN 9781481498548 (hardcover) | ISBN 9781481498555 (paperback) |

ISBN 9781481498562 (eBook)

Subjects: | CYAC: Healers—Fiction. | Missing persons—Fiction. | End of the world—Fiction. | Miracles—Fiction. | Virgin birth—Fiction. | Science fiction.

Classification: LCC PZ7.H96183 (eBook) | LCC PZ7.H96183 Apo 2018 (print) |

DDC [Fic]—dc23

LC record available at https://lccn.loc.gov/2017020322

*To Amy Boggs: Thank you for helping
me end the world one last time*

# ONE

THE APOCALYPSE BEGAN at Starbucks. Where else did you expect the end of the world to start?

The man standing at the pickup counter lowered his cell phone and glowered at me. "Did you hear me say nonfat?"

I'd heard him say it the first time. And the second, third, and fourth. I pressed the button on the espresso machine and lowered the steam wand into the pitcher of nonfat milk, blasting the surface with bubbles. "Hold up," I shouted over the hiss. "You wanted nonfat milk?" The name on his cup said "Greg." He looked like a Greg. Or a serial killer. Maybe both.

"Yes," said Greg. "It's the milk with no fat in it."

"Glad you were here to clear that up for me. Who knows what I might have put in your drink otherwise."

My shift manager, Kyle, stood at the register and flashed

me a quick grin while simultaneously rolling his eyes. I finished the man's double tall nonfat with whip mocha and passed it across the counter to him. He didn't need to know I'd slipped him two shots of decaf, but I was sure whoever he was going home to would thank me for it.

Fadil Himsi had been standing unobtrusively on the other side of the counter, waiting for me to finish. "What a dick," he said when the man was out of earshot. Fadil had thick dark hair, wide eyes accentuated by heavy black-rimmed glasses, and full lips that hid an almost buck-toothed grin. More geek than chic, he had a body built for running rather than fighting, which kind of worked for him. Not that he did much of either, preferring to spend his time playing his trumpet or tinkering with his computer.

"I wish he was the exception." I washed out my milk pitcher and cleaned the area behind the bar. I was a little overzealous about keeping my station orderly, and it bugged me when I took over from someone who left dirty spoons lying around and dried milk caked on the wands.

"So what're you doing here?" I asked. "Don't you have band practice?"

Living in Arcadia, Florida, meant that there was little to do aside from slowly develop skin cancer at the beach, complain about how there was nothing to do in Arcadia, or hang out at the only Starbucks in town and complain about how there was nothing to do in Arcadia. I both loved and hated my job. Loved because it let me help Mama with the bills and got me out of the apartment; hated because half of my classmates eventually showed up there at one point or another, and I wasn't exactly popular at Arcadia West High.

Fadil shook his head. "Mrs. Naam's sick. And I was kind of hoping to run into someone here."

"Is it Gemma Darville? I've seen the way she gives you the googly eyes."

"It's not Gemma."

"Then who?"

Fadil didn't get the chance to answer because a horde of customers, who must have coordinated their entrance to overwhelm us, rushed in all at once and I was distracted by cappuccinos and Frappuccinos and getting yelled at for not steaming the milk to exactly 173 degrees like I'd been ordered to. People take their stupid coffee way too seriously. It goes in the face hole and comes out an entirely different hole, but it probably doesn't taste much different coming out as going in.

Look, I know Starbucks is like the McDonald's of coffee stores and that all I was really doing was pressing buttons and steaming milk, but when a rush came in and I was making three and four drinks at a time, I felt like I had eight arms. I lost myself in the rhythm of pulling shots and steaming milk and blending ice. It was, in its own weird way, cathartic. Which is why I didn't notice Freddie standing at the counter until I set her drink down—a caramel Frappuccino with whipped cream and extra drizzle on top—and called her name.

Winifred Petrine—Freddie to most everyone—wasn't paying attention and hadn't heard me. She stood to the side, looking cute in a pink jersey top and jeans that hugged her hips, staring at her phone. Curls of sapphire-blue hair fell over her cheeks, and I couldn't stop admiring her.

*Ugh! Just say hi already and stop mooning at her like an idiot.*

"What?" I said.

Freddie looked up. "What?"

"I didn't say anything."

"You said 'what.'"

Was I turning red? My cheeks were hot and I'm sure I was blushing like crazy. I pushed Freddie's drink toward her. "Your caramel Frappuccino with extra drizzle."

Freddie made this face where her right eyebrow arched up, her left down, and her lips puckered as if she wasn't sure whether to thank me or check to see if I'd poisoned her drink. "Yeah," she said. "Thanks."

I turned and glared at the siren logo grinning at me from the stack of cups to my right. "I don't need your help."

*She's only a girl, Elena. And one with horrible taste in frozen drinks. You could do better.*

"Shut up," I mumbled under my breath. I hated the siren

logo, and not simply because she offered unsolicited relationship advice. She was creepy, all smiles with her two tails and
boobs hanging out.

Fadil cleared his throat; I'd forgotten he was standing
there. "Were you whispering to the cups?"

"What were we talking about?" I asked. "That's right. You
were going to spill who you came here hoping to see since
you obviously didn't drop by for my entertaining company."

Fadil knew more about me than any friend I'd ever had.
He knew about my virgin birth, he knew I poured the milk
into my bowl before the cereal, he knew I'd had a crush on
Freddie since sixth grade, and he knew the fastest way to piss
me off was for someone to drag their fork against their teeth
while eating. He did not, however, know about the voices I'd
heard since I was a young girl. There was only so much honesty a friendship could survive.

"Why didn't you talk to Freddie? Wasn't that the perfect
opportunity just now?"

I glanced toward the front of the store. Most of the café
tables were occupied by Arcadia West students pretending
to do homework or by the regulars who came for the free
Wi-Fi, so Freddie had taken her drink to the patio, which
was mostly empty because it was September in Florida and
still ninety degrees. The only other person outside was a boy
I'd seen hanging around before but didn't know.

"I think flirting while on the clock is against company policy."

"Is that in the official employee handbook?"

"Right under the section about not allowing friends to distract you while you're working."

A burst of laughter exploded from one of the tables in the corner where Tori Thrash and her friends were pointing at someone's drink that had fallen onto the floor and spilled everywhere. Michael caught me looking and called out, "Clean up on aisle five, Mary!" which everyone at their table seemed to think was hilarious.

Maya came back from her break reeking of cigarettes and nudged my shoulder. "Kyle said to take out the trash and then go on your ten."

"Great," I said, motioning at the coffee puddle, "then you get to take care of that."

"Elena!"

"Sorry, I'm on my ten." I turned to Fadil. "Meet me around back?" He nodded, and I quickly gathered the garbage and carried it into the stockroom. I stripped off my apron, hung it on my locker, and heaved the pile of trash bags out the back door.

*Whatever happens next, Elena, don't be scared.*

The siren's voice blasted me from every box of coffee and sleeve of cups stacked on the wire racks. I even heard her from the cups in the trash. It was the worst surround sound ever.

"It smells terrible, sure," I said. "But why would I be afraid of the garbage?"

*You'll see.*

"Whatever."

I'd grown accustomed to the presence of the voices. Sometimes they helped me, like when I was six and got lost in the mall and a horse on a broken merry-go-round told me what store to find Mama in. Other times they spoke in cryptic riddles, which I ignored. Either way, the voices were an inconsistent constant in my life. I might go weeks without hearing them, but they never disappeared permanently.

Fadil met me near the Dumpster and helped me toss the trash bags inside.

"What're you doing Saturday?" I asked. "Want to catch a movie and maybe hit the comic book store?"

Fadil sucked air through his teeth. "Yeah. So I was kind of planning to go to the renaissance festival with some of the marching band crew."

"Oh."

"You should come," he said. "I swear it's more fun than it sounds. I'll buy you one of those giant turkey legs you love so much."

I shook my head. "No, it's all right."

Fadil shoved his hands in his pockets and we stood by the

Dumpster inhaling the fragrant scent of spoiled milk and old pastries. "You know what? Forget it. I can go with them next weekend. Jack spent weeks working on his corset and gown and is determined to wear it as often as he can, so it's not like I won't have plenty of chances to go."

"Really?" I perked up, a smile lifting my cheeks. "You don't have to—"

"It's done," Fadil said. "Besides, I've been dying to see that indie film. The one where everyone gets a letter the day they're going to die?"

"You're the best."

Fadil squared his shoulders and held his head high and proud. "I know."

"Kind lord, how can I ever repay you?" I said, affecting my worst British accent.

"Well, since you mentioned it," he said. "I hear you're in a study group with Naomi Brewer."

"Come on." I motioned for Fadil to follow me around the side of the store to the parking lot. My stomach was rumbling and there was a sandwich shop next door. "Trig. As usual, I'll get stuck doing all the work. Why?"

"I was hoping you could maybe arrange for me to randomly run into you guys while you were studying."

I fake gagged when I realized what Fadil was asking. "Naomi? Really?"

"She's cute! And smart and she's into K-pop and did I mention she's smart?"

"Twice," I said. "But didn't she get caught copying off one of your tests freshman year, causing you both to get a zero?"

"That was Callie Schumer."

"Whose best friend is Naomi."

"Was."

"What?"

"Callie was her best friend," Fadil said. "They don't talk anymore."

"How the hell do you know all of this? Do you have audio-recording devices in the girls' locker rooms?"

Fadil frowned. "What kind of boy do you think I am? If I were going to bug the locker rooms, I'd obviously prioritize video over audio."

I laughed in spite of myself.

"Will you do it?"

"I don't know," I said. "It's kind of weird. And it's Naomi Brewer!"

Fadil's thick eyebrows dipped to form a V. "Is it that much stranger than your weird thing for Freddie, to whom you've barely even spoken?"

"No fair."

"Totally fair."

I sighed. "Fine, I'll think about it."

We reached the front of the patio, where Fadil grabbed my arm and pulled me to a stop. "Go talk to her."

"Who?"

He motioned at Freddie with his chin. "She's sitting alone. You couldn't ask for a better setup."

"I smell like trash, my hair is a mess, and what am I supposed to say? 'Hi, I'm Elena and I'll be your creepy stalker for the afternoon?'"

Fadil tapped his chin dramatically. "Well, the first part works, but I'd leave out the stalker bit."

"I'm not doing it."

"What if I go with you?"

"Right," I said. "Because flirting is so much cooler with your best friend tagging along for emotional support." I tugged his shirt. "Besides, I'm hungry and I only have ten minutes."

Fadil gave me a shove and shouted, "Hey, Freddie!" in her direction before scurrying behind a car. Yes, I was going to kill him. Slowly and painfully. But now Freddie was looking at me and I think she was smiling, though she could have been confused, and I had no choice but to approach her and try to make word sounds without accidentally biting off my tongue.

Everyone knows someone they've admired from afar but were too intimidated to ever consider actually talking to because their mere presence triggers spontaneous desert mouth or uncontrollable babbling. That person, for me, was

Winifred Petrine. She was so out of my league that, while I'd definitely had a crush on her for a long time, I'd never seriously entertained the thought of asking her out, because I preferred the people I hit on to not hit me back.

The walk to Freddie's table felt endless even though it was only a few feet. My brain created a million scenarios where I introduced myself. In most, I ended up drooling or tripped at the last minute, face-planted on the sidewalk, and broke my nose. None ended with me asking Freddie out and her accepting. I finally reached the table and opened my mouth to speak. I did not drool. I didn't speak to Freddie either, because someone bumped me from behind.

"Excuse you," I said, turning around.

The boy who'd run into me stood uncomfortably close. He was the one who'd been sitting at the other table, and he looked like a baby freshman with an undercut and the bangs of his soft blond hair swept back and styled into a pompadour. He wore cargo shorts and a short-sleeve green plaid button-up. He was holding a flat-black gun in a hand that seemed too small and delicate to wield it.

"Elena Mendoza?" the boy asked in a soft voice.

I froze. My brain was screaming I should run or hide or knee the boy in the balls, but I couldn't decide which to do, so I stood there unable to move at all.

"I . . ."

The boy raised the gun, aimed, and fired. The shot deafened me, and I was certain for a moment that I was dead. That he'd put a bullet in me and I was going to bleed to death in front of Starbucks. But he hadn't shot me. He'd shot Freddie. He'd shot her and then backed up two steps.

Freddie slid out of her seat, and I fell to my knees beside her, pressing my hands to the wound in her stomach. Blood spread across her blouse and I yelled for help. I heard Fadil calling my name, but his voice was an echo across a vast chasm, too far away.

You're a story. I'm a story. There are 7.5 billion stories on the planet. Two hundred and fifty new stories begin each minute, and 105 stories end. It's easy to allow the world to collapse down to our own stories. To see ourselves as the central figure in the only story worth knowing and forget that every person we encounter is living their own, is the center of their own universe. But that's the nature of the human experience. That's why the patio felt so small as I ignored Fadil's shouting and the boy with the gun and focused on the blue-haired girl who was smiling as she died. Her skin was moist and ashen, her eyelids fluttered, but she was smiling at me like I was the only person in the world who mattered.

*Time to shine, Elena!*

The voice hit me from the siren signs in the window and the one on Freddie's cup and even from the ones on the wad of napkins stuffed under the table leg to level it.

"What am I supposed to do?" I asked.

*Heal her, obviously.*

"How the hell am I supposed to do that?"

*Do I have to explain everything?*

"Yes!"

I kept pressure against the wound in a vain attempt to stop Freddie's blood from escaping, but every beat of her weakening heart pushed more of it through the gaps between my fingers.

*You're wasting time, Elena. Consider that the volume of a human's blood makes up approximately 7 percent of their body weight. Winifred Petrine weighs 156 pounds, which means her body should contain four liters of blood. How much of that do you think is puddled on the ground? How much more do you think she can lose and still survive?*

"Then tell me what to do," I begged. "How am I supposed to heal her?"

*You just do it. If you don't, Winifred Petrine will die. Ticktock, Elena.*

It was ludicrous. The voice from the sirens expected me to magically heal a gunshot wound? I had no idea where to even begin. But the voice was right. Freddie had lost so much blood. Too much. If I couldn't stop the bleeding soon, she wouldn't survive.

A shadow fell over me. Over us. I didn't need to look up to know who it was.

"Are you going to shoot me?" My voice trembled, but my hands remained steady against the wound in Freddie's stomach. I looked over my shoulder at the boy. He appeared even younger than I'd first thought. His cheeks were dusted with downy hair, freckles dotted his nose, and he had this dimple in his chin. I'd expected to find nothing in his eyes. A cold, inhuman vacancy. Instead they were red-rimmed and broken. They were hurting. He was hurting.

The boy pointed the gun at me. I'd never seen a real one up close. It resembled the toys my little brother was constantly begging Mama to buy him. "Hi, Elena," he said.

He knew my name. I tried to recall ever meeting him, but I would have sworn I hadn't. "I don't—"

"Was your mom really a virgin when you were born?" The gun twitched.

"Yes," I whispered.

"Did God make you?" he asked. "Do you think he'd intervene if I shot you?"

"I don't believe in God." Kneeling on the patio of a Starbucks while the girl I had a crush on was dying and a strange boy was pointing a gun at me was the wrong place to start a theological debate, but the words had spilled out before I could stop them.

The boy blinked mechanically, like he was a computer processing what I'd said instead of an actual human being. "I don't think I do either." He pointed at Freddie with the gun. "She's bleeding to death."

"Because you shot her."

*Come on, Elena! Heal her! Heal her now!*

I choked off my fear, reaching inside for every ounce of courage I possessed to look the boy in the eye and speak without my voice quivering. "I'm going to try to help her now. If you're planning on killing me, I'd appreciate it if you'd wait until I finish."

The boy chuckled. With a gun pointed at me and Freddie dying, he had the nerve to laugh. "My mom would have liked you."

It was such an unusual thing to say that I nearly faltered. But then Freddie groaned, drawing my attention back to her. If the boy was going to shoot me, I couldn't stop him, but maybe I had the power to save Freddie.

Since the siren hadn't told me how I was supposed to heal Freddie, I closed my eyes and hoped for the best.

I felt like I'd been plunged into an isolation tank. No sight or sound or touch or taste or smell. But there was something else. A sense of Freddie where there'd been nothing before. I reached out to her and I wasn't alone in the dark anymore. She was there with me. Her body was traced in lines of impossible colors of liquid fire. And in her stomach was a gaping hole. A density that was sucking in the outlines of her body, devouring her quickly dimming light. Instinctively, I understood that the black hole was the gunshot wound. All I had to do was reach out and heal it. The darkness in Freddie's stomach evaporated and the light of her body flared so bright I thought it might blind me.

Freddie gasped. She screamed. I opened my eyes and lifted my blood-covered hands. It was real. I'd done it. I yanked back Freddie's shirt, which still sported the bullet hole, and found no wound. Nothing but smooth, flawless, blood-covered skin.

"How did you—" the boy began. He never finished. A bright, narrow beam of light streaked from the sky to envelop him. It was molten gold and it reached from the heavens to the ground in a straight line. It was beautiful and awful, and then I blinked and it was gone. I blinked and the boy was gone. The gun fell where he, only a second earlier, had stood, prepared to shoot me.

But Winifred Petrine was alive. She'd seen me and she'd smiled and I'd healed her, and she was going to live.

# TWO

MY MOTHER NAMED me Elena after a character in her favorite book; Maria, as a dig at her own mother's religious beliefs; and Mendoza because, even though my grandmother hadn't tried to stop him, it had been my grandfather's decision to kick Mama out of the house when they'd found out she was pregnant, and not keeping his last name was my mother's way of telling him that he exerted no power over her anymore.

Despite the stories floating around on the Internet, I wasn't born in a barn or at the beach at sunrise. I wasn't born in a hospital, either—which is one of the few things the stories usually get right. I actually entered the world bloody and squalling in the parking lot of a 7-Eleven. My mother's water broke while she was standing in line to purchase a blue raspberry slushie and a pack of Camels. It's pretty easy to crap on my mother for smoking while she was pregnant, but she was sixteen, homeless, and not exactly known for making awesome life choices. Also, she hadn't asked the Holy Spirit to knock her up and ruin her life.

The same way I hadn't asked to be born of a virgin.

So the whole "virgin birth" thing. I get that it's difficult to accept. No one believed my mother at first either. They called her a liar. Her parents, the paramedics who picked us up from the parking lot of the 7-Eleven, the social workers who occasionally popped by to check on her for the first couple of years of my life. Most thought my mother was too scared to admit who the father was. Some thought she might have even been raped, but my mother continued insisting she was a virgin.

Some mothers in Pakistan give birth in an isolated building called a Bashleni, which men don't enter for fear of "polluting" themselves, and which only other women who are menstruating enter to assist the mother during birth. And the Wolof people of Mauritania believe that saliva retains the power of words, so when a baby is born, the women spit on its face and the men spit in its ears in order to bless it. No one spit on me, but they may as well have spit on my mother, and it wasn't to bless her. In the early days of my life, strangers called her a whore, a slut, a liar. Later some of those same idiots would call her holy and sainted, but I never forgot what they'd first named her.

My story, and my mother's, attracted the attention of Dr. Willard Milner, who eventually proved that I was, in fact, the product of parthenogenesis. It's a process that occurs in some insects where an offspring is born from an unfertilized egg—though, in humans, the process had never produced a viable child.

Until me.

Parthenogenesis is derived from the Greek words "parthenos," which means "virgin," and "genesis," which means "creation."

The truth is that parthenogenesis isn't unheard of in humans, though two rare events are required to occur for it to take place. The first is that an unfertilized egg needs to detect a spike in cellular calcium, which is usually provided by the attacking sperm, in order for it to begin to behave as if it's been fertilized. Then the process of meiosis, during which the egg loses half of its genetic material, needs to be interrupted.

Both of these things actually occur in the eggs of one out of every couple thousand women. The problem is that without the sperm to provide specific genetic instructions, the parthenogenetic embryo grows tumorlike and quickly dies. For the embryo to develop into a healthy child, a pair of the mother's genes needs to be eliminated.

It's theoretically possible but practically improbable. Outside of a lab, anyway.

In 2004, scientists in Japan successfully manipulated a mouse's genes to cause an unfertilized egg to develop parthenogenetically into a viable and healthy baby mouse, and in 2016, scientists at the University of Bath successfully bred mice using a parthenogenetically created embryo that they later added sperm cells to, proving that it wasn't necessary to start conception with an egg and sperm.

I, however, was not created in a lab.

Depending on who you ask, I am either a miracle from God or a statistical aberration. According to Dr. Milner, my mother was not the first to claim her child was the product of a virgin birth, but she was the first to have that claim tested, tested again, and verified.

There was initially some outrage from religious groups over the claims that I was the product of a virgin birth, and I was a scientific oddity for a while, but eventually, especially after I didn't grow horns by my second birthday, I drifted into obscurity. I became a footnote in scientific journals and on rarely visited Wikipedia pages. My mother chose not to hide the nature of my miracle birth from me, but we rarely discussed it. When asked about my father, I usually said he didn't exist, which was literally the truth, though most assumed I meant he was a deadbeat or in prison. For sixteen years I lived a normal life—I went to school, took care of my little brother and sister, hung out with my best friend, Fadil, and complained about my ex-boyfriend, Javi—but due to the unique circumstances of my birth, I'd spent most of my normal life waiting for the chance to do something extraordinary. And the voices—which I was pretty certain were not a symptom of an undiagnosed mental illness—had only reinforced my belief that I was destined for more, though they hadn't given me any hints as to what "more" might entail.

The healing and the light from the sky? Yeah. Those were new.

# THREE

DEPUTY AKERS STOOD in front of me with her hands on her hips, staring with this bewildered expression, like I'd handed her a Rubik's Cube with all the stickers peeled off and had ordered her to solve it in ten seconds or less. She was kind of hot for an older woman, though her ponytail was tragic.

"Walk me through it again, if you would, Ms. Mendoza."

I sat on the curb, as far from the spot where Freddie had been shot as possible, and took a deep breath. Fadil glanced at me from where he was giving a statement to a different police officer. We hadn't had time before the police and paramedics had arrived to decide whether we were going to tell the truth. Kyle had rushed out from inside, along with twenty kids from my school, to gawk and ask what had happened.

I hadn't had the chance to speak to Freddie, either, because the paramedics who rolled up had taken her immediately to the hospital, even though they couldn't find an injury. I wondered what she was going to tell the police when they got around to questioning her.

"I was on a ten-minute break. I walked to that table to talk to Freddie—"

Deputy Akers broke in. "That would be Winifred Petrine?"

I nodded. "Some boy I swear I don't know bumped into me, asked me if I was Elena Mendoza, and then shot Freddie."

"And your claim is that you healed this gunshot wound?"

"Yes."

"Have you ever healed anyone before?"

"Not to my knowledge."

Akers bit her lip in a way that might have been cute if this weren't the third time I'd gone over my story. "Are you sure that Ms. Petrine was actually shot?"

I held up my hands, still tacky with Freddie's blood, and pointed toward the quickly drying stain on the cement. The police had cordoned off the area, and Kyle had closed the store. "That's not menstrual blood on the ground, Deputy."

"Uh . . ." Akers cleared her throat. "Could the shooter have injured himself? Is that possible?"

This was getting me nowhere. "Right," I said. "He walked

up to us, shot himself, and then vanished in a beam of light."

"About that," Deputy Akers said. "Now, you claim that after you healed Ms. Petrine, the shooter disappeared? If your friend was injured, you would have been under a great deal of stress. Is it possible he simply ran away?"

"Sure, whatever. Maybe he ran away after he hurt himself and splattered his blood all over me, Freddie, and the ground."

"There's no need to get defensive. I'm simply trying to understand what happened here." Akers paused. "Can you recall what the shooter looked like? Would you be willing to sit with one of our sketch artists and provide a description of the attacker?"

The boy's face was burned into my memory. But before I answered, a white van with a picture of a smiling cocker spaniel under the words MOBILE GROOM WAGGIN' tore into the parking lot and screeched to a halt at the edge of the police line. My mother practically fell out of the driver's seat and ran toward me, pushing past cops and onlookers and reporters.

"Mija!" She was still wearing her khaki shorts and Groom Waggin' T-shirt. I stood as she reached me and let her pull me into a hug that threatened to squeeze the breath from me. "Are you hurt? What happened?"

I diplomatically detached myself from my mother.

Genetically we were identical, but she had better hair and legs than me and at the moment she reeked of wet dog. "I'm fine," I said. "I'm not hurt."

Mama caught sight of Fadil and said, "Is it Fadil? They told me someone was shot, but they wouldn't tell me who. Where are his parents?"

"Fadil's fine too. His mom's in surgery at the outpatient clinic, and they're still trying to get ahold of his dad."

Everyone reacts differently to extreme situations. Freddie's shooting had been my first, and apparently I reacted by turning into a sarcastic robot. I felt flat and emotionless. Like everything had happened to some other version of me and the event was a movie I'd watched, instead of my life. Fadil got angry. I'd had to calm him down when the police had first arrived because he was shouting at one of the officers for not immediately trying to find the boy who'd shot Freddie. My mother, on the other hand, took control. It wouldn't have mattered who she was speaking to—the police, a doctor, the president of the United States—she would have ordered them around, and the funny thing was that most people did what she said without question.

"Have these children been looked at by the paramedics yet?" Mama asked Deputy Akers like she had finally realized someone else existed other than me and Fadil.

The deputy started to shake her head. "No, but—"

"No more questions," my mother said. "For either of them." She turned toward Fadil. "Come here, Fadil."

"I assume you're Elena's mother?" Akers asked.

"Yes, and I'm taking these two to the hospital like you should have done." My mother's voice whip-snapped in the air between her and the deputy.

"Well, they're not hurt, and we still have a few more questions—"

"Call your father, Fadil," Mama said. "Tell him I'm taking you and Elena to the emergency room to be checked out. He can meet us there."

"Mrs. Mendoza—"

"Ms." Mama said. "Do you have their information? Elena, did you give her my phone number?"

"I did, Mama."

Deputy Akers's shoulders fell as she nodded. She knew she'd lost. "If I could just—"

"You can just call and arrange to ask your questions after they've been examined by a medical professional. And you had best hope neither are hurt or you'll be hearing from my lawyer."

It was difficult not to laugh, because there was no way we could afford a lawyer. Hell, an emergency room visit was going to stress Mama out, even with our insurance.

Akers held up her hands and backed away. "You're free to

go." She caught my eye specifically. "I'll call you to arrange for that sketch artist, all right? We'll have a better chance of finding the boy who did this that way."

"Okay," I said.

Mama took my hand and Fadil's and pulled us toward the Groom Waggin' van. It wasn't until we were all inside—me and Fadil squeezed together in the front passenger seat—that Mama began to cry.

"I'm fine, Mama. It's okay. I'm not hurt. Neither of us is hurt." I kept my hands out of sight to hide the blood.

Fat tears rolled down my mother's cheeks and snot dripped down her upper lip. "I kept thinking you were dead. The whole drive here I thought you were dead and I didn't know what I'd do if you'd died."

"I'm not dead, Mama."

"Neither am I," Fadil added, which made Mama laugh.

"I'm glad you're not hurt either, Fadil." She wiped her nose with the back of her hand and turned the key in the ignition.

A wild yelp from the back of the van caused me to turn around. A wet, wide-eyed Yorkie stood in the tub, panting so hard I thought it would pass out.

"Mama?" I said. "There's a dog back there."

Her eyes flew open. "Lily!" Mama grabbed her phone out of the cup holder and handed it to me. "Gloria's number is in there. Call her and tell her what happened. We'll drop Lily off on the way to the hospital."

"You left in the middle of a grooming without giving the dog back?" Fadil said.

"When it comes to you kids, I'd run through hot broken glass to reach you." Mama put the van in reverse. "Now climb in back and give Lily a treat to shut her up, and wash the blood off your hands while you're there."

# FOUR

IT TOOK OVER four hours in the emergency room for a frazzled doctor to declare me healthy, uninjured, and fit to go home.

Mr. Himsi had shown up shortly after we'd arrived at the hospital, and by then Fadil and I were both over having to explain that we weren't hurt and nothing was wrong with us. I'll admit it gave me the warm fuzzies to see my mother and Fadil's dad so messed up thinking we might be hurt, if only because it reinforced how much they cared. Not that I'd doubted it. Soon after Mr. Himsi showed up, Fadil was moved to his own little examination room and I lost track of him.

Mama didn't speak as we drove back to the store, where she dropped off the Groom Waggin' and got her car. The little gray Corolla had over two hundred thousand miles on it, but it kept on chugging, which was a good thing seeing as I doubted we could afford to replace it. It also happened to be the same car Mama was driving the day I was born. There was a stain on the front seat that she used to joke was from her water breaking. I was pretty sure it wasn't.

We started home, but after a mile, Mama pulled into the parking lot of a Publix, parked the car, and turned to me. "Tell me what happened."

I'd been dreading this. Explaining everything to the police had been one thing. Cops were suspicious by nature. Even if the boy who'd shot Freddie had still been there and Freddie had died, they would have questioned every detail of my story. But this was my mother. She was predisposed to believe me, especially given the unusual nature of my conception, but I was terrified she wouldn't.

I opted to tell her the truth. Most of it, anyway. I left out the part where the siren had told me to heal Freddie, because the last time I'd told her an inanimate object had spoken to me she'd said it was adorable that I had such a vivid imagination. When I finished, I waited for her to say something.

"Mama?"

She held up her hand. "Give me a minute, Elena. This is a lot."

"Understatement of the century," I mumbled. Even as I'd

told her the story, I realized how ridiculous it sounded. While Freddie lay bleeding on the pavement, it had been easy to do what the voice from the creepy siren told me. And then the police arrived and I hadn't had time to think through all that had happened. But now? I'm not sure I would have believed the story if someone else had told it, and I was the so-called Miracle Girl who'd been born of a virgin.

"Have you ever done anything like this before?" Mama asked.

"No."

"And you're sure this boy who shot your friend didn't run away?"

She was starting to sound like Deputy Akers. "A beam of light shot from the sky and took him. What else could it have been?"

"A hallucination," she said. "Stress can play tricks on your mind."

"I didn't hallucinate, Mama!"

My mother bowed her head. "Okay, mi hija. Calm down."

"Why did this happen?" I asked. "Why did some boy I've never met shoot a girl I hardly know? How was I able to heal her? Where did the boy go?" The wall I'd been hiding behind finally cracked and tears welled in my eyes. "I had her blood on my hands. She was dying!"

Mama pulled me across the seat to her and I cried

into her shoulder. "It's over now. You're safe. Fadil's safe. Everyone's safe."

"The boy might still be out there."

"Then the police will find him."

I felt stupid crying on my mother. I was sixteen, not six. Eventually, I returned to my own seat and grabbed a wad of napkins from the glove box to blow my nose on.

"You don't remember what it was like after you were born."

I couldn't help laughing. "Obviously," I said. "I was a baby."

"No one believed that I was a virgin. Not even my own parents. After Dr. Milner proved I was telling the truth, most still thought I was a liar. But it was the believers who wrote the most terrible things about us." She turned to face me again. "You're a miracle, Elena. My miracle, and I don't want you to forget that, but whatever you did, I don't think you should do it again."

The thought of healing anyone else hadn't even crossed my mind. But as soon as my mother mentioned it, the implications loomed over me. "Why not?"

"You never complain, but I know school is difficult for you. Even though I've done my best to make people forget that you were the Miracle Baby, your birth still follows you around."

Another understatement. It had started in middle school

when Jess Maldonado found an article about me. The others were curious at first, but then the name-calling started. Mary was their favorite.

"I don't want that for you," Mama went on. "I want you to have a normal life."

"There were kids from my school there," I said. "They saw what happened." I wondered if any had recorded it on their phones. If there was video proof, the police would have to believe me.

Mama shrugged. "Then tell them they saw wrong. Tell them you don't know what happened. And then keep your head down until it passes."

I hadn't been sure how my mother was going to react, but this was not what I'd expected. If healing Freddie hadn't been a one-time thing, how could I pretend I couldn't perform miracles? How was I supposed to continue marching through life ignoring those who were in pain when I could possibly help?

I didn't expect I was going to find any answers sitting in my mother's car in a Publix parking lot.

"If that's what you think is best," I said.

"Good." Mama brushed my hair off the side of my face. "And let's not tell Sean or the kids, either, okay?"

"Yeah," I said. "Okay."

But it wasn't okay; I just didn't know it yet.

# FIVE

I DIDN'T HAVE to keep the shooting a secret from Mama's husband, Sean, or my little brother and sister, Sofie and Conor, because they saw it on the news that night.

**LOCAL GIRL ALLEGEDLY SHOT OUTSIDE OF STARBUCKS. EMPLOYEE CLAIMS TO HAVE HEALED HER.**

That was only one of the headlines. The others were less charitable. None of the news stations appeared to have any video of the shooting, and I thought my name was going to stay out of it until I sat huddled on the couch with Mama that night and watched Kyle giving an interview about how one of his baristas had performed a miracle and that the shooter had been lifted to heaven in a beam of light. He gave them my full name. I was definitely quitting my job.

My phone started blowing up after that. Mostly reporters

looking to interview me, some jerks who thought it was funny to breathe heavily into the phone, and one weirdo who kept trying to order two large pineapple pizzas. I didn't know how they'd gotten my number, but I eventually shut my phone off.

Mama took Sean aside and explained the situation to him, and he spent the rest of the evening giving me side-eye, and she'd told Sofie and Conor not to bother me even though they were bursting with questions.

Deputy Akers called Mama's phone around eight p.m., and when I got on she told me that the gun found at the scene was registered to Dan and Sue Combs, who had a son named David who was missing, and did I know David Combs? I didn't, but I Googled and found a picture of him. He was definitely the boy who'd shot Freddie. Akers asked me if I was absolutely positive I'd never seen Combs at school or anywhere else, and after I told her I was certain, she said it wouldn't be necessary for me to provide a sketch after all.

Mama said I didn't have to go to school the next day, and she sent Conor and Sofie to bed early. Then she went to her job as a night stock clerk at Walmart because she couldn't afford to call out, especially not after seeing the bill we'd racked up at the emergency room. Sean went out drinking, leaving me alone.

I hopped on the computer to look up David Combs, but there was virtually nothing to find. He had a Snowflake page he hadn't updated in months, and searching for his name brought up few other hits. He was practically a ghost.

There was plenty about me, though. Stories on reddit and Twitter. Never read the comments. It's good advice that I didn't take. They were predictably horrible. According to trolls hiding behind anonymity on the Internet I was either a liar so desperate for attention that I'd created this entire hoax to get my name on the news, or I was some kind of freak with alien powers who should be taken into custody and dissected for science.

I wasn't a liar, but I couldn't prove that without trying to heal someone else. And I wasn't entirely sure I could do it again or what other powers I might have. I'd hoped the voices would tell me more, but they'd been quiet since Starbucks. That wasn't new, though. The voices were fickle. Sometimes they'd speak to me nonstop for days, and then I wouldn't hear from them for weeks, not even if I called to them.

I tried to sleep but all I did was toss and turn on the couch, so I went outside to walk around. Even without the sun, it was sticky and hot, the humidity so oppressive that I felt like I was breathing through a wet strip of cloth. I considered calling Fadil, but I was scared to turn my phone back on. Besides, his parents were probably fawning all over him and wouldn't let him out of their sight for a while.

I sat on the curb and pulled my knees to my chest. As I

sat, Lucifurr, a cat that roamed the neighborhood, limped toward me. He was a beautiful Maine Coon with intelligent eyes who'd belonged to a renter and then been abandoned when they'd moved out. He'd earned his name the first time I'd tried to pet him and he'd clawed my arm.

"Hey, Luce." I held out my hand and waited for the cat to limp over to me. Mrs. Haimovitch often left food out for the cat so that he didn't starve, and though he had been on his own for a while, he hadn't turned feral. He'd had a bad back leg for as long as I'd known him, and Mrs. Haimovitch had told me that she'd learned from Lucifurr's owner that he'd hurt it during a run-in with a car.

Lucifurr swished his tail back and forth and finally crossed the remaining distance, rubbed his head against my hand, and flopped down beside me.

"I don't suppose the voices would talk through you, would they?"

The cat didn't answer, though I hadn't expected he would. The more distance that separated me from the shooting, the more doubt began to creep into my mind. Maybe I hadn't healed Freddie at all. Maybe David Combs hadn't disappeared in a beam of light. Maybe I was still standing behind the espresso machine at Starbucks and the events of the last few hours were an elaborate delusion created out of sheer boredom.

Except, I knew it was no delusion. Freddie's blood had stained my hands. It had been real, and it had been Freddie's. I couldn't explain how I'd healed her, but I knew I had. The question remained: Could I do it again?

Lucifurr purred and squirmed onto his back. He was such a slut for attention.

A thought occurred to me. The voices might not be speaking to me at the moment, and I couldn't explain what had happened to David Combs after he'd shot Freddie, but I could test whether healing Freddie had been a one-time deal. I just wasn't sure I should.

"You okay with this?" I asked. "I'm pretty sure it won't hurt." Lucifurr didn't appear to care so long as I didn't stop rubbing his tummy.

I closed my eyes the way I'd done with Freddie. The cat's lines of energy spread out before me, bright and electric. They were different from Freddie's, maybe because Lucifurr was a cat instead of a person, but where his back leg was seemed encased in concrete. The currents of light were hidden behind a slab of darkness. I reached out and shattered the block and watched as the cat's energy brightened in his bad leg.

Lucifurr leapt up, startled, his hackles raised. He stared at me like I'd shocked him.

"Did it work?"

I waited, and then finally the cat took off across the parking lot into the bushes. And he did it without limping.

"Well, that answers that," I said to myself. I possessed the power to heal with a touch. I didn't know why, how it was possible, or what it meant, but I really was the Miracle Girl.

# SIX

SOFIE STIRRED HER maple brown sugar instant oatmeal, but didn't eat it, while Conor ignored his breakfast completely as he raced through the homework he'd "forgotten" to finish. Sofie had her father's red hair and pale freckled skin, while Conor was tawny with brown eyes like me and Mama. Sometimes it was difficult to believe we were all related.

"Come on, Sofie. Hurry up and eat or you'll miss the bus." I stood at the sink washing yesterday's dishes. Mama was still at work, and Sean's snores trumpeted from the bedroom, loud even through the closed door.

"I don't want to go today," she said.

"Can I stay home too?" Conor asked immediately after.

"No one is staying home," I said.

"You're staying home," Conor countered.

I gave him my "today is not the day to screw with me" frown. "Someone tried to shoot me yesterday. When someone tries to shoot you, we'll talk." I pointed toward the bathroom. "Go brush your teeth."

Conor groaned but pushed his chair back and trudged into the bathroom. "You feeling okay?" I asked Sofie when we were alone.

Sofie wore her emotions openly, though I didn't know whom she'd inherited that from. Sean buried his anger at the bottom of a six-pack, and Mama was a master at pretending everything was fine even when her world was a flaming garbage fire. But Sofie rarely lied and was incapable of hiding her feelings, which I loved even though it would make her a target for unscrupulous jerks.

"Gwen Bettany called me a liar."

"What for?"

Sofie twisted her hair around her finger. "I told her how you didn't have a daddy and she said everyone has a daddy, even Andrew Smitt-Reyes who has two mommys."

I dried my hands on a towel, crouched beside Sofie, and rested my arms on the edge of the table. "Have I ever lied to you?"

"I don't guess so," she said.

"Sometimes things don't make sense," I said. "So people

replace the truth with an explanation they can understand."

Sofie's green eyes filled with concern and skepticism. "Did you really heal that girl we saw on TV last night?"

"I did."

"But everyone's gonna call you a liar, aren't they?"

I brushed Sofie's cheek. "Even if I stood on TV and healed a hundred people at once, there'd still be some who'd call me a liar."

Sofie pursed her lips thoughtfully. "Like how Mr. Randall says there's nothing wrong with the planet even though the ice in the north pole is melting?"

I nodded. "Exactly. Sometimes a person can believe a thing so hard that not even beating them over the head with facts will change their mind."

"But what do I do?" Sofie asked. "It's not fair for people to say you're a liar when you're not."

"You know the truth. I know the truth. Conor and Mama know the truth. You're the only ones who matter to me." I motioned toward her room with my chin. "Go get dressed for school, and if Gwen calls you a liar today, ignore her. If that doesn't work, tell her I can make her hair fall out."

Sofie hugged me and ran off to get dressed. I ate a few bites of her now-cold oatmeal and then washed the bowl. Twenty minutes later, after the chaos of making sure Sofie had brushed her hair and Conor hadn't forgotten his homework, and after they'd left to catch the bus to school, I stood alone in the bedroom we shared, though most nights I slept on the couch.

Usually Fadil picked me up before Sofie and Conor left, but since I was skipping school, I was determined to take advantage of the peace and quiet to take a shower without someone banging on the door. I washed my hair and face and used every last drop of hot water in the tank.

I was grateful Mama had let me stay home from school. I'd barely slept the night before because I'd kept imagining my classmates welcoming me as the hero who'd dragged one of their own back from the vicious jaws of death, their personal high school miracle worker who healed the sick while somehow managing to maintain a decent GPA. The more likely scenario was that my peers would whisper behind my back, mock me to my face, and generally stare at me between classes like I was an animal in a cage who might fling hot feces at them without provocation.

Growing up, Mama had treated me as though my birth and conception were anything but miraculous. My being the only human ever scientifically proven to have been conceived parthenogenetically hadn't stopped her from announcing to the stock boy, cashier, bagger, and cart attendant at Target that she was buying me my first ever box of pads because I'd finally become a woman when I was twelve, or from telling every boyfriend and girlfriend I'd ever had that I farted in my sleep, which is not true and she'd better stop telling people that. It also hadn't stopped me from wondering if I might actually be special or from dreaming that my miraculous birth meant I had a destiny that would one day be revealed. I longed to fit in, to discover whether I was playing a lead role in the grand cosmic drama or merely a bit part with no lines. My miraculous birth and the voices had, for years, fueled my convictions that I had a purpose—that I would lead a significant life—and all I'd wanted was for someone to notice me.

People were definitely going to notice me now, but probably not for the reasons I wanted them to.

I ran into Sean when I walked out of the bathroom, still wrapped in my towel. "Excuse me," I said, and tried to brush past him. He grabbed my arm.

"Where you going?" The toxic cloud of his morning breath—a putrid combination of cigarette smoke and cheap beer—rolled out of his mouth.

"To my room to get dressed."

"I hope you're not planning on hanging around the house all day."

"Afraid I'll interrupt all the ball scratching and pretend job hunting you've got planned?"

"Don't be like that."

Sean stood six foot three, wiry and thin with tufts of red

hair on his chest and shoulders. He had a mean mouth persistently set in a grimace, and meaner words depending on how much he'd had to drink and whether or not my mother was around.

"Let go of my arm." We locked eyes, and I refused to blink first. If you subscribed to the belief that everyone has at least a little good in them, then Sean Malloy had squirted what little he'd had into my mother to produce Sofie and Conor, and nothing remained in him now but impotent rage.

After a moment, Sean released me and I walked to my room.

"I don't believe you healed that girl, no matter what Natalia says," he said to my back. "But others might."

"So?"

"There are folks dumb and desperate enough who'd pay."

I slowly turned around to face him again, and I sure as hell wasn't smiling. "You want me to charge for miracles?"

Sean shrugged. "You'll get your fifteen minutes of fame out of this. We might as well make some money off it."

"There's no 'we,'" I said. "And for the record, you're disgusting." I stormed into my room and slammed the door behind me.

# SEVEN

TURNING ON MY phone was a terrible idea. My messages were a hot mess of reporters asking for interviews and strangers begging me to heal them. I deleted them. I added "change phone number" to the top of my mental to-do list, texted Fadil to pick me up and rescue me from having to spend the day with Sean, and shut my phone off again.

I waited outside my apartment for Fadil, whose parents had also let him ditch school, because, even though it was sticky and hot, it was better than sharing breathing space with Sean. Lago Vacia wasn't in what anyone would consider the fancy section of Arcadia, but it was decent enough. The apartments were old, but not rundown, and mostly occupied by folks struggling to survive on life's jagged edge. Like Mrs. Haimovitch, in the apartment below us. She was an elderly woman on a fixed income who cooked dinner every Sunday for a family that never visited. Then there was Missy Tanner, which I doubted was her real name, who'd run away from an abusive boyfriend and who read more than any person I knew. Mike D. sold weed to pay his rent and cover his video game habit. We were each living our own story, and while some, like Mama, were fighting to change the narrative, others struggled to escape the circumstances of their past and the specter of the future, while a few had given up completely.

"Are you Elena Mendoza?" A tall blond woman in a tight blouse and short pencil skirt walked around the side of a black SUV with dark tinted windows. She had the kind of face most men would call bitchy, but which I suspected simply reflected determination.

"No." I craned my neck to look for Fadil, but didn't see him and considered running back upstairs to the apartment to wait for him.

"Elena, my name is Carmen Ballard, and I'm an attorney for a party who would prefer to remain anonymous." She walked toward me slowly as she spoke, like I was a stray dog she was attempting to corner.

"Yeah, because that's not creepy at all." I let my purse drop from my shoulder to my hand, figuring I could take a good swing at Carmen if she got too close.

Carmen Ballard, if that was even her real name, flashed a pearly, toothy smile. "I grew up in a place just like this," she said. "But if you can do the things you claim, you wouldn't have to anymore." She was talking about the place I lived like there were coke dealers hiding under the stairs and rats chewing our toes while we slept.

"Look, I don't know who you are, but if you don't get the hell out of here, I'm going to call the police." I reached for my phone.

She backed up a step. "I get it," she said. "You're overwhelmed. Have you been approached already? Whatever you're being offered, I'm authorized to beat it."

"No one's offered me anything, lady." The squeal of car tires caused us both to look toward the entrance of the apartment complex, and my entire body unclenched when it turned out to be Fadil in his little orange hatchback. He pulled up in front of my building and rolled down the passenger-side window. "Elena Mendoza?" he said. "I'm looking for a miracle worker named Elena Mendoza."

I quickly slung my purse into the car and hopped in after it. "Get me out of here." I watched Carmen Ballard out of the back window as Fadil drove off.

"What's going on?"

"Nothing," I said. "Just crazy people showing up at my apartment."

Fadil glanced in his rearview mirror. "Should we call the police?"

"I'd rather not," I said. "Let's just go."

"Where to?" he asked.

"The mall? I need to change my number. I think someone doxxed me online."

"Seriously?"

"I'd turn on my phone and show you all the calls and texts from random strangers, but I'm afraid it might burst into flames. Plus, you know, creepy lady outside my apartment on behalf of an anonymous party."

Fadil pushed his glasses up on his nose. "Should we skip the mall? You can change your number online."

The offer was tempting, but I shook my head. "I refuse to hide in my apartment for the rest of my life. Besides, Sean's there."

"My house, then? Dad spent the night stress-baking."

That offer was even more tempting, especially since Fadil's dad was an amazing baker, but I didn't want to deal with anyone asking me any more questions about what had happened. "How'd your mom react to everything?"

"I'm not sure she believes what I told her." Fadil drummed the steering wheel with his fingers. "If I'm being honest, Elena, I'm not sure what I saw. You did heal Freddie, right?"

"I think so."

"Did you make the shooter disappear?"

"His name's David Combs," I said. "Deputy Akers called last night and told me that the gun was registered to his father and that David is missing."

"Okay. David Combs. Did you make him disappear?"

"If I did, it wasn't on purpose."

"What'd he say to you?" Fadil asked. "He said something to you after he shot Freddie."

My memory flashed back to those brief moments. The entire encounter had lasted barely a minute, and yet it had expanded to fill every second since. I remembered healing Freddie. Her smiling when she saw me. That the boy who'd shot her had known my name and had said his mother would have liked me. That he'd had the opportunity to shoot me but hadn't.

"Nothing important."

"Come on, Elena. I told the cops you freaking healed someone and that the shooter got raptured into heaven. They think I'm crazy. My parents think I'm crazy. I deserve the truth."

I clenched my fists and dug my fingernails into the palms of my hands. "Can we not talk about it? All I want is to forget it happened."

Fadil muttered under his breath but kept driving. We parked at the mall and went in. He browsed the phone selection while a short-tempered salesperson changed my number. When we were done, I texted Fadil and Mama the new one, and we walked toward the food court. It was still early, but we bought pizza anyway and found a table in a corner.

As much as I didn't want to discuss what had happened or what I'd done, Fadil did deserve the whole ludicrous truth. Of all the people in my life, he was the most likely to believe me.

"The siren told me to heal Freddie," I said. "The creepy mermaid logo? She told me to heal Freddie, so I did. I have no idea what happened to David Combs or where he went." I poked at my greasy pizza, unable to eat.

Fadil had eaten only a couple of bites of his pizza, and now as he sat across from me, his lips pursed and his brow furrowed, I wanted to crawl through his ear into his brain and see his thoughts.

"So the Starbucks siren told you to heal Freddie?" I nodded. "Was that the first time she's done that?"

"Yes."

"And do inanimate objects often command you to perform miracles?"

"They don't order me around, but I've heard them for as long as I can remember."

Fadil fell quiet again. I assumed he thought I was delusional or lying or worse. Not that I could blame him.

"I healed a cat last night," I added. "Lucifurr. He has

a bum leg—had. I fixed it. I needed to find out if healing Freddie was a one-time thing, but I guess it isn't."

"Did anyone disappear?"

"Not that I know of."

Fadil picked up his pizza, folded it down the middle, and took a bite. "That's good, I suppose?"

"Is it?" I said. "How do we know if it's good or bad or whatever?"

"We try again."

"Try what?"

Fadil wiped the pizza grease off his fingers. "Heal someone."

"Here?"

"Why not?" He scanned the food court. "What about him?" Fadil motioned toward an elderly man in a wheelchair.

"What am I supposed to do? Casually bump into him and make him walk again?"

"Sure."

"I'm not doing that," I said. "And screw you for suggesting it." I stood and started walking back toward the parking lot. I didn't care if Fadil was following me or not; I'd walk home if I had to. He caught up to me outside and was out of breath from running.

"Don't you want to see what you're capable of?" Fadil asked.

I stopped and rounded on him. "I'm not some carnival freak."

"I didn't say you were."

"This morning Sean suggested we charge to heal people," I said. "He doesn't even believe me, but he's already trying to figure out how to make money off this."

Fadil took my hand and held it. "I'm not Sean, but I am curious. Aren't you?"

"Yes," I said. "Which is why I healed Lucifurr."

We kept walking back to Fadil's car. When we got in and he'd cranked the engine, he said, "Will you heal me?"

"You're not even hurt."

Fadil reached over me into his glove box and pulled out a Swiss Army knife. He unfolded the blade and held it to his palm. "Do this," he said, "and I'll drop it."

"Are you serious?"

"Totally," Fadil said. "And this is win-win. If you heal me, then we'll have proof Freddie and Lucifurr weren't flukes. If you can't, all it will have cost me is a minor injury, and at least we'll know."

I hadn't been able to speak to Freddie since she'd been shot, and Lucifurr was a cat. If I healed Fadil, he could tell me what the experience felt like from his end. Besides, I needed answers and the voices were not being particularly accommodating. "Fine. But don't cut too deep."

Fadil gritted his teeth and slashed the fleshy spot under his thumb with the knife. He hissed in pain, but the cut was so clean it took a second before blood welled up and streamed out of the gash to pool in his cupped hand. The fatty layer poked out, meaty and white.

I touched Fadil's arm and closed my eyes. His light was brighter than Freddie's and Lucifurr's had been. I knew I wasn't looking at him with my eyes, but I still felt blinded by Fadil's energy. Having already done it twice before, I was able to quickly find the hurt. It looked like a toothless, gummy mouth trying to find a teat to nurse on. It was so real in my mind that I heard the suckling sounds from it. I healed it and opened my eyes.

"Whoa!" Fadil grabbed a rag from his backseat, wiped the blood off, and held his hand out for me to see. The cut was gone. No scar, nothing to indicate he'd been injured.

"What was it like?" I asked.

"Nothing," he said. "One second my hand was throbbing and then it wasn't. I thought it would tingle or that I'd see the skin stitch back together, but it was instantaneous." Fadil sat there and gaped. "You really can perform miracles. I feel like this moment should be bigger."

"I feel like I'm going to puke. Can you take me home now?"

# EIGHT

ON FRIDAY, MAMA decided I should go to school. The upside meant not having to spend time with Sean in the apartment. The downside was that we had a pep rally instead of our first and second periods. I hitched a ride to school with Fadil and then we headed toward the gym. Forced cheer that early in the morning should be against the law. Fadil needed to run to the restroom, so I hung out in front of the gym waiting for him. As I stood outside, kids passing whispered in my direction and gaped in disgust, not even bothering to hide what they were doing.

"You planning any miracles today, Mary?" shouted a boy I thought I'd had a class with once.

"Sorry," I said back, "nothing I can do to fix your micro-dick."

I'd done my best to prepare myself. This was no worse than how I'd been dragged on social media. I didn't understand them, though. I'd saved someone's life and they were treating me like I was the shooter. I'd performed an actual miracle, but they still thought I was a freak. I wasn't sure if there was anything I could do to change their minds, and I was even less sure I cared enough to try.

Fadil bumped my shoulder and grabbed my hand, pulling me into the gym. We found a couple of seats at the top of the bleachers and settled in. Fadil was a nerd. He was a math-and-science-loving geek who played video games and loved his parents and was serious about his religion and did the extra credit in his classes even though he rarely needed it. He'd been a target of bullying in middle school when he'd been the new student—mostly by idiot boys who thought a brown-skinned kid with a Middle Eastern name was automatically a terrorist—but he hadn't let it bother him. Once they'd gotten to know him, they'd loved him, even the ones who'd initially taunted him. It didn't make sense that he chose to hang out with me. He had his marching band friends, but he spent the majority of his time with me, and I'd never understood why.

In high school, your reputation is the only real currency you have. Some of us were perpetual paupers. Some, like Tori Thrash, were born into wealth and could have run naked through the halls in a clown mask and not exhausted that wealth. Then there was Fadil. He was sweet and kind and helped those who didn't deserve his time, which earned him bankable reputation that he spent slumming it with your local neighborhood social reject. I didn't question it out loud because without Fadil high school would have been a much lonelier place.

Ten minutes into the Arcadia West Otters' dance routine, I noticed Freddie watching me. Her eyes were narrowed and the space between her eyebrows creased. I couldn't tell whether she was disgusted or confused or about to stand up and declare that I was a witch who should be burned alive for what I'd done. It was disconcerting no matter which way I interpreted it. I'd considered calling Freddie after Fadil had dropped me off from our trip to the mall, but I didn't know her phone number. I was desperate to talk to her and discuss what had happened. Maybe she'd known David Combs and could tell me why he'd shot her. Dylan Hartman caught Freddie staring and started whispering to Ned Powell and soon Freddie wasn't the only person looking at me.

Before the shooting, I would have given my left toes, and probably my right, to have captured Freddie's attention, but now that I had it I wished I didn't. I wondered if turning invisible was part of my Miracle Girl powers. I shut my eyes and imagined my body becoming transparent, my molecules refracting the light around me instead of reflecting it. But when I opened my eyes again, Freddie and the others were still gawking at me, so I slumped down and tried to make myself as small as was humanly possible.

*Cheer up, Elena,* said a voice coming from the Otter mascot painted on the wall beside me. *You're special and they're not, and when the end comes, most of them will die horrible deaths after suffering unspeakable agony!*

"Yeah," I said under my breath. "At least I've got that going for me."

Fadil nudged me with his elbow. "What?"

"Nothing." I risked a glance up, but instead of Freddie, I caught Javier Matos Vidente watching me, and I kept my eyes down for the rest of the presentation.

Javi and I had dated for six weeks during sophomore year. He'd been new to Arcadia West and hadn't known asking me out was social suicide. I'd liked him because he was outspoken and handsome and hadn't tried to kiss me until our third date. After that first kiss, I'd spent the next month and a half wondering why we were together, especially when he was on top of me, pawing at me with his sausage fingers and panting at me with his onion breath—two things that are great on pizza but not boyfriends. Our relationship eventually became a protracted siege in which he attempted to starve me out from behind the protective wall of my cotton underwear because he'd assumed I'd be an easy lay. Ugly girls are always easy, right? It's an honor just being nominated, right? We should feel special that some boy, any boy, wants to stick his penis in a part of our anatomy he can't even say without giggling. Right?

Wrong.

Javi reacted badly when we broke up, retroactively deciding that I wasn't the type of girl he wanted to associate with anyway. We hadn't spoken since. He thought he was a "nice guy," and that, being a social outcast, I was practically obligated to want to sleep with him. To boys like Javi, being nice was a means to an end, where to boys like Fadil, being nice was the end itself.

When Principal Gonzalez released us from the pep rally, Fadil walked with me to my third-period class, which was gym.

"You see Freddie checking you out?" Fadil asked.

"If by 'checking me out,' you mean 'staring in utter revulsion,' then yes. Yes I did."

"That wasn't revulsion." Fadil nudged me. "You saved her life. If there was ever a better opening than magically healing the girl you're into, I don't know what it is."

"I healed her because I wanted to. She doesn't owe me anything."

"Of course not, but don't you want to talk to her?"

"Freddie, sure, but what about her friends? The ones who call me Mary?"

"They don't understand," Fadil said. "Give them time."

"Drop it, all right?"

Fadil pulled me out of the flow of students heading to their own classes and leaned against a bank of lockers. "I get that this is difficult, and I read what they wrote about you online—"

I flared my nostrils. "It was hard when I was the freak whose mother conceived her as a virgin. Now I'm the girl who claims she can perform miracles. It took them less than a day to turn me into a joke, so they can go to hell for all I care."

"You can't hate everyone," Fadil said. "Not if you refuse to give them a chance."

"Javi tried to stick his chance down my pants."

Fadil let out a long sigh. "They won't all turn out like Javi. Some of them might even surprise you, and you owe yourself the opportunity to see if Freddie is one of the ones who could."

"You always think the glass is half full, don't you?"

Fadil nodded. "And you think it's full of poison. That's why we make such a great team."

"I'm not sure that's how it's supposed to work."

"Yet it does." Fadil flashed me a bright smile and I couldn't help laughing.

I tugged his shirt. "Come on. Coach Foster will give me detention if I'm late."

"Promise you'll at least consider talking to Freddie."

"Fine," I said. "I'll consider it. I promise."

# NINE

WHO CAME UP with the incredibly brilliant idea of putting locker rooms in high schools? Being a teenager means surviving puberty. It means dealing with acne and awkward changes to our bodies that don't make any sense. It's the most vulnerable time in our lives, even though we're all going through it, and often the easiest way to deflect our insecurity is to make fun of anyone who's different. So, sure, let's dump gasoline on that fire by forcing us to publicly expose our freaky, misshapen bodies before and after mandatory athletic competition. Sounds like a super plan.

Coach Foster loved volleyball. It was more than a game with a ball and a net to her. It was life. I fully believed she spent her evenings making little dolls of her students that she set up on a miniature volleyball court so she could work out game strategies while she watched TV shows about people competing to live in the tiniest house or cooking competitions where all the chefs were required to prepare a meal using some weird animal's tongue.

I hated volleyball. No, I loathed it. I'd never been athletically gifted, and nothing showcased my lack of skills better than trying to hit a ball over a net that someone had spiked at my face.

To make matters worse, Tori Thrash was in my gym class. Usually she ignored me, but sometimes she'd get in a mood and take every opportunity to embarrass me and prove that she was awesome and I wasn't and, oh hey! Look at the freak who can't even hit the ball! I wished Friday was one of the days she'd chosen to ignore me, but I was not that lucky. She and her friends had been loudly talking about me when I'd walked into the locker room to change, and they'd continued when we'd gotten to the court. I could hear her whispering nearby since she was on my team. Not that Coach Foster noticed.

"Come on, Mendoza!" Coach Foster shouted. "Get your head in the game!"

I stood in the back right corner, trying to pray the ball away. I'd healed Freddie, so maybe I could deflect the volleyball with my mind. Turning invisible during the pep rally hadn't worked, but surely this would. Corinne Spieler served the ball in a high graceful arc that sent it hurtling directly toward me. I held my hands out and closed my eyes, bracing for impact. Instead of being hit with the ball, Tori rammed into me, shoving me to the ground. I slammed into the floor, banged my elbow, and yelped in pain. Telekinesis wasn't one of my powers either.

Coach Foster blew her whistle.

"What the hell, Tori?" I sat up and rubbed my elbow. Currents of electric pain scurried up my arm into my fingers.

"What're you going to do, Mary?" Tori asked, standing over me. "Vanish me like you did Combs?"

"I—"

Coach Foster helped me to my feet. "You can't hit the ball with your eyes closed, Mendoza." She clapped Tori on the back. "Nice hustle, Thrash."

Nice hustle? Was she kidding with that? Tori practically body-checked me and she got commended for it? I started to argue, but I didn't want to draw more attention to myself and make it worse.

"I don't think I can play anymore, Coach," I said. "My elbow."

Coach Foster rolled her eyes. "Fine. Bleachers. But you better pay attention to the game. Watch how the other girls play."

I nodded and trudged to the bleachers. Without me playing, my team evened the score and then pulled ahead to win. I was grateful when Coach finally told us to head back to the locker room to shower and change. I hadn't played long enough to need a shower, so I sat in front of my locker after I'd gotten out of my gym clothes and checked my phone. Only two days since the shooting and I'd already become a nonstory. Every credible news source had decided the shooting and healing were hoaxes, and had changed their focus to the search for David Combs.

A slamming locker door broke my concentration, and I heard Tori talking to Ava Sutter. I shouldn't have eavesdropped, but I couldn't help myself.

"Fuck her," Tori said. "Mary didn't do anything. She was probably blowing that weirdo."

"But Freddie said—"

"Freddie's lost it, Ava. Girl hardly even talks to me anymore."

"But what if it's true?" Ava said.

"You don't seriously believe that shit, do you?"

I quietly slipped away.

The bell rang and I grabbed my backpack out of my locker. As I walked toward the exit, I passed Ava and stopped. Tori glared at me. "What're you looking at?"

"Nothing," I said. Then to Ava, "I did heal Freddie."

"Don't talk to her," Tori said. "Don't even look at her." She pulled her arm tight around Ava.

I left the locker room without another word.

# TEN

A PRETTY DECENT drawing of me dressed as the Virgin Mary was decorating my locker in black marker after third period. The detail and shading were quality work, but whoever had drawn it had ruined it by writing "slut" underneath.

I forgot to mention that after our breakup, Javi told his new friends that we'd definitely had sex and that I was a nymphomaniac, even though I'd only let him feel me up. I hadn't bothered disputing the rumors, because Javi had already written my story and nothing I said would change it. The same way others were writing the story of what had happened in front of Starbucks with Freddie and David Combs. Soon the whispers would solidify and their version of the truth would be the only one that mattered.

Fourth period was anatomy with Mrs. Burchfield. It was

the class I slept through most often and was also the one class I shared with Freddie. She was already at her desk when I arrived, and I walked to my seat without looking at her.

I sat near the front of the room, and I felt Freddie's eyes burning a hole through me while Mrs. Burchfield lectured us on the musculature system. I tried to put what Tori and Ava had said out of my mind, but I couldn't. I'd gotten the impression that Ava wanted to ask me to heal someone she knew, or possibly even herself. I'd already healed Freddie, a cat, and a cut on Fadil's hand; maybe I could use my newfound powers to get on Ava's good side. Only, that felt exploitative. No better than Sean's suggestion.

*Hey! What's a skeleton's favorite musical instrument?*

My head jerked up. "What?"

*A trombone. Get it? A trom-bone?*

Mrs. Burchfield stopped speaking and turned her attention to me. She was standing next to an anatomy skeleton that I was 99 percent sure had told the worst joke I'd ever heard. "Did you have a question, Elena?" A couple of kids behind me snickered.

I dipped my head. "No. Sorry."

Mrs. Burchfield continued identifying the individual muscles in the hands and arms.

*Could this lecture get any more boring? Seriously. How can you tell which one of us is dead?*

I did my best to ignore the skeleton. I squeezed my eyes shut and counted backward from a thousand in an attempt to drown out his voice. As much as I wanted to interrogate the voices, I didn't want to do it in anatomy class.

*Real talk time, Elena. What you did when you healed Winifred Petrine? That was only the beginning. We have plans, and we need to know we can count on you. Nod your cranium if you understand.*

876, 875, 874, 873.

*I understand you're scared, but we don't have time for you to be all emo about it.*

851, 850, 849.

The bell finally rang. The other students around me grabbed their books and surged toward the door. I hung back.

"Did you need something, Elena?" Mrs. Burchfield asked.

"I wanted to finish filling in the names of the muscle groups off the board before I forget." It was a stupid excuse, seeing as they were in my book, but I hoped she'd buy it.

Mrs. Burchfield gathered her purse and stood. "Well, this is my lunch period and I need to leave," she said. "Shut the door behind you when you're done."

"Yes, ma'am."

Mrs. Burchfield took off, leaving me mostly alone.

Wasting no time, I stood and moved closer to the

anatomy skeleton. "What plans?" I asked. "And what's with the terrible jokes?"

*You're going to save the human race. The jokes are a bonus. Get it? Bone-us?*

I chose to ignore the obnoxious wordplay. "Enough with the games. Tell me what's going on."

*You're no fun today, Elena.*

"And you're a dick." I wasn't sure it was wise to piss off the voices, but I also didn't care.

If the skeleton could have sighed, I think it would have. *Fine. You need to keep healing people. As many as you can.*

"Are you serious?"

*Dead serious.*

"What happens if I don't?"

*The explanation is complicated, and I'm not certain your brain is sufficiently developed to understand the intricacies.*

"Then give me the dumbed-down version," I said, ignoring the insult.

*Your world go boom.*

"Not that dumb."

*Humanity is in danger. We—and please don't ask who "we" are because you really are too stupid to comprehend even the idiot version of that answer—are attempting to preserve as many lives as possible. You, regretfully, are the vessel through which we are forced to act.*

"I have questions."

*Of course you do.*

"First: You're a jerk. Second: How am I supposed to help?"

*You've already begun by healing Winifred Petrine,* the skeleton said. *Keep healing the sick and we'll take care of the rest.*

"The rest of what?"

*I wish I had eyes to roll.*

"How am I able to heal people? What happened to the boy who shot Freddie? And how, exactly, is humanity in danger?"

Someone cleared her throat behind me, and I stopped, frozen where I was standing, afraid to turn around.

"Are you talking to a skeleton?"

I was relieved the person who'd interrupted me wasn't Mrs. Burchfield, but my relief vanished when I realized I recognized the voice. I slowly turned and found Freddie standing in the doorway. She was wearing jeans and a gauzy seventies-inspired top flared at the bottom. Her face was inscrutable. The pinched mouth and furrowed brow might have been curiosity. Or it might have been revulsion. I couldn't tell.

"Obviously not." I tried to laugh it off. "I was thinking out loud and the skeleton made for a captive audience."

"Oh." Freddie moved two steps deeper into the room.

"How are you?" I asked. "Which is a stupid question seeing as neither of us is okay even though we're trying to act like we are. I mean, someone shot you and now we're back in school dealing with classes and homecoming and all the stupid nonsense—"

"Why did you heal me?" Freddie said, interrupting.

That wasn't the question I'd been dreading. I'd expected her to ask me *how* I'd healed her, which, despite what the skeleton had told me, I still couldn't explain, but she hadn't and it caught me off guard.

"We're not friends, I've never been nice to you, so why did you do it?"

I flashed back to Freddie bleeding out on the sidewalk. I'd healed her and she was alive, but that moment where I wasn't sure she'd survive still haunted me.

"Everything happened so fast and you got shot and I reacted."

"Before the shooting, I actually thought your name was Mary."

I frowned. "But we've had classes together for years. I figured you called me Mary because that was the joke."

Freddie shook her head. "People called you Mary, so I assumed that was your name. Honestly, I didn't care enough about you to know I was wrong."

I'm not sure if it was worse believing she'd called me Mary as an insult or the truth that she'd been too indifferent to my existence to learn my real name.

"My name's Elena Mendoza."

"Yeah," Freddie said. "I got that from the news." She took another step toward me. I resisted the urge to move back. "So then why?" she asked again. "Why heal someone who couldn't be bothered to learn your name?"

"Don't you want to know how?" I asked. "Most people want to know how I did it; even the ones who think we planned the whole thing as some kind of hoax."

"Most people are idiots. Tell me why."

"He shot you and you were bleeding and dying and I . . . What do you want me to say?"

Freddie didn't speak for a moment. She looked at me with her soft leather-brown eyes, stripping me down one layer at a time. Clothes, skin, muscles, until I was as naked as that dumb-joke-telling anatomy skeleton. She wanted answers that I didn't have. Answers that I also wanted.

Then she said, "So you didn't bother asking yourself whether I wanted you to save my life?"

"Wait, what?"

Freddie moved in closer, and now she was barely an arm's length away. "That boy shot me. I felt the bullet tear into my side and I knew I was dying." Her husky voice had dropped low, so much that she was almost whispering. "And I was happy. For the first time in as long as I can remember, I was happy."

I thought she'd been smiling when I healed her because of me. Because she'd seen me. But she hadn't been happy to see me or grateful I'd saved her life. She hadn't even known my name. A killer had, but the girl I had a crush on, whose life I'd saved with a miracle, hadn't.

"I should go." I started to make my way past Freddie when she grabbed my wrist.

"The next time someone shoots me," she said. "Let me die."

# ELEVEN

FADIL'S VOICE ROSE and fell from the back of the apartment as he prayed. The rhythm of it was soothing and peaceful, and I wondered if I could hand my worries over to a force greater than myself and trust that they had a plan. All I had were the voices, and though they'd spoken to me my entire life, I didn't entirely trust them.

"Does he have to do that here?" Sean asked, coming from the bedroom. "Natalia's trying to sleep." He shut the door gently behind him and padded into the kitchen, where I was sitting at the table with Conor and Sofie, helping them finish their homework.

"He's praying," I said. "It's not a crime."

Sean growled, grabbed a couple of beers from the fridge, and plopped down in front of the TV, where he'd spend the rest of the night getting drunk and watching sports.

"I think it's nice," Sofie whispered. "His voice is pretty."

"I think so too."

Conor rolled his eyes. "I wish he'd hurry up so he can help me with my science project."

"Can you do that another time?" I asked. "Fadil and I have to take care of some things."

Mr. Murakami had given me lunch detention for showing up late in fifth period without a good excuse, so I hadn't had time to talk to Fadil since my run-in with Freddie. He'd brought me home after school, but had spent the entire drive telling me what I'd missed at lunch, which had included Mr. Grossman bursting into tears for no reason and running from the cafeteria. Then Sofie and Conor had gotten home and I'd had to throw together dinner using what little we had in our fridge, since Sean had "forgotten" to go grocery shopping.

Conor didn't argue, but his adorable pout was evidence enough of his disappointment. I was glad Conor had a guy to look up to, seeing as Sean wasn't someone you looked up to so much as looked down on.

"Hey, Mr. Malloy!"

Sean grunted at Fadil as he traipsed through the living room into the kitchen.

Before Conor or Sofie could steal Fadil's attention, I

dragged him out of the house. I would have preferred to hang out at his place—especially since he had his own room—but Sean would have fed the kids cereal for dinner, and they deserved better.

We walked in silence around my neighborhood, toward the lawsuit-waiting-to-happen that stood in for a playground, and sat on the swings. The sun's light was draining from the sky, signaling to the mosquitoes that it was time to attack. I swatted them away absently.

"So I talked to Freddie after anatomy."

Fadil kicked off on the old brown mulch until he was swinging in a long, lazy arc. "Did you ask her out?"

"Sure, 'Hey, since I totally saved your life, we should go out.'"

"Or maybe with a little more enthusiasm."

I'd been replaying the conversation in my head, looking for some other way to interpret Freddie's words. They didn't make sense based on what I knew of her. She wasn't the most popular girl in school, but everyone liked her. She took dance classes and was in theater and she fought to make the world better. In ninth grade, the school had put up posters in the cafeteria for Taco Tuesdays, which had included a pudgy-faced Mexican with a bushy mustache who was wearing a sombrero. I couldn't look at those stupid posters hanging in the cafeteria without wanting to tear them all down and set them on fire in the middle of the quad, but Freddie actually created protest posters highlighting the racism inherent in the Taco Tuesday posters. She'd made one for every day of the week, each more offensive than the last, including posters for Matza Mondays, General Tso's Tuesdays, and Fried Chicken Fridays.

By the time Freddie was done, Taco Tuesdays became Turkey Tetrazzini Tuesdays and all the posters were replaced with goofy cartoons depicting the dangers of gonorrhea, genital warts, and herpes. She'd gotten a week's worth of detention for her trouble.

That was when my crush had gone critical. And I didn't know how to reconcile that girl with the one who was upset I'd saved her life.

"Well?" Fadil asked. "What did she say? Did she thank you, at least?"

"Hardly." I was afraid to swing too high, out of fear that the groaning structure would collapse on top of me. "She asked me why I'd healed her, if I'd considered whether she'd wanted to live, and then she told me not to bother next time."

"Next time?" he asked. "Does she think someone's going to try to take another shot at her?"

"Maybe."

I stood and walked to the slide and sat on the edge. There was an empty condom wrapper a couple of feet away and dried dog shit someone had neglected to pick up. Who the hell saw dog poo and thought, *Let's get naked!*

"Why do you think she was upset you healed her?"

"PTSD?" I said. "David Combs shot her. I'm not sure what kind of mess I'd be if he'd shot me."

"Did she know him?"

"I didn't get the chance to ask."

Fadil eventually followed me to the slide and leaned against the pole connected to the jungle gym. "I've been trying to think this through," he said. "You, the first person scientifically proven to have been born of a virgin, hears a voice from a corporate logo that tells you to heal Freddie, which you do. Moments later, David Combs, a boy you'd never met, vanishes in a bright light. And since then, you've healed a cat's leg and a cut on my hand." He cocked his head to the side. "Is that everything?"

I stared at the ground and drew circles in the sand with the toes of my shoes. "According to Mrs. Burchfield's anatomy skeleton, I'm apparently supposed to save humanity."

"A skeleton talked to you?"

"Mostly he made bad jokes," I said, "but he also warned me that the world is in danger and I have to heal more people to stop it."

"How many more?"

"Freddie interrupted before he could tell me."

Fadil was silent for a moment. "Do you believe him?"

I brushed my hair off my face. "For as long as I can remember, the voices have guided me. Before Mama married Sean, she was supposed to go on a date with this guy she'd met online, but my Barbie told me she shouldn't, so I faked being sick and she canceled. A few days later we saw on the news he'd been arrested for kidnapping a woman. The voices told me to take anatomy this semester when I really wanted to take chemistry, and they told me to sit with you at lunch your first day of school.

"The voices have been this constant presence in my life and I didn't always understand the things they said or asked me to do, but I believed they were looking out for me. Now, though?" I caught and held Fadil's gaze. "Telling me where to sit at lunch so that I'd meet my best friend is one thing; telling me I'm supposed to save humanity is a whole different level of weird."

Fadil pursed his lips. A light sheen of sweat coated his face. "But do you believe them?"

"Should I?" I asked. "Would you?"

"I talk to Allah five times a day," he said. "I'd be surprised if he answered, but I'd probably believe him."

"I don't think it's Allah who's speaking to me."

"It might be."

"I doubt he would make silly puns."

"You might be right, but the divine being who came up with human sex organs definitely had a sense of humor." Fadil put on his thinking face. It was a cute scrunching of his nose and forehead, and it made him look a little constipated. Which, okay, doesn't sound cute, but trust me, it is. "So if the voices aren't Allah or any god, though you shouldn't rule that out, how do you feel about them asking you to save humanity?"

Fadil was treating this seriously, and I loved him for it.

"Confused? I'm not sure how healing will save the world unless I heal everyone in it at once."

"Okay, then," he said. "Do you think the voices are connected to the light that took David Combs?"

"I doubt it was a coincidence," I said. "But why would they take him?"

"Punishment? Maybe they zapped him into the middle of a volcano."

My mind began to race at the implications. "Or maybe they took him as a reward for shooting Freddie," I said. Fadil tried to interrupt, but I cut him off. "Follow me, here. I'm supposed to heal people in order to save humanity. The voices encourage David to shoot Freddie in front of Starbucks because I have a crush on her and they believe her nearly dying would make a compelling catalyst to bring out my ability to perform miracles. Then, as his reward, they beam him up and away to spend the rest of his life in paradise."

Fadil's jaw muscles twitched. "Or, David Combs was a violent kid who wanted to kill someone, the voices had nothing to do with that part of it, and we don't know why they raptured him or where he went."

I took Fadil's hand and squeezed it gently. "I wish I had answers."

"Can't you go back to Starbucks and ask the siren? Or the skeleton or some other inanimate object?"

"They don't answer when I call."

"That's inconvenient."

"Can't we forget any of this ever happened?" I asked. "You go back to being a band geek and I'll go back to being Mary and we can pretend our lives aren't a science-fiction movie."

Fadil squeezed onto the slide beside me. "You were chosen by some higher power, and I don't think you can ignore that. Maybe you could go on TV and start your own Miracle Elena Healing Hour show."

"Not likely," I said.

"How else are you supposed to heal enough people to save humanity?"

"I'm not sure," I said, "but Deputy Akers called and told me at least three people claimed to have recorded the 'miracle,' but that all they'd recorded was empty footage."

The lack of video evidence hadn't helped my credibility. "Besides, if the voices wanted me to have my own TV show, they would have told me to answer one of the hundreds of phone calls or e-mails I got after the shooting."

"Either way, you've been given a special ability, Elena, and I believe you have a moral obligation to use it for the betterment of humanity."

"Even if I don't understand why I have this power?"

"When Allah offers you a gift, you don't refuse it so you can decide whether it's a worthy gift."

"But you do if you're not sure it's God that's given it to you," I said. "There are things I don't understand, Fadil, and I think I should if I'm going to move forward."

Fadil frowned with one side of his mouth. "What do you have in mind?"

"David Combs," I said. "He's the connection. If we can figure out why he shot Freddie, whether the voices took him, and where he went, maybe we can understand why I have this power and what I'm meant to do with it."

Fadil leaned into me and I wanted to hold him there forever. I felt safe when he was near, like there was no question I couldn't answer, no battle I couldn't fight. "This is bigger than you. Bigger than Freddie or David Combs. And sometimes we have to do what's asked of us and trust that it's the right thing."

"There were people who thought my birth was a miracle," I said. "And some who thought otherwise. Then a doctor came along and proved it was science and not a miracle. Remarkable, improbable, but still science. We can do the same here, and I believe David Combs is the key."

"I'm on board with whatever you want to do," Fadil said. "But I don't think Combs is the key. I think you are."

# TWELVE

SEAN WAS ALREADY drunk when I returned inside after saying good-bye to Fadil. I wished I had Fadil's faith. My life would have been easier if I trusted the voices implicitly. If I believed the shooting and David Combs disappearing and my newfound abilities were part of a larger plan to save humanity. And maybe they were, but I needed to know for sure. I couldn't blindly follow the orders of the voices when I didn't know where they came from or whether they were being completely honest with me.

"Kitchen's a mess," Sean said. "Clean it up and then put the kids to bed."

"I cooked."

"So?"

"It wouldn't kill you to get off the couch and help," I said.

Sean took a long swig from his beer can and then stretched his free hand behind his head. He was stringy and scruffy and I didn't understand what my mother saw in him. "You're lucky, you know?"

I rolled my eyes. "So lucky."

"When I was your age, I was going to do shit." His eyes got this glassy, far-off look. "Work with computers. Make a shit-ton of money and never have to worry about nothing."

I bit back the smart remark that leapt to my tongue. "What happened?"

Sean scrubbed his patchy beard and relaxed. "Life. My dad got sick and I got a job to help my mom with the medical bills. Then I met Natalia. You were here for the rest."

"So go back to school," I said. "It's not as if you don't have the time."

"It's not that easy."

"Sure it is," I said. "Go online, enroll in classes, attend them, find a job. See? Easy."

"You think it's easy because you never had to make a difficult choice in your life. But one day you'll see. You'll make compromises you wish you'd never made. You'll wake up and look at your life and wonder how the hell you ended up there. Then you'll understand."

"The only choice you seem to be making these days is whether to drink at home or drink at the bar."

Sean's mouth and eyes hardened. I saw the moment the walls snapped up between us. He stood, tossed his empty beer can on the floor, and stormed into the bedroom. A couple of minutes later, he returned in different clothes, grabbed the car keys, and left.

I started cleaning the kitchen. I felt like a jerk. Sean had been trying to tell me something and I'd shut him down without bothering to listen. But it was difficult to feel sympathy for him when he could have helped make our lives so much better if he'd only put in a little effort. If he found a job, we might have been able to afford a bigger apartment and maybe a car that didn't threaten daily to crap out on us.

I heard the shower turn on in Mama's bedroom while I was washing the dishes, and she came out a few minutes later as I'd settled at the dining room table to attack my mountain of homework, which included my makeup work from Thursday. I had all weekend to do it, but I didn't want to leave it until Sunday.

Mama was wearing her uniform—khaki pants and a blue shirt—and she'd pulled her wavy brown hair into a messy bun. The smears of purple and green under her eyes from lack of sleep weren't part of the uniform.

"Do I smell coffee?"

I motioned to a travel mug I'd set by the pot. "I already put cream and sugar in it."

She kissed the top of my head as she passed through. "What would I do without you, Elena?"

"Fall asleep while restocking creamed corn?"

Mama poured her coffee and stirred it before taking a long sip and sighing. She turned and leaned against the counter. "What did you say to Sean that got him so worked up?"

"That he was a lazy asshole."

"Elena . . ."

"All I did was suggest he go back to school instead of wasting his time at a bar."

"Sean's a good man who's going through a rough time." She leaned against the counter. "He wasn't always like this, you know."

"Yeah," I said. I remembered how good he'd been with Conor and Sofie when they'd come along, and despite the way he acted these days, they still loved him.

Mama carried her mug to the table and sat down perpendicular to me. "How was school?"

I wanted to tell her the truth. About the lawyer who'd approached me outside the apartment and the kids saying I was a liar and how Freddie had told me I shouldn't have healed her. I even wanted to tell her about healing Lucifurr and Fadil, and the voices, but I didn't. It was the look on her face that stopped me. The one that said she was treading water in lead boots and that worrying I was running around performing miracles might be the thing that pulled her under.

"It was fine," I said.

Mama reached across the table and took my hand. "I count on you to watch after Sofie and Conor when I'm not around." She flashed me a tired smile. "Which means you need to learn to get along with Sean. He's not a bad person; he's just—"

"An asshole," I finished.

"Sometimes." Mama cupped my cheek in her hand and kissed the top of my head.

"How do you do it?" I asked. "How do you go to work and deal with Sean and me and the kids?"

"I have no other choice," she said. "If I stopped to worry over all I have to accomplish, it would overwhelm me. So I do the thing in front of me, then move to the next and the next." Her phone buzzed in her pocket. She slid it out and peeked at the screen. "And now I have to go. Lydia's out front waiting for me and I want to say good night to the kids." Mama got up from the table and headed to Sofie and Conor's room.

I sat at the table after she'd left, considering what she'd said. Humanity was in danger, I had healing powers I didn't know what to do with, I didn't trust the voices, David Combs shot Freddie and I needed to figure out why, and why the voices had raptured him, and Freddie seemingly wished I'd let her die. Mama was right. If I attempted to solve all my problems at once, they'd drown me. My best option was to focus on the issues immediately in front of me and keep moving forward, so that's what I decided to do. I hoped the world didn't end in the meantime.

# THIRTEEN

NORMAL IS STUPID. Who got to determine the baseline for what was normal and what wasn't, and who appointed them to make that decision? Why did they get to declare that I wasn't normal because I was born without a father? Why did they get to decide that I was weird for healing a girl who'd been shot?

Freddie's shooting hadn't affected most of my classmates. They hadn't seen her body; they hadn't washed her blood off their hands. All the majority of them knew was that I'd either performed a miracle or lied about performing one, and they were quick to label me a freak and retreat into the safety of their routines. While I was attempting to learn why David Combs had shot Freddie and why the voices had taken him, everyone else was pretending the world was awesome and, nope, nothing happened, nothing to see here; go back to your stupid, normal lives.

Fadil and I spent our lunch periods slowly peeling back the layers of David Combs. He didn't have any friends that we knew of. He'd tried out for the marching band but had been cut, and hadn't been involved in any clubs or teams. He'd been a ghost at Arcadia West long before he'd disappeared in a beam of light. We'd learned nothing that explained why he'd become violent or why the voices had deemed him worthy of saving. To say it was frustrating was an understatement.

"So then Mr. Benson's sleeping at his desk and he starts going, 'Who's a good boy? Are you a good boy or are you a naughty boy?'" Fadil had dropped his voice an octave to mimic Mr. Benson.

We were sitting at our usual table near the wall, lost in our own world while a hundred boring conversations went on around us. Most of the time the rest of the school could have vanished and we wouldn't have cared.

"While you were taking a test?" I dipped a greasy fry into my paper ramekin of ketchup and ate it. I didn't know what they'd been fried in, but they were delicious.

Fadil nodded. "And we were trying not to laugh so we could find out whether 'he' was naughty or not."

"Please, dear God, tell me Benson has a dog."

"It's creepy either way."

*You guys are so boring. Take me out of this bag.*

I paused and dipped under the table to dig around in my backpack. The voice yelped when I grabbed the slender box of tampons I'd bought on the way to school that morning because I'd felt crampy and annoyed, which usually meant the communists were invading. I set the tampon box on the lunch table. It was decorated with a faceless sketch of a girl bending a soccer ball under obnoxiously festive lettering.

"That explains the french fries," Fadil said, motioning at my lunch.

"Excuse me?"

"What? You only buy cafeteria fries right before your period."

"Are you keeping track? Is there an app for that?"

"There is," Fadil said. "I don't have it. But I've known you long enough to recognize the signs. So what? We're friends."

It was annoying enough that Fadil was able to guess when I was having my period based on my dubious food choices, but somehow worse that it didn't bother him. When I'd dated Javi he'd practically gagged and run away when I'd mentioned it.

"That's not why I got them out." I spun the tampons so the girl on the box was facing Fadil. "She told me to. Apparently we're boring."

*Why aren't you healing people? Didn't we make it clear that you have to actually perform miracles in order for us to save humanity?*

"She's asking why I haven't gone on a healing rampage," I said.

"Have you told her your plan to uncover all of David Combs's deep dark secrets?"

"You tell her."

*I hear everything you idiots say. I know about your stupid plan.*

"She thinks we're idiots," I said.

Fadil furrowed his brow. "Why are the voices so rude?"

"They didn't used to be." I picked up the box to stuff the sketchy tampon girl back in my bag.

*Wait!* she said. *If you insist on doing this, talk to Javier.*

"Great plan," I said, dropped her in my backpack, and zipped it up.

"What?"

I rested my elbows on the table and leaned forward. "She says I should talk to Javi, as if that's ever going to happen."

Fadil tapped the tip of his nose with his index finger. "Actually, that's not a terrible idea."

"How is talking to my obnoxious ex not the worst idea in the history of bad ideas?"

"It's not worse than the time you went platinum blond."

"You swore never to mention that again on pain of excruciating death," I said. "And talking to Javi is definitely worse."

"Hear me out, okay?" Fadil continued wolfing down his lunch, which one of his parents packed daily in an adorable bento-box-style container, as he spoke. "You heard the rumors that David Combs was bullied? Well, Naomi told me—"

"When did you talk to her?"

A goofy grin practically ate Fadil's entire face. "After you failed to arrange our totally random meet-cute, I had to do it myself. Except it really was an accident. I saw her at the bookstore on Saturday reading manga, and I went up and talked to her. We met; it was cute. And then we hung out again on Sunday."

I held up my hands to stop him. "Wait. You've been spending time with Naomi Brewer? How did I not know that?"

Fadil offered up a shrug. "There hasn't been much to tell so far."

As much as I wanted to dive into the romantic entanglements of my best friend, I thought it best to hold off. "Let's table the Naomi Brewer discussion for later—though you will tell me all the details even if I have to tickle them out of you—and get back to why I should talk to Javi about David."

"So, Naomi told me that a few of the guys from the baseball team pulled a prank on him at the start of the school year."

"And?"

Fadil talked with his mouth full, which annoyed me, but I let it slide to keep from getting off track again. "If Javi was in on it, talking to him is a decent place to start. Besides," he added, "we have no other leads."

I'd managed to avoid speaking to Javi since we'd broken up and I wasn't eager to end my winning streak, but Fadil and the girl on the tampon box had a point. I only wished it didn't involve my narcissistic ex.

"Fine," I said. "I'll talk to him."

"Good." Fadil chewed and swallowed the last of his lunch, wiped the crumbs onto the floor, and tossed his lunchbox into his bag. "Gotta run. See you after last period."

Fadil took off for Dhuhr prayers, leaving me alone at our lunch table. Okay, I wasn't exactly alone. There were some freshmen at the other end of the table, but they pretended to ignore me the way everyone else did. There hadn't been any more anonymous graffiti drawn on my locker, but that didn't mean there wouldn't be. Like I said, my classmates were eager for life to return to normal, which meant pretending the girl who'd practically raised someone from the dead was nothing more than a typical social outcast.

Speaking of social outcasts, though definitely of the non-typical sort, Freddie was eating her lunch alone instead of with her friends. I couldn't figure her out. She seemed as determined not to return to her normal life as everyone else seemed to do the opposite.

Try though I might, I couldn't ignore that Freddie was

also part of the puzzle. Why Freddie had been at Starbucks at that moment was as important as figuring out the whys and whats of David Combs. Of course, it was easier to investigate someone who wasn't around than it was the girl I had a crush on and who'd suggested she would have been happier if I hadn't saved her life. But I might not get a better opportunity to talk to her.

I dumped the rest of my fries into the trash, carrying only my bottled water, and walked to Freddie's table. She'd changed her hair, shaving it on one side and braiding the other, though it was still my favorite shade of blue. The style looked good on her, but I never would have guessed she'd change her hair so drastically.

"Mind if I sit?" I asked, and then sat across from her without waiting for an answer.

Freddie looked up, her lips set in a scowl, and pulled an earbud out of her ear. "What?"

Where she'd said "what," I'd heard "what the hell do you think you're doing here, freak?" Not exactly the welcome I'd hoped for.

"How come you're not with your friends?" I motioned to the table where Corinne Spieler and Tori Thrash and Wendy Nguyen were sitting.

Freddie crinkled her nose and sniffed loudly. "They're not my friends."

"Since when?"

"Since I decided they weren't," Freddie said. "What do you want?"

This was not going well. Winifred Petrine and I weren't friends, and during our previous conversation I'd learned she'd hadn't thought of me at all or even known my name.

"To talk?" I said. "You seem different since—"

"Some loser asshole tried to shoot me?" she said. "Like you care. Besides, I'm not the one who's different."

"What does that mean?"

Freddie sucked in a long breath and blew it out through her nose. "Nothing."

The conversation stalled. I fought to reconcile this Freddie with the girl I'd had a crush on. She was the same girl who'd fought against racist lunch posters and had given a speech in eighth grade about her desire to travel the world with the Peace Corps, and being near her turned my brain to oatmeal, but she was also not that girl. Like someone had cut out the parts of her brain that made her remember how to smile and encased her in metal.

"Look, what I said the other day." Freddie clenched her jaw. "I'm not depressed or suicidal or whatever."

"Okay."

"Everything is weird."

I thought my inability to form coherent sentences was a

liability, but the less I spoke, the more Freddie kept talking.

"I was already having a bad day and then this random kid shoots me. And for a second, one fucking second, I think I'm okay with it. I can die and go on to whatever is next and I'm totally fine with that. Then a girl I've been calling the wrong name for years heals me—which is totally fucking abnormal, by the way—and suddenly, depending on who you ask, I'm either the girl who was saved by an angel or the accomplice in a ridiculous hoax."

Since the shooting, I'd been so worried about my own problems that I hadn't considered how it had affected Freddie. All I'd heard were the insults and jokes directed at me, but it made sense that she'd become a target too, and I felt like an idiot for not realizing it.

"And the cherry on the shit pie is that everything is off somehow. My mom and my so-called friends, they're all the same, but different. Out of focus or something, and I can't stand to be around them."

"You went through a traumatic experience," I said. "It's normal for things to feel strange."

"You sound like my therapist."

"Is that a good thing?"

"She's mostly okay, but I'm convinced she sleeps with her eyes open while I'm talking."

"I'll take it as a compliment anyway," I said. "But she

might be right. Maybe your perspective's changed and the things you used to think were important aren't anymore." I frowned. "Or maybe we're all alien imposters and you're the last human left on Earth."

It took a second, but Freddie let a smile peek out. It was subtle and small, but it was there, like the first fingers of the cresting sun.

"You're fucking weird."

"And you swear a lot," I said.

"My mom said the same thing the other day."

I was doing it. I was having a conversation with Freddie and I hadn't drooled or ended the world. It was a miracle. And then the bell rang. Freddie sighed, shoved her phone in her purse, and stood.

"Hey, wait," I said. "If you ever want to talk about what happened, I'm around. Or we could hang out and not discuss it. Whatever you want."

I expected her to sneer and say no, or to tell me that I was the last person on the planet that she'd want to be caught talking to. Instead, she paused and said, "Maybe," before walking away.

Maybe. I could live with maybe.

# FOURTEEN

THE ONLY CLASS I shared with Javi was English, immediately following lunch. The universe was conspiring to give me the finger or make me vomit.

Javi played the role of stupid well, but it was an act carefully designed to keep his friends from learning he had a brain under the veneer of dick jokes and sports statistics. He read voraciously, and his tastes ranged from Harry Potter to Naked Lunch, though he favored medieval and renaissance literature for reasons I failed to understand. Sometimes it felt like two Javier Matos Videntes existed. One who'd spent weeks trying to convince me to sleep with him and one who couldn't help grinning when he attempted to explain why *The Canterbury Tales* was the most important book written in the English language. I didn't mind brainy Javi, but he rarely allowed that version out to play.

I arrived to class early and pulled out my copy of *The Perks of Being a Wallflower*. I'd done the reading, but I expected Mrs. Czukas to quiz us and I wanted to be prepared. I was deep into the chapter when I overheard Roshani and Jason talking behind me.

"And no one knows what happened?" Roshani asked.

"Nope. Strangers all over the world vanished and it's not on the news or anything."

"But it's a hoax like . . . you-know-who saying she healed that other girl?"

Really? I was sitting only a couple of desks away. Did she honestly believe I wouldn't realize she was talking about me or did she simply not care? The answer was probably a little bit of both.

"Don't think so. There was a kid in France, some woman outside a bookstore in West Jordan, Utah, a couple of dudes in Fruitland, Idaho. People who saw it said a light shot out of the sky and Hoovered folks into it."

"Someone recorded it though, right?"

"One guy said he tried, but that his phone recorded literally nothing."

"That's impossible."

"Maybe it's the end of the world."

The warning bell rang, cutting off Jason and Roshani's discussion. Students poured in, rushing to their seats to avoid being marked late. Two seconds before the final bell rang, Javi strolled into class through the front door.

Javi had a Picasso-painting face. Taken individually, the parts shouldn't have added up to something beautiful, but they did. His ears were wide, his nose was long, and his brown eyes too large. Any one of those things could have doomed him to a life of awkwardness, but together they worked for him. Javi grinned at me and winked as he passed. I resisted the urge to scowl in return.

Mrs. Czukas cleared her throat and sat on the edge of her desk. I was pretty sure she owned the same bland dress in different shades of boring, which she wore every day, and I kind of admired her commitment. If she had any fucks to give about what we thought of her, she hoarded them jealously.

"Settle down," she said, and then waited for the various conversations to end. "I hope you all had a nice weekend."

A couple of students mumbled.

"The good news is that we will not be having a quiz today," Mrs. Czukas said. "The bad news is that we won't be reading *The Perks of Being a Wallflower* anymore."

"Why not?" I asked without thinking. I didn't love the book, but I assumed it was better than the alternative.

Mrs. Czukas took a deep breath through her nose. "A

parent filed a complaint regarding the content, and Principal Gonzalez decided it would be best to pull it from the curriculum for now." She waited for the talking to die down. "I'm not happy about it either. I fought the decision, but lost. You can drop your books off at my desk at the end of class—"

"That's so messed up."

The voice had come from the back. I recognized it instantly and turned around to look.

Javi had his arms crossed over his chest and was wearing a frown I knew well.

"If you want to keep your book, Javier, you're more than welcome to, but I have my orders. Instead we'll be covering—"

Javi cut her off again. "How's that even fair?" he said. "I mean, what? Some kid's parents have to ruin it for the rest of us because they don't want him reading stuff they're too scared to talk about at home?"

"Mr. Vidente," Mrs. Czukas said. Her voice was hard, but there was sympathy in her eyes.

"Come on, Mrs. C.," Javi said. "You know it's dumb. How are they gonna say it's not okay to read a book with gay stuff or jerking off in it, but they're cool reading *Romeo and Juliet*, where a dude in his twenties hooks up with a thirteen-year-old girl and where Benvolio tells Romeo the best way to get over Rosline is to find a girl who's into backdoor action?"

The class erupted with puerile laughter, but Javi wasn't

laughing. Anyone who didn't know him well might have believed he'd said it for the attention, but Javi was passionate about four things other than his dick: his family, food, baseball, and literature. I couldn't help smiling.

"Out," Mrs. Czukas said. "Go to the office and share your concerns with Principal Gonzalez."

"Don't be like that, Mrs. C.," he said. "You know I'm right."

"Good-bye, Mr. Vidente."

Javi grabbed his books and stomped out of the room, slamming the door behind him.

# FIFTEEN

I TOLD MRS. Czukas that I needed to use the restroom in order to chase Javi down the hall and talk to him. I'd considered waiting until the next day and finding him before lunch, but I thought my best chance to get the information I wanted from him was when he was righteously angry about literature.

Javi was loitering in the hall, reading posters stuck to the wall outside the library, clearly in no hurry to reach Principal Gonzalez's office. He didn't even notice me walking toward him until I spoke.

"Hey, Javi."

Javier Matos Vidente turned slowly to look at me. A smile pricked up the corners of his lips. "Elena Mendoza," he said. "The Miracle Girl. Or the girl in love with David Combs. Depends who you talk to. Were you actually banging that psycho?"

"Seriously?"

"It's fucked up if you let that guy get on you when you wouldn't even give me a hand job."

"And there it is," I said.

"There what is?"

"The reason I broke up with you."

Javi rolled his eyes. "I broke up with you."

"Keep telling yourself that."

He turned to continue walking toward the admin office. I jogged to catch up because I'd already come this far and it would have been a waste to turn back now.

"Wait up, Javi."

"What do you want?"

Javier, like most boys I knew, was fragile. Oh sure, he fronted a tough exterior, especially when his friends were around or when he was trying to impress a girl, but inside he was a delicate glass ballerina who longed to show the world his pirouette. "I appreciated what you said to Mrs. Czukas. I was actually enjoying *The Perks of Being a Wallflower*."

"Whatever. Now we'll get stuck reading *The Great Gatsby* or some shit." He shook his head. "I get that the story's supposed to show how fucked up the 'American dream' is, but there's nothing familiar to me about those privileged, rich white people. I can't feel bad losing something I never had."

This was the Javi I'd enjoyed spending time with. The one who talked books like they were part of his soul. It was a shame he hid this version of himself from his friends. They might not have appreciated it as much as I did, but it would have been honest.

"Maybe you can change Mr. Gonzalez's mind."

"You ever talked to Gonzalez?" Javi asked. "If he won't change his seventies perm, he won't change his mind about a book. I'm going to get a month of detention unless I say my outburst was because I'm having problems at home or something."

"You don't have any problems at home," I said. "Your parents treat you like a little prince."

"That's not how I'll be selling it to Gonzalez."

"There's not a universe where that's not messed up."

Javi stopped walking and turned to me. "What do you want, Elena? I know you didn't come out here to thank me for using Shakespeare's butt fetish to stop Mrs. C. from banning *Perks*."

"No. No I didn't," I said. "I wanted to ask you about David Combs."

"The dude who shot Freddie?"

"I heard some of the guys from the team pranked him last year."

"And?"

"Were you in on it?"

Another smile cut Javi's face. "Yeah. It was funny."

"Maybe not to him?"

"Oh, I get it. Everything's my fault."

"I'm not—"

"Anyway," Javi went on, "I'm not the one who helped him run away."

This was not going the way I'd intended. I'd put him on the defensive without meaning to and now he'd activated full attack mode. "I didn't help him do anything."

"So you say." Javi crossed his arms over his chest, his sleeves pulling back to reveal his thick, muscled biceps. I could lie and say they weren't impressive, but they really were.

"I'm just trying to learn more about David," I said.

"He could've killed you," Javi said. "I tried calling when I heard, even though you blocked my number, and then I couldn't sleep all night thinking you might've been hurt."

I faltered. I knew that under the hormones and the act he put on for his friends, Javi had cared for me, but I hadn't considered he'd been worried. It hadn't even crossed my mind to call and tell him I wasn't hurt.

"I'm sorry I didn't call you," I said. "And I didn't block your number. I had to change my number because of all the weirdos."

Javi gave me one of his emotionless shrugs. "Whatever. Why're you so interested in Combs, anyway?"

"It's difficult to explain here in the hallway," I said. "But it's important."

Javi slid seamlessly from pouting to grinning. There was something sinister about his dimples. I felt in a strange way that, even though I'd thought I was the hunter, I'd become the prey. "Let me take you out."

"Excuse me?"

"On a date? That ritual where one person picks another person up, takes them to a movie or dinner, and then goes home at the end of the night with blue balls or whatever the female equivalent of blue balls is?"

I still wanted information from him, which is why I tried hard to hide the frustration creeping onto my face. "We already broke up once. What makes you think I'd go out with you again?"

"You need information. I got information. Go on one date with me and I'll tell you what I know."

Sure, Javi had strong arms and a handsome face and I'd liked him once, but that was a lifetime ago. I'd never regretted our breakup or considered giving him a second chance, and I didn't see why that should change now. Except that David had been bullied, and Javi knew why and by whom. One night wouldn't be the end of the world. I hoped.

"Fine," I said. "But you're still going home with blue balls at the end."

"I expect nothing less."

# SIXTEEN

FADIL LAUGHED FOR a solid five minutes when I told him on the drive home from school that Javi had ransomed his David Combs info in exchange for a date with me.

"This isn't funny," I said. "Going out with him the first time was bad enough."

"It's a little funny."

"No, it's really not." Then I told him about the conversation I'd overheard Jason and Roshani having during English. "Do you think those people disappearing are my fault?"

Fadil pulled into my apartment complex and parked. "You can't take anything that comes from Jason Carpenter seriously. I had speech with him last year and he gave a presentation on how the government is using the smart devices in our homes to create profiles of us so that it can replace us with obedient artificial machines."

"I get that," I said. "But the way he described it was exactly how David Combs disappeared."

"Then he heard it from someone who was at Starbucks that day."

Though Fadil had a point—Jason's love of conspiracy theories, no matter how far-fetched, was widely known—I wasn't prepared to blow off what I'd overheard quite yet.

Fadil had plans with Naomi—again, Mama was sleeping, and Sean was out, so I took Conor and Sofie outside to the playground to burn off their excess energy. I used the time to hunt through the Internet for information that supported Jason's claims. I didn't find much, and I didn't trust what little I did find. One site that talked about other disappearances also had an article purporting that David Combs had been an alien and would soon return to transport all of humanity back to his planet. So, not exactly credible. But if even one person other than David had been raptured by a light from the sky, then that had to mean there was more going on than the voices were telling me.

I was so distracted by my phone that I didn't hear Mrs. Haimovitch shuffle up beside me until she lowered herself onto the bench with a huff.

"You kids and your cell phones."

Mrs. Haimovitch was beautiful. Age may have traced lines across her face and gravity may have dragged her skin downward, but time couldn't erase her beauty, only change it, like a tree's leaves that shift from green to gold.

"Hey, Mrs. Haimovitch. How's the hip?"

"Hurts," she said. "And my stupid insurance won't pay to replace it. Not until I'm completely unable to walk, so they claim."

"Bastards."

"You got that right." She watched Sofie and Conor chasing each other around the park, laughing and fighting. "How's your mother?"

I shrugged. "Tired all the time. It doesn't help that Sean does absolutely nothing to help her."

"She's too good for that man."

"That's what I keep telling her."

"And how are you holding up?" Mrs. Haimovitch asked. "Some sleazy reporter came around asking after you."

I froze. "What'd you tell him?"

Mrs. Haimovitch let slip a devious laugh. "Oh, I invited him in for brownies and told him about my hip and my gout and the damn insurance company, and I showed him pictures of my grandchildren and the video of my colonoscopy. He didn't have any questions for me after that. Also, he ate two brownies, so I made sure he took a taxi home."

Now I was the one laughing. Mike D. often gave Mrs. Haimovitch his skank weed, which she used to whip up brownies and cookies and other edibles, which she shared with him and some of the others in the apartment complex. She claimed the brownies helped her manage her pain. If the reporter had eaten two, he'd likely spent the rest of the day staring at pretty lights seen only by him.

"So you invited a strange man into your house, drugged him, and showed him a video of your lower intestine? You might have missed your calling as a supervillain."

"All these folks harassing you after what you did," she said. "It's obscene. But he left me his card."

"I get it. I'm a story. Either I'm a girl who performed a miracle or a girl responsible for perpetrating a hoax to help a mentally unstable teenage boy escape."

Mrs. Haimovitch tilted her head to the side and offered me a sweet smile. "No one here believes you helped that troubled boy."

"I might have," I said.

"How so?"

"I'm not sure." My thoughts drifted back to that afternoon at Starbucks. "When I healed Freddie, I think I might have caused the beam of light that took David Combs."

"I've known you and your mother for a while, Elena," Mrs. Haimovitch said. "You're a sweet, kind girl. Whatever you did or didn't do, I'm sure your heart was in the right place." She shifted on the bench, wincing even from such a small movement.

"Thanks, Mrs. Haimovitch."

"I do have one question, though."

"Ask away."

"Have you always been able to perform miracles?"

I fidgeted with my fingers and glanced at the kids. Sofie had climbed on Conor's back, and he was carrying her around while she raised one of her arms in the air like she was taking a victory lap on a prize horse. "I don't think so. I'd never tried before."

Mrs. Haimovitch nodded and smiled. "How's that nice Muslim boy you spend so much time with? Has he worked up the nerve to ask you out yet?"

I coughed to cover my laugh. "Fadil? We're just friends."

"Oscar and I were 'just friends' for years before he finally found the courage to ask me on a date."

Mrs. Haimovitch had told me countless stories of her husband who'd passed away, and I let her because those were the moments she seemed most alive.

"You miss him, huh?"

"I do."

"Well, there's no chance of that with Fadil. He's got a girlfriend now anyway. I think. I'm not sure what they are."

Mrs. Haimovitch wore a knowing smile and I hoped she wasn't going to push the issue. I loved him like a brother and nothing more. "Is there anyone special in your life, then? I'm living vicariously through you, so don't leave me hanging."

"There is a girl," I said. "But I'm pretty certain she's not interested in me."

"Who is she? Have I met her?"

I shook my head. "It's the girl I healed. Winifred Petrine."

"Now, that's interesting," Mrs. Haimovitch said.

"Not really. I had a crush on her. Maybe I still do. Either way, she's made it clear my feelings will go unrequited."

"People change," she said. "Why don't you invite her to dinner?"

"At my apartment?" Mrs. Haimovitch was only trying to help, but the idea of her in my home with Sean and Mama and the kids was ludicrous. One minute with them and she'd probably run away.

"Mine," Mrs. Haimovitch said. "Sunday. I always cook in case Katie and the grandkids drop by, and it's a shame to waste all that food."

"Thanks," I said. "But we've barely been able to have a five-minute conversation. I'm not sure I'm ready for a dinner date."

"The offer's always open."

"I'll keep that in mind."

"I should get back inside. Help me up?"

I took Mrs. Haimovitch's hands and anchored myself to the ground while she pulled herself to her feet. Pain creased her face with every movement, and an idea formed.

"Let me fix you," I said. "Your hip I mean. Why wait for the insurance company when you have a miracle worker living above you?"

Mrs. Haimovitch steadied herself before letting go of my hands. "Don't waste your miracles on an old lady like me. Save them for those who really need them."

"You've done so much for us." I'd lost track of the number of times she'd babysat Sofie and Conor on short notice, and she'd even drugged a nosy reporter to protect me. "Besides, I don't think the healing is a limited resource."

Mrs. Haimovitch caught my eyes. The creases around her mouth deepened. "There's a good reason my daughter and grandchildren don't come around for Sunday dinner," she said. "I don't deserve a miracle."

While Mrs. Haimovitch spoke frequently of her deceased husband, she rarely spoke of her daughter and grandchildren. Mama might have known why they were estranged, but I didn't, and I found it impossible to imagine anything Mrs. Haimovitch might have done that would cause her daughter to shun her. Then again, we all have secrets we're ashamed of. We're all capable of hurting the people we love, even if we do so unintentionally. But that didn't mean Mrs. Haimovitch wasn't worthy of a miracle.

"You don't deserve to suffer, either. Not when I can help you." When she still hesitated, I added, "Please?"

Finally, Mrs. Haimovitch nodded. I made sure Conor and Sofie were on the other side of the park and then I took Mrs. Haimovitch's hand and closed my eyes. Her fire was dimmer than Freddie's and Fadil's had been. It was tinged with shadows and flickered in places. I didn't think it was in any danger of dying out, but it was evident it had burned for a long time. I zeroed in on the area where her hip was and found sharp teeth gnawing at the bone. Slowly grinding away at it, patient and unyielding. Her pain must have been constant, and I'm not sure how she'd managed to live with it for so long. I guessed there was more strength in her than I'd given her credit for. I pried the teeth from her bones and threw them into the void, healing her.

Mrs. Haimovitch drew in a sharp breath and stumbled against me. I opened my eyes. Before I could ask if she was okay, Mrs. Haimovitch pulled me to her and wrapped her arms around me and cried.

"It doesn't hurt anymore," she said. Over and over and over. "It doesn't hurt anymore."

# SEVENTEEN

TWENTY-ONE PEOPLE VANISHED from the earth when I healed Mrs. Haimovitch. There was no way I could have known that at the time, but if I had, I might not have done it.

Sofie was taking her shower and Conor was watching TV with Sean while I enjoyed a few moments of quiet alone in the bedroom with the computer in my lap, searching for any news about lights from the sky or strange disappearances. I stumbled across a new article about David Combs with a quote from his parents pleading for anyone who had information to contact the police. I felt sorry for them. There was no scenario where they wouldn't be living a nightmare. If the light from the sky hadn't raptured him, David might have shot others, and I might not have been able to heal them. Or he could have taken his own life rather than face being arrested. In some ways, I think not knowing where he was or what had happened to him was worse. If he were dead or in prison, at least they wouldn't be stuck in limbo wondering.

*Woooo! Elena! Your dread god commands you to listen!*

I looked up from the computer and scanned the room, pausing on a stuffed baby Cthulhu Javi had bought me as a joke after our first date. We'd spent the evening arguing over whether it was appropriate to teach stories written by a heinous racist and anti-Semite to high school students, and Javi had given me Baby Cthulhu to remember the conversation by. It had been a weird, sweet gesture.

"Good," I said. "I have questions. Did I cause David Combs to disappear when I healed Freddie? And was it only him or did others vanish?"

*Do not demand answers from your deity! Grovel, worm, and despair.*

Baby Cthulhu had wide cartoon eyes and a horde of fat tentacles for a mouth. He was cute and not at all intimidating, and I found it difficult to take him seriously. "Or you could stop being a prevaricating dick and answer me."

*Come on! Show some respect to your dark lord or I will set fire to the world and watch you burn with it!*

I wasn't certain how to respond to the bratty, stuffed god.

If I pissed him off, he might go silent and I'd never learn anything. But I also wasn't in the mood to allow him to talk down to me. "What do you want?"

*We have given you gifts of might, the ability to perform miracles, and you have squandered them on old ladies and cats. We command you use your powers to heal the sick and dying or face our eternal wrath.*

"I can't run around healing people at random."

*Of course you can! That's the whole point, you sweet, ignorant fool.*

"How would you like it if I stuffed you under the bed?"

*You would demean your god by treating him like an unwanted toy?*

"I'd shove you in a blender if it would shut you up."

*Time is running out. Use the abilities we have given you, Elena Mendoza.*

"Stop messing around and maybe I will," I said. "Did I cause David Combs to vanish?"

*Fine. Yes.*

"Did I cause others to disappear?"

*Yes. Yes, it's all your fault. Now get on with the healing or suffer the consequences.*

The implications caused my brain to run wild. "How many?"

Baby Cthulhu didn't answer immediately, and I thought

I'd scared him off. But he hadn't left, and after a moment he said, *Twenty-one.*

"Total?"

*Twenty-one when you healed the old woman's hip, five when you saved Winifred Petrine, eight when you healed the cat, and thirteen when you wasted a miracle on that boy's cut hand.*

I did the math in my head, and when I came up with the total my mouth fell open. "Forty-seven? Are you serious?"

*We told you that you were saving humanity.*

"I thought you meant by healing them!"

*That's why we're responsible for the thinking and you for the healing.*

I felt sick to my stomach. Eight people had vanished because I'd healed Lucifurr's leg on a whim. There were eight families out there wondering what had happened to someone they loved, and it was my fault. "Are they still alive? Where did they go? And why twenty-one? Why thirteen before that? Are the numbers random or significant?"

*The explanations would cause your puny brain to explode, and while I would greatly enjoy that, we need you, Elena. You have a divine purpose. Do not question the will of your gods!*

I laughed without meaning to. "You're not my gods."

*Could anything but a god give you power over life and death?*

Fadil might have been willing to take Baby Cthulhu's assertion that he was a god at face value, but I wasn't. He saw the will of Allah in the sunrise and in every smile and human interaction. I, however, saw science. Cause and effect. The sun didn't rise because Allah or God or gods willed it; it rose due to of the rotation of the earth, which was controlled by gravitational forces.

Still, Baby Cthulhu had asked me a question I couldn't answer. If the voices weren't divine, then where had my ability to perform miracles come from?

"I don't know," I admitted. "But I'm not ready to believe that you're God or even a little-G god."

*Your belief is not as important as your obedience. Do as we command or your world will end in flames. The world will burn and everyone you care for will burn with it!*

I'd had enough. Clearly, Baby Cthulhu wasn't going to tell me anything useful. I stood, grabbed him off the dresser, and stuffed him under the bed.

*Elena! What are you doing? Get me out of here this instant! Your dread god commands it!*

I headed for the door, stopped, and said, "Try not to burn the world down while I'm gone."

# EIGHTEEN

RUNNING AROUND HEALING strangers wasn't as easy as Baby Cthulhu had tried to make it sound. I couldn't walk into a hospital, find a room full of cancer patients, and zap them well. There were likely rules against it. I'd read an article about a boy who'd secretly lived in a hospital in Central Florida for a few months after his parents died there. He'd eventually been caught. And there was another story about a kid who'd masqueraded as a doctor at a hospital down south for a while before he was discovered. So I guessed it might have been possible to sneak in, perform some quickie miracles, and sneak back out, but doing so felt too risky.

And I still hadn't processed the new knowledge that healing people caused others to vanish. I didn't care that Baby Cthulhu had said they were being "saved," whatever that meant. I was responsible for tearing mothers and fathers and sisters and husbands and kids from those who'd loved them. Even the worst human beings on the planet had at least one person out there who would miss them if they were gone. Making the lives of some better by healing them couldn't balance out the pain caused by the disappearances of others.

Ever since I was little and Mama told me that I was unique, I'd thought that meant I was destined to do something special, to be someone special. Hearing voices that no one else heard had only reinforced that belief. And I wanted it to be true. I wanted my life to have meaning. For the kids at school and my family to see me for who I really was. I wanted Freddie to see me. But if I did what the voices wanted, Miracle Girl is all I would ever be. And eventually someone would make the connection between my ability to heal and the random beams of light that shot from the sky. When that happened, it would only be a matter of time before shadowy government agents came knocking on my door to whisk me away to a secret underground base where they'd force me to use my abilities for them, or cut me open to understand how I worked.

But if I did nothing, all of humanity might suffer. I couldn't expose myself to the world and remain hidden at the same time. Eventually I was going to have to make a choice, but I needed more time to figure out what to do.

On Friday, I hung around after class to discuss our homework with Mr. Murakami, and I was late heading to the cafeteria. The normally chaotic hallway was quiet, and I caught the faint echo of music in the distance. It was fast and frenetic and not the sort of music I would have expected a teacher to be listening to. I was anxious to get to lunch so I could tell Fadil what Baby Cthulhu had said, but curiosity drove me to follow the music instead, and I found myself standing in front of one of the art rooms. I peeked through the door's window. Freddie was dancing in front of a pile of garbage, wearing a rubber apron and work gloves, uninhibited the way someone is when they're certain no one will see them.

I shouldn't have watched. I was stealing a private moment from her, one that I didn't deserve to see, but I couldn't leave. No. That's not true. I didn't want to leave. This was the real Freddie, the one I'd had a crush on. Gone was the girl who'd been angry with me for saving her life, replaced by this goofy, beautiful woman, and I couldn't look away. I watched her bounce on her heels and bob her blue-haired head to the manic music's beat as she sorted through the metal bits and wires on the table. Then she suddenly stopped what she was doing and performed a guitar solo in the air. A laugh escaped my lips that was so loud, Freddie stopped and turned around.

She'd caught me. I suppose I could have run away. That

might have been the prudent action, but instead I opened the door and walked inside and said, "If there was an air guitar competition, you'd totally win," which was definitely a terrible line heavy on the cheese, but it was the first thing I thought of.

Freddie reached behind her, grabbed her phone, which was plugged into a portable speaker, and turned the music down. "Why are you spying on me?"

For a brief second, I'd seen her content. Happy, even. But now she was scowling, clearly annoyed I'd interrupted her. "I wasn't spying. Well, I mean, I was, but not intentionally. I heard the music and was curious, and then I saw you dancing and I shouldn't have watched but I did and—oh! What's that you're working on?" I pointed at the sculpture behind Freddie. It was approximately four feet tall, five counting the pedestal, and made of copper tubing and ribbon cables and wires.

Freddie practically glared a hole through the center of my chest while I prayed my flimsy diversion would succeed. Finally, she said, "My end-of-the-year project for Mr. Aydin."

I moved toward the whatever-it-was and circled it slowly. "Is it a person?"

"Possibly. I'm not sure what it'll wind up being."

"You don't work with clay or marble or normal stuff?" I motioned at a couple of the other projects sitting out. There was a brownish lump that looked like it might grow up to be a vase one day, and another that resembled a disembodied mouth full of crooked teeth.

Freddie motioned with her hand like those other projects were so lame. "Garbage is kind of my thing."

"I didn't know that."

"Why would you?"

*Uh, because I had a crush on you and I thought I was the foremost expert in all things Winifred Petrine, but clearly I was wrong and am a gigantic moron.* None of which I actually said because she'd already caught me spying on her and I didn't want to make the situation any creepier.

"So you're not sure what you're building?"

Freddie ran her hands across a sheet of chicken wire that was stretched between two metal supports. "I'm not big on worrying about the end result. I let the materials dictate the form."

"What if the materials dictate a crappy form?"

"Then I build something crappy." Freddie stopped. "Why are you here, again?"

The question sucker punched me in the gut. "I can leave." I turned toward the door.

"Wait," she said. "I'm sorry. That was mean. You saved my life and all, and I repay you by being bitchy."

"You're not bitchy. I was the one spying on you, after all."

"True." She walked to a cabinet, grabbed a pair of gloves

off a shelf, and tossed them to me. "But since you're here, you can help me." She motioned at the pile of trash. "Pull out whatever looks interesting."

I was kind of hungry, and Fadil was waiting for me in the cafeteria, and this wasn't how I'd intended to spend my lunch period, but I dropped my bag on the floor and slipped the gloves on. "How will I know what's interesting?"

"You just will."

Freddie cranked the music back up. I didn't know the band, but they screamed a lot.

"Who is this?" I asked.

"You wouldn't recognize the name." Freddie stood on a stool, bending what I thought was supposed to be an arm from the legs of a camera tripod.

"Probably. It's not the kind of stuff I usually listen to." I prided myself on having decent taste in music, but I wasn't a connoisseur.

"Not because . . ." Freddie trailed off. "It's old stuff. My dad gave it to me. He called it a history lesson. Some of it's really, really bad. There's this one band called The Suicide Machines. They're pretty terrible. But there's other stuff that's cool. Patti Smith and the Yeah Yeah Yeahs, and this one is Operation Ivy. It's from my dad's short-lived punk rock phase."

It felt weird to be having a conversation about music with Freddie instead of discussing her being shot and me healing her and what it meant. "I have no idea what they're saying, but I like it."

"Me too."

"And it was nice of your dad to do that."

Freddie paused. "Yeah, well, I guess he didn't want to die without completing my music education."

I froze, a circuit board dangling from my hand. "Sorry. About your dad, I mean."

"It's fine. He died last year. You don't have to be weird."

And now I couldn't stop being weird. "I don't have a father at all."

"Right," Freddie said. "Because you're the Miracle Girl."

I tossed the PCB into a pile of stuff I thought Freddie might want to use and kept pawing half-heartedly through the junk. "It wasn't a miracle. It was parthenogenesis."

Freddie climbed down off the stool. "Partheno-what?"

"Parthenogenesis," I said. "It's a form of asexual repro- duction."

Freddie stared at me like I was speaking French. "You're not making this shit up? It's a real thing?"

I nodded. "This scientist, Dr. Milner, proved it and every- thing. There's even a Wikipedia page."

"Honestly," she said, "I always thought someone had made that virgin birth shit up."

"It's all true."

Freddie moved closer and started looking through the pile of trash I'd added to. She smelled like dust and copper and melted plastic, and I think that was the first time I'd been turned on by the scent of garbage. She picked up a bundle of wires and began stringing them around and through the bars of one of what I thought might be a leg. "How come you don't stand up for yourself when people mess with you about it?"

"No matter what I say, they're going to believe what they want. Besides, the words 'virgin birth' call to mind Jesus and the Virgin Mary, and the idea that a lower-middle-class Cuban girl could be in any way associated with Christ makes people uncomfortable. It's really not that important."

"Of course it is. Those assholes are shitty to you because they think you made it up to get attention, and they're wrong."

"It's not like I care what anyone says."

"Lie."

"No it's not!"

"Of course it is. Everyone cares what others say about them. Especially the ones who claim not to."

The music shuffled to a less angry band. "Whatever. Besides, usually when I can talk to someone, like we're talking now, they understand. I don't need to change everyone's minds, just the people who matter."

Freddie screwed up her face. "And you think I matter?"

"I healed you, so you're probably predisposed to believe

the rest of it," I said, sidestepping her question. "What's one more miracle compared to coming back from the dead?"

"I'm not sure I'd call that a miracle."

"Are you really not glad you're alive?"

Freddie sighed. "Sometimes. I guess. Can't a girl have a bad day or a bad month or whatever without someone coming along and trying to tell her to smile more or be happy even when she's not? None of this shit matters. Alive, dead? There's no point to any of it."

"What if this is the point?" I said. "This moment and every moment that comes after." She eyed me skeptically. "It's all connected, I think. Like two hundred years ago some guy in a small town in rural Pennsylvania bumped into a woman and they started talking and got married and popped out babies and now we're here having this conversation. Everything we've done leads to everything we're going to do."

"And I suppose that includes David Combs shooting me?" Freddie said. "I'm supposed to believe there was a reason for that, too?"

"Maybe."

Freddie shucked off her gloves and tossed them onto the table. "That's pretty fucked up. I'm not okay with a world where a fucked-up loser has to try to murder me in order for us to have this boring conversation."

Her words caught me off guard. She thought the

conversation was boring. Which meant she thought I was boring. I'd dreamed of the day we'd finally talk and she'd realize she thought I was pretty and wanted to go out with me and it all felt stupid in light of everything else that had happened, but that didn't make her words hurt less.

I took off my gloves and grabbed my bag from the floor. "Sorry. I didn't mean to bore you."

Freddie started to speak, but the door opened and Corinne Spieler, Tori Thrash, Wendy Nguyen, Ava Sutter, and Tori's boyfriend, Daniel, rolled in laughing and talking. They stopped when they saw me.

"Hey, Mary," Tori said. "How's your arm?"

"What's she doing here?" Daniel asked. He'd been nice in middle school. And then he'd gone through puberty and had come out the other side a smoking-hot asshole.

"I thought you were coming to lunch today," Ava said to Freddie. "We have a party to plan for tomorrow."

Corinne, Ava, Tori, and Wendy were the kind of girls who had the things I was supposed to want: beauty, popularity, friends. And they made having them look easy. But they also made it difficult for someone like me to have those things. Popularity was a zero-sum game. There was only so much room at the top, and I didn't rank.

"See you later," I said to Freddie, making my way toward the door.

"Later, Mary," Daniel said.

"Jesus Christ," Freddie said. "Her name's not Mary. It's Elena."

I hesitated, pausing to see if Freddie said anything else, but she didn't, so I left.

# NINETEEN

FADIL WAVED AT me from the field where he was practicing with the marching band, and then promptly stumbled
into Jennifer Swan's back. I was watching from the bleachers,
trying to do my homework, which I'd gotten a little behind
on due to all the excitement with performing miracles. You
know how it is. Two rows down and a few feet to the right, a
small-framed girl with her hair in twists appeared to be working on a school assignment of her own. I kept replaying my
conversation with Freddie in the art room. Look, I wasn't stupid enough to believe that real life would play out the way it
had in my many, many daydreams. I knew that my crush was
based on my imagined perception of a girl who wasn't real.
Freddie wasn't my soul mate. She wasn't going to swoop in
and rescue me from my life. We weren't destined to begin an

everlasting romance so passionate that poets would compose glorious sonnets in our honor that would wind up being used to bore future high school students. She was a girl I'd idealized because she was beautiful and seemed like a decent human being from afar.

That's how crushes work. They're not based in reality. If they were, we wouldn't call them crushes because we wouldn't wind up crushed by the inevitable truth of the person.

So, no, I wasn't navigating our new whatever-it-was under the fallacious notion that we were going to fall in love and spend the rest of our lives together. I did, however, hope that we could continue to get to know each other. The way I saw it, there were only two ways to get over my crush. Either I realized she was a horrible person not worth my time or I got to know the real Winifred Petrine and built new feelings for her on a solid, honest foundation. Of course, there existed the very real possibility that Freddie would never share my feelings. But friendship with someone you like isn't a second-place trophy; it's a win all its own, and I thought I could be happy with that.

Mrs. Naam shouted at the band, yanking me from my thoughts. Fadil was constantly complaining about how tough she was, but Arcadia West's marching band was one of the best in the state, so her methods clearly got results. The girl I'd noticed earlier had moved closer, and she kept slyly stealing glances at me.

"Hey," I said.

As if I'd given her the opening she'd been hoping for, the girl flipped on like a spotlight, beaming at me with a hundred-and-fifty-watt smile. "You're Elena Mendoza, right?"

"Yes."

"I'm Justina. Smith. Justina Smith."

"Okay."

Justina took the opportunity to scoot even nearer. I hadn't been looking for a conversation, but she wasn't going to give me a choice. "Did you really heal that girl who got shot at Starbucks?"

"If this is some thing where I tell you I did and then you call me names or preach at me and tell me I'm going to hell, please do it so that we can move on with our lives."

Justina flinched. She had this whole wounded baby bird thing going on that made me instantly feel crappy for going off on her.

"Sorry," I said.

"I hear the stuff they say about you," Justina said. "It's trash. You saved a girl's life. And I don't believe you helped that boy get away, either."

"Is that so?"

Justina moved fractionally closer. "I go to Lakeview Unitarian Church, and Pastor Stephanie says God works through us, you know? She says the world is full of miracles and that it's regular folks who are performing them."

"Are you sure she wasn't speaking about metaphorical miracles, like feeding the poor or whatever?"

"She might have been, but that doesn't mean you aren't doing real stuff." As she spoke, Justina's hands zoomed through the air like they were controlled by wires. "There's a girl in São Gonçalo who can heal the sick, and there are stories about miracles all over the Internet. I'm a believer."

"Is this the part where you tell me how your mom is sick and ask me to save her life?"

Justina bowed her head. "My brother; he has cystic fibrosis. He's a good kid, annoying sometimes, but what eight-year-old isn't? I hate sitting with him watching other boys his age play sports and tag and knowing that, even though he doesn't complain, he'll never do those things. I just want Ben to get to run."

I was surprised it had taken this long for someone at school to approach me. Even with the world full of skeptics, there were those desperate enough to take a chance, no matter how slim. But aside from that creepy lawyer who'd stalked me at my apartment, Justina was the first.

"Please?" Justina caught my eyes, and I wanted to say yes, but there were so many unknown variables. I didn't know how many people would wind up sucked into the sky if I healed Justina's brother, or where any of them went. The uncertainty was crushing. But then I remembered what Mama had said. Focus on one thing at a time and keep moving. I couldn't answer all the questions I had, but I could help one boy breathe.

"Does your brother go to our school?"

"Arcadia Elementary," she said.

I sighed and nodded. "I'm not saying I'll do it, but meet me here Monday after last period, and if I show up I'll heal him."

Justina cranked up the wattage of her smile to dangerously bright levels. Brighter than a lighthouse. It was the second most beautiful thing I'd ever seen. She jumped up and nearly tripped down the bleachers in her haste to leave before I changed my mind.

"And, hey," I called after her. "Can you not tell anyone?"

"I won't," she said. "I promise."

# TWENTY

FADIL SAT ON my bed with Sofie, playing checkers, while I tried to find clothes to wear on my stupid date with stupid Javi.

"I still can't believe you're doing this," he said.

"We agreed that I need to figure out why David Combs"—I paused and looked over my shoulder at Sofie—"did what he did. If Javi has answers, I can suffer through a few hours of dodging his grabby hands."

Sofie jumped two of Fadil's red pieces and threw her hands up in victory. Then she said, "I liked Javi. He made me laugh."

"That's because he has the mentality of an eight-year-old." I settled on a pair of jeans and a plain gray scoop-neck top. It was an outfit that said, "I know I'm hot, but touching me will cost you your balls."

Fadil moved another of his pieces. I couldn't tell whether he was letting Sofie win or was the worst checkers player in history. "You do realize this whole date thing is a lame attempt to win you back."

"A) I'm not a trophy. B) Javi doesn't want me back."

"He might."

"His friends hate me."

"Men throughout history have risked the wrath of their friends for a girl they loved."

I mimed gagging. "Javi loves books. He loves his grandma. He loves himself. And he loves a good frita. He does not love me." I couldn't figure out what to do with my hair, so I gave up and let it fall loose around my shoulders. "Javi can't stand the idea that I'm not soaking my jeans every time he flashes his grin at me, and he only wants me back to prove that he's irresistible."

Fadil wrinkled his nose. "That's gross. And graphic. Do you think all guys are like that?"

"You're not, but you might be the exception."

"I hope that's not true," Fadil said. "Anyway, have you decided if you're going to heal that girl's brother?" On the ride to my apartment I'd told him about Justina and what

Baby Cthulhu had said the night before, but he hadn't said much about either until now.

"What girl?" Sofie piped up.

"Her name is Justina," I said. "Her brother Ben goes to your school. He's got cystic fibrosis."

"What's cysta fi—"

"Cystic fibrosis," Fadil finished for her. "It's a genetic disorder that causes mucus in the lungs and makes it difficult to breathe, among other things."

Sofie picked up one of her checkers and held it to her lips. "There's a boy who carries a breather thing at my school, but he's in Mr. Campbell's class so I never talk to him."

"That's probably the same kid. And I'm not sure what I'm going to do." I made Fadil turn his back while I changed. "You should have seen Justina's face, all sad and hopeful at the same time. The most cold-hearted villain in the world would've struggled to say no to that girl."

"I think you agreed to do it because you want to," he said.

"Of course I want to—I'd be a horrible human being if I didn't—but that doesn't mean I should."

"You're afraid of who might disappear."

I finished wriggling into my jeans and buttoned them. "You can turn around again." I pulled a couple pairs of shoes out of the closet from under Conor's box of LEGOs and decided to go with the red Converse. "Would you be Team

Miracle if one of your parents got raptured, or is it only okay when it's people you don't know?"

Fadil sat frozen in the middle of a move, his checker dangling from his fingers.

"Are you going to make Daddy go away?" Sofie asked.

"Not today," I said. "Why don't you go find Conor and get your stuff together to stay with Mrs. Haimovitch?" Mama was working and Sean had informed me he was going out, so Mrs. Haimovitch had offered to watch Sofie and Conor. Since I'd healed her hip, she had so much energy. I'd even seen her jog-walking around the neighborhood.

When Sofie was out of the room, Fadil said, "I have to believe there's a plan. Even when I don't understand it."

"How could I live with myself if you lost one of your parents?" I asked. "Or if I lost you or Mama? That's the risk, right? The voices aren't going to only take strangers and boys who try to shoot us. Eventually someone we know and care about is going to vanish, and that'll be on me."

"But if those people are being saved," Fadil said, "if humanity is being saved, then the alternative is allowing everyone to die. I could live with losing my parents if it meant they were safe."

*Listen to Fadil,* Baby Cthulhu said from under the bed. *At least he's not a total moron.*

I ignored the stuffed deity. "It's easy for you to say. You're not the one in charge of the fate of the world. Anyway, does the world look like it's ending? Things suck, yeah, but that's nothing new. Things have always sucked for the majority of people, and the world hasn't ended yet."

"What do you want me to say, Elena? You heal people. You hear voices that are warning you the world is in danger."

"Which is totally normal."

Fadil clenched his fists and looked like he was two seconds from flipping the checkers board across the room. Then he took a deep breath. "Joan of Arc heard voices from God. Maybe you're like her."

My phone buzzed from the dresser and a message flashed on the screen. "It's Javi," I said. "He'll be here in a few minutes."

Fadil swung his legs around and stood. "Then I'll take off. But think about what I said, okay?"

"Fine," I said. "But you know they burned Joan of Arc at the stake, right?"

Fadil rested his hands on my shoulders. "If anyone tries to burn you at the stake, Elena, they'll have to burn me with you."

# TWENTY-ONE

I GOT INTO Javi's car, buckled my seat belt, turned to him, and said, "These are the rules: No touching. No trying to touch. We're not going to have sex. You're not going to make some awkward attempt to kiss me that I'm going to have to fend off. If you do, I'm going to slap you and you're not going to act offended and claim I was giving you signs that I wanted it. There are no signs. There will be no signs. This will be our one and only date, and by the end of it you are going to tell me what your friends did to David Combs. Understand?"

Javi was wearing clean jeans and a nice plaid button-down shirt. Clearly he'd put some effort into his outfit, but he'd wasted it on me.

"Jesus, Elena. It's a date, not an inquisition."

"It's not even really a date."

Javi raised one eyebrow. "The deal was a date. If this isn't a date, then I don't have to tell you about Combs."

I gritted my teeth. "Fine, it's a date. Whatever."

"Would it kill you to pretend to have fun?"

"Kill me? No. Turn my stomach and possibly make me vomit onto the floor of your sister's car? Probably."

Without another word, Javi put the car in drive and took off. Maybe it was a side effect of a mother who doted on him, or maybe he was born that way, but Javi was an eternal optimist when it came to dating. No matter how many times I told him no, he still believed he had a chance. Instead of moving on and finding a girl who was actually interested in him, he hung on to some small, misguided sliver of hope that he could change my mind and make me see that he was worthy of my time and affection. But there was nothing sexy about wearing me down. If Javi was honest with himself, he'd have realized I'd only gone out with him to get the information I wanted and so he'd quit asking.

"And for the record, Fadil is tracking my location on my phone in case you try anything sinister."

"Sinister?" Javi said. "I'm not a comic book villain. This is a date. And I'm taking you somewhere awesome. I promise."

I actually had activated the friend finder on my phone for Fadil, but not because of Javi. I'd done it after Carmen

Ballard, attorney to the anonymous creeper, had shown up at my house, so that if I ever vanished Fadil could find me.

"How's Izzy?" I asked. "And how'd you convince her to let you borrow her car?"

"She offered when I told her I was taking you out."

"You told her we weren't getting back together, right?"

Javi stopped at a red light and glanced at me. "She said you'd be stupid not to give me another chance."

"But did she really?"

Javi shook his head. "No. She actually said you'd be stupid to give me another chance. She also says hi."

I liked Javi's sister. She was in college and smart and I should have dated her instead of Javi.

"So how're you holding up?" Javi asked. "I'm sure things are kind of crazy for you, what with you performing miracles and shit."

"Mrs. Haimovitch fed pot brownies to a reporter who'd come around asking questions."

"Nice."

"We've gotten some hate mail, and someone keeps tagging my locker with 'slut,' among other things."

Javi held up one hand but kept his eyes on the road. "Totally not me."

"But you know who's doing it."

"Possibly," he said.

"Whatever. I changed lockers, so now they're defacing an empty one."

I tried to guess where Javi was taking me based on the direction we were driving, but we were heading north on I-95, which made our destination difficult to predict. Previously, Javi's attempts to take me on dates had included movies, mini golf, and parking at the beach. The beach was east, mini golf in the opposite direction, and we wouldn't have needed to get on the interstate to go to a movie, so I assumed he was taking me somewhere new. I prayed it was a place with crowds and bright lights. It was easier to fend off Javi's roving hands if I could see them properly.

"What was it like?" he asked. "Healing Freddie, I mean."

"Bloody."

"Did you see Freddie's memories or form a psychic bond with her?"

"No." I would have been content to sit in the car in silence until we reached our destination, but Javi was going to continue pestering me if I didn't offer him more than one-word answers. "It was freaky. I closed my eyes, but I could still see her, only it wasn't her. She was made of light, and there was this black hole where she'd been shot. And I made it go away. I don't know how to describe it."

Javi bobbed his head. "I read this book about the multiverse. It was fiction, but the science was based on the real theory that every time we make a choice, the universe branches off, with the choices we didn't make forming new universes and shit."

I'd seen enough sci-fi movies to be familiar with the concept. "So there's a world in which I didn't agree to go on this date?"

"And one where we didn't break up."

"How about one where we didn't elect a narcissistic reality-TV personality to be president?"

"God, I hope we got that shit right in at least one universe."

I laughed in spite of myself; I didn't want Javi to think we were having a good time. "Okay," I said. "I'll play along. Are you trying to say you think I'm—what?—healing people in other universes?"

"Hell if I know." Javi took an exit in Port Saint Lucie and headed east. "But the power to heal Freddie came from somewhere. Why not an alternate dimension? In comic books, healers sometimes draw the wound into themselves."

"I definitely didn't do that."

"So where'd the power come from?"

I didn't have an answer. I didn't have a lot of answers. The power to heal could have been given to me by the voices or it could have been part of me all along and the voices simply helped me learn to use it.

"Of course," Javi said, "it might have come from God."

"So I'm Saint Elena now?"

Javi grinned, and it was cute, but as soon as the thought surfaced, I mentally slapped myself back to reality. Javi wasn't cute. He wasn't charming. The moment he sensed weakness, he'd try to get into my pants. "You're no saint, but that doesn't mean God can't still be involved."

"Do you really believe in God?"

"Five years of Catholic school."

"But you don't believe the earth was created in seven days or that humans rode dinosaurs to work, right?"

"That's messed up, Elena. Going to church doesn't make you an idiot." He gave me a sour look. "Science and God aren't mutually exclusive."

In a million years I never would have guessed I'd be enduring a lecture about religion from my ex-boyfriend on the way to our mystery date-not-date.

"You sound like Fadil," I said, not wanting to argue.

"How is Fadil? Still playing his trumpet solo?" He laughed at his own joke. I did not.

"Actually, I think he's hooking up with Naomi Brewer."

"Huh," Javi said. "How're you handling that?"

"Me? Why would I care?"

"Don't play like you don't keep Fadil around as your safety boyfriend."

"I don't even know what that means."

Javi's mouth twisted into a smirk. "It's the sweet loser guy you keep around, stringing him along so that if you wind up alone you have a boyfriend ready to fall back on."

"First of all, I don't have those feelings for Fadil. Second, he doesn't have them for me. Third, not everyone is you, Javi. It is possible for boys and girls to be friends without it being about sex."

"If you say so."

I let the conversation die as we drove to our destination. I still had no idea where we were going, and was confused when we finally pulled into the parking lot of a botanical garden. Of all the places I would have expected Javi to take me, this hadn't even made the list.

"You're surprised, aren't you?" Javi said. "It's okay, you can admit it. I won't gloat too much."

"And here I'd almost forgotten how charming you could be." There's no way he missed my sarcasm, but I was surprised. "You asked Izzy for suggestions, didn't you?"

Javi wriggled his shoulders with pride. "I came up with this idea all on my own."

Surprise number two.

We walked through the gift shop, which was full of kitschy Florida crap—flamingo key chains and palm tree T-shirts—and Javi paid for us to get in. The woman behind the register gave us a suspicious look because she probably didn't see many high school kids in the botanical garden on a

Friday night. Then we started walking aimlessly. I didn't know much about flowers or plants, but they were pretty to look at and their myriad scents filled the air with ginger and jasmine and smells I couldn't identify. We strolled along, admiring the beauty under the starlit sky. It was muggy and mosquitoes roamed the night in vicious swarms, but if I ignored them it was almost wonderful.

We stopped in a section devoted to bonsai trees. It was walled off from the rest of the garden, with koi ponds that burbled and decorative plaques and informational signs over each tree. I sat on a bench and watched the enormous fish swim to the surface.

"These things are unnerving," I said.

"Koi?"

"They belong in a bad B movie. *Koimageddon!* Or *Attack of the Giant Goldfish!*"

"You know they're not the same thing, right?" Javi said. "Goldfish and koi?"

"Really?"

"Koi can cost thousands of dollars, but you can't give goldfish away."

"They're still creepy."

"Definitely."

Javi had opted not to sit with me, instead roving around the pond, reading each of the signs over the bonsai. To his credit, he hadn't tried to hold my hand or give me one of those longing glances that told me he was thinking about trying to kiss me or was picturing me naked. I mean, he didn't deserve that much credit for basically acting like a normal human being, but some was warranted.

"You ready to tell me about David Combs?" I asked.

"Answer me one question first."

"That wasn't the deal."

"Don't be like that, Elena."

"Fine."

Javi turned to face me. He kept his hands behind his back. The light framed his broad shoulders and mischievous dimpled cheeks. If I hadn't known what an asshole he could be, I might have been incredibly attracted to him.

"Why'd we break up?"

I couldn't help rolling my eyes. "That was last year, Javi. Get over it."

"I'm serious. Out of the blue you ghosted me and I didn't even know something was wrong until our relationship was over. I kind of feel like I deserve an explanation."

What Javi thought he deserved and what he actually deserved were two different things, but this was the price I had to pay, and if he wanted to wade into the septic tank of our dead relationship, I could play.

"Are you sure you want to hear this?"

"Want?" he asked. "No. Need? Yes."

I sighed and rubbed my hands on my jeans. This wasn't a conversation I'd expected to be having, so I was unprepared. "All you thought about was sex. We'd barely been dating for two months, and it was like I'd become nothing but a sex doll to you."

"That's not true!"

"And you couldn't say 'vagina' without giggling. If you can't say it, you don't get to go near it." Even though we'd been broken up for a while, all the old resentments flooded back. "It's a word! You come out of them, you come in them, but I say it and you get all giggly and stupid."

Javi's face and ears were turning pink. "It's funny!"

"It's really not. But it proves how immature you are that you think it is." Maybe yelling at Javi wasn't the best way to put him in the appropriate mood for telling me about David Combs, but he'd asked and I felt obligated to tell him the truth. "It was more than that, though. You asked me out when you were still new to Arcadia West. You treated me like a normal human being. And then you met Adam and Clay and Ram, and suddenly I was nothing but some girl you were banging, even though we weren't banging."

"You know how guys are." Javi's voice had risen an octave.

"Not the kind of guy I wanted to date."

Javi's shoulders slumped. He sat down on the bench beside me, wise enough to leave space between us. "I get stupid around the boys."

"And I might have been able to deal with that, but then you called me Mary."

"I never did that."

"I was waiting outside of Mr. Greene's class because we were supposed to go to my house to study. You walked by with Adam, nodded in my direction, and said, 'Sorry, Mary. Rain check on tonight?' Then you and 'the boys' laughed your asses off and left. That's the moment I knew we were over."

Javi screwed up his face like he was trying to recall that day but couldn't. "I didn't mean . . . I don't remember that."

"Well, it happened."

"I'm sorry."

"I don't want your apology. I get it. I'm the school freak. I'm the girl whose mother was a virgin when she was born. Which, by the way, calling me Mary doesn't make any sense since Mary was the virgin and I was the one born of a virgin."

"You're not a freak," Javi said.

"No, I am. It's okay. In our school hierarchy, I'm barely a rung above the kid who eats paste. And it's fine. I've accepted that." I took a breath and went on. "But for a few weeks, despite the pressure you put on me to sleep with you, I thought you saw me as more than that. When I realized you didn't, I knew we were through."

I sat quietly and waited for Javi to protest that he hadn't meant to hurt me and that he'd only been joking—because saying he's only joking is how every dick defends being a dick—but he didn't argue or attempt to defend himself.

"I'm sorry," he said.

"Okay."

Javi turned to me and caught my eyes. "No, really. I'm sorry."

"I accept your apology," I said. "We're still not getting back together."

"I wouldn't take me back either if I were you." He hung his head. "Why didn't you tell me I was such an asshole?"

"You wouldn't have heard me."

"Probably not."

Despite my trepidation, I reached across the space between us, took Javi's hand, and squeezed it. His apology didn't make his actions less horrible, but it was a difficult thing to look in a mirror and see the ugly parts of yourself clearly for the first time, and I think that's what Javi was seeing right then. Whether it would change him remained to be seen, but for this one moment, he wasn't so bad.

"This isn't a sign," I said. "I'm not sending you any signals."

"Message received. Or, not received."

I let go of Javi's hand and walked to the edge of the pond, leaving him to think for a while. The monster fish huddled together at the surface when I approached like they expected me to feed them or hoped I'd fall in so they could eat me. I didn't hear Javi behind me until he spoke.

"David Combs danced ballet," Javi said. "Did you know that?"

I shook my head.

"He took classes in West Palm, probably because he didn't want anyone in Arcadia to find out." Javi's voice was low now, almost a whisper. "Pete's sister took classes at the same place, and one day Pete went to pick her up and saw David dancing. He recorded it on his phone and showed the rest of us at practice the next day. The thing was, he was really good. But then Clay got the idea to set the dance to some funny music and add glitter trails and other shit and post it on Snowflake. It didn't even seem like a big deal. No one really saw it. But I heard David stopped dancing after that."

"You're a horrible person," I said.

"Yeah."

"Was that all?"

"We stole his clothes a couple of times during gym. And Adam hung sugarplum fairy decorations all around his house over Christmas break."

From everything I'd learned, David had been as much of

an outcast as I was. He could have sat with me and Fadil at lunch. I could have noticed him at Starbucks and tried to talk to him instead of Freddie. He'd still tried to kill Freddie, and that was on him, but maybe, just maybe, he wouldn't have wanted to if I hadn't been too involved in my own world to see him.

"Do you think he intended to only shoot Freddie?" Javi asked. "I heard he had a whole list."

"Where'd you hear that from?"

"Ram. His dad's a cop."

"Oh," I said.

"Is it my fault?"

"If I say yes, I'd only be doing it to make you feel like the dog crap you deserve to feel like, but if I tell you no, it'd only be to make you feel better, and you don't deserve to feel better, either." I leaned my head back and looked at the stars. "I don't know, Javi. I'm sure what you and your friends did to him didn't help."

"I wish I could tell him I'm sorry."

"I wish you'd thought to tell him before he shot Freddie."

"Me too."

Our date was over. We weren't going to kiss at the end of the night. We weren't getting back together. Though Javi had to have known neither of those things was likely to happen, I imagine he'd hoped for them regardless. But we stayed at the botanical garden until they closed, gazing at the sky and not talking, because, for this moment, in this bubble of time, I wasn't a freak and he wasn't a bully, and we could be friends without anyone knowing, and at least for now, that was enough.

# TWENTY-TWO

DEPUTY AKERS WAS sitting in her cruiser when Javi dropped me off in front of my apartment. He asked me if I wanted him to wait around, but I told him it wasn't necessary. I wasn't certain why Akers had decided to pay me a visit, but I figured if I was in trouble, she wouldn't have waited for me to come to her.

"Hi, Officer," I said when she got out of her car. She wore jeans and a thin zipped hoodie instead of her uniform, though she still kept her hair tied back in that sad ponytail.

"Evening, Elena," she said. "Do you have time for a chat?"

"It's a little late."

"I'm not here officially."

"Oh."

Deputy Akers crossed the lot to stand in front of me.

She'd seemed taller the day Freddie had been shot, but we were nearly the same height. "I only want to talk."

I weighed my options. Either we stood in the parking lot and discussed whatever it was she'd come to speak to me about, or I invited her into the apartment. Seeing as I was being eaten alive by mosquitoes, I figured it couldn't hurt to talk inside. Mama's car wasn't in the lot, so Sean was still out, and I didn't get the impression Akers meant me any harm.

"My apartment's upstairs."

"I was thinking we could go for a ride."

The last thing I wanted to do was get into the cruiser with Deputy Akers, but I didn't know how to decline. If she wanted to arrest me, she would have done it already, but my brain spun out a hundred possible scenarios and none of them ended well for me.

"Am I in trouble?"

The deputy shook her head. "Nothing like that."

I pulled my phone out of my purse and said, "Let me just tell my mother I'm going to be home a little late." Akers nodded, but instead of texting Mama, I tapped out a message to Fadil and then returned my phone to my purse. I'd told Fadil if I didn't call him in an hour to call Mama and the police. Then I got into the car with Deputy Akers.

"What's this about?" I asked.

"You'll see when we get there," was all the deputy said.

Fear gnawed at me as we drove. I had no idea where she was taking me or what she was going to do with me when we arrived at our destination. I briefly considered throwing open the door when we were at a stoplight and trying to make a run for it, but I didn't think I'd get far. Besides, Akers knew where I lived.

We drove to Saint Mary's Hospital in West Palm and parked in the visitors' lot.

Deputy Akers unbuckled her seat belt and climbed out of the cruiser. "Come on," she said.

I followed Akers into the hospital. The nurses on duty waved at her and smiled as we passed.

"Isn't it a little late for visitors?" I asked.

"Being a cop has advantages," she said. There was an aloofness to Akers that bothered me. She'd shown up at my apartment, she'd brought me to the hospital, but she was acting like she didn't care whether I was there or not.

We stopped outside a dark room in which a young girl a little older than me lay sleeping in a bed. She was thin, had no hair, and was connected to various machines by wires and tubes.

"My sister, Ashlyn," Akers said. "Leukemia. Doctors have done everything they can, but the disease is too aggressive and they've run out of options."

"You brought me here to heal her?"

"If you can."

I'd imagined Deputy Akers was going to throw me in a dark room in an undisclosed location from which I'd never escape. That she would ask me to heal someone had never crossed my mind. I was still struggling with whether or not to help Justina's brother, and now Akers was asking me to cure her sister's cancer.

"And if I refuse?"

"Then I take you home." The emotionless quality in her voice was maddening. It was like she'd brought me here and asked me to do her taxes instead of perform a miracle.

How many people were going to disappear if I did this? I didn't know, and that's why I hesitated. I would be responsible for anyone who vanished as a result of performing this miracle. But they weren't lying in a bed dying. Those hypothetical people weren't standing beside me asking me to save their sister's life. Ashlyn Akers was in front of me and I could help her right now.

I walked into the room, took her hand, and closed my eyes. The girl's light was so dim it was almost nonexistent. Where her light should have been I found spiders scurrying over her, driving their mandibles into her body and sucking the life out of her. They weren't really spiders, of course. I didn't understand how healing worked, but I guessed what I saw was my mind's way of interpreting the illness. It was still creepy as hell. With a single thought, I obliterated the spiders, killing them all. They would never hurt her again.

Deputy Akers was still standing outside the room when I opened my eyes. "It's done," I said. "I think it'll take time for her body to recover, but the cancer is gone."

"I didn't see anything," Akers said.

"Were you expecting heavenly light or fireworks?"

"Something like that."

"Sorry to disappoint you."

Akers took a couple of steps into the room. "Her color looks better, but how do I know you really healed her?"

"You could have her doctors run some tests?" I said. "I'm sorry, but how are you so calm about all of this?"

Freddie had smiled, Fadil had been amazed, Mrs. Haimovitch had wept, but Akers wore an armor of stoicism. "All you did so far was walk in and touch her arm. If it worked, I'll send you a fruit basket. If it didn't?" She shrugged. "You hungry? I'm hungry." She led me to the cafeteria and bought us turkey sandwiches. We sat at a table under the sickly fluorescent lights and ate.

"I didn't believe you, and I'm still not sure I do." Akers caught my eyes when she said it. I imagined her strong gaze unnerving the criminals she questioned. "When you told me David Combs shot Winifred Petrine and then vanished in a beam of light from heaven, I assumed you were on drugs."

"I'm a drug-free zone," I said. "Not even Mrs. Haimovitch's brownies."

The deputy's brow furrowed. "Brownies?"

"Forget it."

"I've been treating what happened like a missing person's case. Working under the assumption that David Combs ran away from home and that you and Winifred Petrine staged the shooting to help obfuscate his whereabouts."

None of what Akers was saying surprised me. I'd read the news and the statements from the Sheriff's Department and had known that they were focusing on finding David rather than figuring out why he'd shot Freddie.

"If you believe I helped David run away, why haven't you been back to question me about it?"

Deputy Akers resumed her thumb fidgeting. "I'd planned to, but I was removed from the case. My lieutenant handed it off to another officer and I was warned to drop it."

"I'm still not sure what you want from me, Deputy. Other than healing your sister, of course."

"Do you know a woman named Leslie Dippold?"

The name didn't sound familiar. "No, ma'am."

"You sure?"

"Pretty certain," I said. "Should I know her?"

Akers chewed the bottom corner of her lower lip and nodded like that was the answer she'd expected, but was still disappointed. "Ms. Dippold disappeared from her office four days ago. She was last seen entering the restroom, and witnesses claim she never came out. The restroom had no windows or other exits, and her car was found in the parking lot."

Four days. I'd healed Mrs. Haimovitch's hip four days earlier. I fought to keep my expression neutral, though if Akers was telling me about the missing woman she obviously believed I was connected.

"Again, I thought it was a routine missing person's case," Akers went on. "People dissatisfied with their lives abandon them sometimes. They leave to start fresh in a new city with a new name. It happens."

"Why are you telling me all of this?" I said.

Deputy Akers flashed me a chilly look that told me she knew I knew exactly why she was revealing this information to me. "Two days ago, I was removed from that case as well and warned to leave it alone. I became a sheriff's officer because I enjoy solving puzzles, and I'm damn good at it. I wouldn't have connected your missing shooter to Leslie Dippold if my lieutenant hadn't made such a fuss about me staying away from the cases. So I did a little digging, and did you know that on the day you claim David Combs shot your friend, there were other reports of strange lights from the sky and missing persons? At least three around the exact time of the shooting, and more later that night."

"I was not aware of that."

"Of course you weren't."

Deputy Akers finished her sandwich, pushed the wrapper away, and sipped her coffee. "The strangest part of all of this is that yesterday two agents claiming to be from Homeland Security showed up, spent ten minutes in my captain's office, and left with all the files on you, Winifred Petrine, David Combs, and Leslie Dippold. Now, I didn't know why Homeland Security would be interested in a missing woman or in you kids, but it didn't sit right with me."

I suppressed a shiver from the glacier floating in my stomach. Homeland Security had taken over the case? Did that mean it was only a matter of time before they came to question me? Had they made the connection between me healing Freddie and the disappearances? They couldn't have known that I'd healed Lucifurr or Fadil or Mrs. Haimovitch.

"Did you bring me here to test me?" I asked. "What are you going to do with me?"

Deputy Akers drummed her fingers on the table and stared into me. Her gaze made me want to confess to every terrible thing I'd done since I was a little girl. After what felt like forever, she said, "One of the most important lessons I've learned from being a cop is that the simplest explanations are nearly always the correct ones. If it looks like a man shot his wife, he probably did regardless of the convoluted story he spins. In your case, I'm either to believe that you and Winifred Petrine planted a large volume of her blood at the scene, faked a shooting witnessed by multiple parties, and also faked a pyrotechnic display in order to help David Combs run away from home, or the story you told about a shooting and miracles and lights from the sky. Neither is simple and one defies belief."

"You just saw me heal your sister."

"Maybe," she said. "We'll know after her doctors run their tests." Akers swirled her cup and stared into the watery coffee. "Do people always disappear when you heal someone?" She cut me off before I could answer. "No, wait. Don't answer that."

"If you didn't believe me," I said, "then why'd you bring me here?"

Akers fidgeted with her fingers for a moment before saying, "After the last treatment, when Ashlyn's doctors said they were out of options, I prayed. I was hoping for spontaneous remission or something. Instead, I got you." She shrugged. "Like I said before, I'm still not sure I believe you, but I want to, and I don't think it was a coincidence I was on duty the day of the shooting."

How was I supposed to respond to something like that? Akers believed I was the answer to her prayers. It was too much for me to wrap my mind around. "I'd like to go home now," I said.

Deputy Akers didn't argue. She drove me back to the apartment. Neither of us spoke on the drive. Fadil was blowing up my phone, so I texted him that I was all right and promised to call him the next day.

When Akers pulled up in front of my building to drop me off, she grabbed my arm to keep me from getting out of the car and said, "I think you're in trouble, Elena. If you really healed my sister, I'll do whatever I can to protect you, but you need to be careful either way."

"What would you have done if I'd refused to help her?"

"I don't know," she said. "Just, watch your back, all right? If people keep disappearing, I think it'll end badly for you, and I'd rather not see that happen."

Akers let go of my arm.

"Thanks for the warning," I said, got out of the car, and watched her drive away.

After I'd picked up Conor and Sofie from Mrs. Haimovitch's and gotten them to bed, Baby Cthulhu told me thirty-four people had vanished.

# TWENTY-THREE

"SHE SERIOUSLY SENT you a fruit basket?" Fadil said on the other end of the phone.

I hadn't called him right after Deputy Akers had dropped me off because I was unsure what her warning meant for me and I needed time to think about it, but he'd pestered me all day Saturday until I finally filled him in on what had happened.

"I healed her sister's cancer," I said. "A fruit basket seems like a small price to pay for that." I'd thought it was a joke or maybe from that creepy lawyer until I'd read the card.

"Maybe you should tell your mom."

"About the fruit?"

I could hear Fadil roll his eyes over the phone. "About what Deputy Akers told you."

"Mama's got enough to worry about," I said.

"And you don't think she deserves to know that men in black suits might bust down your door and kidnap you at any minute?"

"If that were to happen, and I'm doubtful it will, there's nothing she could do to stop them."

"Maybe you should hold off on healing Justina's brother."

*Tell him not to be such a whiney bitch. Your dark master will protect you.* Baby Cthulhu had been in a good mood most of the day, likely because I'd healed Ashlyn Akers, but he was already growing impatient for me to get back to work.

"Baby Cthulhu says he'll protect me."

"Baby . . ." Fadil paused. "I'm worried is all."

"Weren't you the one saying this was all part of a grand plan?"

Fadil growled. "Anyway, how'd your date with Javi go? Did he tell you anything about David?"

"It wasn't a date," I said. "And, honestly, it helped me less with understanding David than it did with understanding Javi." I told Fadil about the nondate and he listened patiently until I'd finished.

"Kids get bullied," Fadil said. "Most of them don't become attempted murderers."

"I told you it was a waste of time." Only, it kind of wasn't. No, I hadn't found a definitive answer for why David shot Freddie or whether the voices had been involved, but I felt like Javi and I had gotten to a place where we could put the past behind us and become friends. Maybe. We still had a long way to go, but it was a start.

"You said Javi mentioned a list with other names on it?"

"What about it?"

"If Deputy Akers wants to help you, she might be able to tell you if it's real and who's on it."

I considered it for a moment. "I'm still not sure I trust her."

Fadil was quiet on the other end of the phone. Then he said, "What other leads do we have? Look, you're the one who needs to understand David's motives. That list, if it exists, could help. Either way, you need to be careful."

He had a point, but we ran out of time to debate it further because Fadil had plans with his parents and couldn't hang out, leaving me alone on a Saturday night, which, admittedly, didn't bother me much. I wanted to do some research into Leslie Dippold. I was working under the assumption that the voices weren't rapturing people at random, and that if I could find some common threads connecting her with David Combs, I might be able to predict who would vanish.

A few hours later, around ten p.m., my phone rang. I didn't recognize the number, and normally I would have ignored it, but I was frustrated by my search, more specifically by the lack of information my search had turned up, and I answered without thinking.

"Elena?"

"Who is this?" Music and the chatter of faint voices echoed in the background, but the person who'd called remained silent. "Look, I'm not interested in doing your show or giving you a quote or whatever it is you want from me."

"Um. It's Freddie."

That stopped me cold. Freddie was on my phone. This was how all my best dreams began. Freddie called and told me she'd been thinking about me and we talked all night, sharing our lives and our dreams, and, yes, I had the lamest fantasies ever.

"Freddie?"

"Look," she said, "I'm at this party at Tori's house and I'm hiding in a closet in one of the upstairs bedrooms and Ava gave me a ride but she's drunk and I really don't want to be here anymore."

So she'd called me. Freddie had called me, though I didn't know how, seeing as I'd only given my new number out to Fadil, Mama, Javi, and . . . Nope, that was it. They were the entirety of my social circle. But it didn't matter at the moment. What mattered was that she'd called and I'd let five whole seconds pass in silence and she probably thought I'd hung up, so I'd better speak before she changed her mind.

"I can come get you."

"I'll text you directions to Tori's house."

"Be there in ten."

# TWENTY-FOUR

GETTING OUT OF the apartment was easy. I didn't even have to sneak. Sean had practically grown roots into the couch and I didn't see him moving anytime soon, so I pretended I was getting a drink from the kitchen, pocketed the keys, and walked out the door. I only knew he'd noticed because he yelled at me not to block the TV when I passed in front of it.

Tori Thrash lived in a private community near the ocean with a sign on the gate that read "Smile! You're on camera!" It might as well have said "You don't belong here, Elena Mendoza!" Thankfully, in addition to directions, Freddie had texted me the code so that I didn't have to use the call box.

Even without the house number, I would have been able to figure out where Tori lived. There were cars packed into the cul-de-sac and spilling out into the one road that led in and out of the development. I imagined the neighbors standing in their windows watching the Thrash house with naked disapproval, debating whether or not to call the police. It was certainly different from where I lived. No one there would willingly call the cops, and if police did show up for some reason, it was a given that someone was leaving in handcuffs.

I drove to the end of the neighborhood, turned around, drove past the house again, and parked by the sidewalk so that I didn't get blocked in. I checked myself in the car's mirror before getting out, wishing I'd taken the time to change into nicer clothes instead of the shorts and *Star Wars* T-shirt I was wearing. My one hope was that I could slip into the party, find Freddie, and sneak back out unnoticed.

A small, cynical voice in the back of my mind wondered if this was a trap. It was weird that Freddie had called me or even had my phone number, and I couldn't help thinking that she and her friends might be setting me up for a prank. I'd walk into the house and they'd kidnap me and throw me into the pool or they'd hose me down with pig's blood, while recording video of it, and post the whole ordeal online. It was the sort of "joke" Javi and his buddies might have played on David Combs. If Fadil hadn't been with his parents, I would have begged him to come with me for protection, but

Freddie was inside, and she'd asked for help, so I sucked it up and went in.

The Thrash house was the opposite of what I'd expected. I figured there'd be fancy art on the walls and expensive furniture no one was allowed to sit on. Instead, it was homey with a weird Southern charm. Framed photos of the Thrashes were strategically placed throughout the house, and the couch was a plaid monstrosity that sagged in the middle. The mantle over the fireplace and the end tables and every other flat surface were stuffed with knickknacks that looked like they'd been purchased at a flea market.

The house was objectively trashed. The kitchen counter was covered with beer bottles and red cups and plates with the crumbs of eaten meals on them. The party, it seemed, had moved outside to the screened-in patio, which was a good thing for me. I didn't even have to sneak around. Freddie had texted that she was in one of the upstairs bedrooms, so I climbed the stairs to the second floor, which was decorated as eclectically as the downstairs, though it was less of a disaster. I poked my head into a bathroom, a linen closet nearly as big as my shared bedroom, and then into a room that I was guessing belonged to Tori.

"Freddie?" I whispered. "It's Elena."

No answer. The room was dark, but the light from the full moon shone through the windows. A bed stood in the middle of the room, and there was a desk and TV against the wall opposite it. I turned until I saw the closet doors, and walked toward them. I flipped on my phone's flashlight and opened the closet. Instead of Freddie hiding under hanging clothes, I found shelves full of My Little Ponies. There must have been hundreds of them neatly displayed in organized rows.

*Elena! You're here! I've been waiting so long for you to arrive!*

"Shhhh!" I hissed. "I'm trying to be stealthy."

*No one else can hear me, silly.*

I pinpointed the voice coming from a pink pony that was smaller than the others and had a pink-and-yellow mane, antennae, wings, and weird pixie ears. I picked her up and held her closer to my face. "What do you want?"

*World peace. Pizza. Not to be in this fucking closet anymore. Those other ponies are bitches.*

I was taken aback by the pony's profanity. It was weird. "Do you know where Freddie is?"

*Obviously not here, dummy.*

"I don't have time for this." I started to return the pony to its shelf.

*Wait! Wait. Please don't leave me here with them.*

"Then tell me where Freddie is."

*She's in the master bedroom.*

"Thank you." I hadn't brought my purse inside, so I held

on to the little pony after I shut the closet doors.

*You're going to heal Ben Smith, right?*

"I don't know." I crept down the hall, looking for the master bedroom. "If there are more disappearances, won't those Homeland Security agents come after me?"

*Let us worry about that. We've been planning this for a long time, and we won't allow anyone to screw it up. Not even you.*

"You could save us some time by telling me how the world is in danger and why you're stealing strangers every time I heal someone."

*Why do you have to question everything? Do your damn job and heal some fucking sick people already!*

"Do you want me to put you back with the other ponies?"

*I'd rather you melted me into a bubbling pool of plastic.*

"Don't tempt me."

*Elena!*

"Whatever," I said. "I'll deal with you later."

The hallway of a house I wasn't technically invited into wasn't the place for this discussion, so I tabled it and turned my attention to finding Freddie.

The master bedroom was at the end of the hall, with double doors that led in. There was a king-sized four-poster bed dominating the room, and a pillar of books stood on the bedside table. I found the closet and slid open the mirrored doors. Freddie was sitting in the back corner with her knees drawn to her chest, playing a game on her phone.

"Freddie?"

She held up one finger and continued tapping her screen and tilting it around as beeps and explosions popped from her phone's speakers. "Damn! I almost beat my high score," she said, and then finally looked at me. "It's about fucking time. Why are you carrying a My Little Pony? Did you steal that from Tori? She's going to kill you. I knocked one of her ponies over once and she didn't speak to me for a week."

"It's a long story," I said. "You ready to go?"

Freddie nodded. I offered her a hand up, and she heaved herself to her feet. "Did anyone give you any trouble getting in?"

"No. They're all out on the patio."

"Even better."

I wasn't sure what that meant. Would Freddie be embarrassed for Tori and her friends to find out I'd come to rescue her? And that was only one of the many questions I wanted to ask. Why had she called me? Why was she hiding in a closet? How did she get my number? But I figured it was best to wait until we'd successfully escaped.

"Thanks for doing this," Freddie said. We walked down the hallway back to the stairs.

"Sure. It's not like I was doing anything tonight."

"Shit. Did I fuck up your plans?" I shook my head.

"Good." She frowned at what I was wearing. "Nice shirt?"

"I was serious about not having any plans."

When we reached the bottom of the stairs, I heard someone moving around in the living room. Whoever it was, we were going to have to walk past them to reach the door. Freddie pulled me along, either oblivious or unconcerned with the person blocking our path to freedom.

"Elena?"

Fadil paused in the midst of pulling back the couch cushions and stood up straight, furrowing his brow.

"What're you doing here?" I asked. "I thought you were with your parents."

Fadil hung his head. "Yeah, about that."

"You lied to me?"

"Naomi invited me to the party." Fadil wouldn't look me in the eyes. "I wanted to tell you, but—"

Anger flushed my cheeks. "But you thought I'd want to come and then you'd have to choose between your best friend and your new girlfriend?"

"It's not like that," Fadil said. "She's not my girlfriend."

"Whatever."

Fadil's voice rose high and broke. "Come on, Elena. You don't like these people, and if I'd invited you, you would have sat alone and not talked to anyone and then I would have had to sit with you and neither of us would have had any fun."

Freddie nudged my arm. "Can we go?"

"Yes." I walked to the door, refusing to look at Fadil.

"Elena, wait."

*Go to hell, Fadil,* the pony said.

"Go to hell, Fadil," I echoed.

I didn't speak again until we were in my car. I sat staring at the dash. I wouldn't have been so angry if Fadil hadn't lied. All he'd had to do was tell me he wanted to spend time with Naomi and didn't want me along to cock-block him, but instead he'd lied, probably figuring I was the last person he'd run into at Tori Thrash's house.

"I'm not ready to go home," Freddie said. "You want to go to the beach?"

I nodded, started the car, and drove toward the beach to find a place to park. Freddie and I carved a path through the sea oats and morning glories down to the water's edge. The tide was ebbing, but I slipped off my sneakers anyway, to avoid getting them wet.

"Sorry about your friend," Freddie said.

The full moon cast shadows on the sand, and without the lights from the houses, the stars hung brightly in the sky like fireflies. They were so beautiful that if I hadn't been so pissed at Fadil I would have enjoyed watching them with Freddie.

"I get that he's into Naomi and wanted to hang out with her, but the rest of those people are jerks."

"Those people?"

"Yeah. The ones who call me Mary and write 'slut' on my locker?"

"A couple of assholes don't make them all bad."

I heaved an angry sigh. "Then why were you hiding in a closet begging me to rescue you?"

"It's a long story and I'm not in the mood to spill my guts at the moment."

"Fine," I said. "Then tell me how you got my number."

Freddie grinned. I could see the outline of her teeth even in the dark. She dug into her pocket and handed me a phone. "I kind of stole this from your friend. I think that's what he was looking for when we ran into him."

I triggered the screen and there was Fadil's background image—a picture of the superhero from his favorite comic book, Patient F. It was definitely his phone. Served him right. I slipped it into my pocket.

"He didn't have to lie to me," I said as we walked.

"Probably not. But haven't you ever lied to spare someone's feelings?"

"Not to Fadil."

"Maybe he's never put you in a position where you needed to."

"So it's my fault?"

"I'm not saying that. But look at it from his point of view.

He likes a girl whose friends you dislike. He wants to hang out with her. You're judgmental, obviously. And he figures if he tells you where he's going, you'll shit on him for it."

"I wouldn't have done that." At least, I didn't think I would have. Either way, it hurt that Fadil thought I would.

"If you say so."

"Now who's being judgmental?"

"Me, I guess," Freddie said. "But I own that shit, so whatever."

We continued trudging down the beach toward a cluster of high-rise hotels in the distance, and there was no one else around. In another universe, this might have been a perfect date. Except this wasn't a date, and the night was far from perfect.

"So why'd you'd steal one of Tori's ponies? Don't get me wrong, I think it's fucking fantastic—she's going to lose her mind when she realizes it's missing—but you're not a klepto, are you?"

"Says the girl who stole a phone. Anyway, you'll just judge me for it if I tell you."

"Don't let that stop you. My opinion doesn't count for much."

It counted far more than she thought. Telling Fadil I heard voices had been one thing—I knew he wasn't going to out me to his new friends about being a freak who talked to tampon boxes and sirens and stuffed baby gods—but I didn't know Freddie well enough to trust her. And yet I suspected she would believe me. Especially seeing as I'd practically brought her back from the dead.

"Fine," I said. "I stole the pony because it asked me to. Begged is more like it. It said the other ponies were bitches."

"I've always thought those ponies were bitches."

"I'm not joking."

"I didn't think you were."

Freddie was nothing like I'd imagined she would be, in countless ways. I'd dreamed that when we finally talked, she'd be this sweet, understanding girl I could pour my secrets into and fall in love with and she'd understand me in a way that no one, not even Fadil, was capable of. Instead she was crass and pessimistic and caustically blunt.

"I hear voices," I said. "From inanimate objects. Tori's pony, for instance."

"Do you take medication for it?" Freddie asked.

"I'm not . . . It's not a mental illness."

"Are you sure? It's cool if it is."

"The Starbucks siren told me to save you the day of the shooting." I blurted it out. And as soon as the words left my mouth, I wasn't sure saying them had been a wise idea, but I'd said them, so I kept going. "She told me I could heal you— she told me I *should* heal you—so I did."

Freddie pursed her lips, her eyebrows dipped down, and

I didn't know what she was thinking, but I really wished I did. Why couldn't mind reading have been one of my miracle powers? It would have made my life so much easier.

"So that day in anatomy," Freddie said, "when you were talking to the skeleton?"

"It told me the world might be in danger and that I'm supposed to help save it."

"You hear voices and you have a savior complex?" Freddie shrugged. "You're a psychiatrist's wet dream."

"I'm not making this up."

"Isn't that exactly what a person with schizophrenia might say?"

It was a fair point. And I didn't even have to be suffering from a mental illness to have created a lie that I myself believed. We—human beings, I mean—believe our own lies all the time. Sean, for instance, had convinced himself he was a victim of the system, that forces beyond his control had conspired to keep him jobless instead of his own drinking and laziness. I couldn't blame Freddie for thinking I might be so entangled in a delusion that I couldn't see the truth, but I was determined to convince her otherwise.

"Fact: My mother was a virgin when I was conceived and born. It was proven by a doctor beyond all doubt. Fact: David Combs shot you at Starbucks, and you were bleeding to death on the pavement. Fact: I healed you." I paused to see if Freddie was going to add anything, but she remained silent. "So with those things being true, isn't it possible that the voices I'm hearing, and have been hearing for as long as I can remember, are also real?"

Freddie turned abruptly away from the water, walked toward the dunes, and plopped down in the sand. I followed and sat beside her. "What's the point?" she asked. "Not of the voices. Of any of it? All of it?"

"That's what I'm trying to understand."

"The pony didn't tell you?"

"The short version is that, supposedly, humanity is in danger. I'm not sure from what. The voices, whatever they are, want to help us. I'm their means of doing so."

"How?"

"Remember when David Combs disappeared?"

"Not really," Freddie said. "I was kind of out of it, but I heard what happened."

"Right. Well, according to the voices, every time I heal someone, they 'save' other people by rapturing them or whatever you want to call it."

"And they chose a killer?"

I held up my hands. "Don't ask me why they took him—I've been working to figure that out—but four others disappeared at the same time as David."

"So they're using you. That figures."

"I don't understand."

Freddie shifted so that her body was angled toward mine. "You're their tool, Elena. They tell you what to do and who to heal, and you do it. Then they rapture fucked-up killers and who knows who else, and you don't even get a say in it. You're the one with the power, but they're making the decisions."

"I can choose not to heal anyone," I said.

"Which is equally fucked." Frustration vibed off of Freddie in waves. "They've given you an impossible choice. Either you're their miracle-performing chimp and they take others without your permission or input, or you do nothing and people suffer and die. They rigged the game, Elena. You won't refuse to heal someone in need because you're sweet and kind, and these voices or whatever they are, are playing you."

I struggled to counter her argument, but she was right. I didn't think I was actually that sweet or kind—though hearing Freddie say I was made me smile involuntarily, and I tucked that memory away to savor later—but there was never a real possibility I would have let Freddie die or Mrs. Haimovitch suffer or Ashlyn Akers lose her fight to cancer, and though I still hadn't made up my mind regarding Justina Smith's little brother, I was leaning toward helping him despite the consequences.

"Does this mean you believe me?"

"Yeah, no," Freddie said. "But pretend I do for now."

The way she'd said it was less than reassuring. "Fine," I said. "Then how do I keep from being used by the voices?"

"You don't."

"Well, that was helpful."

"There's power in knowing that you're being used. All you have to do is look for an opportunity to flip this shit on the pony and the siren and the skeleton. Maybe you can't stop playing the game, but now that you know it's rigged, you can figure out how to beat them."

What Freddie said made sense and reinforced my belief that I needed to understand why David had shot her. That by doing so, I could win the game or change the rules or at least understand what the voices were playing at.

"You're not who I expected you to be," Freddie said.

"Who did you expect me to be?"

"The shy girl who spilled milk on her skirt in sixth grade and started crying so hard Mrs. Dawson had to take her to change."

My eyes flew wide and I covered my mouth with my hand. "Oh my God! I'd totally forgotten about that."

"I didn't," Freddie said. "It was sad but adorable."

"Yeah," I said. "Well, you're not who I expected you to be either."

Freddie shoved herself to her feet and offered me her hand. "We should go."

It took us a while to find the path back to the road, and we didn't speak while we walked. Before I got in the car, I leaned across the hood and caught Freddie's eye. "Hey," I said. "You never told me why you called me to come get you from the party."

Freddie paused. Shrugged. Then said, "You were the only person I knew who would come."

# TWENTY-FIVE

SUNDAY WAS A rare day off for Mama. She worked her second job on the mobile grooming van only three or four days a week, but sometimes she'd pick up odd jobs helping friends out, which meant there were stretches when she worked seven days a week for a month straight. She'd wait tables for Dom—the only one of her ex-boyfriends I actually liked—or help Elle clean houses. I asked her once why she worked so much and she told me there was no job she wouldn't take to make certain we had a roof over our heads, food in our bellies, and clothes on our backs. I'm ashamed to admit that I resented her for not being there all the time when I was younger, but then I grew up and realized no matter how much I'd missed her, she'd missed me more.

I did my best to take care of the house, but Sean and the

kids made more of a mess than I could keep up with, so we all knew what it meant when Mama had a day off: cleaning party! Sean, of course, always managed to have "somewhere important to be" on those days, but Mama said she didn't mind because anything he did, she'd have to go behind him and clean again anyway.

A cleaning party is exactly what it sounds like. Mama cranked up the music—mostly music from the 1980s, which adults her age seem really nostalgic for despite the fact that Mama wasn't even old enough to listen to music when she was alive in the eighties; and sometimes Pancho Amat or Pedro Luis Ferrer when she was thinking about her mother, which didn't happen often. Mama didn't talk much about her life before she'd had me. She'd taught me to cook some of the Cuban meals she'd grown up with, but hadn't taught me or Conor or Sofie more than a few Spanish words and phrases. She wasn't ashamed of her heritage—Cuban from her mother and whatever white European mix my grandfather was—but rather was ashamed of the parents from which it had come. Getting to her roots required digging through the barren and rocky soil of her mother and father, and that was one of the few jobs she refused to do.

I danced and worked on the kitchen, Mama sorted through a mountain of laundry, Sofie vacuumed, and Conor cleaned the toilet—a job he would own until he learned to stop pissing on the seat. It seemed like we'd only lip-synced with a duster to a couple of songs before we were finished and the house was spotless. Which was coincidentally around the time Sean returned and offered to help. Mama surprised him—and me—by telling him to watch Sofie and Conor so she and I could go out.

After we'd taken turns in the shower and changed into nicer clothes—jeans for me, jean shorts for Mama, who had better legs, which seemed unfair since I was basically a clone of her—we drove to a nearby animal shelter where her friend Lilah worked and where she sometimes volunteered grooming the dogs to help give them a better chance of being adopted.

When I'd been younger, we'd gone to the shelter often. I'd loved playing with the dogs, who were stuck in their cages for most of the day, taking them for walks in the grassy lot behind the building and letting them run around. It'd been a while since Mama had brought me there. Once she'd had Conor and then Sofie, she'd had to work more to keep us afloat and there hadn't been time for much else.

I was tossing a ball with a dog called Meatloaf—a stumpy-legged pug who was eager for me to throw the ball but didn't actually want to give it to me—while Mama walked an arthritic pit bull named Nell around the grass, whispering to her that she was a good girl and someone would take her home and love her for the rest of her days. She loved animals, and they loved her right back. Mama said that animals could see through our walls, straight to the heart of who we truly are.

"How are you, mija?" Mama asked. She'd sat in the grass to rub Nell's belly and let the old dog soak up some sunshine.

"Fine," I said. "I guess."

"We haven't talked in a while."

"You've been busy."

"So have you." There was an edge to her voice. A question that wasn't really a question.

On a day like this, it was easy to forget the shooting or that voices in my head wanted me to save humanity from an unknown threat. If I could have stolen this moment from time—the breeze soft with the last dying gasp of summer, the sunshine, the freedom from responsibilities and these moments with my mother—and existed in it forever, I would have been content.

"I'm surprised you're not with Fadil today," she said.

Meatloaf had grown bored with the ball and had decided to dance around Nell in an effort to lure her into playing. The old pit bull slapped a giant paw across his back, requiring him to wriggle free, which Meatloaf decided was an even better game.

"I think we're fighting."

Mama frowned. "That's a shame. You two shouldn't fight. Is it about a girl?"

"Sort of. But not really."

"Does this have to do with you sneaking out with the car last night?"

My head jerked up, but I avoided looking her in the eyes. Sean had been passed out when I'd gotten home, and I'd thought my nighttime excursion had gone unnoticed.

"Helen told me you came home after one in the morning," Mama said as if reading my mind.

"Mrs. Haimovitch ratted me out?"

"Don't blame her. I asked her to keep an eye on you kids."

I found it impossible to stay mad at Mrs. Haimovitch, even though she'd turned informant on me after I'd healed her hip. And Mama didn't seem too upset.

"A friend was stranded at a party," I said. "Her ride was drunk and couldn't drive, and she asked me to pick her up. Fadil told me he was hanging out with his parents, but he was at the party because he's totally into this girl, and I'm not upset he's interested in her, but he lied to me about it."

Mama shifted to a more comfortable position, which earned her a grumpy look from Nell. "Why do you think he did that?"

"I don't know."

"Have you asked him?"

"Not yet."

"It would probably be a good place to start."

Of course she would think it was that simple. Everything

was that simple to her. When you had a problem, you faced it. When you needed information, you asked for it. Mama was blunt that way. She never made excuses for herself, and she did what she needed to do to survive. It was a quality I both admired and despised. She believed there was no obstacle in life she couldn't bulldoze her way through, but it often blinded her to life's nuances. Not every problem had a simple solution.

"So who's the girl you picked up?" Mama asked. "Do I know her?"

I shook my head, not wanting to tell her it was the same girl who'd been shot and whom I'd healed only a couple of weeks ago. "Just a girl."

"Do you have feelings for her?"

"Yeah. But I'm pretty sure it's one-sided."

"What about Javier? Didn't you go out with him Friday night? He was nice."

I laughed so loudly that it startled Meatloaf. He turned his pug bug eyes on me, and his ears twitched, waiting to see if I was going to play with him. When I didn't, he returned to harassing Nell.

"Javi is not a nice boy."

"I thought he was so polite when I met him."

"That's because he wasn't trying to convince you to sleep with him."

Mama's lips turned downward, her smile gone. "Did you? If you need condoms, I'll buy them for you."

"There's a higher probability that I'll be killed by a falling coconut than that I'll sleep with Javi, but if I ever did choose to sleep with him, I'd prefer you pay for me to see a therapist rather than for prophylaxes."

My mind began to wander to Justina Smith and her brother. I still hadn't decided what I was going to do, and, worse, I didn't know how to decide. Fadil was in one part of my brain telling me that Allah or God or whatever wouldn't have given me the ability to heal if I wasn't meant to use it, but Freddie was in another part telling me the voices had rigged the game and that if I did what they wanted I was allowing them to control me. And then there was Deputy Akers hanging out in the shadows warning me that secret agents might come after me if I wasn't careful.

"There's more going on than your fight with Fadil, isn't there?" Mama said.

"No."

"I can read you, Elena. Is this about Helen? She told me what you did for her."

"Please don't be mad," I said. "I know you told me not to heal anyone else, but she was in pain and—"

"I'm not angry. Just worried." She patted my leg. "Now tell me what's got you all twisted up."

"Have you ever had to make a choice, but you weren't sure what to do?"

Of course she had. I doubted there was a fool alive who hadn't been put in a situation where they'd needed to make a choice, and I'd expected Mama to tell me so, but she took a breath and watched me thoughtfully for a moment before saying, "I had you."

I rolled my eyes. "Come on. I'm being serious."

"So am I."

I'd never considered that my mother had thought about not having me, but it made sense. "I get it, I guess," I said. "You were sixteen, enjoying your life and then—bam!—miracle baby. I suppose it would have been easier to abort me so you didn't get kicked out of your parents' house."

"It was more complicated than that."

"How so?"

Mama scratched Nell behind the ears. The dog lay there with its tongue hanging out of its mouth, looking happier than it had ever been. "Mama was Catholic and felt that my claims about the nature of my pregnancy were a way of mocking her devotion to la Virgen, while Papa was Baptist and thought everything I did was a sin, and though they didn't agree on much, both adamantly opposed abortion." She sighed. "The moment I found out I was pregnant with you, there was no way for me to go on living in their house."

"Wait, so they threatened to kick you out for getting pregnant without being married, but they would have also kicked you out for ending the pregnancy?"

My mother nodded. "That's the way my parents were. I had to make up my mind whether to wind up a homeless teenage girl or a homeless teenage girl responsible for a baby. It would have been easier to finish high school and find a way to go to college and become a veterinarian without a child, and I worried I wouldn't be able to provide you with the life you deserved."

"So why did you have me, then? Your life might have been so much better if you hadn't."

"Different," she said.

"What?"

"My life would have turned out differently, but who's to say it would have been better?"

Mama and I were sitting in the grass at that moment because of a decision she'd made before I was even born. Her choice to keep me had directly affected every choice she'd made since then, like dominoes lined up and knocked over. If she'd chosen to abort me, she might have stayed in school, might have even convinced her parents to let her move back in, and gone to college and met a man with a job who didn't drink. She never would have had Conor or Sofie. My mother's entire life would have unfolded differently.

But it wasn't solely her life that would have changed. If

I'd never been born, Freddie would have died at Starbucks. David Combs might have gone into the store and kept shooting until he ran out of bullets. Or, if the voices had instigated the events of that day, he might have stayed home and played video games.

One choice in the past had set off a chain reaction with repercussions still being felt sixteen years later. Mama said it wouldn't have necessarily been better, but I wasn't so sure.

"Fine," I said. "Different. But you still haven't told me why you chose me."

"Even though I didn't know how I'd wound up with a baby in my belly or why, you were still my responsibility. I didn't get to choose whether or not to become pregnant with you, and I didn't get to choose whether or not my parents threw me out of their house, but I couldn't live with my first act as a mother being to strip you of the ability to make your own choices. To decide your own future. I committed myself to making sure you had the freedom to choose your own path through life, and I don't regret it. I am proud every day of the young woman you've become."

"Without me, though, you could have gone to college and become whatever you wanted to be."

"That's true. And I would never judge any woman who might have made a different decision, but you were my choice. I chose you. I chose your future."

I was the same age Mama had been when she'd sacrificed her future for mine, and I doubted myself capable of acting so selflessly. I'd long considered my mother the strongest woman in my life, but now I knew she was superhuman. As proud as she was of me, I was equally proud of her.

I'd wanted to tell her all my problems. The voices and Freddie and the end of the world. Mama would have known what to do. I was sure of it. But she'd given me life, she'd given me the freedom to choose, and I needed to honor that by making this decision on my own.

"Have you talked to your parents?" I asked. "Since they kicked you out, I mean."

Mama rolled her head on her shoulders like she was trying to exorcise the tension from her neck. As if she feared the mere thought of her parents might summon them. "They called me after Dr. Milner went public with the proof that you were conceived parthenogenetically."

"And?"

"They apologized," she said. "We were living in this disgusting, tiny efficiency. The roaches were so bad I covered your crib with mosquito netting and slept with wax in my ears so none could crawl inside and lay eggs."

"Gross!"

"Be thankful you were too young to remember," Mama said. "Your grandparents offered to take us in. They said they'd been wrong and that you were a miracle sent by God and we were welcome to live with them."

"But you didn't."

"I forgave them for what they did," she went on. "But I refused to allow them the opportunity to hurt me, or you, ever again." I waited for her to say more, but she stood and we walked the dogs around for a few minutes more. Then we traded them out for a lazy Pomeranian named Chewie, who resembled a furry football, and a golden retriever named Guster, who had patches of his coat missing and was so skinny I could count his ribs.

"I'm sorry," I said. "That I'm the reason for all the crap you've gone through."

Mama scowled at me. "Don't be sorry. I'm not. Look at all you've accomplished. You're as beautiful as your mother but smarter than I ever was. You're kind and sensitive. You saved a young woman who'd been shot and healed Helen's hip." Her frown morphed into a soft smile. "No matter what you're going through, I'm Team Elena all the way."

"I know, and I appreciate that." Chewie refused to walk, forcing me to carry him to the grass to do his business. "Everything just sucks. There are no good decisions, everyone's messed up, and no matter what I do, I risk hurting someone. I thought it was supposed to get better. When does it get better?"

Mama followed Guster around with a plastic poop bag, waiting for him to go. "There's no light at the end of the tunnel."

"That doesn't give me the warm fuzzies."

"It's not supposed to. But that's life. One long tunnel. There are lights along the way. Sometimes they feel spread farther apart than others, but they're there. And when you find one, it's okay to stand under it for a while to catch your breath before marching back into the dark."

"So it never gets better, then?"

"Not the way you think. But walking through a stretch of dark doesn't mean you can't be happy. And if you're lucky, you'll bump into someone willing to walk through the darkness with you."

"Like Fadil."

"And you," she said. "And Sofie and Conor."

"What about Sean?"

Mama glanced at her feet. "Sometimes we walk with people. Other times we carry them."

"Only because he's usually too drunk to stand on his own," I said. "You should leave him behind to find his own way."

"Do you remember the first time you met Sean?"

"Not really. He sort of blew into our lives and became permanent without me noticing."

Guster finally dropped a load. Mama scooped it up in the

bag, tied it off, and tossed it on the ground. "I'd been dating him for a few weeks, and he'd been begging to meet you, but I didn't want to introduce him to you until I was sure he was going to stick around for a while. Then the fair came to town and he bought us all tickets. You were so excited when I told you, you demanded to dress yourself in a special outfit of your own choosing."

"I did no such thing."

"You most certainly did." Mama's eyes grew unfocused like she was reliving that memory. "You wore a black tutu, a striped shirt, pink leggings, little high heels that you abandoned after ten minutes of walking in them, and you even convinced me to let you put on hideous red lipstick. You looked like you'd been dressed by a circus clown."

I was horrified, but Mama was laughing, and that made me smile. "I'm glad my terrible fashion sense was so amusing to you."

"Some things never change."

"Hey!"

"Anyway," Mama said. "Sean picked us up and we went to the fair, but when we got to the merry-go-round, you started to cry and cry. You said the animals were saying mean things about your clothes, and you refused to go near the ride."

"Really?" I didn't think the voices had started being rude and demanding until after I'd healed Freddie.

My mother nodded. "So Sean picked you up and told you that it didn't matter what the animals said because you were the most beautiful princess in the world. Then he got on a proud white stallion with you and held you as you both spun around and around. You made him ride with you at least five times."

"What happened to that guy?" I asked.

"He's still in there," Mama said. "And I keep hoping if I carry him long enough, the man I married will learn to walk on his own again."

"You shouldn't have to carry him at all," I said. "And I hate that he makes everything so much harder for you."

Mama crossed to where I was standing with Chewie, draped her arm over my shoulder, and hugged me to her. "It's not hard, Elena. It's life."

Her phone rang, and I led the dogs back to their kennels while she took the call. When I returned she said, "Speaking of life. Kelly's sick, so my day off is officially over."

Talking with Mama hadn't exactly made me feel better, and it hadn't helped me decide what I was going to do about Justina's brother or the voices or the end of the world, but she'd bet her entire future based on her belief in me, so I owed it to her to try to believe in myself.

# TWENTY-SIX

IF I HADN'T needed a ride to school, I would have let Fadil stew. Dragged it out and allowed his guilt over lying to me about the party eat at him until he finally crawled to me to apologize. I'm not necessarily proud of the impulse, and I'm actually glad that I needed a ride so that my less-than-better nature didn't have a chance to assert itself.

Fadil frowned when I got into the car and handed him his phone. "How did you—"

"Let's go," I said. "I don't want to be late for first period."

After Fadil plugged his phone into the charger in his car, we took off. He stopped at a Dunkin' Donuts and bought me an OJ and a bagel. Bribery wasn't going to make me forgive him, but I couldn't say no to carbs and juice.

"Can I explain?" he asked.

"What's to explain?" I said between bagel bites. "You wanted to hook up with Naomi; you didn't want me around. Easy enough to understand."

"It's more than that, though. Naomi and her friends aren't so bad, but you act like they're monsters."

"Maybe because they call me names and treat me like a freak?"

"I know, but I thought if I could tell them how great you really are, they'd see you the way I do."

I wiped the crumbs off my hands onto the floor, but only because I knew it would drive Fadil crazy. "Don't pretend you lied and went to that party for my benefit. The only person's interest you were serving was Little Fadil's."

"Not true."

"Totally true."

"Fine," he said. "So what if I was? Is it so horrible that I wanted to get to know a girl I like without worrying someone was going to hurt your feelings?"

"Do you really think I'm that fragile? Christ! Do you even know me at all?"

"Of course I do, which is exactly why I didn't invite you."

"Look, Fadil. I don't care if you hook up with Naomi or date her or screw and make a million adorable baby Fadils. And I'm sure that under the layers of wealth and privilege and expensive foundation, those girls she hangs out with aren't venomous harpies, but please don't lie to me."

I thought I'd slammed the door on our argument, that Fadil was going to tell me he understood and was sorry for lying, but he banged his hand on the steering wheel.

"I didn't lie to protect you," he said. "I lied so that you wouldn't act like I'm a horrible person for being into a girl whose friends are mean to you."

"Don't I have a right to?"

"No!" he said. "I didn't see you dumping Javi for calling me Abdul all the time."

"I didn't—"

"You ignored the way he treated me and only broke up with him when he annoyed you."

"But Javi thinks you're nerdy cool."

"That doesn't mean I like him," Fadil said, "or being called shitty racist names."

I tried to recall Javi calling Fadil Abdul, but it didn't matter if I remembered it; Fadil obviously did, and it had hurt him.

"At least when Tori called you Mary at the party, I spoke up for you and told her it was rude and that you had a name. Something you never did for me."

"Fadil, I'm sorry."

We pulled into a space and Fadil parked the car. "I don't want you to be sorry," he said. "Everyone's shitty in their own way. You dated a boy who called me names and now you like a girl who didn't even know your name until you saved her life. I like a girl whose friends can be mean and petty, and I hate that they are, and I will always stand up to them for you, but none of it changes that you're my best friend, so stop acting like it does."

Here I'd expected to have Fadil groveling for forgiveness by the end of the ride to school, but I was the one feeling ashamed, and I deserved it. "I'm sorry I never called Javi out on the things he said to you."

"And I'm sorry I lied," Fadil said.

We'd apologized to each other and I thought that was the end of it, but I still felt awkward. I'd been blindsided by the things Fadil had said, and it made me think of what Javi had said to me on our nondate. "Javi thought I'd be pissed about you dating Naomi because I keep you around as my safety boyfriend. Isn't that stupid?"

Fadil shook his head. "Not really."

"You know I would never—"

"I know," he said. "Not intentionally, anyway." He turned in his seat to face me. "It's just, you act like I should sit on a shelf waiting for you to need me—like I don't have a life of my own—but it's not fair. I love you, Elena, and I will always be there for you when you need me, but I can't always be around when you want me."

I'd had no idea Fadil felt like I'd been taking advantage of our friendship. "I want you to be happy," I said. "I want you to do whatever it is that makes you happy, even if it doesn't include me."

"I know."

"And I'm totally cool with you and Naomi. Honestly."

"I know that too."

"Can we be friends again?"

He nodded. "Obviously."

"Good."

He shut off the car. "Now that that's settled, how in the world did you get my phone?"

# TWENTY-SEVEN

FADIL THREW ME curious side-eye when Freddie joined us at lunch on Monday. She didn't bring any food with her; she simply took a seat across from me and acted like it was totally normal and we sat together every day. Which isn't to say I wasn't simultaneously freaking out and dancing inside that she'd decided to grace us with her presence, but I was definitely confused.

"Word is you're going to heal a bunch of people after school," she said.

I'd done my best to push Justina Smith and her little brother out of my mind. It wouldn't have been a big deal if using my ability to heal others didn't come with such huge consequences, but it did and I couldn't ignore them.

"What?" Fadil said with his mouth full.

Freddie shrugged. "Elena? Going all Miracle Girl on the football field after last period?"

"I said I might heal Ben Smith. And I still haven't decided."

"Yeah, that's not what I heard at all."

Fadil might have been worried, but it didn't stop him from stuffing his face. "If you do it, you know I've got your back."

"Thanks," I said, though if Homeland Security agents decided I was a threat, I doubted there was anything Fadil could do.

"Uh, I don't," Freddie said. "How many people did you say have disappeared in your magic sky lights?"

I did the math in my head. "Around eighty, I think."

"That's not nearly enough," Fadil said.

"Are you serious?" she asked. "Is he serious?"

"Usually not," I said. "But this time he is."

Freddie stared at Fadil and me like we had eight heads between us, each speaking a different language. "How are you pretending this isn't a big deal?"

Fadil ate the last of his sandwich and swept the crumbs off the table. "No one's saying it's not, but Elena's part of a bigger plan. She can't ignore that."

"Sure she can."

The way Freddie was eyeballing Fadil, I worried she was going to punch him if I didn't intervene. "Can we talk about anything else?" I asked. "I haven't made up my mind what I'm going to do, and arguing about it isn't helping."

Fadil pushed his chair back and stood. "I have to run anyway." He caught my eye. "Think about what Deputy Akers said, okay?"

"I will."

"What was that about?" Freddie asked when Fadil was gone.

"Afternoon prayers," I said.

"Not him leaving, the thing about the deputy."

"Oh, that." I'd been serious about not wanting to talk about it anymore, but Freddie was part of it, so I figured she deserved to know. I explained what Akers had told me about the case and the Homeland Security agents and healing her sister.

Freddie was shaking her head as I finished. "If a cop's telling you it's a bad idea, don't you think you ought to listen?"

I didn't expect I'd ever be eating lunch with Freddie, wishing the bell would ring so I could escape, but I was tired of talking about healing and miracles and the end of the world. "You never told me why you were hiding in the closet at Tori's party."

My abrupt subject change must've caught Freddie off guard, because she sputtered and looked everywhere but at me. "I wasn't in the mood to party."

"Then why'd you go in the first place?"

"My favorite movie when I was a kid was *The Little Mermaid*. I loved that shit and I would sit and watch it, like, five times a day."

"Okay?" I said.

"I thought it would be so cool to live underwater and then fall in love with a prince and live happily ever after."

"Sure," I said. "Who wouldn't want to be a mermaid, though don't you think it's a little disgusting, them swimming around and breathing the same water they go to the bathroom in?"

Freddie grimaced. "Gross."

"Seriously though."

"You have issues," Freddie said. "But anyway, I watched the movie a few months ago, expecting to love it as much as I'd loved it when I was little."

"Let me guess: You hated it."

Freddie's eyes widened. "Like, what kind of fuckery are we teaching kids? If you want someone to love you then all you need to do is change every fucking thing about yourself? What a crock of shit!"

"You're not wrong," I said, "but what does that have to do with the party?"

"The way I felt watching that movie is the way I've felt about my entire life since Starbucks. I'm seeing all the things

I used to love with these new eyes, and I hate it." She chewed on her thumbnail. I hadn't noticed before that she bit her nails, most of them down to the quick. "I was sitting on the couch listening to Tori and Corinne argue about prom and I flipped out. Who gives a shit about prom? It's one night in our lives. A blip. If you hadn't been working the day David Combs shot me, I wouldn't have been around to worry. But you were, and I am, and I still don't give a shit about it."

Nothing existed outside of me and Freddie and our lunch table. Not the other kids eating, not the school, nothing. We were suspended in a moment, just the two of us. "You're not . . . ? Should I be worried? Should I tell someone?"

Freddie snorted derisively. "Tell them what? That I'm having an existential crisis?"

"You said you were happy you'd been shot. You told me if it happened again not to heal you."

"I'm not suicidal," Freddie said.

"This is serious."

"You don't have to tell me how serious suicide is," she snapped. "I know."

The force of her words caused me to flinch. "Okay," I said. "But if you need to talk, you can always call me, no matter what closet you're calling from."

Freddie opened her mouth, shut it, and looked down at

the table. "I promise I'm not suicidal," she said. "It's just that my life doesn't make sense anymore. You healed me and part of me feels like I have to prove I was worth saving."

"You were," I said. "You are."

"How would you know?"

"Because either we're all worth saving or none of us are."

"And yet you pick and choose who lives and who dies."

"I didn't ask for this," I said.

"Like that matters."

The bell rang, and now that it had, I found I didn't want to leave. Freddie stood and slung her bag over her shoulder.

"Freddie?" I said. "What if I make the wrong choice? What if the voices are right and the world is literally ending and I screw everything up?"

Freddie shrugged. "Then we all die. No big deal."

"Right. No big deal."

"Exactly," Freddie said. "I've already died once. I can do it again."

# TWENTY-EIGHT

JAVI CAUGHT UP to me in the hall after Mrs. Czukas's class. "When're we going out again, Elena?"

"When you get an A in algebra and hell freezes over." Javi was flashing me his best smile. "I told you it was a one-time thing."

"Come on," he said. "Admit you had a good time."

"I didn't have a terrible time."

"See?"

"You know that's not the same thing, right? I also don't have a terrible time at the gynecologist, but that doesn't mean I do somersaults every time I have to go back."

Javi's grin grew impossibly bigger. "But you do go back."

"What do you want? I'm going to be late to my next class."

"I'll walk you," he said.

I didn't particularly want to walk with Javi, but letting him tag along was easier than arguing.

"Is it true that you're going to heal some kids on the football field after lunch?"

"Who told you that?"

"I heard it around."

I'd kind of been hoping Freddie had been exaggerating, but if Javi had heard the rumor then it had spread further than I'd thought.

"Whatever," I said.

Javi held the door out of the building open for me. I turned my face toward the sun to soak it in as we crossed the quad. "You get any sleep last night?" he asked. "You look tired."

I shook my head. "Sofie wouldn't go to bed until I'd read her the next Harry Potter chapter, but I kept putting it off because we're getting to the part where Cedric's going to die."

"Too scary for her?"

"For me," I said. "I hate that part. Up till then everyone who gets hurt winds up fine. Hermione survives her encounter with the basilisk, Ron and Harry escape the creepy spiders, Ginny is returned unscathed from her encounter with Tom Riddle. There's no actual loss. And then Voldemort kills Cedric Diggory and suddenly everything becomes real. We have to face the possibility that we won't all live long enough to lose our hair or become those crotchety old folks who yell at dumb kids like us. Good people die and bad people don't always get what they deserve. Death stops being this abstract concept that happens to other people and becomes something that could happen to the people we love. Or even to us."

"It's not true, you know," Javi said.

"You don't think Cedric's death was the turning point in the series?"

"No, about Cedric being the first real death."

I rolled my eyes because I'd been expecting this. "Yeah, Harry's parents, but—"

"Professor Quirrell."

"Quirrell?"

Javi nodded. "He dies when Voldemort leaves his body."

"He was Voldemort, though."

"Voldemort possessed him. He wasn't in control. Quirrell didn't deserve to die any more than Cedric. He was just this random nerd who winds up a prisoner of Voldemort, and kicks it as a result. And Quirrell's death is fucking tragic because no one mourns him. He dies, and everyone goes on levitating feathers and conjuring dinner like whatever. His death is senseless and cruel, but we all shrug that shit off and move on. Why is that?"

I sat on one of the benches, no longer concerned about being late to class. "I guess we're meant to assume that Quirrell isn't innocent. That he was somehow complicit."

"But why? Did he ask Voldemort to possess him? Was he given a choice?" Javi cast his shadow across my face. "No one's innocent, Elena. Not even the Cedric Diggorys of the world."

"That doesn't make me hate it any less."

Javi nudged me. "I gotta run, but listen, I'd skip that shit on the football field if I were you."

"Is that so?"

"Yeah." Javi had the emotional IQ of a potato, so his casual warning was the equivalent of another person's frantic concern and was worth taking seriously. "I think it's good and all what you're doing, but you don't want the kind of shit this is going to bring down on you."

"Thanks," I said. "I'll keep that in mind."

# TWENTY-NINE

JUSTINA SMITH DIDN'T care about saving the world. When she'd asked me to heal her little brother, she hadn't been concerned with who might vanish or whether my miracles were part of a larger plan. All she wanted from me was to fix what was wrong with someone she loved. Saving the world was a task so enormous that thinking about it made me sick to my stomach.

When a doctor takes a patient into surgery, she doesn't worry over the other patients who might need her help. She doesn't consider who might die while she's patching up a bullet hole or removing a tumor. She focuses on the person in front of her. She turns all her attention to the life she can save.

Maybe the world was in danger, maybe it wasn't. I didn't know if I was capable of saving humanity, but I could heal one boy who couldn't breathe.

Part of me expected to walk onto the football field and find it empty except for the marching band and the few students who sometimes sat in the stands to watch and do their homework like I did when I was waiting for a ride home from Fadil. Another part of me expected to find the stands packed to capacity; to see reporters with video cameras and microphones who'd snuck onto campus to witness a miracle. The reality was closer to *A* than *B*. The marching band was on the field, though they were clustered in small groups while they waited for Mrs. Naam to arrive, and there were about a dozen students waiting by the bleachers. Included in the group were Javi, with a couple of his annoying friends, Freddie, standing alone, and other students whose faces I knew but whose names I couldn't recall. Some of them had their phones out, waiting to record whatever was going to happen here so they could be the first to post it to Snowflake or whatever. I was surprised Freddie had shown, but glad she had. Even though I'd saved her life, even though she knew my name and I'd talked to her and rescued her from a party and she'd sat with me at lunch, I still felt like she didn't really see me, and I hoped watching me heal Ben Smith might finally open her eyes.

Trying unsuccessfully to hide behind the bleachers stood Carmen Ballard in a cream suit, wearing oversized sunglasses that made her look like a glamorous alien. She smiled in my direction and I ignored her. There was something slimy about her that freaked me out, and I wondered if I should tell Deputy Akers about her.

Justina Smith, surprisingly, was not part of the crowd. Instead, she sat with her brother on the bleachers, huddled close to him, pointing at a book he was reading. He was a small boy, gangly and thin. His face lit up every time Justina spoke. A nasal cannula was positioned in his nose, and the tubes ran back over his ears to an oxygen tank on wheels, decorated with patches of superheroes and Dora the Explorer.

The crowd fell quiet as I strode across the field. Justina saw me and stood, still holding her little brother's hand. She said something to him I couldn't hear, and he smiled, all bright teeth and dimples.

Out of the corner of my eye, I saw a few of the members of the marching band pointing at me. Some moved closer to the small crowd that had assembled. A couple of the people nearest to Justina held up their phones, waiting for me to perform a miracle. I ignored them.

"Hi," I said to Ben Smith when I reached him. I knelt down so he didn't have to stand. "I'm Elena."

"I'm Benjamin Jefferson Smith." He spoke his full name like he was applying for a job. It was the cutest thing I'd ever heard, and he reminded me a little of Conor.

"Your sister tells me you have trouble breathing."

Ben nodded. "It's hard walking up stairs and Mommy says I'm not supposed to run."

"Would you like to be able to run?"

"I think so," he said, though he sounded confused.

"Did your sister tell you why you're here?"

"Just that you were her friend and she wanted me to meet you."

I admired that she hadn't told him why she'd brought him to the field, likely to avoid getting his hopes up in case I didn't show or couldn't do what I'd promised. I didn't need to know anything else about her to understand how much she loved her brother.

"I'm going to help you," I said. "I'm going to heal you. It won't hurt, though; I promise."

Ben's wide, deep-set eyes remained unskeptical and curious, but I'm not sure he believed me. "Will I be able to breathe better?"

"I hope so."

"Okay, then. I'm not scared."

At least one of us wasn't. My hands were shaking and I felt the eyes of everyone on the field watching me. There were more onlookers gathered than I'd expected, and I thought about what Javi and Deputy Akers had said. Even if no one managed to capture my "miracle" on their phones, they would still see it. They would still know, and I wasn't sure what that would mean. There would be more disappearances, for sure, and that could bring the agents Akers had warned me about down on me. But I'd already made up my mind to do this, and there was no turning back.

I took Ben's hand and closed my eyes.

Ben Smith shone brighter than anyone I'd ever seen. He might have been sick, but he was fire and electricity and his brilliance threatened to blind me. But there, in the center of his light, chains wrapped around his chest, squeezing tighter. Every second I watched, the chains constricted, and Ben's light grew fractionally dimmer. He wouldn't die today or tomorrow, or even a year from now, but eventually those chains would crush the life from him, so I reached out and broke them.

I opened my eyes and Ben was smiling. He pulled the tubes out of his nose, dropped them on the ground. And he ran.

# THIRTY

I HEALED BRENDAN Landsman of his asthma and Sylvia Griffith of her type 1 diabetes before leaving the football field that night. Two hundred and eighty-eight people disappeared, including Ava Sutter from our school and the manager of a McDonald's in town. Snippity Snap, which turned out to be the name of the My Little Pony, congratulated me when I got home and told me the number saved. I learned about Ava and the McDonald's guy from the news. Despite the number of phones recording what I'd done, none actually managed to capture video of the event. Apparently the voices didn't want me to have my own television show after all.

I'd expected Fadil to change his mind on the whole healing thing after the light raptured Ava Sutter. It was one thing to say it was part of a divine plan when the voices were taking killers and strangers, but Fadil had known Ava. We'd gone to school with her and sat through classes with her. She was a real person rather than a hypothetical. But Fadil held on to his belief. He might have been scared that exposing my abilities would attract the kind of attention that could land me in a dark hole somewhere, but he still trusted that I was following the path laid out for me and that everything would work out for the best. It's difficult to knock that kind of optimism, but I didn't share it.

Freddie left without saying good-bye sometime after I'd healed Ben Smith, and I didn't know whether she was proud I'd healed Justina's brother or disappointed. Everything about that girl confused me. Then again, after the conversation we'd had at lunch, I was pretty certain she confused even herself.

My life didn't change overnight and I didn't become a superstar at school. Sure, I'd converted the students who'd been on the football field and had seen me perform a miracle into believers, but the majority of my classmates and teachers still considered me a fraud. They claimed the entire thing was a hoax perpetrated by a disturbed young woman desperate for attention. I'm not entirely certain if I became famous or merely infamous for healing Ben, Brendan, and Sylvia.

At school the following day, someone wrote "lying bitch" on my locker, which was better than "slut" I supposed. Another left flowers. I heard my classmates whispering everywhere I went. What I'd done on the football field might have turned me into even more of a social pariah, but that didn't stop them from asking me for help. They had sick grandparents, dying parents, brothers and sisters with cancer or born with genetic ailments. Sunni Myers had a deadly peanut allergy and asked me to help her. I did. Two hundred and thirty-three vanished. Daniel Kokie caught me and Fadil on our way to the car after school and asked me to heal his cystic acne. He cried as he explained that the bullying he endured had gotten so bad he'd tried to buy generic Accutane over the Internet, but it had been a scam. Three hundred and seventy-seven strangers were raptured when I gave him blemish-free skin.

And on it went. The number of people taken in beams of light increased dramatically each time I healed someone, and I kept waiting for agents in black sunglasses to show up at my house and whisk me away in the middle of the night.

Fadil brought me stories of strange happenings around the world as proof that the voices had told the truth regarding humanity being in danger. An unexplained patch of darkness in the Sahara Desert, slowly spreading, that killed everything it touched; a sinkhole in New Zealand that grew incrementally wider every day; and more mundane events like a blight in Iowa killing cornfields and outbreaks of a virus in seemingly disconnected towns that spread fast, killed mercilessly, and then disappeared. There was an earthquake in Alaska that knocked out power to tens of thousands for a week, the sudden meltdown of the sole remaining nuclear power plant in Japan, and rolling, intermittent brownouts across the United States that the government couldn't explain.

Fadil insisted these were signs, but I wasn't convinced. I couldn't simply attribute every bad event that happened in the world to the voices in my head. Were the riots at Harvard University that ended in the death of three caused by whatever danger the voices said we were in or by the reaction to a racist ideologue who'd been scheduled to give a speech at the school? Was the bombing of the US embassy in Germany a symptom of the world's end or a response to the aggressive actions of our incompetent president? Horrible things were happening all the time, and I didn't know whether I was the cause, if they were the effect, or if what I was doing was helping at all.

# THIRTY-ONE

I'M NOT SURE anyone would have blamed me if I'd jumped out of the speeding car into the road and prayed for a nonlife-threatening injury.

"I can't thank you enough for doing this," Naomi said from the front seat. Yep, I'd been relegated to backseat passenger for the first time in the history of my friendship with Fadil, and I wasn't handling the demotion gracefully.

"I haven't done anything yet," I said.

Fadil glanced back at me in the rearview mirror. I'd reluctantly said yes when he'd called and asked me to go with him and Naomi to the nursing home where her grandfather lived to heal his COPD. There was nothing the doctors could do for him except keep him comfortable, and without help he wouldn't survive the year.

"I'm not doing this to help you get laid," I'd said.

"You're not doing this for me at all," Fadil had countered. "You're doing it for Naomi."

"But I don't even like Naomi."

"Fine," he'd said, "then you are doing it for me."

I would have felt less weird if Naomi had asked me to do it herself, but Fadil asking made me feel like he was using me to score points with the girl he liked, and I wasn't sure I was okay with that. But I'd agreed because I never wanted it said that I'd stood between Fadil and what he wanted.

"Still," Naomi said, "thank you."

"Yeah," I said. "Sure."

The Shady Lane Nursing Home was an okay place as far as nursing homes went. This might make me sound kind of horrible, but old people freaked me out. Not all of them—obviously I loved Mrs. Haimovitch—but the ones who were on the verge of dying. I still had an ocean of years between where I was in life and where they were, but I couldn't look at them with their wrinkled skin and gray hair and failing health and not see my own distant future. And it scared me. It terrified me that one day I might not be the person I was, that one day I might not even remember who I used to be. Like I said, maybe it makes me a horrible person, but I think anyone who says they're not afraid of the future is lying.

Naomi led us through the home. We signed in at the

front desk, and she said hi to everyone we passed, nurses and residents alike. I might have only tolerated her presence for Fadil's sake, but I couldn't deny that she was a pretty decent person. Sometimes she talked too much, but she offered a smile to everyone she met, and she honestly did know more about K-pop than anyone had a right to. If I was going to lose my best friend to someone, I grudgingly accepted that he could have done worse than Naomi Brewer. Not that I would ever admit that to either of them.

Mr. Brewer, who insisted we call him Nelson, was exceptionally tall and made the chair he was sitting in look child-sized. He spoke haltingly, stopping every few words to catch his breath, and he told the filthiest jokes I'd ever heard. Healing him took barely a minute. Around the world 610 people vanished. Nelson hugged me and hugged Naomi and hugged Fadil, and he even hugged the nurse who came to see what was going on. I slipped out in the confusion to avoid the inevitable questions from the nurses and doctors who were beginning to show up, but also to dodge Naomi's inevitable awkward attempt to hug me too.

I wandered through the nursing home until I found myself standing in front of an open door leading into a room filled with photographs. An elderly woman lay on her bed napping, and I tiptoed in to look at the pictures. The walls were covered with them. Framed photos of the woman's life,

I suspected. Next to each one were pages from a journal, also framed. I paused to read one from the day she was married. She'd been beautiful in her wedding dress, smiling at a handsome man who gazed at her with naked adoration.

"You look a little young to be a nurse."

I turned and found a guy barely older than me with wavy brown hair and brown eyes standing in the doorway watching me, the hint of a smile on his lips.

"Sorry," I said. "I wandered by and saw the pictures and . . . I'll leave."

"It's fine. Breakfast foods are about the only things that wake Nana up these days."

"Your grandmother?"

He nodded. "I'm Henry."

"Elena."

A nurse ran past in the hallway. "What's going on out there?" Henry asked.

"Not sure," I said. "What's the deal with all the pictures?"

Henry walked into the room and stood near me, but not so close as to make me uncomfortable. "They were a Christmas present," he said. "She has Alzheimer's, and I wanted to make sure she'd never forget the amazing life she led."

"That was sweet of you."

"You look familiar," Henry said. "Did you go to Calypso High?"

"Arcadia West. I'm a junior."

"Then how—" He snapped his fingers and his eyes lit up. "You're the girl from Starbucks. The one who . . ."

"Yep," I said. "That's me. The one who claimed she healed someone."

"Is that why you're here?" he asked. "Is that why the nurses are all freaking out? Did you heal someone?"

"Don't you mean 'supposedly'?"

"If I meant 'supposedly,' I would have said it."

I couldn't tell if Henry was mocking me or if he sincerely believed. "You don't think I'm lying?"

"You'd be surprised at what I'm willing to believe."

"You're weird."

"Says the girl who performs miracles. Supposedly." He said the last with a wink.

I walked to where Henry's grandmother was sleeping. "I could heal her."

"So why don't you?"

I'm not sure I would have reacted so calmly to a strange girl in my grandmother's room who claimed to have the power to heal.

"I'm not sure I should."

"You already healed someone here though, right?"

"Yeah, but it was for a friend. And I'm not even certain I should have done that."

"Why?"

"Would you believe me if I said it involved the fate of the entire world?"

Henry laughed, and the sound filled the room. "Is there a red button?"

"Uh, no. Why would there be?"

"No reason," he said. "Go on."

"Forget it. You wouldn't understand." I started to leave, but Henry blocked the doorway.

"Try me."

I had no reason to trust this strange boy. For all I knew the sleeping woman wasn't even his real grandmother. Maybe it was his smile or the way he seemed to accept that I really could perform miracles, but he made me want to trust him.

"The short version is that I have the power to heal, but each time I do, strangers around the world vanish, and these voices say that the disappearances are part of the plan to save humanity, but I'm not sure I believe them and I don't know what to do."

Henry didn't blink. He stood there with his hands in his pockets and listened. When I finished, he said, "It's always the end of the world, isn't it?"

"What?"

"Nothing," he said. "Look, I can't tell you what to do. No one can, though trust me when I say that everyone will have an opinion. You have to do what you think is right. Forget the end of the world, forget saving humanity. Those things aren't your responsibility. The only things you can control are the choices you make, and that has to be enough."

"How do you know?"

"This is one area I have a little experience with."

"I should go."

Henry stepped out of the way, and I moved to leave. But before I did, I crossed the room to the old woman in the bed, touched her arm, and healed her. Nine hundred and eighty-seven souls were raptured.

"Did you . . . ?" Henry said.

I nodded. "I hope it's enough."

# THIRTY-TWO

FADIL FINALLY WORKED up the nerve to ask Naomi to sit with us at lunch. All through high school, Fadil and I had been our own lunch group, and I was content for it to remain that way. But I couldn't argue the point, because I'd allowed Freddie to squeeze in between us whenever the mood struck her, and denying Fadil the chance to sit with the girl he liked at lunch would have been hypocritical. Still, sometimes I wanted to hog-tie Naomi and tape her mouth shut, but I managed to restrain myself.

"You should go on *Ellen*," Naomi said. "She could bring a hundred kids on her show for you to heal all at once and then no one would be able to doubt you."

"That's a fucking ridiculous idea," Freddie said. "She's not one of those religious faith healers bilking the ignorant and desperate out of cash. She doesn't need to go on TV."

"It wouldn't work," I said. "Javi said he tried to record me healing Ben Smith, but that nothing showed up on video."

"Then what's the point?" Naomi asked. "Aside from healing the sick, I mean? Tori says—"

"I don't care," I said. "Tori's mean." And she'd become meaner since Ava had vanished. No one was openly blaming me, but I knew they did anyway.

Freddie, who was picking at a slice of greasy pizza, stopped and looked at me pointedly. "Actually, she's not."

"She is to me," I said.

"Tori's difficult, judgmental, and opinionated," Freddie said. "But she's also one of the most loyal friends I've ever known."

Fadil's phone vibrated, and he started gathering his trash. "Then why aren't you sitting with her?"

Freddie glanced at her old table, where Tori and the others were sitting. They'd left a chair empty for Ava. "They're not my friends anymore."

Naomi either couldn't sense the tension or was actively attempting to ignore it. "I only wanted to understand what the point of all this is. You healed my grandpa, and I can't thank you enough for that, but what's the endgame? Are you going to keep doing it forever? And what's with the people disappearing? Ava's mom thinks she was kidnapped.

Did anyone disappear when you healed my grandfather?"

Fadil hadn't told Naomi about the terrible tradeoff of performing miracles. I wasn't sure she would have understood it when I didn't understand it myself.

"Wanna walk with me?" Fadil asked Naomi, nudging her shoulder. She nodded and they left.

When Freddie and I were alone, I kind of wished we weren't.

"That girl's nice and all, but damn does she talk a lot."

I laughed. "Right? I keep wondering if she talks while they're making out." I put my hand over my mouth and mimed kissing it. "Mmmphm let me tell you what I think. Mmmphm."

Freddie busted up and smiled, and my crush, which I'd managed to drag down to manageable levels, exploded. "She does have a point, though."

"About?"

"The endgame. Why you're doing this. You can't ignore the disappearances." When I started to talk over her, she held up her hand. "Yeah, I get that you're looking for answers and focusing on helping those you can until you find them, but you're still playing by someone else's rules."

My smile had faded. In the weeks since the shooting, since I'd healed Freddie, I'd learned practically nothing. Not about the voices or the end of the world or David Combs. "I heal people. Isn't that enough?"

"What if you were capable of something greater? Like cleaning the oceans or solving world hunger or resurrecting the dead or getting rid of all the garbage in landfills?"

"I tried to make myself invisible during the pep rally after the shooting," I said. "Does that count?"

Freddie snorted. "Not really."

"If I had the power to do more, the voices would have told me," I said.

"Would they?" Freddie asked. "You've wasted weeks agonizing over what you should do, but you haven't bothered to ask yourself what you can do. You think you're the one making the choices, but you're choosing between the options those fucking voices laid out for you."

"That's not true," I said. "I make my own decisions. I healed you."

"Because the Starbucks mermaid told you to!" Freddie looked at me thoughtfully. Her eyes had this lazy quality to them that made her look like she was on the verge of falling asleep and that I found insanely attractive. "Why did they choose me, Elena?"

"What?" I stumbled over the word.

"You'd never healed anyone before—you weren't even aware you could—so I figure the voices had to choose someone you'd be really motivated to heal. Why me? Why not Fadil or your mom?"

The question caught me totally off guard. I was still considering the possibility that my powers extended beyond mere healing, and I blurted out, "I had a crush on you, all right?"

Freddie narrowed her eyes. "You had a crush on me?"

"It was before I knew you," I went on. "I mean, you're beautiful, and you made those posters protesting Taco Tuesdays, and you seemed nice."

"Even though I called you the wrong name?"

I pretended to brush it off, trying desperately to regain my composure and certain I was failing. "Crushes aren't rational."

Outside, I was trying to act like admitting I'd had feelings for Freddie was no big deal, but inside I was flailing and freaking out because I'd tossed it out there and now she knew and I had no idea how she was going to react.

"But you don't have a crush on me anymore?"

"I don't know! Like I said, you're not who I expected you to be."

"Neither are you." Freddie stated it like a challenge.

"Then we should go out sometime and settle the question once and for all."

It slipped out. I mean, I'd had these feelings for Freddie even when I didn't know who she was, and now that she was sitting at my lunch table, eating with me and Fadil and talking about the end of the world, I wanted to find out if those feelings could become something real.

Because here's the thing about falling in love: It's an illusion. We watch television and movies, we read books, and we see all these examples of how two people meet and fall in love over the course of a couple of hours or a couple of hundred pages, and we think that's how it's supposed to be. But it never is. Not really. Falling in love is about hormones and pheromones and powerful emotions that overwhelm our better judgment. Staying in love requires time and effort and knowledge and trust that has to be earned over the course of lifetimes. Falling in love is the illusion. Staying in love is the real miracle. And while I knew I wasn't in love with Freddie or even if we could pretend to fall in love for a while, I was still hoping for a miracle.

Freddie stared at me for a moment. Then she stood and walked away without saying a word.

# THIRTY-THREE

MAYBE I SHOULD have let Freddie go. My feelings for her before I'd healed her at Starbucks had been, admittedly, irrational. That Winifred Petrine had been a two-dimensional construct onto which I'd projected my desires. The real person was more complicated than I'd imagined and didn't seem to like me so much as tolerate me. Despite that, I didn't want to let her go. Even if she wasn't interested in me romantically, I genuinely believed she needed a friend, and not in the way that boys often think befriending a girl is merely a stepping-stone to getting into her pants.

I went to the art room because that was the only place I could think to look for her, and I heard the music before I reached the door. She was listening to Sharon Jones, whose voice was unmistakable. I opened the door and walked in.

In the couple of weeks since I'd last seen Freddie's sculpture, she'd refined and changed it so much that I hardly recognized it. Wings of wires and aluminum grew from its back, frayed copper wiring made up its hair. One arm was raised over its head while the other was bent in front of its body like it was defending itself. The details had transformed it from a mess of scraps into a figure both menacing and divine. It was a mad warrior angel, or a demon looking for redemption.

"Wow," I said over the music. "It's looking really good."

"It's shit." Freddie stood with her back to me.

"Hardly."

"So you're a fucking art expert now?"

I moved farther into the room. "About what I said—"

"It's already forgotten."

"Who says I want to forget it?"

"You fucking embarrassed yourself back there," Freddie said. "I'd want to forget that if I were you."

"What is your problem?"

Freddie yanked the cord from her phone, killing the music instantly, and suddenly everything was too loud. "You put your life in danger and practically brought me back from the dead because you have a thing for me? I called you by the wrong name, my friends think you're a joke, and all you really know about me is that I did some shit freshman year. Who the fuck does that?"

"An idiot, apparently."

She leaned against the worktable and crossed her arms over her chest. "You think I made those posters, why? Because I was protesting the school's shitty racism?"

"Well, yeah."

"Nope. Sorry to disappoint you. I was trying to get expelled. I hate this fucking school and I hate this fucking town and my parents kept threatening to send me to live with my uncle in Utah because he's military and they thought he'd whip me into shape, and I wanted to go. I didn't give a shit about you or anyone else." Freddie laughed bitterly. "You act like there's this grand design to our lives, but there's not. It's all pointless. Our lives, our deaths, and all the bullshit in between. Nothing happens for a reason, Elena. Everything just happens, and none of it matters."

"Do you really believe that?"

"Yes!" Freddie threw her hands up. "You think David Combs shooting me and you healing me and everything else are all connected, but they're not! Combs was a fucking psycho. He didn't shoot me at Starbucks so that you would heal me and we would fall in love and fuck like bunnies or whatever bullshit you've worked up in your head. Combs shot me because he wanted to kill me. I was fine with it because I didn't care if lived or died. And you healed me because you were tripping on some weird fantasy that you loved me or whatever."

"I never said I loved you. And, in fact, I kind of hate you right now."

"Good!" she said. "You should hate me, Mary. You should hate me and hate Tori and hate everyone. None of us give a single fuck about you. Those people who say you're a miracle or a messiah? They only want to use you to heal their sick whatever, after which they won't care whether you heal the rest of the world or get hit by a bus. You're nothing to them but a thing to be used."

My cheeks flushed and pressure built behind my eyes, but I wasn't going to cry in front of her. Winifred Petrine didn't deserve my tears. "Maybe I should have let you die," I said.

"You definitely should have let me die, Mary."

"Stop calling me Mary."

"But you didn't just bring me back; you brought me back wrong."

"Screw you," I said. "You were probably wrong from the start."

"That's the first smart thing you've said since I met you." She plugged her phone back into the speaker and turned on the punk band she'd been listening to the first time I'd walked in on her. "Get out," she said.

I managed to hold back the tears until I made it to the restroom.

# THIRTY-FOUR

I STOOD BEHIND Fadil as he pawed through the bins of the mostly useless and broken toys at the Goodwill he'd dragged me to. He was looking for a birthday gift for his father, who collected action figures from the 1980s, though I didn't think Fadil was going to find any hidden gems in that sad mess of plastic body parts.

"And then she called me Mary," I said, still fuming. "I don't understand what her problem is. One minute she's laughing at my jokes and flirting and the next she's acting like my face is a giant scab."

"Gross mental image," Fadil said. He was bent at practically a 45-degree angle with his ass sticking into the air while he searched. "But can you blame her? If someone shot you, would you want to be reminded of it every ten minutes?"

"I didn't—"

"You never shut up about it." Fadil put his hands on his hips and faced me. "Humanity's in danger. I don't know who to heal. All those people are vanishing. Poor me." Fadil said it all in a deeply offensive falsetto.

My face turned red and the tips of my ears burned. "I do not sound like that."

"Lately you have."

"Screw you." I stomped off to another part of the store and left Fadil to sort through his dirty toys. I would have gone home and stranded him there if he hadn't driven. I walked up and down the aisles, scanning them for anything we could use at home. Almost everything we'd ever owned had belonged to someone else first. Furniture, dishes, clothes. Not that I minded. When we died, the only things we'd leave behind of importance were our deeds. Our corpses would rot and our treasured belongings would wind up in someone else's house or in a landfill. Our clothes don't tell the stories of our lives, and no one would remember what kind of dishes we had. But they'd remember the things we'd done. Our actions would live on and tell the stories of our lives long after we'd vanished from the earth.

*Hey, girl! Stop being such a downer!*

I closed my eyes and prayed for the voice to go away. The last thing I wanted was to deal with that noise in the middle of Goodwill right after Fadil had insisted Freddie was annoyed because I made everything about me.

*You best listen to me, Miss Thang.*

"Oh my God, stop," I said under my breath. I finally had to open my eyes, and the first thing I saw was a six-inch-tall statue of the Virgin Mary, because of course the voices would choose her to speak to me through.

*There's no stopping the miracle train, Elena. Choo! Choo!*

I grabbed the Virgin Mary off the shelf and held her close to my face. "Why are you doing this to me?"

*Stop frowning and get clowning, Miracle Girl! We got work to do!*

"Why does the Virgin Mary sound like a fifty-year-old high school teacher doing her worst impression of teen slang?"

Fadil turned the corner and spotted me holding the statue. "See?" he said. "This is exactly what I was saying."

"She talked to me first!"

"I'm not the one who has a problem with it," Fadil said, walking toward me.

*Elena. Elena. Elena. Elena. Listen to me. Listen. Are you listening? Listen. Elena. Elena.*

"Well, I do," I said. "She's annoying the hell out of me."

"Then tell her to shut up," Fadil said.

"I told her I should've let her die."

Fadil frowned. "Are we still talking about Mary?"

"Freddie."

"Oh."

I started to put the statue back, but changed my mind. "I'm buying this."

*Elena! Elena, Elena bo-belena!*

"Why?"

"So I can smash it with a hammer." I marched to the cash register and paid for the stupid statue, though three dollars was far too expensive.

When we were back in the car, I tossed the statue onto the floor. I didn't have to tell Fadil that I didn't want to go home, and though I wouldn't have been able to tell him where I wanted to go, he knew the perfect place to take me.

*Banana-fana fo-felena. Fee-fi-mo-melena. Elena!*

Fadil and I had made a pact when we'd first discovered the Pie Hole that we would go there a maximum of three times a year. If I had my choice, I would have eaten there every single day. I also would have had to run ten miles daily or buy a new wardrobe, which is why we limited how often we allowed ourselves to go.

I left Mary in the car, because if I had to hear her sing one more verse of "The Name Game" song I was going to light Fadil's car on fire with her in it. The only reason I'd bought her was because the voices rarely spoke to me unless they had something to tell me or a job they wanted me to do, and since she hadn't told me what it was yet, I needed to keep her around until she did.

Pie Hole was—surprise!—a pie shop. They had, at any given time, over thirty types of pies baked fresh daily. Now, as I understand it, there is an uninformed faction of the population that thinks cake is superior to pie, but they are clearly wrong. There is no cake, only pie. Seeing as we limited our Pie Hole trips to three times a year, I had to take advantage of it, so I ordered slices of blueberry crumble, lemon meringue, and sweet potato pie. And, yes, I was going to eat every bite before going home, because leftovers wouldn't last five seconds in the fridge.

Fadil and I sat on the trunk of his car eating pie. I stabbed a bite of his chocolate cream—and was lucky he didn't stab me back—and leaned my head on his shoulder.

"Did I tell you I tried to kiss Naomi?" he asked.

I shook my head. "How do you try to kiss someone?"

"You lean across the armrest in the middle of the movie, all smooth and debonair, and when your lips are almost touching, you accidentally crush the soda you're holding and spill it in your lap."

I laughed for a solid minute while Fadil grimaced, reliving his shame. "Good thing you didn't spill it on her."

"Next time."

"At least you know there'll be a next time."

"True."

"So you're really into her?"

Fadil nodded. "She's curious about everything. It's like you can't just tell her something. You have to explain it and prove it and offer supporting evidence."

"Sounds exhausting."

"Not really."

"Well, she's a lucky girl," I said. "You're kind of a catch."

Fadil finished off his chocolate cream pie and started in on his peach cobbler. He ate his in order, finishing one before moving on to the next, while I put in a valiant effort to eat them all at the same time. "How come you never tried to catch me?"

"Apparently I only date guys who disgust me and like girls who disgust them," I said with my mouth full of pie.

"I'm serious. I'm not saying I wanted you to, though, so don't get your hopes up."

"You're just . . . Fadil. I didn't ever have those kinds of feelings for you."

"Fair enough. And, for the record, I only had those feelings for you for a minute in eighth grade."

My eyebrows shot up in surprise. "Really?"

"It was the Halloween dance. You showed up wearing that Valkyrie costume and I thought you were the baddest warrior I'd ever seen."

"How come you didn't say something?"

"The moment passed," he said. "Plus, I tried picturing us kissing and it made me laugh."

"Which would have been a total mood killer if it'd actually happened."

"That's what I thought too."

We fell quiet for a moment. It was weird to think that Fadil had ever had those feelings for me. There had been times when I'd wished I could have fallen in love with Fadil. He was sort of the perfect human being. Good-looking, sweet, smart, generous. He was the kind of guy girls should have been beating each other down to date. But love is a feeling you can't fake and you can't force.

"I feel like I'm falling, Fadil," I said. "Faster and faster, and I'm fairly certain I don't have a parachute."

"Are we talking about Freddie or the voices?"

"Yes."

*Uh, Elena? It's kind of hot in this car. Wanna maybe get me out of here before I suffocate? Oh, that's right, I can't suffocate because I'm a statue. Get me out or I'll keep singing.*

Fadil set his pie aside and angled his body toward me. "You've got a lot to figure out, Elena, but you're making it more difficult for yourself. It's not that complicated."

"That's easy for you to say; you're not the one a Virgin Mary statue is serenading with 'Sixteen Going on Seventeen.'"

"Let's ignore that you actually know any song from *The Sound of Music* for a second. You're right; this is happening to you and not me, but that doesn't mean I don't know what I'd do in your place. I wouldn't waste my time trying to understand David Combs, for one."

"Why?" I asked. "Because you think Allah explains everything?"

"No, but thanks for shitting on my religion."

"I wasn't—"

"You were," Fadil said. "But let's move on. No, the reason I wouldn't waste my time with David Combs is because I don't give a crap why some entitled, middle-class white boy tried to commit murder."

"And I'm the dismissive one?"

"We're living in a world where a bunch of rednecks can literally take over a federal building armed with guns and wind up not getting any jail time, but a kid with brown skin can't walk around in public without worrying about getting shot by some overzealous neighborhood watch asshole. So no, I don't care if the voices or Allah or your stupid stuffed Cthulhu doll told him to shoot Freddie. It doesn't change what he did."

"I know that," I said.

"Do you?" Fadil seemed to have lost interest in his pie, which was sacrilege. "If he'd left a note saying he shot Freddie because he was bullied, half of Arcadia would be holding anti-bullying rallies. If he'd done it because some girl he'd liked wouldn't go out with him, we'd be talking about how boys need to learn to deal with rejection. If the voices told him to do it, then we'd have to ask ourselves if he even had a choice in the matter. I'm tired of watching the world bend over backward to make excuses for boys like him."

I scraped the remains of my three pies into one container and closed it, thinking I could hide it in the fridge at home long enough for Mama to finish it.

"I'm not trying to absolve David Combs," I said. "I'm trying to absolve myself."

"What have you got to be sorry for?"

"I want to know why David shot Freddie, because I need to know it wasn't my fault. I want to figure out where the people who are 'raptured' are going, because I need to know Ava Sutter is somewhere better than this." Tears began to well in my eyes and I blinked them back. "Her parents have no idea where she is or what happened to her. They're wrecked, and it's my fault."

Fadil growled. "It's not your fault. It's the voices' fault. You didn't take anyone. They did."

"Only they can't take anyone unless I heal someone, but you're acting like this is an easy choice, and it's not! I've got you in one ear telling me to trust the voices, Freddie in the other telling me the voices are using me, Deputy Akers showing up at my house in the middle of the night telling me Homeland Security might be investigating me, and the Virgin Mary in the front seat of your car singing Spice Girls songs." I turned and shouted at the back window. "I don't give a fuck what you really, really want!"

I wasn't sure what Fadil was going to do when he slid off the trunk of the car, opened his door, and leaned inside. Honestly, part of me was scared he was going to abandon me. My problems had become too tangled around him and he was going to sever the threads and leave me behind. Instead, he returned to the trunk where I was sitting, holding the Virgin Mary statue.

"This is a statue, Elena," he said.

"A talking statue. Though currently it's trying to rap."

"Whatever." Fadil held the statue up to me. "It can yell at you, sing at you, and annoy you. But that's it."

*Remind him that David Combs could have shot him instead of Winifred.*

I pursed my lips and breathed in deeply. "She wants me to tell you that David could have shot you instead of Freddie."

Fadil nodded. "Maybe, but the voices wouldn't have had anything to do with it."

*Says him.*

"What do you mean?"

"If Combs had shot me, it would have been his choice. He shot Freddie of his own free will. It doesn't matter why."

"But—"

Fadil held up his hand. "No buts, Elena. Even if a statue told Combs to shoot Freddie, it couldn't have forced him to steal his parents' gun, carry it to Starbucks, and pull the trigger. Just like the voices can tell you who to heal and when, but they can't make you do it."

*That's not a theory you want to test, Elena-bo-belena.*

"They can rapture people."

"Only if you heal someone first," he said. "I told you the choice was easy because the voices don't matter, David Combs doesn't matter, Freddie doesn't matter, and I don't matter. The only person who can choose is you."

*He's a damn dirty liar.*

"She says you're a liar."

"Really?" Fadil glared at the statue, cocked his arm back, and threw the Virgin Mary across the parking lot. She sailed in a high, graceful arc, yelling, *Elena, noooooo!* before smashing into the asphalt and shattering into hundreds of shards. "How do your voices like me now?"

I climbed down off the trunk and wrapped my arms around Fadil. "Thank you," I whispered into his ear.

When I let go, he said, "You still have no idea what you're going to do, do you?"

"Not really," I said.

"Well, it was worth a try, and at least we both got pie out of it."

# THIRTY-FIVE

THERE'S NOTHING GOOD on TV after mid-
night on Wednesdays when you only have basic cable and
can't afford Netflix. How do I know this? Because it was
Wednesday night and I couldn't sleep and there wasn't a damn
thing to watch that wasn't an infomercial or some dumb show
where sexy characters, who are supposed to be my age but are
really in their twenties, make terrible life choices. Or buddy
cop shows. There's always a show about a cop and someone
weird. A cop and a writer. A cop and an interpretive dance
instructor. A cop and an alien from the future. No, I got it.
A cop and a disgruntled librarian team up to track down the
worst late-book offenders. And with one idea, my career as a
writer for television ended before it had even begun.

Anyway, Mama was at work, Sofie and Conor were in

bed, and I was curled up on the couch under a blanket when Sean stumbled through the door reeking of cigarette smoke and defeat.

"What're you still doing up?" he said, his words crammed together like rush-hour traffic.

"Can't sleep."

"Oh." Sean wandered into the kitchen. I expected him to take some aspirin and then pass out, but he grabbed something from the fridge, which turned out to be a beer, and then flopped down on the couch beside me.

"You smell worse up close," I said.

Sean shrugged. "Seriously. Why're you awake? Don't you have school tomorrow?"

"I do," I said. "But I have a lot on my mind."

"Like what?" Sean's eyelids fell heavy over his bloodshot hazel eyes, but there was a sincerity in his voice that made me think he actually cared, though it might have been the alcohol talking.

I pulled the blanket tighter around me. "I have to make a choice, but it feels impossible. No matter what I do, it's going to so suck for someone."

Sean sipped at his beer and tried to swallow a burp, but it came up despite his attempt. "College or my dad," he said.

"What about them?"

"My dad got sick and I had to decide whether to go to

college or whether to get a job to help my mom and stay home to spend time with him in case he died."

"How'd you decide?"

"Let me tell you the thing about shitty choices. They make you feel like you're deciding the rest of your life in a single moment. If I went to college, my mom could've lost everything, my dad could've died, and I wouldn't have gotten to make peace with him. Without college, I worried I'd never make much of myself."

Sean's father had died before he'd married my mother. "How do you make that kind of choice when it can affect everything?"

"Everything doesn't matter," Sean said. "All I was deciding was one thing. Do I stay with my dad or do I go to college?"

"But your decision had consequences."

"Fuck the consequences."

"That may work for you," I said, "but we can't all ignore the effects of our actions."

Sean rolled his eyes, but I didn't know whether he was sleepy or annoyed. "Shit, Elena, I'm not stupid. Sometimes, though, you gotta focus on your actions in the here and now and forget the future."

"But—"

"Look, some guy has a heart attack on the sidewalk. You do CPR and try to save him, right?"

"Of course."

"But what if you knew he was going to kill a hundred folks in ten years? Would you still save him?"

"I don't know."

Sean waved me off. "Yes you do. You'd do CPR on him because you can't possibly foresee what's going to happen ten or twenty years from now. Shit, you can't see what's going to happen a week from now. The only information you got to make your decision is what's in front of your face." He drained the last of his beer and let out a belch, not bothering to hold it in this time. "That's what I did with my dad. He was sick, my mom needed me, so I stayed."

My phone rang and I picked it up. Freddie's name flashed on the screen. Sean nodded at me and stumbled into his bedroom.

I answered the phone.

"Elena?"

"What?" I hadn't forgotten the last time we'd spoken, and I wasn't about to act like everything was normal even though my stomach was squirming and I was starting to sweat. "Are you hiding in another closet?"

"Can you meet me somewhere?"

"It's almost one in the morning," I said. "On a school night."

"I'll pick you up."

"Why should I?"

Freddie didn't immediately answer and I wondered if she'd hung up, but the phone said she was still connected. "Look, I'm sorry for what I said to you earlier. And this is important."

The only thing I thought she could have said that would have made me agree to meet her was that she'd harbored a deep and abiding love for me since the moment she first saw me and that she hadn't been able to admit it sooner because the tidal wave of her emotions was simply too great and would have dragged her out to sea and drowned her.

She did not say that thing. She said another thing. I hadn't fantasized about her saying it, but it was equally compelling.

"I have information about David Combs."

# THIRTY-SIX

THE TEST ADMINISTRATOR at the department of motor vehicles who'd passed Freddie and allowed her to menace the streets of Arcadia should have been shamed and fired. Freddie didn't seem aware that her blue Prius had a turn signal. In fact, she didn't seem aware that she was sharing the road with other drivers at all. Luckily for them, and me, there were few other cars out at one a.m. on a Wednesday night.

I'd quickly changed out of my pajamas and met Freddie in front of my apartment. She took me to a twenty-four-hour diner, and that's how I found myself staring across a coffee-stained table at her when I should have been asleep. I got the impression that she didn't want to be the first to speak and that we could have stared at each other until the sun rose and it wouldn't have bothered her in the slightest. It did, however, bother the hell out of me.

"You said you had information about David Combs." Okay, yeah, it came out like I was interrogating her, but all I'd done was agree to meet her to discuss Combs; I hadn't agreed to be nice.

"Have you learned anything new?"

"What the hell?" I said. "You were the one who told me I had to meet you, so start talking or I'll walk home."

Freddie's lips pulled back in disgust. "What the fuck is your problem?"

"My problem?" I said. "You're lucky I'm even sitting here after what you said to me yesterday."

"What about what you said?"

"You started it."

"I'm not the one who said you should have let me die."

"Only because you said everyone hated me, and then kept calling me Mary."

Freddie raised one eyebrow. "I was trying to get a rise out of you. Mary."

I clenched my fists and dug my nails into my palms. "Oh my God! I hate you so much right now."

An impish smile crept onto her face. "Then you don't still have a crush on me?"

"I don't get you," I said. "One minute you act like I'm your nemesis and the next you're flirting? Is this a joke to you?"

"Look, I'm sorry for the things I said. I was having a day. And then you told me you only saved me because you had a thing for me and I kind of lost my shit a little."

"A little?"

"Okay, a lot."

"Fine," I said. "Then I guess I didn't mean it when I said I wished I hadn't healed you."

"You guess?"

"It's fifty-fifty at the moment."

Freddie winked and nudged me under the table with her foot. "You wouldn't have let me die."

"Now it's sixty-forty."

"I knew you still liked me," Freddie said.

"Sixty-forty against healing you," I said. "Now tell me what was so important you had to drag me out of my house in the middle of the night."

Our waitress wandered up, looking bothered and exhausted, and waited for us to order even though we didn't have menus. Freddie asked for coffee and I did the same.

As soon as the waitress left, Freddie said, "Did you tell me you liked me because you think I'm into girls?"

"Obviously," I said. "You went out with Ellen Cho for a few weeks last year. And don't change the subject."

"I'm not changing the subject, and I most certainly did not. I can't stand Ellen Cho. For one, she turns every word into a verb—"

"You don't like her because she verbs things?"

"I'm gonna verb you in a second."

"Tease."

"You wish," Freddie said, but there was a hint of a smile playing on her lips. "Second, Ellen Cho's been with Kelly Greenway since fucking conception."

"Kelly who?"

Freddie threw up her hands and groaned. "Forget it. Back to Combs. I'll tell you what I know if you tell me one thing about yourself you've never revealed to anyone else."

"Deal."

"Good," Freddie said. "You first."

The waitress dropped off two mugs of coffee that were stained on the outside. It didn't inspire confidence in the food, but I ordered a plate of onion rings because they were nearly impossible to screw up and dunking them in the deep fryer would likely kill any lingering bacteria. While Freddie was quizzing the increasingly irritated waitress about the type of cheese used in the omelets, I tried to think of a secret to tell her that wasn't too embarrassing. Finally, Freddie settled on a patty melt and fries and then folded her hands on the table and waited for my offering.

"The first time I got my period, I was hanging out with my mother at this animal shelter where she sometimes volunteers. I was twelve. Mama was always open with me about that stuff, but I still had no idea what to expect. Anyway, I went to the bathroom in the shelter, and when I pulled my pants down there was blood on the crotch. It wasn't a lot, but the second I saw it, I fainted and hit my head on the side of the toilet. Mama found me ten minutes later passed out on the restroom floor."

Freddie waved her finger in front of my face. "Lame. That doesn't count."

"Of course it does."

"No it doesn't," she said. "You're supposed to tell me a story no one else knows."

The only thing that kept me from walking out was my desire to find out what Freddie had learned about David Combs. "Fine," I said. "Something I've never told anyone else?"

"That's the game."

"I'm glad David Combs shot you."

Freddie's mouth fell open and her entire body tensed. She'd been expecting another embarrassing story about how my bikini top fell off at a public pool or how Mama caught me masturbating on the couch once, but she clearly hadn't expected what I'd told her.

"That day at Starbucks, Fadil was trying to get me to

talk to you. That's why I approached your table. But I would have chickened out. I would have asked you if you wanted another drink or taken your trash or something stupid like that. David shooting you gave me the chance to heal you and finally get to learn who you really are. And I hate that he shot you, but I'm also glad."

When Freddie finally recovered her ability to speak, she said, "That's really fucked up."

"Freddie—"

"You know what your problem is?"

I rolled my eyes before I could stop myself. "I'm sure you're about to tell me in great detail using colorful language."

"You're scared," she said.

"I can heal people, beams of light shoot from the sky when I do, I hear voices, and the world might be ending. Of course I'm scared. Your powers of observation are astounding, Dr. Freddie. Please, tell me more obvious things."

Freddie went on like I hadn't spoken. "Not just of that shit. Of everything. You play this shy, bullied, innocent routine, hoping one day everyone will magically realize how special you are. Meanwhile, you're so afraid to even talk to a girl you like that it took some psycho shooting me for you to work up the nerve. It's no wonder you can't make a decision about the end of the world."

The waitress dropped our food off wordlessly. For the

record, I'd made a good choice with onion rings; Freddie's patty melt looked like a soggy, grease-soaked mush platter, which didn't stop her from digging in.

"You're not worried about the end of the world," Freddie said around a mouthful of greasy meat and cheese.

"Of course I am!"

Freddie shook her head and waited to speak until she'd wiped her mouth with her napkin. "Maybe you don't know why the world is ending or why Combs shot me or how the world is ending or any of that shit, but you know what to do. You know what you want to do. You're just so terrified it's the wrong thing that you're going along with what Fadil tells you and I tell you and the voices tell you. That way if you fuck everything up, you can blame it on someone else and no one will realize you're not the special snowflake you're so desperate to be."

My face flushed to the tips of my ears as Freddie spoke. "That's easy for you to say. You didn't grow up a freak. You don't have people calling you a slut or Mary one moment and then begging you to heal their grandpa the next. If the voices had given you this ability, you'd probably hide out in your stupid art room, working on that crappy garbage sculpture."

Freddie set her patty melt down and wiped her hands on her napkin. I was so certain she was going to walk out that

I touched my phone through my pocket, preparing to call Fadil or Mama to beg one of them to pick me up.

"A) My sculpture may be garbage, but it's not crappy. And B) if I did have your abilities, I'd be doing a fuck-ton more with them than you are."

"Really? Like what?"

"For starters, I wouldn't be stressing out over the kid who shot the girl I healed."

"Except you called me claiming to have information about Combs, so obviously you have been," I said.

"I'm the girl he shot. It's different."

"Oh yeah? How?"

Freddie pushed her plate out of the way with half the patty melt uneaten. Her voice had softened. The edge dulled. "Some nobody, some kid I never met before that day, shot me. He decided I didn't deserve to live. He decided my life didn't matter and that I would be better off with a bullet in me." Freddie caught my eye and held it for a moment.

My own anger began to fade. "Maybe you were a convenient target."

"Because convenience is the best reason to shoot a person. That clears everything up."

"You're twisting my words."

"Why didn't he shoot you?" Freddie asked. "You were closer. Why didn't he fire into the store and hit one of a dozen people on the other side of the window? He shot me for a reason, and I need to know what it was."

"You also wanted to know why I'd healed you, and look how that turned out." A grim laugh escaped my throat.

Freddie narrowed her eyes and clenched her jaw. "David Combs didn't profess his love for me before shooting me."

"I never said I was in love with you. And you still haven't explained why you get to care why he shot you but I don't."

"Since you healed me," Freddie said, "everything feels different. My friends feel different; my family feels different. Either something is wrong with me or with the rest of the world. I can still see the person I was before, but I don't recognize her. Hell, most of the time I don't even like her, and I need to know if I deserved to be shot."

I flared my nostrils, and my voice took on a tone that reminded me of Mama's. "No one deserves that. Not you, not anyone."

Freddie nodded like she understood, but her downcast eyes said maybe she didn't. "Fine. Then I need to know if David Combs thought I deserved to be shot."

I started to tell her "Of course he didn't," but I didn't know that for sure. I was no closer to divining Combs's motives than I had been that day in front of Starbucks. I wanted to tell her that there was nothing she could have done that would have justified David shooting her, but it worried me that she needed to hear it. I couldn't comprehend how she could think for a moment that she'd deserved to be shot. If I'd been having the same conversation with Fadil, I would have slid around to his side of the booth and hugged him and leaned my head on his shoulder, and we wouldn't have needed words, but Freddie wasn't Fadil, and despite what I might have imagined was flirting, she'd made her opinion clear where my feelings for her were concerned.

"Anyway," Freddie said. "Forget it."

But I didn't want to. "Do you think you deserved to be shot? Do you think you didn't deserve to be healed?"

"I said to forget it!"

"I'm trying to help," I said. "I wish I had answers, but I don't."

"Why don't you ask the voices in your head? They've been super useful so far."

"You don't have to be so mean."

"You're right. I don't."

"Then why?" I asked. "I get that you're not into me, but I saved your life. You could at least pretend to be nice."

"Why bother?"

"Forget it," I said. "Let's go."

I dug a few bills out of my purse—it was most of what little cash I had—and tossed it on the table. Freddie, however, hadn't moved.

"Have you ever stopped to consider that this is what your voices wanted to happen? You're all about how things are connected. How two strangers bumping into each other forever ago can cause a nuclear explosion a hundred years later. I'm thinking you were set up to save me so that you'd learn I wasn't worth saving. So that you'd understand that none of us are worth saving."

"That's a load of crap." I said, unable to stop myself. "If the voices didn't want me to help them save the world, they could have let you die."

Freddie shook her head. "No. You needed to learn the truth about me so that you'd help everyone and not just fucked-up girls you're in love with."

"I'm not in love with you!"

"At some point, if you're really going to rescue humanity, you've going to have to save rapists and murderers and Wall Street bankers. So maybe learning that I'm not the person you thought I was is part of that process."

"Except I don't think you're really this person. You want me to think you're mean, but I don't believe you actually are."

Freddie's face remained emotionless. "Luckily, what you think doesn't matter."

"You didn't find out anything new about David Combs, did you?"

Freddie didn't say anything. "Yeah," I said. "I didn't think so. Keep on telling yourself what I think doesn't matter, but you're the one who called me tonight, not the other way around. And if this is the way you're going to act, maybe next time you call, I won't answer."

# THIRTY-SEVEN

I LIKED SEEING Fadil happy. Not that he hadn't been happy before, but when Naomi was around, his smile seemed permanently etched on his face. That alone was enough to make me ignore her annoying questions.

"Can you fly?" Naomi asked while she picked food out of Fadil's lunch. Yes, they'd become the couple who ate off of each other's plates. It was gross, and it took all of my strength not to vomit in my mouth.

"I heal people," I said. "I can't fly."

"But have you tried?"

I waited for Fadil to jump in and shut her down, but he was munching on a carrot stick he'd gotten from Naomi and grinning like the world wasn't ending. "No, I haven't tried to fly. I haven't tried to set things on fire either, but maybe I should." I squeezed my eyes shut and was sure I looked like I was trying to poop.

"No!" Naomi said. "It's cool. I don't need you to set anything on fire."

"Are you sure?" I peeked one eye open. "It probably wouldn't be a big fire."

Fadil finally tagged in to the conversation. "How do you think the healing actually works?" Before I could answer, he said, "I know how you describe it, but I'm talking about the science stuff. Like with Ben Smith. You corrected a genetic defect. Shouldn't that have changed him?"

"It did," I said. "It got rid of his cystic fibrosis."

Naomi was shaking her head before I'd finished. "No, he's right. If you made changes to someone on the genetic level, it might affect more than the disease."

"Then maybe I didn't fix his defective genes," I said. "Maybe I only fixed the thing that they were doing wrong."

"What about mental illness?" Naomi asked. "Could you fix that?"

"Should you fix it?" Fadil added.

All I'd wanted to do was enjoy my chick'n nuggets and tell Fadil about my argument with Freddie at the diner, but that was a conversation I didn't want to have with Naomi around. Plus, I was cranky from lack of sleep. "Why wouldn't I?"

"Not even doctors really understand the causes of mental

illnesses," Naomi said. "My uncle has OCD for real. He's not one of those people who likes a neat house and says they have OCD. He really has it, and he takes medication for it."

"Don't you think he'd rather not have OCD?" I asked.

"Possibly, but if we're talking about someone's brain chemistry, wouldn't changing that change who they are fundamentally? It's not a broken bone; it's a brain."

"It's a hypothetical at this point," I said, "since no one's asked me to heal their OCD."

Fadil leaned closer to Naomi, and I could tell they were holding hands under the table even though I couldn't see it. Yuck. "She's got a point. What about, like, autism? There are those who claim it's a disease, but we don't understand it well enough to say that it is. For all we know an autistic person's brain works in a way we don't fully understand and it might be an evolutionary advantage."

These were questions I hadn't asked myself, but probably should have. "I don't know," I said. "I guess it would depend."

"On what?" Naomi asked.

"If someone with autism asked me to heal them." I dipped one of my nuggets into a pool of honey mustard and bit the end off. It was disgusting and I was sure it wasn't even real chicken. "I'm not running around healing people against their will, but if someone with autism asked me to 'heal' them, why would I say no?"

Naomi's eyes opened wide. "Because there's nothing wrong with them, that's why!"

I held up my hands. "Calm down. It's a hypothetical, unless you know someone with autism who wants me to heal them."

"I don't, but—"

"Then it's pointless to get worked up about it."

Naomi's eyes looked like they were going to bulge out of their sockets, but thankfully Javi walked up to our table, casting his shadow over us, before she could say anything else. He wore tight jeans and his baseball jersey even though the season was over.

"What do you want?" I asked, grateful for the interruption.

He dipped his head at Fadil and Naomi. "What's up?"

"Hey, Javier," Naomi said. I thought they knew each other, but wasn't sure how well.

"Javi," Fadil added.

"Can I talk to you outside?" Javi said.

"I'm kind of busy with eating and building my imaginary world where you and I were never a couple."

Javi fidgeted with his hands, and when he looked me in the eyes, there was something curious in them. A pleading I'd never seen. "It's important, Elena."

I didn't want to keep arguing with Naomi and Fadil, so I heaved a sigh, gathered my stuff, said bye to Fadil, and followed Javi out of the cafeteria. As soon as we were outside, I said, "What's so important?"

"I need you to come with me and not ask any questions."

"Yeah," I said. "Because that's not the opening scene to a movie where I end up at the bottom of a pit massaging lotion into my skin."

He clenched his jaw and the muscles pulsed. "Look, I've been thinking over what we talked about on our date—"

"It wasn't a date."

"—and how the shit I did to David might have contributed to what set him off. I'm not saying I'm to blame, but it probably didn't help. And I wish I could, like, go back in time and not be such a dick to him, but I can't, so I've been thinking of other non-time-travel ways to make it right."

I had no idea what Javi was going on about, but I was losing my patience with him. "Get to the point."

"I got some people together, and I thought you could help them."

"People who need healing?"

Javi nodded.

"I'm not a rent-a-healer, Javi!"

"I didn't rent you out." He took my hand, and it was all I could do not to yank it back. "Just, please? Meet them or whatever, and if you don't want to do it, then you don't have to, but talk to them first. That's all I'm asking."

I flared my nostrils. "If this is some weird scheme to get me to take you back, it won't work."

"It's not."

"Then what is it? You think you can balance out being a bully with your dickhole friends by getting me to heal strangers?"

Javi's chin dipped to his chest and his lower lip puffed out. I knew the look on his face. I'd seen it once when his mother had yelled at him for flunking the second quarter of geometry. This was genuine. It was real. "Kind of," he said. "I know I can't undo being an asshole, but I can try to not be one going forward, right?"

I looked into his eyes, searching for some hint of an ulterior motive, but found nothing. Finally, I said, "Take me to them."

# THIRTY-EIGHT

JAVI LED ME to the chorus room, where four students and, surprisingly, a teacher, were waiting. They each sat in a different part of the room, looking like they were trying to pretend that the others weren't there. I still wasn't thrilled that Javi had essentially told a bunch of strangers that I would help them without asking me first, but since they were already there, I didn't feel like I could say no.

"Not her," I said, pointing at Tori Thrash. She stood with her arms folded over her chest, looking down at me like she was doing me a favor by gracing me with her presence.

"Elena—" Javi said.

"I'll talk to the others, but I'm not going anywhere near her."

Javi pulled me to the side and whispered, "I get it, you don't like her, but hear her out, okay?"

"I'm not promising anything."

I used Mrs. Eaton's office, assured she wouldn't be back for a while, to talk privately with each person. The first, Elias Morales—whom I recognized from the baseball team—told me he was addicted to painkillers. He'd started taking them when he'd hurt his knee the year before, and now he couldn't stop. I wasn't even sure I could cure addiction, but I tried anyway. I placed my hand on his arm and closed my eyes. There were dark spots inside of him that felt like toothless, sucking mouths. I reached out and healed them, hoping they were the source of his addiction. It was the best I could do; the rest was up to him.

The second was a girl who had been diagnosed with endometriosis. The teacher, Mr. Holden, who taught history and sociology, suffered from debilitating migraines. I healed them both.

The third was Michael Graudin. We'd had a couple of classes together, but I couldn't remember talking to him. He was the type of boy who flew under the radar. Not popular, but not a freak, either. I suspected after high school no one would even remember he'd been in our class. Michael was tall and lanky with hair that swooped back, smooth skin, a perfect roman nose, and bright white teeth. Cute in a Ken-doll kind of way.

"What's wrong with you?" I asked.

"I'm gay," he said. Michael's voice was low and smooth.

"What?"

Michael folded his hands in front of him, but looked me straight in the eyes. He spoke slowly and deliberately. "I met a guy off this dating app and he didn't know I was seventeen. We went out a couple of times. He told me he loved me and then he stopped answering my texts and taking my calls."

I slowly sat back down on the desk.

"Did you catch something from him?" I asked. "An STD?"

"No!"

"Then what? Did he hurt you?"

He shook his head violently. "Nothing like that. I want you to make me not gay anymore."

The enormity of what Michael asked took a moment to sink in. "Being gay isn't a disease," I said. "I'm bi, so I get that it can be difficult sometimes, but there's nothing wrong with you."

Tears welled in his eyes and his knees started shaking so badly he had to sit down. "I love him," he said. "And I don't want to, and if I'm not gay then I won't anymore."

"Michael, I—"

"He was the first guy I ever . . . And he fucking threw me away without even telling me why."

I crossed the room and touched Michael's hand. Not to heal him, just to let him know I was there. "I'm sorry for what you're going through, but I can't change who you are. I wouldn't even if I could."

Michael scrubbed the tears away with the back of his hand. "Then can you change how I feel?"

"Only time can do that."

"You're the worst miracle worker ever."

"Yeah," I said. "I know."

We sat there for a few minutes. When Michael stood to leave, I said, "You'll fall in love again."

"What if I don't want to?"

"That's the miracle. Love happens whether you want it to or not."

*Give me a break, Elena. Are you really dicking around healing addicts, headaches, and broken hearts when you should be finding a way to save the whole fucking world? I wish you'd been a boy. A boy would have gotten shit done already.*

I searched the room for the source of the voice, because I hadn't brought Snippity Snap or Baby Cthulhu with me. I finally found a Lego Gandalf propped up beside Mrs. Eaton's computer monitor, picked it up, and held it in front of my face. "No one asked you."

Javi poked his head in. "Everything all right in here?"

"Yeah," I said. "Just talking to Lego Gandalf. He's being rude."

*I wouldn't have to be if you'd do your fucking job.*

"I'm sending in Tori now," Javi said. "But you need to hurry. Lunch is almost over."

I braced myself to deal with Tori Thrash. I was still pissed off at Freddie for what she'd said the night before, but I think she'd gotten one thing right. At some point I was going to have to heal people I disliked. My personal feelings for someone didn't make them less worthy of my help.

Tori walked in, shut the door, and leaned against it, staring at me with her long-lashed blue eyes like she was the queen of every room she entered. She had tanned skin, blond hair, and a toned body she'd clearly spent hours at the gym sculpting. I couldn't deny she was beautiful, but that didn't mean she wasn't also ugly.

"Is it genital warts?" I said.

"Hey, Mary."

"My name's—" I stopped myself and took a deep breath. "Give me one good reason I should help you with anything. Freddie says you're a decent person, but I don't see it."

*Quit wasting time with this child. You've got more important things to concern yourself with.*

"Tell me something I don't know," I said.

Tori smirked. "I'd heard you talked to yourself, but I didn't know you talked to toys."

I looked at the Lego Gandalf I was holding and set him back on the desk. "I can't fix you being a bitch, so unless you've got something else wrong with you, we're done here."

"You're not special, you know?" Tori said. "You might have fooled Freddie, but you're nothing but a wannabe, and you'll never amount to anything more."

"Great talk," I said. "Later."

I crossed the room to the door, but Tori refused to move. "Bring back Ava," she said. "It's your fault she's gone, so bring her back."

"I can't," I said.

"Don't give me that," Tori said. "You made her disappear; you can make her reappear."

*No you can't. It doesn't work that way. Tell her.*

"It doesn't work that way," I said.

"Bullshit!" Tori's cheeks flushed red. "If you don't give her back to me, I swear I'll tell everyone it's your fault. I'll tell the police." Tears welled in her eyes.

"I'm sorry," I said. "I really am. I can't explain it, but Ava's gone."

"She's my best friend, Mary! I need her."

*Tell her she's gone to a better place. People eat that shit up.*

I almost felt sorry for Tori. And maybe Freddie had been right about her. It took a lot of guts to show up here and demand her best friend's return.

"Can I do it?"

"Of course you can!" Tori said.

But I wasn't talking to her. I turned back to the desk and picked up Lego Gandalf. "Can I bring Ava back?"

*No, but maybe you should rapture this girl so I don't have to listen to her whine anymore.*

"I thought I didn't get to choose who vanished?"

*Forget I said that. Just get rid of her; I'm bored.*

I stuffed Lego Gandalf into my pocket and turned my attention back to Tori. "I don't think I can help you," I said. "I would if I could, but it's not possible."

Tori wiped her tears away with the back of her hand, smearing her eyeliner. She squared her jaw and stood up straight. "You're a fraud, Mary, and I'm going to expose you." She opened the door and stormed into the chorus room as the bell rang.

"Tori, wait!"

Javi peeked in. "What'd you do to her?"

"I stole her best friend," I said. "And I'm pretty sure she's going to find some way to make me pay for it."

# THIRTY-NINE

I DIDN'T KNOW if Javi's theory regarding parallel worlds was true, but a universe didn't exist where I wouldn't answer the phone when Freddie called, regardless of what I'd said at the diner that night. And, as I'd predicted, she did call and suggested we see a movie at the luxury theater in Cloud Lake. If I'd been totally honest with myself in that moment, I would have realized that she could have offered to take me alligator wrestling in the Everglades and I would have found a way to justify going, but instead I told myself I was only accepting her offer so that I could discuss my disastrous encounter with Tori and see if Freddie knew how much trouble I might really be in.

Which is how we ended up wandering the strip mall before the movie to kill time, talking about the weather and the test in anatomy neither of us had studied for, and nothing of actual consequence. I pulled her into a quaint local bookstore where a frumpy hipster sat at a table off to the side, typing on an old-style mechanical typewriter of all things, and a young man with umber skin and a warm, inviting smile, stood behind the register helping a customer.

"I'm sorry about how I acted the other night," Freddie said. She was wearing tight jeans with a tear across the right thigh, and an oversized printed tank top. I couldn't pinpoint whether it was her makeup or the way she'd styled her hair, but she seemed to glow. Like the light I'd seen when I'd healed her was so bright now that it was leaking out, her body no longer able to contain it. It was likely nothing more than a combination of wishful thinking and my overactive imagination, but I couldn't help hoping I was the cause of her illumination.

"Wow," I said. "I thought I was going to have to tickle an apology out of you."

"Nope," she said. "When I fuck up, I apologize. But maybe save that tickle plan for some other time."

Was she flirting with me? She was definitely flirting, right? I never knew how to tell. Franklin Rowan had stolen and eaten most of my lunch throughout seventh grade because he thought I was pretty, which I hadn't known and had assumed he'd done because he thought I was a troll. He finally worked up the nerve to tell me how he felt on the last day of school, but by then his parents had already decided to move to Montana and I never saw him again after that. I'd come a long way since seventh grade, but I was still clueless when it came to boys and girls, and I didn't want to interpret Freddie's comment in a way she hadn't intended. God, then I'd be just like Javi. But if I let it go unanswered, she might think I'd lost interest. Why was this so difficult?

"I'll do that," was the less-than-amazing response I finally came up with. "And it's okay."

"It's not," Freddie said. "I'm not."

"What do you mean?"

We wandered through the stacks, ignoring the books. "Forget it," she said. "What's new with you?"

I didn't want to forget it, but the one thing I'd learned about Freddie—the real Freddie and not the imaginary version of her I'd been crushing on for years—was that the force of her obstinate desire not to do something was inversely proportional to how much someone else wanted her to do it. In other words, if I pushed her, it would probably shut her down completely, so I let it drop.

"Well," I said, "Javi pimped my healing abilities out to a teacher and some students, including Tori Thrash, who wanted me to bring Ava back from wherever the voices took her and then threatened me when I told her I couldn't. Also, she cried. Does she do that often?"

Freddie stopped in the middle of the biography section and grabbed my wrist. "Tori doesn't cry," she said. "I mean, in all the years I've known her, I've never seen her shed a single tear. Not even when she had to put down her dog two years ago, and Shortcake had been with the Thrashes since Tori was born."

"So I'm guessing I should take her threat seriously?"

"I would." Freddie let go of my arm, but I kind of wished she hadn't.

We kept walking. "I feel terrible," I said. "It was one thing when I didn't know the people who vanished—"

"Or when it was someone who'd attempted to kill me?"

"Exactly," I said. "But Ava was a real person. These are real lives I'm wrecking."

"I told you that Tori is one of the most loyal friends I'd ever had. If you'd offered to rapture her in Ava's place, she would have taken you up on it."

Freddie's comment reminded me what Lego Gandalf had said about making Tori vanish, and I wondered if I could have done that. I still didn't know the extent of what I was capable of, and the truth was that I was afraid to try. People disappeared when I healed and I had no idea what might happen if I performed another type of miracle. I could set the world on fire or kill everyone on the planet. But I couldn't change that Ava was gone, and though it might sound callous, I had to put her out of my mind or the indecision would break me.

"You never told me why you stopped hanging out with Tori," I said.

Freddie pulled a book off the shelf and flipped through the pages. It was a photo book full of pictures of a woman who'd posed for her death over and over. The pictures were macabre but playful and beautiful. "Have you ever heard of jamais vu?"

"Not that I can recall."

"It's the opposite of déjà vu," she said. "The feeling of knowing you've experienced something before or should know it, but can't. Have you ever written a word over and over so many times that it suddenly looks unfamiliar?"

"My teacher in third grade used to make us write lines as punishment. Every time I had to do it, I'd end up staring at the words thinking they couldn't be real. I knew they were, I knew I'd spelled them correctly, but they just looked—"

"Alien," Freddie finished. She returned the book she'd been flipping through to the shelf. "That's how my life has felt since you healed me. There are pictures of me doing things I'm supposed to remember but can't. Friends tell me stories that sound familiar but aren't. Hell, even my friends all seem like those lines you wrote. Strange."

"And you think it's my fault?"

"Or David Combs's fault."

Freddie and I wandered to one of the tables and sat. It was

kind of hard to concentrate with the sound of the clicking keys behind us, but it was also kind of meditative. I imagined losing myself in the rhythmic tapping and letting the world fall away, but I needed to remain in the present with Freddie.

"What was it like?" I asked. "Getting shot, I mean."

"It hurt."

"Oh, I see," I said. "Someone's being sassy? The tickle interrogation technique can be used to extract more than an apology."

"You keep acting like that's a threat," Freddie said. "But, fine. Getting shot was surreal. My body knew I'd been hit before my brain did. I was sitting there, watching you be all awkward and waiting for you to do that thing normal people do where they open their mouths and make words, and then I had a bullet in me. There wasn't one part of me in more pain than another; it was like my marrow had been swapped out with molten lead."

"And when I healed you?"

"That was weird too." She chewed her thumbnail. "I thought I was hallucinating from blood loss or whatever, but you were there and you opened me up and found the thing inside of me that hurt and switched it off."

It was the first time anyone had described what it felt like to be healed. "When I heal someone, I close my eyes, but I can still see the person. And whatever's wrong with them looks different, which is how I know what to fix."

"So you really don't understand how it works?"

I shook my head. "Not so much."

"That's disappointing." Freddie nudged my leg with her foot under the table. "Like learning Santa Claus isn't real."

"He's not?"

Freddie laughed and smiled, and I think this was the longest we'd gone where she hadn't cussed at me or cut me down.

"When I first talked to you after the shooting, why'd you tell me I should have let you die?" I held my hands up in front of me. "I know you said you're not suicidal, but why did you say it?"

The laughter on Freddie's face vanished so completely that I had to wonder if I'd imagined it in the first place. She cast her eyes at the table and redoubled her effort to gnaw her fingernail to the quick.

"People who're suicidal believe they want to die. They make a choice to actively end their lives, and they're determined to do it. There are others who simply give up. Whatever happens, happens, even if it's death."

I tried to wrap my brain around what Freddie was telling me, and I had a strong urge to call Freddie's mother, whom I'd never spoken to before, to warn her that something was wrong with her daughter, but I wasn't entirely certain what Freddie was getting at and I didn't want to jump to conclusions.

"It's the same thing, though," I said. "If I walk out into the street, see a car speeding toward me, and let it hit me because I can't be bothered to get out of the way, it's the same thing as walking in front of the car on purpose."

Freddie shook her head. "Do you believe pacifists are suicidal?"

"Like Quakers?"

"Sure," Freddie said.

"I guess not." I felt like Freddie was luring me into a trap, but I wasn't sure how to avoid it.

"If someone hits a pacifist, they roll with it. They don't hit back; they turn the other cheek."

"There's no way anyone hits you without you punching them back," I said. "And if you're trying to claim pacifism is the same thing as giving up on life, you're doing a terrible job."

"How so?"

Freddie was trying to tell me something important, I thought, so I chose my words carefully. "A pacifist might not physically fight back against someone threatening to kill them, but that doesn't mean they wouldn't attempt to talk them out of it. It doesn't mean they don't care if they die."

"Fine," Freddie said. "But then it's no different from the way you keep healing people even though you're not sure the voices are being honest with you. No matter what you say, you're not doing it because you want to, but because it's easy."

"There's nothing easy about it," I said, "and how did this become about me?"

"Do you perform miracles because you want to? Look what you did to Tori. To Ava's parents and David Combs's parents. You did that, but did you do it by choice or because of inertia?"

"The voices said—"

"Answer the question, Elena."

"I healed you because I wanted to, though sometimes you're so frustrating that I wish I hadn't."

"That makes two of us." Freddie scrubbed her face with her hands. "I need to use the restroom." She walked off before I could stop her.

It was the second time Freddie had said she'd wished I hadn't healed her, and I couldn't help wondering if she actually meant it. Every time I got too close to the walls she'd erected, she started lobbing boulders at me until I retreated.

"Trouble with your girlfriend?" The tall boy from the register stood over my table.

"She's not my girlfriend."

He laughed. "If you say so. I'm Tommy."

"Elena."

Tommy sat down without asking. "What'd you do to upset her?"

"Why is it my fault?" I asked. Tommy had kind eyes and

a bright smile that inspired trust. "Fine, maybe it is my fault. I made a choice that affected both of us, and now we're dealing with the fallout."

"So," he said, "basically life."

"Excuse me?"

"Life," he said again. "Look, I made a choice once. Did what I needed to do for myself, and it hurt someone I loved very much."

"And?"

"Some days I'm not sure if it was the right choice, but we do the best we can with the knowledge we're given and hope we don't fuck it all up too badly."

"What if we do?"

"Then we live with the consequences and try not to make the same mistakes twice."

"What about the person you hurt?"

"He made his own choices." Tommy's smile grew wider. "Did what was best for him. Went off to college in Colorado."

"You miss him?"

Tommy nodded. "Every day. But I'm kind of hoping to fix that soon."

"How so?"

"Going to visit him in a couple of months. I needed to see what my life looked like without him; I had to figure out my own path without his shadow cast over it. And I think I have. So now I'm going to see if he's still interested in carving out a path together."

"I hope everything works out," I said.

"Me too."

Freddie walked toward us, returning from the restroom. Tommy saw her and stood.

"But, hey," I said. "Don't wait a couple of months. Go now. The sooner the better."

"Why?"

"Trust me, all right?"

Tommy left, and I hoped he made things right with the person he hurt and that they were able to find their way back to each other before the end of the world, whenever it might be.

"Who was that?" Freddie asked when she returned to the table.

"No one," I said. "You ready for the movie?"

# FORTY

I CAN'T RECALL what movie we watched because I spent the two hours it was playing sitting next to Freddie wondering if she really didn't care whether she lived or died. If Fadil had said to me what Freddie had, I'd have dragged him to his house, sat him down in front of his parents, and forced him to get help. But that was because it would have been out of character for him to say something like that. Freddie's admission could have been a cry for help or it could have been hyperbole. The only way to know for sure was to spend more time with her, which I resolved to do.

After the movie, Freddie and I walked around the outside mall. We didn't talk much, but she kept bumping into me, which might have been one of those flirty things I was supposed to recognize but didn't.

We ducked into a candy store and grabbed plastic bags to fill.

"Twizzlers?" I said, eyeing Freddie's bag. "That's it, we can't be friends anymore."

"Are we friends?"

"You tell me."

Freddie seemed to think about it. "I suppose my reputation can take the hit."

"Good to know," I said. "But, seriously, we've got to talk about the Twizzlers."

Freddie laughed and held her hand to her chest like I'd stabbed her. "What've you got against the greatest candy ever invented?"

"Aside from the fact that it tastes like ass-flavored earwax? Nothing, I suppose."

"Let's see what you bought." Freddie swiped my bag. "Gobstoppers, SweeTarts, and M&M's?" She looked down her nose at me. "M&M's? Really? All these sweets to choose from and you pick the most generic candy in the world?"

I snatched my bag back. "They're peanut butter M&M's, thank you very much."

"Even worse!" Freddie's smile basically lit up the entire store. It was the kind of smile that made me think kissing her might be nice. Of course, I doubt she had a single facial expression in her repertoire that I wouldn't have considered kissable. I also assumed there was less than a .00005 percent chance of Freddie actually wanting to kiss me, which put a damper on my feelings. "M&M's are the leftover scraps of better chocolates, mixed together, shat out into a ball, and coated with a crappy candy shell."

I reached into my bag, scooped up a handful of M&M's, and tossed them into my mouth. My cheeks bulged, and I think a SweeTart had gotten mixed in.

"But they're so delicious," I said, syrupy drool leaking out and diving for the floor.

"Hey!" called the woman behind the register. "You can't do that!"

Freddie and I both broke into fits of laughter, and I nearly choked on the glob of gooey chocolate. When I'd swallowed, I said, "Next I suppose you're going to tell me your favorite candy bar is Snickers."

"Obviously."

"I knew it!" I said. "Also, you're wrong. The only candy bar worth eating is a Butterfinger. Anything else may as well be a sweetened poo log."

Freddie tried to look serious, but she couldn't erase her cheeky smirk. "I think our differences in what constitutes candy may be too vast for this friendship to work."

Okay, I know I said there was an almost zero percent chance of Freddie wanting to kiss me, but there was this moment when she was looking at me with her beautiful brown eyes, and she bit her bottom lip, and I swear she was leaning in to do it. I might have imagined it, but there's an electrical charge that fills the space between two bodies in that inevitable second before they kiss—an energy that draws them together—and I felt that. My entire body tingled. I forgot the names she'd called me and how she didn't seem sure if she deserved to live or deserved to die and about the end of the world and all of it. All I saw was Freddie.

And then I blinked and cleared my throat. "Yeah," I said. "If we can't overcome the Great Candy Divide, we don't stand a chance."

The woman at the register was dancing from one foot to the other. Either she really needed to pee or she was working up the courage to ask us to leave.

The electricity between us had dissipated. "I should get home," I said.

"Cool. Have fun walking."

I slapped her shoulder. "Jerk."

"It's a good thing I'm cute, then."

"You're not that cute."

"Yeah," she said. "I'm pretty adorable."

We paid for our candy—the cashier added a couple of dollars for the M&M's I'd eaten—and walked to Freddie's car.

# FORTY-ONE

FREDDIE DROVE ME home in silence. We'd had a moment—this brilliant, beautiful moment when we'd laughed and had fun and forgotten everything else—but it had felt stolen. Unearned. We had no right to be carefree and happy when the world might be ending and our lives were in shambles.

Freddie parked in front of my apartment building and idled, waiting for me to get out.

"I'm not sorry I healed you," I said. "But I am sorry if I'm the reason David shot you."

"You're not." Freddie's voice barely rose above a whisper.

"But if I was," I went on. "And I also don't care that you know I had—have—a crush on you, though to be honest, you've really tested its limits, especially considering your irrational love of Twizzlers."

I was afraid bringing up my crush would upset her again, but Freddie laughed. Her entire face brightened. Her cheeks rose and her nostrils flared and the laugh lines around her eyes deepened to depthless trenches. She was always beautiful, but in that moment she might have been the most beautiful girl in the world.

"What's so funny?"

"Nothing," Freddie said, still laughing. "Just, you're this miracle girl. Your birth was a miracle, you can perform miracles, and you hear voices that have given you the responsibility for deciding the fate of the world. Why would you even be worried about a nobody like me?"

I wrinkled my forehead. "Because you matter. Isn't that obvious?"

"Everyone matters, Elena."

"But don't some people matter more than others?" I asked. "I mean, if we're talking about saving humanity, doesn't it make sense to save the best and brightest of us?"

Freddie's laughter had faded. "So you're saying it's better to save a world-famous physicist rather than say, a modest merchant who was a partner in a bed feathers company."

"That's a really odd comparison, but yeah."

"Except no," Freddie said. "That merchant and his wife would go on to birth and raise Albert Einstein." She paused dramatically. "Hermann and Pauline Einstein might not have seemed like anyone special at the time, but their son changed how we look at the universe."

"That's one example."

"Here's another. Who should you save? A genius mathematician admitted to Harvard at sixteen or a single mom living on welfare?"

"This is a trick question."

"Are you allergic to answering questions, or what?"

"The mathematician," I said.

"Ted Kaczynski. Otherwise known as the Unabomber. And that single mom would go on to write Harry Potter."

I raised my hands in surrender. "Fine. I get it."

"Do you?"

"Yes. Everyone deserves the chance to survive. And that includes you."

"Forget me for a minute. You can't judge someone based on who they are right now, because you never know who they'll become or who their children will become."

"The voices saved David Combs after he'd shot you. Are you really okay with the boy who attempted to kill you being among those who're saved?"

"Yes."

"Even if he didn't think you deserved to live?"

Freddie opened her mouth, closed it. Opened it again. "I . . . I don't get to judge, Elena. And neither do you."

"First nothing matters, and now everyone matters? Make up your mind."

"You do realize it's possible to hold two opposing ideas in your head at one time, right? I can believe all this stupid bullshit is pointless and simultaneously believe it's not my right to decide who matters."

"Why not? Why shouldn't we get to decide someone like David Combs doesn't deserve to be saved over someone like you?"

"Because," Freddie said, "the moment we forget that even the evil among us are still human is the moment we forget that even the most human among us are capable of evil."

"You sure have a lot of opinions on life for someone who thinks it's bullshit."

"I have a lot of opinions on everything. Most of them are crap."

"What's your opinion on me?" I asked.

Freddie reached across the emergency brake and took my hand. I froze, not sure what to do. I was pretty sure Freddie had made her feelings—or lack thereof—for me clear, and I didn't want to read more into her holding my hand than might really be there, despite what I'd felt in the candy store.

"I like you, Freddie. Though you don't make it easy."

"I know."

"Do you like me?"

"I think . . ." She paused. Slipped her hand out of mine. "I'm not sure."

I wanted to kiss her. To lean across the distance between us and press my lips to hers. I wanted to forget the voices and the world ending. I wanted her to kiss me back. I wanted a miracle for myself.

Light blasted through the darkness and someone was yelling and I turned to see Sofie in her pajamas running down the stairs and banging on Mrs. Haimovitch's front door. I fumbled for the handle and scrambled out of the car.

"Sofie? What's wrong? Sophia!"

Sofie grabbed my hand and tugged me back toward the stairs. "Conor's hurt, Elena! Hurry!"

# FORTY-TWO

I STOOD BESIDE Mama while Dr. Berko explained that Conor had a concussion but was going to be fine. That he was resting and they were going to keep him overnight for observation. She had a soothing voice that gave me hope that Conor really was going to be all right and that she wasn't sugarcoating it to keep us from freaking out. She told us a nurse would be out soon to take us to Conor's room.

"You should have let me heal him," I said to Mama when Dr. Berko had retreated back behind the double doors.

Mama shook her head. "I'd already called 911. There would have been too many questions. And, see? He's okay."

She was being far too calm about all of this.

"Was it Sean?" I asked.

"Mija . . ."

"That son of a bitch," I said. "I want him in jail."

Mama sank into the hard plastic emergency room chair and buried her face in her hands. "It was my fault—"

"You did this to Conor?"

"Sean spent the grocery money on pain pills. His back has been hurting him so much lately. We got into a fight and Conor was in the way and Sean didn't mean for it to happen. He's not a bad man, Elena."

"Like hell!"

"It was an accident."

"Are you—" I stood and walked away from my mother. Already the nurse at the window was giving us side-eye, and I didn't want to complicate matters even more. When I'd taken a few deep breaths, I returned to my mother.

"You can't defend him," I said. "I get that he's Sofie's and Conor's father, but you can't carry him forever, Mama. He's dragging you down."

"We don't abandon the people in our lives when things get difficult."

"The way your parents did with you?" I leaned my head on her shoulder. "You're not them. They threw you out because you got pregnant. Kicking Sean out because he's a loser who hurt Conor isn't the same thing. You didn't deserve what happened to you, but he does."

Tears had welled up in the corners of her eyes. Her face

THE APOCALYPSE OF ELENA MENDOZA ✸ 307

was a battlefield, and the creases that etched her skin and the deep circles under her eyes were the scars of a war she would either win tonight or lose forever. If she threw Sean out, she'd feel responsible for anything that happened to him. If she let him stay, she'd blame herself if he hurt Conor again or Sofie or me.

"No matter what you do, someone is going to wind up getting hurt. Sean made his choices, and he should have to live with the consequences."

"I care about him."

"But does he care about you? About us?" I took her hand and squeezed it. "When the police come to question you, tell the truth. Promise me you'll do that, at least."

A nurse strode through the double doors. "Mrs. Malloy? I can take you back to see your son now."

Mama stood, but I gripped her hand tightly. "Promise me."

She didn't speak, but she pursed her lips tightly and nodded.

# FORTY-THREE

I STOOD IN the center of my mother's room trying to decide where to begin.

"We could burn it all." Javi stood in the doorway with his arms crossed over his chest. He was wearing Power Rangers pajama bottoms and a tank top, and his fingernails were painted bubblegum pink.

"It's definitely an option," I said. "But not a good one."

Javi shrugged. "You want me to start in the closet?"

"Yeah. Grab whatever looks like his and pile it in the plastic tub."

It might have seemed like Javi was the last person I'd call to help me, but he was actually the best person for the job. Freddie and I didn't know each other well enough for me to ask her for this kind of favor—plus, I wasn't sure what might have happened in that car if Sofie hadn't interrupted, and I needed some space to figure it out—I didn't want to bother Fadil on his date with Naomi, and Mrs. Haimovitch was watching Sofie, whom I didn't want around while we rid the house of Sean's belongings. Javi, however, worked fast, didn't ask a lot of questions, and if Sean was stupid enough to return to the apartment, Javi would kick his ass, chop his body into tiny pieces, and make sure no one ever found the remains.

I went through the dresser, pulling all of Sean's clothes out, grimacing when I had to touch his dingy, nasty underwear, and tossed it all in the plastic tub. For someone who'd lived in the same house as us for nine years, he didn't have a lot of belongings.

"You look nice, Elena."

"Focus on what you're doing."

"I'm serious." Javi was staring at me, letting his eyes wander up and down. I was wearing tight jeans and a thin light-blue hoodie that I had thought looked fabulous when I'd dressed to go out with Freddie earlier. "You look hot."

"Well, at least someone noticed," I said under my breath.

Javi chuckled and shoved a bunch of dress clothes into the tub, not bothering to fold them neatly. "You stepping out on me, Mendoza?"

"We're not dating."

"Who's the lucky dead man or woman? I'm an equal-opportunity bruiser."

Though I still didn't trust Javi's motivations, it was different now that we definitively were not and would never be a couple. Talking to him was easy in a way that talking to Freddie sometimes wasn't.

"It was nothing," I said. "I went out with a friend."

"You only have one friend, those are the jeans you think your ass looks best in, and you don't care what Fadil thinks of your ass."

I swiped Sean's cologne bottles and other junk into the box. "Well, you look like you're dressed for a slumber party," I said, dodging the question.

Javi stood on his toes to pull a stack of old DVDs off the shelf. "In fact, I am. Cristina invited a bunch of her friends over and I was keeping them entertained."

I motioned at his fingernails with my chin. "I can see that."

"It's a good color on me, don't you think?"

"Your friends will love it." I scanned the bedroom, decided we'd gotten everything, and moved into the living room. I was determined to exorcise our apartment of Sean Malloy by the time Mama brought Conor home from the hospital. "And speaking of friends, I have more than one."

"Yeah?" Javi asked. "Who?"

"Mrs. Haimovitch."

Javi barked out a laugh so loud I was sure the neighbors had heard it. "I like Mrs. H., don't get me wrong, but she's five times your age."

"Don't be ageist."

"Was it Freddie?" Javi asked. "I've seen her sitting with you at lunch. She's hot. I'd totally bang her."

I rolled my eyes. "You'd bang a warm sandwich." Javi opened his mouth to speak, but I cut him off. "I swear to God if you make a mayonnaise joke I will shove you into that box and put you out with the rest of the garbage."

Javi held up his hands in surrender. "You got anything to drink?"

"Fridge," I said. "And bring the beer while you're in there. I want it out of this house." The tub still had room in it, but when I looked around, I saw nothing else that belonged to Sean. His entire life with us fit in one plastic container. I went into the bathroom, grabbed all of his toiletries, and dropped them in the tub as well. That was it.

Javi was sitting at the kitchen table drinking a soda. Two six-packs of beer sat on the counter, and I grabbed them and set them with the rest of Sean's stuff.

"So, you and Freddie?" Javi said.

I didn't have the energy to argue. It was late and I was physically and emotionally exhausted. "She's not into me," I said.

"Then she's stupid."

"She's not stupid."

Javi swirled the ice in his soda, watching it spin around and around. "She is if she's not into you."

"That's oddly sweet of you, Javi, even if it's not true."

"Yeah it is." Javi snorted. "If I could do it all over again . . ." He paused. "I'd make all the same mistakes, but I'd try hard not to because you're kind of worth it." I watched him for a few seconds, not sure what to say. "Truth is, I'll probably end up like this asshole." He motioned at Sean's box. "Some girl tossing my shit in the middle of the night because I did something stupid."

"You're better than Sean," I said.

Whatever self-pity Javi was feeling, it quickly passed. "Yeah, I am. And you're better than Freddie. If she's not into you, find someone who is. You deserve it."

"What I want and what I deserve are two different things." I sat at the table and scrubbed my face with my hands. "Twice tonight I felt like she was going to kiss me, but she didn't. And we can be talking and laughing and everything's fine, and then she turns mean and tells me she's not sure I should have saved her and that nothing matters."

Every time I thought back to the candy store and the moment in the car, I imagined what might have happened. How differently the night could have unfolded.

"Why didn't you kiss her?"

I shook myself free of my thoughts. "She didn't—"

Javi cut me off. "Not what I asked. Why didn't *you* kiss *her*?" He waited for an answer, but I didn't have one. "You're upset and you figure she's not into getting down because she didn't kiss you when she had the chance, but what if she was waiting for you to make the move? What if she's sitting home in her little jammies thinking the same mopey shit you are? That you're not into her because you didn't kiss her when you had the chance?"

I hadn't thought of that. She knew how I felt about her, so I assumed that if anyone was going to break the awkwardness and make the first move it would be her.

"Good point." Which was a phrase I never expected to say to Javi. "But it's complicated. Especially with all the other stuff going on."

Javi laughed. "You make everything complicated, Elena."

"I do not!"

"You totally do," he said. "World's ending, right? You can do something about it, right? Then do it. You can heal people and you want to do it, then do it. You want to kiss Freddie, then fucking do it."

"But what if she doesn't want me to kiss her? What if the world isn't really ending and I screw everything up?"

"Then you move on and try kissing someone else. You fix

the world another way. Or you don't fix it at all because you're not in charge of everyone and everything, and taking care of other people's shit isn't your problem."

"Freddie said I was scared of making choices and that I let others make them for me."

"I might've been wrong to call her stupid," he said.

"I just don't want to make the wrong choices."

Javi stared at me. His eyes had these streaks of green amid the brown that I'd always thought were beautiful. "Guess what happens when you don't make a choice?"

"What?"

"Nothing. Maybe you don't fuck anything up, but nothing gets better either."

"Javi—"

"I know you'll never give me another chance, and I don't deserve one, but I don't want to be thirty, kicking myself in the ass, flipping through Snowflake or whatever fucking thing we'll be using when we're thirty, wondering what might've happened if I'd tried."

Javi pushed back his chair. "Come on. I'll help you get this junk out to the curb, but then I have to get home. The girls were gonna teach me how to take care of my oily T-zone."

I stood and kissed Javi's cheek. "You can be really sweet sometimes." He was grinning when I stepped back.

"Does this mean—"

"Nope."

"Are you sure, 'cause—"

"Not even if we were the last humans on the planet."

Javi shook his head. "Damn, Elena, no need to be so harsh."

I smiled and he smiled and I said, "Thanks. Not just for helping me with Sean's stuff, but for everything."

"I got your back, Elena. Always."

# FORTY-FOUR

"THE POLICE LET him go?"

I sat on the floor in Fadil's bedroom, leaning against the side of his bed. Posters of his favorite soccer players hung from the walls and books filled the shelves, leaving room for little else. There was a warm, lived-in feeling to it that made me feel welcome. "Mama told them what happened, but even she had to admit Sean hadn't meant to shove Conor. They offered to help her file for a restraining order, but she refused."

Mama had brought Conor home from the hospital that morning, and before Fadil had picked me up, a locksmith had arrived to change the locks.

Fadil shook his head and sighed. "What'll happen to him, then?"

"I don't know. Javi helped me clear all of his stuff out

of the apartment, so he's not living with us anymore. And I know Mama's hoping he'll check himself into rehab, but I don't see that happening."

"You should have called me," he said. "I would have been there in a second."

I smiled at Fadil. At the fierce gleam in his eyes. "I took care of it. Plus, you were out with Naomi and I didn't want to bother you."

"That's not what I meant when I said—"

"Calm down. I wanted you there, but I didn't need you."

Fadil leaned back in his desk chair and stretched his arms behind his head. I watched the conflicting emotions play across his face. On one hand, he wanted to be pissed off at me for not calling him when Sean hurt Conor, but on the other he couldn't be mad that I'd respected what he'd wanted. Finally, he let out an explosive sigh.

"So how did your date with Naomi go?" I asked. "Does she ever stop talking long enough for you to kiss her?"

"She kissed me, actually."

"Naomi put the moves on you?"

"Yeah."

"Wait, was this the first time?"

"It was."

"And?"

Fadil crinkled his nose. "What was it like when you kissed

Javi?" It was not the question I'd been expecting. Not even a little.

"Frustrating." I paused. "What was it like when you kissed Naomi?"

Fadil pulled his legs up onto the chair and hugged his knees. "Boring."

"Seriously?"

"I thought it would be different. I haven't kissed a girl since freshman year—"

"Olivia Appleby."

A far-off look took root in Fadil's eyes. "At Tori's pool party over the summer. Yeah." He shook off the reverie. "I was bored then too, but I'd only made out with her because it was the stupid game."

"Tell me what happened with Naomi," I said.

"We were watching a movie at her house, which is huge by the way. She's got her own floor, if you can believe that."

"I do." I didn't know what Naomi's parents did, but she lived in one of the nicest neighborhoods in Arcadia, so I'd assumed they were loaded.

Fadil kept talking like he'd barely registered my response. "She wanted to watch *Star Wars*, which we'd both seen a million times, and I took that as a sign she was more interested in not watching a movie. Mr. Brewer had just peeked in to make sure we had enough popcorn, and we were cuddled up together and I was thinking about how to make my move, when she pulled my face to hers and kissed me."

"Maybe her taking the lead threw you off your game?"

"I kissed her back," Fadil said. "There was tongue and heavy breathing and all the stuff that's supposed to happen. But I spent the whole time wondering how Obi-Wan doesn't recognize R2-D2 when he spent three freaking films with him."

"Are you sure you're really into her?"

"I thought so."

"I used to create mental to-do lists when I was making out with Javi." I stretched my legs out in front of me. "Sometimes lists of the chores I needed to do, sometimes lists of all the places in the world I wanted to visit."

Fadil climbed down off his chair and crawled over to sit beside me. "Do you think there's something wrong with me?"

"Wrong with you how?"

"I don't know. But it's weird that she kissed me and I was thinking about Obi-Wan Kenobi."

It didn't actually seem that weird to me, but my only comparable experience had been with Javi, so I wasn't the best person to judge. "Were you thinking about old man Obi-Wan?" I asked. "Or were you thinking about hot Ewan McGregor Obi-Wan?"

"I'm pretty sure I'm not gay," he said. "When you told

me you were bi, I got curious and looked at some naked guys online. They didn't do anything for me. Not even a twinge."

"Maybe you're not into sex or making out. There's an Archie character, Jughead, who's asexual and aromantic, and so is Kamal Jean at school. I met him in the GSA last year. You could talk to him."

"I'm confused."

"There's nothing wrong with that." I kept trying to catch Fadil's eyes, but he seemed so distant. "You are who you are, Fadil. And it's okay if you're not sure what that means yet. Anyone who says they've got it all figured out at sixteen is a liar, and don't let anyone tell you otherwise."

"You know who you are."

"Ha!"

"I'm serious," he said. "You knew you were bi in eighth grade."

"Mama knew before I did."

Fadil perked up. "Really?"

I nodded. "We were at Target and I guess I'd been checking out this girl, though I didn't realize that's what I was doing, and she asked me if I was gay. I didn't think I was because I'd had a big-time crush on Cody Reynolds the year before, and I told her so. She didn't say anything else about it while we were shopping, but afterward she took me to Starbucks and explained what bisexuality was and that she'd suspected I might fall somewhere on that spectrum. It made sense to me. I'd never had a word to describe how I'd felt, and when Mama gave me that word, I just . . . knew."

"What if I don't know yet?" Fadil asked. "What if none of the words fit?"

I took Fadil's hand and held it to my chest. "Then you keep looking until you find one that does. Keep being you and you'll figure it out when you're ready."

Fadil and I sat quietly for a while. In a way, I felt like a terrible friend for not recognizing his confusion sooner. That's the problem with living in a world where everyone was assumed to be heterosexual until proven otherwise. He'd talked about girls, so it had never crossed my mind to ask if he was queer. But it should have. I should have asked.

"Do you think I should tell Naomi?" Fadil's hand was sweaty. "It seems unfair to lead her on if I'm not into her the way she's into me."

"Do you like her?"

"Yeah."

"Do you enjoy spending time with her?"

"Definitely." A smile brightened Fadil's face. "She's a manga encyclopedia. And did you know she taught herself to code?"

"I did not."

"She's working on this app to help connect people who suck at certain subjects with others who are good at them. Kind of like a dating app but for schoolwork."

Only Fadil would get excited about something like that. "Tell her what you want to tell her when you're ready," I said. "If she's as cool as you say, she'll understand."

"Thanks."

I hugged Fadil and then we worked on our homework for a while. It was difficult to think about assignments and romantic entanglements when I still had the fate of the world looming over me, but the world ending didn't mean that our other problems disappeared. We could push them aside for a while, but we dragged them behind us everywhere we went. Whether or not the world really was ending, I was still going to have to make up my mind what to do about Freddie. Fadil was still going to have to figure out what to say—or not say— to Naomi. Sean was still going to have to choose between his family and drinking, and if he chose us, Mama was going to have to decide whether that was enough.

"Do you really believe the voices come from God?"

Fadil looked up from his chemistry worksheet. "Yes."

"Just like that?" I said. "You don't want to take a minute to think about it?"

"I don't need to." The uncertainty written across Fadil's face when we'd been discussing Naomi had vanished, replaced by a calm determination that I admired.

"I thought if I understood why David Combs shot Freddie

I'd understand why the voices took him—why they deemed him worthy of saving—and then I'd know that I could trust them."

Fadil set his pencil aside. "David did what he did because he made a choice. We may never know why he did it, but that doesn't necessarily matter, because it will never justify the choice he made."

"I know," I said. "But I have to make a choice too. Save the world or not. Do what the voices tell me to or not. I want to make sure I'm making the right choice for the right reasons, and knowing why David did it, knowing why the voices saved him, might help me."

"Or it won't," he said. "And then you'll still have to choose."

"I'm scared of doing the wrong thing, Fadil."

Fadil chuckled. "You should be."

"That's not helping."

"Look," he said. "I don't know for sure whether the voices you hear are Allah, if they were sent by Allah, or if they're something else entirely. I know what I believe, but you have to make up your own mind. Don't forget, the voices made their own choice. They chose you. And I believe with all my heart that they made the right choice."

"What if you're wrong? What if I screw up and the world burns?"

Fadil shrugged. "Then I'll buy the marshmallows and we'll watch it burn together."

# FORTY-FIVE

I DIDN'T KNOW many things for certain, which bothered the hell out of me. I liked certainty. Two plus two equals four no matter where you are or what's going on, and that comforted me. I could find myself on the dark edge of the universe, and two plus two would still equal four. If I threw a billiard ball into space, it would continue traveling in a straight line and at a steady velocity until acted upon by another force. No matter what I did, Fadil and Mama would always be there for me. Those were the constants I relied on to keep me anchored.

Unlike everything else in my life, which was mutable or unknown. I didn't know if the voices I heard were telling me the truth. I didn't know if humanity was in danger. I didn't know if the voices were really taking the people they "saved" to a better place. I didn't know why David Combs had shot Freddie.

Despite Fadil's faith in me, I didn't know that I would make the right decision when the time came. How could I when I didn't have a complete picture? How could I when I was forced to doubt the information that I did have? The number of people who'd vanished now totaled 10,938. Stories of their disappearances had cropped up on the news. It was only a matter of time before the Homeland Security agents Deputy Akers had warned me about appeared on my doorstep to question me. And they'd be right to ask, wouldn't they? If I couldn't be sure where the people "saved" were going, how could I make that choice for them? If I didn't know whether I was really healing people or just rotating them out to another world, how could I keep doing it?

What I was doing was wrong. I was deciding people's fates without giving them a chance to make up their own minds. But if I didn't, and the voices were right about the end of humanity, then I was dooming them to death instead.

And who the hell were the voices to coerce me into this impossible situation? I had to admit the possibility that they'd engineered the shooting to force me to heal Freddie and set me on this path. How monumentally screwed up would that be? They'd decided that Freddie's life was less important than the life of David Combs, whom they'd "saved" with their ridiculous beam of light. Hell, they'd practically rewarded him for shooting Freddie. There was no world where that was acceptable. Yet that was the decision the voices had made, and it forced me to question them and everything I'd done since the day of the shooting.

It was too much. Too much for me to handle. I was frozen with indecision. I couldn't, in good conscience, continue following the voices' orders when there was so much I didn't know or trust about their plan. But I couldn't do nothing, either, not if the fate of humanity hung in the balance.

The only thing I could do was continue trying to figure out the truth on my own. On Monday, I skipped lunch and went to the art room, hoping Freddie would be there. We hadn't spoken since the movie, and I was nervous about how she would react. Between Conor and Sean and the voices and the end of the world, Freddie was the last person I should have been worried about—priorities, you know?—and yet she was the one person I couldn't shake from my mind. We'd almost kissed. I'd told her I liked her and she hadn't rejected me outright and I swear we'd nearly kissed, and I know I said the end of the world should have been my primary concern, but I couldn't stop thinking about all the nearlys and almosts that had happened that night in the car. So I was determined to do it. I was going to lay it all out there for Freddie and make a move and see what happened.

I didn't see Freddie when I first walked in, but her phone was plugged into the portable speaker, playing a song sung by a man who sounded like he'd had his heart ripped out of his chest and was being forced to watch someone he'd once loved blend it into a bleeding-heart smoothie. It might have been the saddest song I'd ever heard.

"Damien Rice," Freddie said.

I swung around to find her walking out of the supply closet holding a pair of pliers. She was wearing paint-splattered overalls and her work gloves.

"My dad wrote notes to go with each of the bands he put on the playlist, and he wrote that I should listen to this when I was going through a breakup."

"Are you going through a breakup?"

Freddie shook her head. Her blue hair had faded at the tips, and her auburn roots were growing out. "Not that I know of."

"It's pretty."

"Pretty depressing." Freddie dropped the pliers on the worktable and changed the music to something more upbeat.

"How'd he die?" I asked. "Your dad, I mean."

"Suicide."

"Really?"

Freddie turned on me, her face etched from stone. "You think I'd lie about that?"

"I didn't mean. I wasn't . . . It just came out."

I was a giant ass. I hadn't known her father had killed himself. The more I learned about Freddie, the more I realized I knew nothing.

Freddie sat on the stool by the workbench and hugged her arms around herself. "I only ever saw glimpses of it. The days when he'd lock himself in his workshop in the garage and not come out until after dark. The days when I'd hug him and he'd try to hug me back but he lacked the strength to lift his arms. He and my mom hid what he was suffering through from me. That week he'd said he was going to a comic book convention? He'd really checked himself into a hospital for treatment."

"I'm so sorry, Freddie."

I wasn't sure if she'd heard me, because she kept talking. "I think they kept it from me because they were scared I was like him." Freddie looked up at me. "And I am. Like him."

"You're not—"

"No," she said, shaking her head. "I am. Even when I didn't have a word for it, I knew I was like him. And the worst part is that since he died, I feel closest to him when I'm depressed. When I'm good and everything's good and I don't have this fucking shadow latched to my back, I feel him slipping away, so I pray for the bad thoughts, and when they come, I don't want them to leave because I don't want him to leave."

I hopped on top of one of the workbenches and let my legs dangle over the side. "Did you want David to shoot you that day?"

"No," she said. "But I was glad he did."

"Freddie . . ."

"I'm not—" She shut her eyes and took a deep breath. "I'm not my father. I take my medication and I tell my therapist when things get really bad." Freddie paused, and I kept quiet. "I go to these group meetings a couple times a month for kids whose parents committed suicide. Some of them are depressed like me, and there's this boy who said once that his greatest fear is that he'll never be happy. Mine is that I will be. I understand how depression works. It won't ever go away, but I'm terrified that one day I'll look around and I'll have everything I ever wanted—someone who loves me, a job where I can make a difference, friends who care—but my father won't be there anymore. I don't want to be happy if it means losing him."

More than anything, I wanted to hold her. To tell her it would be all right. But saying a thing doesn't make it so. Empty words can't return what we've lost. "Being happy doesn't have to mean losing your dad. As long as you remember him, he'll be with you."

Freddie laughed derisively. "You sound like a fucking greeting card."

"Maybe. But it's true."

"I wish he wasn't—" she started to say but stopped. "Forget it. Enough about me. How's your brother?"

"He's okay," I said. "Home now."

"That's good."

"Yeah. I moved all of Sean's belongings out and I'm pretty sure Mama won't let him come home again, so hopefully—"

"You're not the reason David Combs shot me," Freddie said suddenly.

"What?"

"I know you've got this idea in your head that the voices told Combs to shoot me in order to motivate you to do your healing thing, and that you blame yourself, and maybe that's true, but it's also not. You're not the reason."

"How so?"

Freddie's shoulders slumped. "Do you remember the Halloween dance when we were in eighth grade?"

"That was the year with dengue fever from the mosquitoes, right? And we had to hold the dance at four in the afternoon?"

"You were a Valkyrie," she said.

"You remember?" I wasn't just surprised that she recalled what I'd been wearing; I was surprised she'd remembered the dance at all.

"You were beautiful in that costume. You're always beautiful, but there was something otherworldly about you that

night." Her cheeks flushed red and she coughed before con-
tinuing. "Anyway, I'd been dancing with Cam and Shannon—"

"Who's Cam?"

Freddie waved the question aside. "No one. He moved to
California a few months later. He's not important. Anyway,
this squeaky sixth grader in a Spider-Man costume that was
at least two sizes too big asked me to go out with him. I didn't
even know who he was, but I'd had my eye on Jacob Gold—"

"Didn't Jacob—"

"Transition," Freddie said with a nod. "Last year. She's
Nissa now, but that's not the point." She seemed to be waiting
to see if I was going to interrupt again. I didn't. "Spider-Man
was all adorable and I couldn't take him seriously, so I started
to laugh. I didn't mean to, but I couldn't help it. He ran into
the boys' room and I didn't see him for the rest of the dance."

"It was David Combs, wasn't it?"

"Yeah." Freddie bowed her head and fidgeted with her
gloves. I noticed the polish on her fingernails was in as bad
shape as her hair. Chipped and faded. "I was going through
my old yearbooks looking for . . . nothing . . . anyway, and I
found a picture of the dance and Spider-Man was in it and
there was a caption underneath with his name."

I tried to recall a Spider-Man at the dance, but I couldn't.
I'd spent most of my time with Fadil, pretending we were
too cool to dance, hanging out by the snack table. I'd known

Fadil had wanted to show off his best moves, but he'd stayed with me. "That doesn't mean he targeted you for that reason."

"Why not? It makes a lot more sense than him shooting me because voices convinced him to."

I couldn't argue, even though I thought she was wrong. "I have to tell you something," I said.

"I already know you like me," Freddie said. "And I don't know what to tell you. That you're an idiot? That you should ask out Tabia Fumnaya because she's gorgeous and I hear she's got a massive thing for you? That I can't tell you I like you back because I'm not even sure I like myself much these days?"

Freddie's admission reached down my throat and stole my words. My mouth still hung open, but nothing came out.

"That girl, the one you had a crush on, she's not me. She'll never be me. I'm not sure she ever was. And I feel like a completely different person since you healed me. Wrong somehow in a way I can't describe." Freddie paused, but I still couldn't speak. "But I get it, you know? I've had crushes before. I had a crush on a senior last year. Courtney Winters. She was the first girl I ever admitted to myself that I liked."

I'd known Courtney. Or rather, I'd known of her. She wasn't the type of girl I'd expected Freddie would find attractive.

"We had creative writing together, and I spent last year dreaming that every story and poem she read in front of the class was about me. And all the poems and stories I wrote were about her, and it was pretty fucking transparent. I created this fantasy where I asked her out and she said yes and we fell in love and carried on a long-distance relationship until I graduated.

"Then, right before summer, I asked her out."

"She turned you down?" I said, finally finding my voice again.

Freddie shook her head. "She said yes. I'd planned to take her to dinner and a movie, but when I picked her up, she said a friend was having a party that she wanted to go to. She got drunk and told me she'd stolen her creative writing assignments from her older sister, and she tried to finger me on the couch while her friends were right fucking there, and then she puked on the floor. I swore off girls forever after that."

"That's . . . I'm sorry."

"Don't be," Freddie said. "It was my own fault. I'd never seen Courtney before. I didn't really know her. And when I finally got the chance, she wasn't the person I'd thought she was."

"And you think you're not the person I think you are."

"Exactly."

I'd marched into the art room determined to take a chance. But Javi had been wrong. Sort of. Yeah, I definitely overcomplicated life, but sometimes life really was complicated. Freddie couldn't say she liked me because she wasn't sure who she was, her father had killed himself and she was afraid of being happy, and she'd laughed at David Combs and thought that was the reason he'd shot her. It didn't matter what I wanted. I couldn't tell her I liked her and kiss her and act like it was just that simple.

So I said nothing. I did nothing.

Freddie and I sat together quietly for a few minutes, her father's music playing in the background. I thought I should leave, give Freddie some time to think, but I didn't want to.

Then the bell rang, making the decision for me. I picked up my backpack and headed for the door.

"Elena?"

I stopped and turned around.

"I know it might not seem like it, but I am glad you healed me or whatever."

"Even if I brought you back wrong?"

Freddie nodded. "The girl you had a crush on, the girl you thought I was? I don't think you would have had the guts to tell her you liked her."

"I might have."

"Maybe, but she wouldn't have had the nerve to tell you she liked you back." Freddie cranked up the music before I could respond, and returned to working on her sculpture.

# FORTY-SIX

I STOOD IN front of the gym, looking across the football field. There was a crowd of students gathered near the bleachers waiting for me. I wasn't certain they were waiting for me, but I doubted they'd assembled to watch Mrs. Naam berate the marching band for an hour and a half.

They were the people I was meant to help. But I wasn't sure I was helping them at all.

I dug Snippity Snap out of my backpack and held her in front of my face. "Tell me the truth. Am I helping people when I heal them? Are you really taking those you 'save' to a better place? Why did you rapture David Combs?"

The plastic pony didn't answer. I hadn't expected she would. The voices only spoke to me when they thought they could manipulate me.

I'd healed Freddie, but had chained her to a world where she felt wrong and where her father was dead and she might like me but didn't like herself enough to say so. I'd healed Mrs. Haimovitch's hip, but I couldn't do anything about her daughter refusing to speak to her. I couldn't mend Michael Graudin's broken heart or give Tori back her best friend. I'd healed Ben Smith, but maybe the world was going to end and he'd die anyway.

And somewhere out there David Combs was still alive. He'd gotten to live and would never face the consequences of his actions. It wasn't fair. None of it was fair and none of it made sense and I had no idea what to do.

I turned my back on the field and walked toward the front of the school. It was too late to catch the bus, but I figured I could wait for Fadil to finish band practice without having to face the people who wanted me to solve their problems.

"Elena!"

I'd been sitting on a bench in front of where the busses loaded, and I hadn't seen the gray Honda Civic pull up and idle at the curb. Sean Malloy was sitting in the driver's seat, the passenger window down, leaning toward me. "Hey, Elena! Can we talk?"

"I'm sure there's got to be a law against a known child abuser being parked at a school."

"Don't be that way." I heard the anger crouching in his throat, threatening to attack, but he kept it tamed.

"What do you want, Sean?"

"You need a ride home? Let me give you a ride and we can talk."

My inclination was to give him the finger and walk away, but I didn't have anywhere else to go. I was worried that the people waiting on the football field would grow restless and find me. And if they did, I wasn't sure I could refuse to help them even though I wasn't certain I'd actually be helping. They wouldn't understand why I was telling them no. They would hear my rejection of them and believe I thought them unworthy.

Besides, I wasn't afraid of Sean.

I sighed, lugged my backpack to the car, and got in. "Who'd you steal the car from?"

"I borrowed it from a friend." He rolled up the window and pulled around the circle back out to the road. I noticed he'd taken a right instead of a left, which meant he intended to take the long way home.

"So what do you want?" I did my best to keep my voice neutral and flat.

Sean clenched his fists around the steering wheel, turning his knuckles white. The inside of the car, while clean, reeked of cigarettes, though Sean, surprisingly, didn't smell like booze. "You know I didn't mean to hurt Conor. I love him. And Sofie too. I'd never lay a finger on either of them."

"What you meant to do and what you did are two totally separate things."

"I get that. I fucked up."

"You put your son in the hospital, Sean. My brother. You gave him a concussion."

"But he's all right. He's gonna be okay."

"No thanks to you. And have you even thought about the hospital bills? Do you know how expensive it's going to be? As if Mama doesn't already have enough to worry over." I shook my head in disgust. "At least we won't have to pay for your beer anymore."

Sean breathed shallowly. His chest rose and fell in rapid bursts, and I kept expecting him to yell at me or call me a bitch, but he didn't. "I'm going to pay for all that."

"With what job?"

"I'll find a job," he said. "And I'll pay the hospital bills and I'll make it up to Conor and Natalia and Sofie." Sean slammed his palm on the steering wheel. "I'm not a bad person, Elena!"

"You're not a good one, either."

Sean opened his mouth. Closed it. Then he nodded. "You're right. You didn't have a father, and I never wanted to be one."

"Then you should have worn a condom."

"You think I hate you." He kept on like I hadn't spoken. "You think I hate you because you're weird, but it's not that."

"So you hate me for some other reason?"

"You and Natalia came as a package deal, but I didn't want you." He shrugged, like saying he'd taken me when he married Mama because he'd had no choice wasn't a big thing. "I thought when we had Conor and then Sofie that—"

"That she wouldn't love me as much anymore and you could have her all to yourself?"

Sean nodded. "Something like that."

"Wow," I said. "You really are an asshole."

"Don't—" He stopped himself. "She'll never love me like she loves you and the kids."

"It's not a contest, Sean. Mama can love us and love you and there are no losers there." I cocked my head to the side. "Well, you're a loser, but that's your choice. You choose to sit home all the time getting drunk. You choose not to get a job. Those are your choices, and no matter what you think, your choices do have consequences. If Mama doesn't love you anymore, it's on you."

The thing was, I knew she still loved him. I didn't understand why, but she did. I wasn't about to tell him that, though, because he didn't deserve it. Not after what he did to Conor.

Sean's shoulders slumped. "Help me," he said. "Heal me. You did it for Helen."

How could I, though? I could take away his addiction to alcohol the way I'd done for Elias Morales, but he'd still be a self-centered jerk. He'd still believe the world revolved around him and that nothing was his fault. I could heal him, but I couldn't fix him.

"I can't," I said.

"You're lying, Elena. Please. I want to get better; I want to be better."

"Then you're going to have to do it on your own."

Sean slammed the brakes, screeching to a stop in the middle of Military Trail. The car behind us squealed and swerved out of the way, its driver shouting profanities at us as they passed.

"What the hell?"

"Get out," Sean said. When I didn't move, he shouted, "Get out!"

I scrambled out of the car and onto the sidewalk. I hadn't even shut the door when Sean peeled away, leaving me stranded.

# FORTY-SEVEN

THIS TIME, FREDDIE had rescued me. I'd called her after Sean had abandoned me on the side of the road, because Fadil was still practicing with the band and Mama was working the Groom Waggin', and she'd agreed to pick me up without hesitation. We'd ended up at her house because I hadn't wanted to go to mine in case Sean cooled off and made another attempt to convince me to heal him.

Freddie's house was smaller than I'd expected, but it was on the intracoastal with a dock and a boat, which meant it was worth a fortune. The outside was plain and white with a wood shingle roof, but the inside was modern and chrome and sanitized. Even her dog, Biscuits, had pristine curly white fur.

"Sorry for the mess," Freddie said as I followed her inside.

"You think this is a mess?"

"According to my mom it is."

"This place is cleaner than a sterile operating room. I can't imagine what you'd think of my apartment."

Freddie shrugged. "Mom's allergic to clutter. Everything has a place, and God help you if you put something where it doesn't belong."

Where the kitchen at home usually bore sticky handprints and cup rings as evidence of Sofie and Conor's presence, the Petrines' kitchen was immaculate. There were no bills sitting on the counter waiting to be opened and paid, no aced tests stuck to the fridge, no dirty dishes in the sink. If I'd randomly walked into the house without knowing better, I would have guessed it was a show home that no one actually lived in.

"You sure you don't want me to take you home?" Freddie asked.

"Already trying to get rid of me?"

"I thought your brother and sister—"

"They won't be home from school for a while, and if I'm not there they'll go to Mrs. Haimovitch's house."

"Oh."

"You going to show me your room?"

Freddie motioned for me to follow, and we walked toward the back of the house. "Mom didn't used to be such a neat freak," she said. "Before Dad died, she didn't care how the house looked. I think it helps her feel like she's in control, you know?"

"I guess it makes sense."

Freddie's bedroom wasn't quite as tidy as the rest of the house, but it still had that not-lived-in feeling. Her queen-sized bed was perfectly made, every item on her desk in a precise position, her walls bare but for a framed photo of Freddie with her parents in front of the Eiffel Tower.

"It's not much, but it's where I sleep."

"At least you have your own room." When Freddie frowned at me in confusion, I said, "I have to share a room with my brother and sister, so I sleep on the couch most nights."

"That's terrible."

"It is what it is." I didn't know where to sit or stand. I'd left my backpack in Freddie's car, so I didn't even have that to hold. I spotted a creepy plastic clown on the nightstand by Freddie's bed. It was lumpy and squat with an elongated mouth full of teeth, and it was wearing a pink skirt, a halter top, and had yellow pigtails. It looked so out of place in her otherwise boring room. "What in the world is that?"

Freddie followed my line of sight. She walked to the figure and picked it up. "Winston."

"Winston?"

"My dad designed toys," she said. "Figures and stuff. This one's from a comic book. It was the last one he worked on before . . ." She trailed off and set Winston back down. "Mom boxed up the others and hid them in the attic. She keeps trying to take Winston too."

"Oh."

"So what's the deal with your stepdad ditching you on the side of the road?"

I flopped down on Freddie's bed and told her what happened. About the drinking and how he hadn't had a job in years and how Mama worked her butt off to make sure we had a place to live while he contributed nothing but dirty laundry and empty beer cans.

"And then he expected me to heal him and make all his problems go away."

"Why didn't you?" Freddie asked. She'd sat at the head of the bed, hugging her pillow, while I sprawled out across the end, rubbing Biscuits's belly.

"I can't fix everything. I'm not a vending machine you can pop money into and demand a miracle from."

"But you could have helped him."

"Fixing one of his problems wouldn't have fixed the rest."

"Didn't you say you helped someone with an addiction to painkillers, though?"

"Elias Morales," I said. "But it's different with Sean."

"Why?" Freddie asked.

There's something uniquely meditative about rubbing a

dog's belly. It cleared my head and allowed me to think. "Elias wasn't using pills to escape his life. He got hooked because a crappy doctor prescribed them. He wanted me to heal him because he didn't want to take them anymore." I paused. "Sean didn't want to quit drinking. He wanted an easy fix for his problems, and I think if he wants to make things right badly enough, then he needs to do this on his own."

"Not everyone's as strong as you," Freddie said.

I laughed so loudly I woke the dog, who glared at me for it. "You think I'm strong?"

"All the shit you've gone through?" Freddie said. "I would have broken a long time ago."

"You're the one who got shot."

"But you're the one deciding the fate of the world," Freddie countered. "I couldn't handle that. I can barely deal with the problems I've got."

Freddie was stronger than she gave herself credit for. I tried to imagine losing Mama or Fadil or one of the kids, but even thinking about it carved a hole in my heart. "My mother says there's no light at the end of the tunnel. That it's just more tunnel. More dark, sometimes broken up by light, but that we can find others to walk through the darkness with us."

Freddie shifted toward me. "You offering to walk through the dark with me, Miracle Girl?"

"If that's what you want," I said. "And if you don't, I'll be there if you change your mind."

Freddie leaned forward and gently brushed her lips across mine. It was the lightest touch and the brightest light and I could hardly breathe because I was afraid to ruin the moment. Then she leaned back again and watched me.

"Are you asking?" I said.

Freddie bit her bottom lip, but she didn't pull away. "There is one thing."

"What?"

"My dad," she said. "Bring him back?"

"He's dead, Freddie. I can't—"

"You perform miracles. You could give him back to me. Make it so he never died."

I was shaking my head, unable to believe what Freddie was asking. "That's not . . . I heal people; I don't resurrect them. I don't think I could if I wanted to."

It broke my heart to watch her. The tears that streamed down her cheeks. She hadn't been able to ask me to heal her when David had shot her, or known she could, and she might not have wanted me to, but she wanted this. She wanted me to bring back her father.

"Could I?" I asked. But I hadn't directed my question at Freddie.

*I knew you were going to do this.*

I already disliked clowns, and Winston was a nightmare with its fleshy tongue and thick arms and razor teeth. Oddly, its raspy, high voice didn't match its terrifying appearance, which made it less frightening. "Do what?"

*Fuck up saving the world.*

Freddie was watching me argue with an inanimate object, and it was kind of weird, but she didn't interrupt.

"Can I do it or not? Can I bring back Freddie's dad?"

I got the sense that if Winston could have moved it would have been stomping around and clenching its fists. *It's com—*

"I swear to God if you tell me it's complicated, I will never speak to any of you again."

*You can heal the sick and nearly dead. Why can't that be enough?*

*We're trying to help you save your pitiful world, but you want more. You have to know why David Combs shot your pathetic girlfriend and why we told you to save Freddie and where the people we save go. Instead of saving billions from dying, you want to resurrect someone who's already dead!*

"You chose me," I said. "Why give me these powers if I can't help those who really need it?"

*You're not special. You're a cosmic fuckup. A mistake we exploited to save humanity. You think we wanted you to help us? We used you because we didn't have a choice. You're nothing but a tool. What gives you the right to question us?*

"Go to hell."

*No, Elena Mendoza. Hell is what your world will become if you fail to act. Now do your fucking job or you will leave us no choice but to do ours.*

"Elena?" Freddie said.

I bowed my head. I couldn't look her in the eyes because I knew she'd see that I'd failed. I was a failure. She'd asked me for one thing and I couldn't give it to her.

"Freddie. I'm sorry."

"Elena, please."

"I can't."

"Then what fucking good are you?" She ran out of the room, leaving me alone.

"I hate you," I said to Winston.

*The feeling's mutual.*

# FORTY-EIGHT

IT'S DIFFICULT TO see the stars well from where I live because there are too many other lights competing with them. Streetlights and stoplights and the headlights from cars. All that ambient light overwhelms the stars in the sky, but they're still up there, millions and billions of light-years distant, waiting for us to see them. They're a lot like life that way. The constant noise of our own personal problems drowns out what's happening in the rest of the world. We get caught up in our day-to-day struggles and can't see that everyone is fighting their own battles.

But they are.

Whether we see them or not, they are.

"Everything okay, Elena?"

I sat up on the trunk of Mama's car and found Mrs.

Haimovitch walking toward me. She was wearing a flower nightgown and looked like she was ready for bed.

"Hey, Mrs. Haimovitch," I said. "Yeah. Just thinking."

"About anything good?"

I shrugged. "Can I ask you a question?"

"Of course."

I scooted over so Mrs. Haimovitch could climb up and sit on the trunk beside me, something she wouldn't have been able to do a month ago.

"If I could bring Oscar back for you, would you want me to?"

Mrs. Haimovitch narrowed her eyes. "You can do that?"

"I don't think so," I said. "But Freddie's dad committed suicide last year and she asked me to resurrect him but I couldn't and now she hates me."

"There's been a part of me missing since Oscar died," Mrs. Haimovitch said. "When you spend long enough with someone, they grow to occupy a place inside of you, but you don't know it until they're gone and you have this hole where they used to be."

I slapped a mosquito off my arm. "So you'd want me to bring him back, then?"

Mrs. Haimovitch shook her head. "No."

"Really?"

"Oscar was a good man who lived a good life. He loved

me and I loved him, and he loved our daughter. He worked hard his whole life to provide for us. It'd be selfish of me to call him back now. He deserves to rest."

"But Freddie's dad killed himself."

"And that's terrible," Mrs. Haimovitch said. "It's terrible that he felt taking his own life was his only choice, and it's terrible that he left his daughter behind to wonder why. But it was still his choice, and I'm not sure anyone has the right to undo that choice for him."

Every time I blinked, I saw the devastation on Freddie's face when I told her I couldn't help her. It was like she'd been holding on to this tiny scrap of hope and I'd torn it from her and stomped it into the carpet. "Don't you think if he saw how much Freddie was hurting he'd make a different choice?"

"Maybe, but the cruel truth of life is that it only moves in one direction. All our actions are permanent. We might be able to apologize for the mistakes we make and atone for our sins, but we can't take them back." Mrs. Haimovitch sighed. "We can't make choices for others. That's how I lost Katie."

Mrs. Haimovitch had never told me what had happened between her and her daughter. All I knew was that they rarely spoke and that Mrs. H. had never seen her grandchildren in anything other than pictures. "What happened?"

"I didn't approve of the man she married," Mrs. Haimovitch said. "They met when they were in high school and dated for years before getting engaged. He cheated on her multiple times while they were together and caused my Katie so much pain. When she told me he'd proposed, I tried to be happy for her, but I didn't want to see her end up with a man who would hurt her."

"What if he'd changed?" I said.

"The foundation of every relationship—friendship or otherwise—is trust, Elena." I started to tell her I knew that, but she cut me off. "Just listen. Before Oscar and I married, I told him I only had one rule. If he was thinking about straying, he had to tell me and we'd work it out from there."

I frowned. "You'd let him hook up with someone else?"

"Stay with anyone long enough and the urge is going to strike. It's human nature. But if you trust the person you're with enough to tell them, then it's possible your relationship is strong enough to survive it."

"Did Oscar ever cheat?"

Mrs. Haimovitch chuckled. "He told me after we'd been married ten years that there was a woman who'd been flirting with him and that it made him feel good. I told him if he wanted to sleep with her he could, but he had to tell me if and when he did."

My eyes grew wide. "Did he?"

"No," she said. "He told me having my permission had

ruined it for him. The point is, Larry hadn't trusted Katie enough to tell her he was going to stray, so I didn't think it was right for her to commit her life to someone who wasn't mature enough to be honest with her."

"I'm sorry."

"Don't be," Mrs. Haimovitch said. "That's the point. I tried to make Katie's choice for her. Sometimes we have to let go of people if they're dragging us down, like Natalia did with Sean. But I should have trusted Katie to make her own decisions. I didn't, and now I have to live with the consequences."

I couldn't imagine Mama doing anything that would make me cut her out of my life the way she'd done with her own parents and Mrs. Haimovitch's daughter had done with her. "She might still forgive you," I said.

"I hope she will, but I can't force her. I made that mistake once already."

My thoughts drifted back to Freddie. Even if I had the power to resurrect her father, I think Mrs. Haimovitch had a good point. He'd made his choice, and I didn't have the right to undo it. "I wish there was some way for me to help Freddie," I said.

"You already are."

"What?"

"You're being her friend."

I was trying to be her friend, but Freddie deserved more. And then an idea struck me. I slid off the trunk to the ground. "Thanks, Mrs. H."

"Where are you going?"

"To bring back the dead."

# FORTY-NINE

MAMA WAS OFF on Thursday night, so I borrowed the car and drove to Freddie's house. I didn't call first because I was worried she'd tell me not to come and I needed to see her. It was almost eleven when I showed up at her house. I considered knocking on the door, but I didn't imagine her mother would appreciate being woken up by a strange girl.

I tapped Freddie's name on my phone and then waited.

"Elena?" Freddie's voice sounded froggy and thick.

"Come outside."

"What?"

"Come outside," I said. "And bring your phone." I hung up without giving Freddie time to argue, and then I waited.

A few minutes later Freddie opened the front door and walked outside. She was wearing blue pajama bottoms and a white tank top and her hair was adorably messy and sticking up in every direction, but she didn't look as happy to see me as I was to see her.

"Is this payback for me dragging you out the other night?" Freddie asked as she approached. "Because I'm not in the mood."

I was already walking back around to my side of the car and getting in. "Trust me. That's all I'm asking."

Freddie stared at the car door, sighed, and got in.

I drove to Arcadia West High and parked near the football field. We had to hop the fence, which Freddie grumbled about, to get onto the field. I'd brought a blanket with me, and Freddie waited while I spread it across the dewy grass.

"I hope the sprinklers don't turn on," she said. "If I go home smelling like swamp ass, I'm going to kill you."

"They won't." I couldn't be sure, but there was nothing I could do about it so it was pointless to worry.

I sat down on the blanket and patted for Freddie to sit across from me.

"So what's the deal, Elena? This better not be a date; I told you I don't know how I feel and—"

"It's not a date."

"Then what is it?"

"I can't bring back your dad."

Freddie tensed. "Yeah. We've covered that." Her face became stone.

I was scared I'd lose my nerve, so I ended up babbling. "You told me you were afraid of being happy because you thought you'd lose your father completely if you were. I can't bring him back to life, but I can make sure you don't lose him whether you're happy or not."

"Elena—"

"Trust me, okay?"

Freddie chewed on her thumbnail and looked into my eyes. I wondered what she saw. I'd spent countless hours staring at myself in the mirror hoping to see how I was special, but I'd never found anything other than a strange girl who shouldn't have been born but had been anyway and who could perform miracles. Neither of which made me special. Those things simply made me different.

Finally, Freddie nodded.

"Lie back, then," I said. "And turn on your dad's music."

Baby Cthulhu had told me I was an insignificant moron when I'd asked if I could do this. Snippity Snap had scolded me for wasting my time. Even the girl on the tampon box had suggested using my powers for this purpose was prioritizing the feelings of one girl over the fate of the entire world. But none of them had told me I couldn't do it.

Since Lego Gandalf had let it slip that I could make someone disappear when Tori had asked me to bring back Ava, I'd wondered what else I was capable of. I knew from experience that I couldn't become invisible or control volleyballs with my mind, and the voices had confirmed I couldn't resurrect the dead, but when I healed someone, I saw into them. I saw the parts of them that were broken, and I believed it possible to see into other parts of them as well. In a way, what I planned to do wasn't that different from healing. At least, that's what I hoped.

I didn't recognize the song playing, but Freddie had chosen well. It was soothing and melodic. The notes drifted into the night and swirled around us.

"I'm pretty sure this won't hurt," I said. "But keep your eyes on the sky."

"Hurt?" Freddie said, but I was already kneeling behind her. I put my hands on her head and closed my eyes.

When I healed someone, I saw their pain, and each person's took a different form in my mind. Freddie's gunshot wound had looked like a black hole, Mrs. Haimovitch's hip like teeth gnawing on her bones, Elias Morales's painkiller addiction like hungry mouths. I found another hurt in Freddie when I touched her this time. A pulsating mass with tendrils jacked into her heart and brain and spine. Its body was protected by a thick carapace with sharp ridges, and its soft, invasive arms were sickly green. The thing looked like it was feeding off of Freddie, drawing strength and life from her, and I fought the urge to banish it because I wasn't certain I could have and that wasn't why I was there.

Buried deep inside of Freddie I found a box, the flaps closed and taped tightly shut. This was what I'd come for. I might not have been capable of expelling the parasitic hurt that she was battling, but I could give her a weapon she could use to fight it herself. I cut the tape on the box, threw open the flaps, and let Freddie's memories of her father burst free.

Freddie gasped. I couldn't see what she was seeing, but I imagined I could. I projected her memories of her father into the sky. Every song that played was connected to something she remembered about him. Not only the happy memories, but their arguments and their pain, too.

That's what love is. No one is perfect, no one is flawless, and loving someone means admitting they have faults. It means loving them, not in spite of those flaws, but because of them. And that's how Freddie loved her father. She loved his strengths and his weaknesses equally and without reservation.

The songs played on and on. Sometimes I heard Freddie laughing, and other times I think I heard her cry. I kept my eyes closed and held the box open and let the music play until I was too exhausted to do it anymore, but before I stopped, I taped the flaps open so that the box would never be closed to Freddie again.

I opened my eyes and let go of Freddie's head. She sat up and turned to face me.

"What was that?"

"I couldn't bring back your father, but he never really left, either," I said. "And anytime you need him, you can play his songs and look at the sky, and he'll be there."

Freddie's eyebrows dipped to form a V. "How?"

"Call it a minor miracle," I said. "Only you'll be able to see your father, but you can see him whenever you want."

Freddie crashed into me and crushed me to her. "Thank you, Elena."

When she pulled away, I said, "What was he like?"

"You didn't see?"

I shook my head. "They're your memories."

Freddie scooted around so she was sitting cross-legged. "He had a wicked sense of humor," she said. "Once, he had these life-sized cardboard cutouts of himself made and he hid them all around the house. In the pantry, in the car, in the closets. My mom screamed bloody murder when she found the one waiting for her in the shower. But he loved to make us laugh. He did this impression of Kermit the Frog and Miss Piggy that had me rolling every time."

I stayed up all night listening to Freddie talk about her father, and we went home only when the sun began to light up the sky. Maybe the reason I hadn't been able to bring him back to life is because the dead never truly die.

# FIFTY

MAMA WAS SITTING on the couch when I got home, and she did not look pleased. On the drive back to Freddie's house, I'd checked my phone and seen all the missed calls and text messages my mother had sent me, but I hadn't been brave enough to read them.

"Where the hell have you been?" She stood and got in my face. "No, I don't care. Do you know how worried I was about you? I woke up and you weren't here and the car was gone. I almost called the police!"

"I told you I had to go meet a friend."

"Not for the whole night!"

"I'm sorry."

"Sorry?" she said. "Sorry doesn't even begin to cover it, Elena!"

I was still giddy from spending time with Freddie, but exhaustion was clawing at the edges and all I wanted to do was sleep. "Will you let me explain?"

Mama crossed her arms over her chest. "Well?" she said. "Go on. I'm waiting."

"Someone I care about was walking alone in the dark," I said. "And I went to walk with her."

"That's it?"

"It was important."

"No more using the car," Mama said. "I don't care if you can heal everyone in the world, you're still a child, and I will not let you run around all night with my car."

The anger drained from her face and she flopped down on the couch. "You can't do things like this."

I sat beside her. "I know. I'm sorry."

I could barely keep my eyes open, and I knew Mama was still going to make me go to school as further punishment for sneaking out, so I didn't even ask to stay home.

"I worry about you," she said. "A boy tried to kill you."

"He shot Freddie, not me."

"You think that matters?" Mama said. "He could have killed you. This thing you can do scares me. What if someone else tries to hurt you? I can't watch you all the time, so I have to know that you're being smart."

"I am."

"Staying out all night without letting me know you're alive proves otherwise."

I couldn't argue.

"Do you think the world is ending, Mama?"

"Don't change the subject."

"I'm not," I said. "Just listen to me." I explained about the voices and the choice they'd given me. I kept expecting my mother to tell me it was all in my head like she had the one time I'd told her about the voices when I was little, but she didn't.

"Freddie thinks David Combs shot her because she laughed at him when he asked her out in eighth grade. Javi thinks it was because he was bullied and that Combs had a list of students he wanted to kill. I'm worried the voices told him to shoot Freddie so that I'd heal people and cause the raptures. And if that's the case, then I don't know if I can trust them that humanity is really in danger."

Mama brushed a curl off my forehead. I was smart enough to know she was still pissed at me, but she seemed to be taking what I'd told her seriously. "I don't know, mija. The world always feels like it's in danger of ending. Maybe it is. It could end tomorrow or a million years from now. It's impossible to guess, but I wouldn't run away because of something that might happen."

"You wouldn't?"

She shook her head. "If the world ends, I want to be on the front line, fighting for our corner of it until the bitter end."

"That's morbid."

"We don't give up on the things we care about because they get tough."

"I'm not sure everyone else would agree with you."

"That's their choice to make."

"What about David Combs?" I asked. "If I understood why he shot Freddie, at least I might know whether the voices are lying or not."

Mama looked toward Sofie and Conor's room when she heard one of them stirring. It was time for them to get ready for school. "Have you asked his parents?"

"What?"

"Parents always know, Elena," she said. "I've always known you were special, destined for something great, but I didn't want to admit it, because it scared the hell out of me. Other than David himself, his parents might be the only ones who can tell you what you want to know."

Mama made a good point, but I wasn't sure Mr. and Mrs. Combs would be happy to see me.

"Think about it," Mama said. "But if you go, you're not taking my car. I was serious about that."

I shouldn't have, but I laughed. "I won't," I said.

"And no more staying out all night."

"Okay," I said. "I promise."

Mama frowned. "I don't suppose I could get you to promise to stop healing people and trying to save the world."

"Probably not."

"Well, it was worth a try."

# FIFTY-ONE

I DIDN'T HAVE any reason to think something was wrong when I was called out of Mr. Murakami's class and asked to go to the administration office. I should have, though. My life had been too quiet. Deputy Akers had kept her promise to watch the apartment, and I hadn't seen Carmen Ballard since I'd healed Ben Smith on the football field. So I should have expected I hadn't been summoned to administration to discuss my attendance record.

Mrs. Clarke at the front desk directed me to Principal Gonzalez's office. I'd never been in the principal's office before, and I was surprised to find it so warmly decorated with awards and photographs and artifacts gifted to him by past graduated classes. The only thing that seemed out of place were the man and woman sitting at a side table in the corner.

Principal Gonzalez was a broad, beefy man with a neatly trimmed goatee and mustache, dimples, and a bright smile. Principals sometimes get a bad rap, but I'd always thought Gonzalez looked like the kind of man who truly enjoyed helping students.

"Elena," he said, scooting his desk chair back and standing. "I'm sorry to pull you out of class, but these agents have some questions for you regarding Ava Sutter's disappearance." Principal Gonzalez glanced at the agents warily, and I got the impression he wasn't happy they were there.

"I don't know anything about that," I said. "I hardly even spoke to Ava outside of class."

The woman, who wore black pants, a white shirt, and a black jacket, motioned at a chair at the table. "Have a seat, Ms. Mendoza. You're not in any trouble."

I glanced at Principal Gonzalez, hoping he could see the fear in my eyes. "Where are these so-called agents from?" I asked. "Did you check their badges? Shouldn't my mother be here?"

"Their identification is valid," Principal Gonzalez said.

The man, who wore a light gray suit with a gray shirt and a plaid gray tie, smiled in my direction, though he looked like a predator baring his teeth. "I'm Agent Kraus and my partner is Agent Dunn. We're with Homeland Security. We'd just like to talk with you, if that's all right?"

"And if it's not?" I asked.

Agent Dunn said, "Then we can pick you and your mother up at your apartment—110 Lago Vacia, apartment 305—this evening, take you to our office in Miami, and speak there." I heard the implicit threat in her statement. Talk now or they'd cart me and Mama off to some facility we might never leave.

"Again," Kraus said, "you're not in trouble. This is nothing more than an informal chat."

I didn't see that I had much choice. I should have been prepared for this—Deputy Akers had warned me—but I wasn't. Reluctantly, I took the empty seat at the table and folded my arms across my chest.

"Thank you, Mr. Gonzalez," Agent Kraus said, though he kept his eyes on me.

Principal Gonzalez sat down and folded his hands on his desk. "I believe I'll stay."

Dunn and Kraus glanced at each other, but they didn't tell Principal Gonzalez to leave, for which I was immensely grateful. I doubted the agents would try to do anything more than ask questions with him in the room.

"So," I said, "are you going to tell me what this is about? I'm missing calculus."

Agent Kraus brushed his straight black hair off his forehead as he reached into his inner jacket pocket and pulled out his phone, opened it, and read his notes. "Two individuals have gone missing in Arcadia recently. Ava Sutter and David Combs, is that correct?"

"You tell me," I said.

I didn't like Agent Kraus. Truth be told, I didn't like either of them, but there was something about Kraus that made me think he'd have no problem yanking a pillowcase over my head and throwing me in his trunk if I didn't give him the answers he wanted.

Agent Dunn cleared her throat. "You were involved in an alleged shooting at a Starbucks where you were employed. The shooter, according to the statement you gave to Deputy Akers, was a young man named David Combs. You claimed, as did a witness named Fadil Himsi, that after David Combs shot Winifred Petrine, you healed her and David Combs vanished in a beam of light from the sky."

"If it's in the police statement, then that's what happened."

"Would you care to elaborate?" asked Kraus.

"What's to elaborate on?"

Principal Gonzalez leaned forward at his desk. "Agents, I'm not sure what you're looking for here, but I think it might be best for me to call Elena's mother."

Kraus and Dunn ignored him. "We also spoke to a young woman by the name of Justina Smith who claims that you healed her brother, Benjamin Smith, of cystic fibrosis," Kraus said. "Is that true?"

"Yes," I said.

"And that occurred on the same day Ava Sutter disappeared?" Kraus asked.

"I'm not sure," I said. "When did she disappear?"

Kraus looked like he was sucking on a lemon. "We spoke to a friend of yours, Tori Thrash, who claims that you were responsible for the disappearance of Ava Sutter."

I barely held back a laugh. "Tori is most definitely not my friend." Freddie had been right; I should have taken Tori's threat more seriously.

Agent Dunn had a short blond bob that gave her face the appearance of severe angles, and when she smiled, it looked strained. "Are you aware that since September thirteenth there have been nearly ten thousand reports of unexplained disappearances, often connected with mysterious lights from the sky, worldwide? And that many of those cases reportedly occurred on a day when someone claimed you'd performed a miracle."

Principal Gonzalez stood, shoving his chair back into the wall. "That's enough. I'm going to have to ask you to leave."

"I don't know what you want me to say," I said, stuttering. Sweat rolled down my temples and down my back. I imagined I stank of fear. That the agents could smell it and knew they had me.

"You realize it's a crime to impede a federal investigation, don't you, Elena?" Agent Dunn asked.

"I asked you to leave," Principal Gonzalez said. When the agents ignored him, he picked up the phone on his desk. "I'm calling the police."

Agent Kraus held my gaze for a second before looking at Principal Gonzalez. "There's no need for that," he said. "We'll be on our way."

Both agents stood and headed for the door. Dunn stopped, turned to me, and said, "You may not realize it, Elena, but we've kept the disappearances as quiet as we could because we're trying to help you."

"Don't you mean 'use me'?"

"We don't use people," Kraus said. "We help them. We keep them safe. By whatever means necessary."

"We'll talk again," Dunn said.

Principal Gonzalez waited until the agents were gone before setting his phone down and sitting. "I don't know what you've gotten involved in," he said. "I've heard rumors and I watch the news, but miracles? Disappearances? What is going on?"

"Maybe nothing," I said. "Maybe the end of the world. I'll let you know when I figure it out."

# FIFTY-TWO

I LAID LOW for a couple of days after the visit from Agents Dunn and Kraus, and I decided not to tell Fadil, Freddie, or my mother about it. Doing so would have only worried them unnecessarily. A few times I thought I spotted a suspicious car in the parking lot outside my apartment or tailing me and Fadil on our way to school, but it might have been my imagination.

The one good thing about hiding in my apartment was that it gave me time to decide Mama was right and I needed to speak to David Combs's parents. If anyone could tell me why David had shot Freddie it would be them. I considered asking Fadil if he'd take me, but he'd made it clear where he stood on the subject. I didn't blame him—he had faith that it was all part of a greater plan, so the whys of it all didn't matter to him. I figured Freddie might be as invested in the answers as I was, but we'd had this perfect moment on the football field and I was scared to ruin it. The girl I'd come to know over the past month was replacing the image I'd had in my head, but it was still confusing, and I wanted to make certain I had feelings for the real Freddie and not my fantasy of her. Unfortunately, the DHS agents had convinced me I was running out of options and out of time, so I sucked it up and asked her. Thankfully, she'd agreed without argument.

"I think you might be right about the world ending," Freddie said. We'd agreed to go to David's house after school on Wednesday, and I'd met her in the parking lot after last period.

"How so?" I turned down her stereo.

"You didn't hear about the tsunami?" She glanced at me and I shook my head. "Last night. An earthquake in the Pacific caused a tsunami that hit Papua New Guinea, Hawaii, Indonesia. They're estimating the death toll will be in the millions."

"Millions?"

"It's worse than the one in 2004 that killed almost three hundred thousand." Freddie tapped the steering wheel. "Do you think your voices caused it, to try to force you to do what they want?"

Winston had threatened to do something if I didn't start healing more people, but I didn't believe the voices capable of such extreme and direct action. "Maybe it was just an earthquake," I said.

"It's possible, but the president is sending troops to Crimea, and North Korea had a successful nuclear missile test and—"

"I get it. The world is ending."

"Or it's not. But it's fucking weird to be worried about David Combs if it is."

"I get why Fadil doesn't care, but I thought you'd be curious," I said.

"I am, but not for the same reasons as you." Freddie had dyed her hair again and it was back to a deep sapphire blue. In the story I told myself, she'd done it for me, but most stories are lies anyway.

"So you think I shouldn't talk to them? Because you didn't have to come."

"Did I say I didn't want to be here? Christ, you're in a mood today."

"Sorry." I played with my phone. "I'm not sure I can explain it."

"Try?"

I took a deep breath and let it out. "I can explain the science behind how I was conceived. I understand parthenogenesis. I understand the scientific principals that made my birth possible. But I'm the only person ever proven to be born that way, and I can't explain why. Given enough time, I might be able to explain how I'm able to heal people and how the voices 'save' others—I'm certain there are scientific explanations for both—but I doubt I'll ever be able to explain why I can do these things or why the voices are rapturing strangers. If we don't all die first, scientists will likely explain the mechanics that made the famine and the virus outbreaks and the earthquakes and whatever else happens possible. But they'll never be able to explain why they're happening. Hell, I can even explain hormones and pheromones and all the biological processes that make me like you, but I can't explain why."

Freddie raised one eyebrow and frowned skeptically. "Okay . . ."

"Forget it," I said. "I told you I couldn't explain it."

"Keep going. I'm listening."

I wasn't sure I should, though. "I can't explain why any of the things that have happened are happening, but maybe I can explain why David Combs shot you. And even though explaining why won't change anything, if I can find this one reason, I can continue believing the others exist."

Freddie stared straight ahead, driving, likely rethinking her decision to join me on this foolish trip. I rolled down the window and let the warm breeze blow in. The sky was as blue as I'd ever seen it. On a day like that, it felt impossible to believe humanity was in danger and the world might ever end. And maybe the world wouldn't ever end. Maybe, instead, humanity would be wiped away and the world would keep going on with its blue skies and boundless oceans. It's not as if the world needed us to keep spinning.

"I never wanted to know why my dad killed himself," Freddie said after a few minutes. "It was the depression, yeah, but I was scared there were specific reasons and that I was one of them."

"You weren't the reason he killed himself," I said.

"But you don't know that. And neither do I. He could have hated his life and I was the cause and if I didn't exist he'd still be alive."

"It's like you said, though; it was the depression."

"I did say that. But the thing about depression is that it doesn't create bad thoughts, it amplifies and distorts them. Depression doesn't make me look in the mirror and see a girl who's overweight and has too-wide hips and pudgy cheeks. Those thoughts are already there. Depression just cranks up the volume on them so loud that I can't hear anything else." She glanced at me. "So if I was one of the reasons my dad took his life, depression wouldn't have made him feel that way, but it would have made him feel more that way."

"I get what you're saying, but wouldn't you still want to know?"

Freddie shook her head. "Won't change that he's gone."

I didn't say anything to that because there was nothing to say. Freddie had lost her father, and she was right that knowing why he'd killed himself wouldn't bring him back. But that didn't change my mind about needing to understand why David Combs had tried to kill Freddie.

"I can tell you why I like you," Freddie said.

"What? I—"

"You're fearless, despite what I said."

"Hardly."

"And you think about everything. Everything. You're never content to accept what anyone tells you."

I laughed. "Except weren't you just trying to convince me to stop questioning?"

"So what?" she said. "Doesn't mean I don't like that you do it."

"All right. Keep going."

Freddie snorted. "Maybe I should roll down my window so your swollen head doesn't block my view of the road." She winked at me. "You ask 'why?' instead of 'why me?' when faced with a problem. You're kind of bratty—"

"I am not!"

"And you're beautiful, Elena."

I don't think anyone had ever called me beautiful other than my mother. Javi had said I was hot, and I'd been called cute before, but never beautiful.

"Also," Freddie added, "you saved my life."

I frowned and shook my head. "All I did was heal you."

"Yeah," she said. "But that's not what I was talking about."

# FIFTY-THREE

FREDDIE AND I had parked down the street to avoid looking suspicious. The Combs's house was a two-story colonial with a neatly manicured front lawn, a mailbox built to look like the house, and nothing to signal that it was where an attempted murderer had grown up.

We'd been sitting in the car for ten minutes while I worked up the courage to walk to the front door and confront David's parents, but if I didn't do it soon I was going to chicken out.

"Are you sure you don't want to come in with me?" I asked.

Freddie turned to look at the house and stared for a moment before saying, "I think you need to do this on your own."

"Okay." I took a deep breath, got out of the car, walked to the house, and knocked on the door. I'd spent the last two days rehearsing what I was going to say, but the moment the door opened, all my words vanished.

"Yes?" The woman who opened the door appeared near my mother's age, but she was dressed in jeans and a nice white blouse and stared down her nose at me like I was covered in pus-oozing boils.

"Mrs. Combs?"

The woman shook her head. "I'm sorry, I think you have—"

"My name is Elena Mendoza. I was acquainted with David Combs. I know this is his house, and I'm hoping to speak to his parents for a moment."

The woman stood holding the door half-closed, the slits of her eyes narrow, her lips tight. I thought she was going to slam the door in my face, but she said, "Stay here," and then shut the door.

I looked over my shoulder at where Freddie was sitting in the car. I got the impression that the person who'd answered the door wasn't David's mother, and I didn't know what I would do if his parents refused to speak to me. Drive home, I supposed. I couldn't force them to talk.

A minute later, the door reopened and the woman said, "Come in." The house was a battlefield of toys and books and LEGOs. "You'll have to excuse the mess," she said. "I'm Dan's sister. We've been staying with them since . . ."

"I have a younger brother and sister," I said. "They never put their toys away either." Of course the difference was that Mama couldn't afford all the toys this family obviously could. She led me to the dining room and motioned that I should sit, and then offered me water, which I accepted.

"Dan and Sue will be down shortly."

The woman, whose name I still didn't know and was too embarrassed to ask, left me alone. But it was only for a moment. David Combs's parents entered the dining room from the kitchen. Mr. Combs—Dan—wore a T-shirt with a hole in the neck and hadn't shaved in days, and Sue zombie-shambled to the table, but light and life flooded into her previously dead eyes the moment she saw me.

"You're Elena Mendoza?" She pushed her glasses higher on her nose.

Not "What the hell are you doing here?" or "What did you do to my son?" or even "Get the hell out of this house!" Mrs. Combs's question surprised me.

"I am," I said, unsure of myself.

Sue sat at the table, and Dan reluctantly sat across from her. A smile touched her lips, but it looked painful. Like she hadn't smiled in so long that the muscles had atrophied.

"Davie told us so much about you," Mrs. Combs said.

"He did?"

She nodded. "He was always going on about Elena this

and Elena that. I'm so sorry we didn't meet before . . ." Words failed her. Her smile fled and tears welled in the corners of her eyes.

I sat there confused. I'd hoped Mr. and Mrs. Combs would recognize my name—I was counting on it, in fact—but as the Miracle Girl. I hadn't expected to learn David had told them things about me when I hadn't even known his name until the day he'd shot Freddie.

"Do you know where our son is?" Mr. Combs asked. His voice was sandpaper and his nose was a lattice of burst red capillaries.

"Is he safe?" There was a hint of hope in Mrs. Combs's face, where I'd expected accusation.

"I have no idea where he is." Which was the truth. He'd been raptured, but I was still clueless as to where the voices had taken him.

"I don't understand why he ran away," Mrs. Combs said. "He seemed so happy. He was in the marching band and he had a beautiful girlfriend—"

"Girlfriend?"

Mrs. Combs reached out and touched my hand. "Or whatever you kids call it now. Hooking up? Is that the right phrase?"

David had told his parents that I was his girlfriend? That had to have been how the rumors had started that I'd helped him run away. But why had he lied?

"I told that sheriff's deputy who questioned us that you weren't involved," Mrs. Combs said.

I'd come to speak to David's parents expecting they'd have the answers that I lacked, but instead of answers, they'd given me more questions. Every question I'd meant to ask, every answer I'd hoped to find, evaporated.

"I wasn't involved," I said. "David shot my friend Freddie. She would have died if I hadn't healed her."

"Allegedly shot," Mr. Combs said.

"I had her blood on my hands and—"

"Why are you here, Elena?" Mr. Combs clenched his fists.

"I was hoping you knew, that you could tell me why."

Dan and Sue looked at each other across the table. Unspoken words passed between them, and then Mr. Combs pushed his chair back and stormed out of the dining room.

"You'll have to excuse Dan," she said.

"It's fine," I said. "I understand."

Mrs. Combs's smile turned acerbic. "At least someone does." Without her husband there, Mrs. Combs relaxed a little. "We simply don't know what to believe. You say Davie shot your friend, but the police said the young woman had no gunshot wound. We only want to find him and understand what's going on."

"Your son tried to kill someone."

"Davie isn't capable of hurting anyone."

This was one situation I had come prepared for. I knew it was possible that David's parents would be as skeptical as everyone else that I'd healed Freddie, and I had only one way to prove that I had. "May I?" I asked, motioning at her hand.

She nodded, likely not fully aware of what I was asking. I took her hand and closed my eyes. I hated using my abilities knowing hundreds or thousands of strangers around the world were going to vanish as a result, but Mrs. Combs deserved to know the truth about her son. The energy of her body was strong, though the languid pulse of it showed me how exhausted she truly was. She had multiple problems, none serious, and I focused on the one that would have the most irrefutable impact. A pair of what appeared to be ghostly fingers were pinching her eyes and, with a thought, I swept them away and healed her.

Mrs. Combs let out an "Oh!" She slowly pulled off her glasses, set them on the table, and looked around the dining room as if seeing it for the first time.

"Did you—?"

"I did."

As the weight of the implications of what I'd done settled around her shoulders, the wonder in her eyes and on her face fled, replaced by a tightness around her mouth that turned into a frown. "You were telling the truth."

"Yes."

"About everything?"

"Yes."

Mrs. Combs began to cry. She buried her face in her hands and shook as she realized her son hadn't run away. That he'd tried to kill someone and had vanished, possibly forever. I went into the kitchen and got her a napkin, which she used to dab her eyes and blow her nose.

"Dan blames himself for David running away," she said when she'd recovered. "We were going to send him to a private school, but Davie begged us not to. We thought things were getting better when he met you and his friends from marching band. He still had problems, but I thought having a girlfriend and friends would help him."

"I'm sure this is a lot to take in all at once," I said, "but I was really hoping you could tell me why he shot my friend."

Mrs. Combs's shoulders slumped—I'd given her too much information too quickly. "I didn't want to believe it," she said. "I told myself he ran away. That he couldn't have tried to hurt anyone. Even when the police told us they found Dan's gun, I refused to believe. Davie was sweet and kind and . . . but, of course, you knew that."

"Did he ever mention hearing voices? Maybe from an action figure or a doll?"

"No," she said. "Why would you ask that?"

"What about the name Winifred Petrine?" I said. "Freddie?

Did he ever talk about her? Do you think it was my fault?"

Mrs. Combs shook her head violently. "No. You can't blame yourself, Elena. Davie loved you. You made him happy."

Except I hadn't. Not really. Maybe the idea of me had made him happy the way the idea of Freddie had made me happy before I'd gotten to know her, but it wasn't really me. Right before I'd healed Freddie, David had said that he thought his mother would have liked me, but I didn't think she would if I told her that the things she knew about her son were a lie.

"Why do you think he did it?" I asked.

"I don't know, Elena." Her voice caught in her throat and tears welled in her eyes again. "I don't know and I wish I did and if I could tell you I would, but I just don't know!" She slammed her fist on the table and her whole body shook.

Mr. Combs walked into the room and rested his hands on his wife's shoulders. "I think you should leave now," he said. "I'm sorry you came all this way, but you need to leave."

There were no answers here. David's parents had thought their son was happy. They'd thought he had friends and a girlfriend and a life, but they hadn't known their son at all.

I stood and turned to walk toward the door. I stopped under the archway leading to the living room. "I don't know where David is," I said. "But I think, wherever he is, he's okay."

# FIFTY-FOUR

FREDDIE DIDN'T ASK me what had happened when I returned to the car. I didn't volunteer the information either. I'd learned a little more about David, but nothing to explain why he'd tried to shoot her. David had lied to his parents, convinced them he was happy. He might have even managed to convince himself of it for a while. But in the end, he'd made a choice. Maybe he'd done it because Freddie had rejected him. Or because he'd liked me and knew I'd had a crush on Freddie and thought killing her would make me see him. Maybe Javi had been right and the voices "saving" him had stopped him from trying to kill as many of us as he could. Or maybe the voices had told him to kill Freddie as motivation to get me to use my ability to heal.

There was no way to know short of asking David himself, and he was gone. But regardless of his reason, he'd made a choice, and now it was time for me to make my own.

"I like you because you never back down," I said as Freddie pulled up in front of my apartment. It was the first I'd spoken since we'd left David's parents. "I like you because you never give up. I didn't know about your father or what you've been through, and I wouldn't have known if you hadn't told me, because you defy the world, dare it to fight, and refuse to back down no matter what it throws at you."

Freddie bobbed her head a little as I spoke. "I don't think I'm as strong as you think I am."

"And I think you're stronger than you believe."

"Thanks," she said.

I reached across the emergency brake and held her hand. She didn't pull away. Instead, she simply smiled.

"So what now?" she asked.

A gray Honda Civic screeched to a stop behind us, the tires squealing, and Sean jumped out of the driver's seat and ran around to my side of the car. He banged on the window, so I rolled it down.

"Elena," he said. "It's Natalia. She's hurt and you need to come with me." Sweat had matted his hair to his forehead and his eyes were wide and wild.

"What's wrong with her?"

Sean opened my car door, grabbed my arm, and started pulling me out. "We have to go!"

"What's going on?" Freddie asked. "I'll go with you."

"She's at the hospital, Elena," Sean said. "It's serious!"

"What happened to her?"

Sean kept pulling me toward his car. "We need to hurry!"

"Elena?" Freddie said.

"I'll text you," I called to her. I got in Sean's car and barely had time to shut my door before he slammed on the gas and took off.

# FIFTY-FIVE

"WHAT HAPPENED TO Mama?" I asked as Sean tore out of Lago Vacia.

Sean's skin was moist and pale, and his hands trembled on the steering wheel. "Do you have your phone?"

"Yes, but—"

"I need to call Helen and ask her to watch the kids," he said. "Mine's dead."

"I'll call her, then." I pulled my phone out of my pocket and started to dial, but before I could finish, Sean plucked it from my hand, rolled down his window, and threw it into the road.

"What the hell are you doing?" I yelled.

Sean kept his eyes focused straight ahead. He rolled up his window and locked the doors. A wave of nausea crashed over me, tumbling me and threatening to drown me. I pulled on the handle and tried to unlock my door, but it didn't work.

"Child safety locks," Sean said.

"What did you do to my mother?" I demanded.

"Natalia's fine. She's working the Groom Waggin', I think." He looked at me with contempt, a seething, burning disgust that had, after years, finally boiled over. "Now sit there and shut the fuck up. And don't try anything or this is going to get a lot worse for you."

I was afraid to ask "worse than what?" Unless I could open a door or a window, I was trapped in the car with Sean. I briefly considered punching him and trying to escape, but that would have caused an accident and I didn't know whether my miracle abilities included the power to heal myself.

"I'll heal you," I said.

"Too late," he said. "You told me I was going to have to fix shit on my own, so that's what I'm doing."

Sean drove to I-95 and headed south. The entire drive, I tried to come up with a plan, but I was trapped in the car with nowhere to go, so the best I could do was see where he was taking me, remain vigilant, and hope an opportunity presented itself. After half an hour we drove over the Flagler Bridge onto Palm Beach Island and navigated the side streets until we pulled into the driveway of a sprawling house and parked in a circle, at the center of which stood a fountain crawling with cupid statues. Ornamental columns stood guard along the front of the house, and thick confederate jasmine climbed the walls, covering all but the stained-glass rose windows.

"What are we doing here?" I asked, trying to keep my voice neutral to avoid pissing off Sean.

"You'll find out." He got out of the car, hurried around to my side, opened my door, and yanked me out. I immediately began screaming for help, but he squeezed my wrist so hard it felt like he was going to break it. "Shut your mouth. No one's going to hurt you."

*Run, Elena!* the cupids sang. *You have to get out of here!*

I kicked Sean in the shin and tore my hand free of his grip, but before I could run, he tackled me to the pavement. I threw out my hands as I fell, and they burned as the ground shredded my palms. Sean pulled me up by the back of my shirt and shoved me toward the door.

"You always gotta make things hard, don't you?"

I'd also hit my knee when I'd fallen, so I was limping, and my hands stung like mad and were bleeding, though not badly. "And you always try to take the easy way out."

"Nothing's easy when it comes to you."

The front door opened, and Carmen Ballard stepped out, looking elegant and powerful in a fitted sleeveless dress that was green from the waist down and had light and navy blue geometric patterns on top. Her wavy blond hair shone like sunlight, and she wore a welcoming smile. She held an envelope and her cell phone in one hand, and offered me the other.

"Elena," she said. "It's so nice to see you again."

I scoffed at her gesture. "You had me kidnapped?"

"When you wouldn't agree to meet with my client, I enlisted Mr. Malloy's assistance to persuade you to come."

I barked out a laugh. "So you preyed upon him because he was desperate," I said. "How much are you paying him?"

Carmen stepped aside, and Sean shoved me into the house. The furniture was covered in white sheets, and dust hung in the air, flittering motes that looked like minuscule fairies.

"Up the stairs," Carmen said, motioning toward the grand staircase. I would have been awed by the house if I hadn't been forced there against my will. As it was, the only thing on my mind was figuring out how to escape. My best chance was to run to a neighboring home and hope someone answered the door.

I trudged up the stairs, pushed by Sean and followed by Carmen Ballard.

"You're a very special girl, Elena, and I wish that we were doing this under friendlier circumstances, but my client simply lacks the time to wait."

"I won't heal them," I said. "Just because you got me here doesn't mean I'll do what you want."

Sean snorted. "I told you she was stubborn."

"I'm hoping you'll change your mind," Carmen said. "But if you don't, I believe we can incentivize you another way."

"That sounds like a threat," I said.

"Not against you, of course. We would never hurt you."

I tried not to think of who Carmen Ballard would hurt to make me do what she wanted. Freddie was safe, but I had no idea where my mother or Fadil or Conor and Sofie were. Sean might not have given a crap about me, but I refused to believe he would put Mama or his own kids in danger.

We reached the top of the stairs, and Carmen led us down a hallway to a pair of heavy oak double doors. Without preamble, she pushed them open and walked inside. The room was enormous, decorated like something out of Versailles. Gilded, framed art hung from the walls, and a four-poster bed stood in the middle of the room, surrounded by medical machines hooked into an old man lying in the bed under a heavy comforter, buttressed by an army of pillows. The man himself was bald and frail, with liver spots on his hands and head. His chest rose and fell slowly in time with the beeping of the machines, helped by the breathing mask over his mouth and nose.

Carmen handed Sean the envelope, which I assumed contained cash, and said, "Thank you for your help, Mr. Malloy."

Sean took the envelope and shoved it into the back pocket of his jeans. He glanced at me, and I think he almost looked ashamed. "Don't be stupid, Elena. Just do what they want and go home."

"If you think Mama's ever going to take you back now, you're dumber than I thought."

With nothing more than a scowl, Sean stomped from the room, leaving me with Carmen and the old man in the bed.

"Elena," Carmen said, "I'd like to introduce you to Harrison Bartlett."

"Yeah, hi. Whatever. I'm leaving now."

Carmen stood in front of the exit, and though I thought if I rushed her I might be capable of overpowering her, I wasn't sure. "Hear me out, please."

*Do not listen to them, Elena! Get out of there!*

I scanned the room until I found a stately brass horse clock on an ornate table in the corner. I couldn't answer the horse or Carmen and Harrison Bartlett would ask questions, and I didn't want them to learn about the voices.

*You're in danger! You have to run!*

"Mr. Bartlett is suffering from multiple organ failure and his remaining life is measurable in weeks if not days. He has used his extensive resources to try every means available to extend his life, but none have succeeded. We heard of your story, and I witnessed your miracle work when you healed Benjamin Smith of cystic fibrosis. Mr. Bartlett has asked me to offer you whatever you wish in exchange for your help."

"You want me to heal him," I said.

"Yes."

"Why would I do that?"

"Money?" Carmen said. "Protection? We know about the agents who visited you at school. They're not from Homeland Security."

*Do not help them, Elena!* the horse shouted.

"How do you know I won't heal this old guy and then go straight to the police and tell them you had me kidnapped?"

Carmen offered an unconcerned shrug. "Mr. Bartlett is a valued member of the community, with ties to very important people. It would be your word against his."

The sad truth was that she was probably right. History has proven that in a showdown between a wealthy man and a teenage girl, the girl will usually lose. But I wasn't about to be coerced into healing this guy.

I crossed the room to the bed and stood over Harrison Bartlett. "Why you?" I asked.

Mr. Bartlett withdrew his right hand from under the blankets, moving glacially, and removed the mask. "Because I can." Even those three words, spoken in a dry, raspy voice, seemed to exhaust him. But he had enough life in him to follow it with a smile before returning the mask to its place.

"You're nothing but another rich dick who thinks he can take what he wants."

"In exchange for more money than you would otherwise ever see in your life, Elena," Carmen said. "Enough to buy a house, enough to buy ten houses. Your brother and sister could attend the best schools and your mother would never have to work again."

*She's lying, Elena! They'll never let you leave, and the world will end. Everything we've worked for will be for nothing!*

I believed the horse.

I wasn't foolish enough to think that my life mattered to the voices, but they still needed me and would do anything to protect me so long as I was useful.

"What if I don't want your money?" I asked.

"I thought you might say that." Carmen tapped the screen of her phone and waited. When it lit up, she said, "Are you with them?" A man's voice on the other end acknowledged he was. "Show me." A moment later, Carmen turned the phone's screen to me. Sofie and Conor were running around on the playground at home while Mrs. Haimovitch watched from the bench.

"Mrs. Haimovitch!" I shouted.

Carmen took her phone back. "As you can see, I have a man waiting for instructions. You may leave here without healing Mr. Bartlett if you so choose, but if he dies, so will your brother and sister, Helen Haimovitch, your mother, Fadil Himsi, and Winifred Petrine."

"You can't—"

"Yes, Elena," she said. "We can." There was no malice in her voice. To her, this was nothing more than a business transaction, and she didn't care what happened either way.

*If you heal this man, they will never allow you to leave,* the horse said. *You can't do this.*

"I don't have any choice," I said.

"No, you don't." Carmen hadn't known I wasn't speaking to her. But she was still right.

I turned back to the old man in the bed. He was staring at me hungrily. There'd never been any doubt in his mind that he was going to get what he wanted. Men like him always got what they wanted. I lay my hands on his arm. His skin was rough and thin and repellant to me.

*You can make them disappear.*

"What?"

"Hurry, please, Elena," Carmen said. "The lives of your loved ones depend on you now."

*You can make them both vanish. Close your eyes and we'll show you how.*

Lego Gandalf had hinted that I could rapture people directly, and now the horse had confirmed it. I didn't believe that Carmen Ballard and Harrison Bartlett would allow me to leave the house after I'd healed him. Even if it was my word against his, going to the police would still call more attention to them than they would want. My only chance to save my family and win my freedom was to get rid of Carmen and Harrison myself.

*Quickly!*

I closed my eyes. Bartlett's energy was practically nonexistent, but I wasn't concerned about him.

*Look beyond for the crack in the dark.*

I had no idea what the horse was telling me, but I did as he said and turned my senses outward, past Bartlett. Deep in the darkness, I found a sliver of light leaking out through a crack in the void, just like the horse had said. I reached out and ripped it open. Fire surged through the tear and I aimed it at Bartlett and Carmen Ballard. I found the man watching Sofie and Conor and sent another tendril toward him. The fire tangled around them and sucked them back through the hole in the empty space beyond. I didn't see them leave with my eyes, but I knew the moment they were gone, and I pulled the ends of the tear together, cutting off the light.

When I opened my eyes, exhausted by what I'd done, Carmen's phone lay on the floor, Bartlett's bed was empty, and I knew Sofie and Conor were safe.

# FIFTY-SIX

THE MYSTERY OF life is that there is no great mystery. You were born. You will die. This is an incontrovertible fact. Every human who has ever walked this planet gestated in a mother's womb and was spit out onto the earth. Every human who has yet to be born, even those who might exist in a future paradise where they may never know cancer or hunger or pain, will eventually die.

I'm no cynic, though. I'm not suggesting there are no mysteries or miracles in our world. There are mysteries. There are miracles. I might be one of them or I might be a girl-shaped cosmic oops. It's just that the mystery isn't life itself. The miracle isn't that we're alive. Instead, it's the choices we make and the people we meet and the lives we intersect in the finite seconds between our births and our deaths. It's that we can live in this ugly, cruel world and still find the love to sustain us. Sometimes we don't. Sometimes we lose our way and can't separate the mystery from the misery, and when that happens, sometimes we make bad choices. Horrible choices that ripple through the lives of everyone involved.

And yet, despite being faced with so much hardship and pain, we continue to live. We continue to struggle and fight for our place in the world. We continue to try even when we know we're going to lose. That's the real miracle; not me.

# FIFTY-SEVEN

HUMAN BEINGS ARE stupid. Sure, we've traveled into space, we've built machines that have allowed us to peek into the building blocks of all creation, we learned to replace human organs and how to connect the entire world over wires and screens. We've written beautiful literature and we've created more silly cat videos than, I imagine, any civilization in the universe. We will our most fantastical dreams into reality and believe resolutely that there is nothing we can't accomplish. And yet, despite our ingenuity and genius, we're a fundamentally stupid species.

Human beings actively work against our own self-interest. We know that we're destroying the planet, yet we fill electronics graveyards with cell phones because we need to have the latest model. We toxify our lakes and rivers because we're too lazy to properly dispose of chemical waste. We drive vehicles that spew carbon dioxide into the air because we have to have a bigger and better car than our neighbors. We take drugs that wreck our minds and bodies, we eat mountains of fast food despite knowing it will eventually kill us, we complain about the politicians ruining our country and we devote countless hours to wearing pins and posting protest memes and bitching about it to strangers on the Internet but willfully refuse to sacrifice one hour of our lives to vote.

People make stupid choices. We make dumb, harmful, self-destructive decisions because we can. Because we have free will. It doesn't matter whether you believe free will comes from the divine—God or Allah or Elohim or Krishna—is a result of possessing a soul, or is merely a side effect of humanity's singular biological and neurological processes. Our free will and ability to choose is ultimately what makes us the dumbest intelligent species on the planet.

I didn't know David Combs. I didn't know of him. He may as well have not existed for me on the day I went to work at Starbucks and inadvertently jump-started the apocalypse. I didn't know his name or that he'd been a victim of bullying or had been rejected by Freddie. I didn't know he'd created a fantasy life where I was his girlfriend and he had everything he'd ever wanted.

But the truth is that no matter what series of events led

David Combs to shoot Freddie, he'd made a choice. I regret any part I might have played in causing David to feel that he had no other options, but the ultimate decision—and the blame—belonged to him alone. Nothing could justify his actions, nothing could explain away what he did. He made a choice. And it was the wrong one.

Freddie's father made a choice that devastated Freddie and caused her to believe the only way to cope with life was to stop making choices altogether.

I made a choice when I chose to heal her.

Fadil made a choice to stand by me.

Sean made a choice to ignore his problems, and then he made a choice to attempt to rectify his mistakes by choosing to make a bigger one.

The voices chose me to save humanity, a choice I'm determined to make them regret.

We make choices. We make bad choices. But we still deserve the right to choose.

Carmen Ballard and Harrison Bartlett attempted to take my ability to choose from me. I'm betting they wished they hadn't done that. And while the voices may have chosen me, they also tried to use me to take away the rights of others to choose. David Combs and Ava Sutter and the 17,701 souls who were raptured without their consent. It doesn't matter whether the voices were actually saving them from a terrible fate or that I didn't know about the connection between my miracles and the disappearances until many had already been taken. My ignorance doesn't absolve me of complicity. I am responsible for every life disrupted and shattered. I stole their right to choose the way others tried to steal mine.

I'd spent weeks feeling boxed in and helpless. I thought if I could understand why David Combs shot Freddie, I could make a decision. If he'd done it because he was bullied or in love or mentally ill, then I could trust that the voices were telling the truth. But Fadil was right; it doesn't matter. No reason could justify my withholding the right to choose from everyone else. True, if I did nothing, humanity would perish. That's what the voices promised. And if I continued to heal the sick, I would be involuntarily rapturing countless people, to where I didn't know, and stranding those of us left behind to an unknown but potentially fatal end.

Both options sucked, but after I called Deputy Akers from Carmen's phone and waited for her to arrive at Bartlett's mansion, I remembered what Freddie had said. The game was rigged, but just because I had to play didn't mean I had to play by the rules dictated by the voices.

The siren and the girl on the tampon box and Snippity Snap and Baby Cthulhu and Lego Gandalf had given me two equally terrible choices, but the choice belonged to me, and I chose neither.

# FIFTY-EIGHT

*THINK ABOUT WHAT you're doing, Elena,* the sketchy girl on the tampon box said.

*You shall fail.* That was Lego Gandalf.

"Then I fail," I said. "And humanity dies. But this is my choice to make, not yours."

It had been only a day since Sean had kidnapped me and I'd raptured Carmen Ballard and Harrison Bartlett. When Deputy Akers had arrived at the mansion, we'd spent a while discussing our options. She'd been eerily calm about the whole thing and had advised me not to report it. If I did, I'd have to explain to other police officers where my kidnappers had vanished to, and it was doubtful they'd believe I'd raptured them. But since no one was going to find the owner of the house or his attorney, and they weren't a danger to me anymore, we agreed the best course of action was to simply leave. Then Deputy Akers had driven me home. When I asked her why she was helping me, knowing she could get in trouble, she told me that miracle workers need miracles of their own sometimes, even if they didn't want to admit it.

I told Mama what had happened, and when she'd finished hugging me and crying, I'd had to beg her not to call the police or try to find Sean on her own. If he came back, I'd told her, I knew how to deal with him.

By the next morning, I'd made my choice and I knew what I needed to do. So I'd gathered the voice's proxies together, lined them up on my bed, and told them my plan. Lego Gandalf, Snippity Snap, Baby Cthulhu, the tampon box, the siren peering at me from a coffee mug I'd bought Mama, and even Winston, which Freddie had brought over and given to me.

*Your god commands you not to do this!*

"You're not my god," I said. "You're not even *a* god. For all I know you're some basement-dweller sitting on a fancy future computer in a parallel universe messing with my life because you get off on it."

*How dare you—*

*You've experienced a trauma,* the girl on the tampon box said. *Take some time to consider the choice you're making.*

"Oh, I have," I said. "So will it work or not?"

*Theoretically,* the siren said, *but the risk is too great. Even one mistake and you could burn the entire planet or collapse it into a singularity.*

*Do you think you're smarter than a god?* Baby Cthulhu said. *If what you propose were possible, we would have done it!*

*Enough,* said Snippity Snap. *We can't force her not to do this, and if she fails, the end of the world and the billions of lives lost are on her.*

Winston spoke for the first time. *This will kill you. You will die. Your skin will melt and your brain will explode. And you will visit the same gruesome end on all of humanity.*

"I understand the risk."

*What gives you the right?* Lego Gandalf asked. *If you do things our way, it at least offers some on your planet the opportunity to live. But if you fail, you all die.*

"What gives me the right to decide for everyone you rapture?" I said. "This isn't a debate. I'm not asking your permission. We all deserve the right to choose, and this is the choice I've made."

*Please reconsider,* the siren said. *I didn't save your life to watch you die this way.*

*You have the audacity to defy your gods?* Baby Cthulhu added.

"Yes," I said. "I really do."

I picked up a box that was sitting on my dresser and

swept the figures into it. Freddie, Fadil, and my mother were waiting for me in the living room. I nodded at them as I headed for the door, and they followed me to the playground.

*What are you doing, Elena?*

*This isn't the way!*

*You wouldn't dare.*

*Please, Elena. Don't.*

I dumped them all into a metal trash can and doused them with lighter fluid. Fadil handed me a box of matches.

"You sure it's okay?" I asked Freddie, glancing at the comic book clown. "Your dad made it."

"It's good," she said. "You gave me a better way to remember him."

I drew a match from the box, dragged it across the strike strip, and dangled the tiny flame over the can. The voices had been a part of my life for as long as I could remember, but I wasn't Joan of Arc. They weren't God or gods or any type of divine beings. They were like me—fallible, human, I hoped—trying to make their own choices with the information they had. And though they had more knowledge than I did, they still didn't, couldn't, know everything.

"Hold up." Mama stepped forward, pulled off her wedding ring, and tossed it in the can. "Okay. Now go."

I smiled. The match was burning down toward my fingers. If I held on to it a little longer, it would simply die out.

But this was a choice too, and one I should have made a long time ago. I dropped the match and watched the voices burn as they continued screaming at me to stop.

"What was that?" I asked, cupping my hand to my ear. "I'm sorry; I can't hear you anymore."

# FIFTY-NINE

MEET ME IN the art room. That was the message I received from Freddie during last period on what might have been the day the world ended.

I had a simple plan, but that didn't mean I wasn't terrified, and I was grateful to procrastinate a little longer, especially since that meant a few more minutes with Freddie.

I wasn't sure what to expect, but Freddie's sculpture was the first thing I saw when I walked into the art room. A girl with wings of wires and copper tubing spread wide stood on a pedestal. Her head was tilted toward the sky and her arms both pointed groundward. She was painted gold and silver and blue, and struck a pose both beautiful and strong, like she was prepared to hold back an army equipped with only her resolute smile.

"It's a Valkyrie," I said.

"It's you." Freddie stood back, admiring her creation.

I shook my head. "You didn't even know me when you started it."

"That's why I call it Mary," she said with an impish grin. "Besides, my job is simply to peel back the layers and discover the truth hiding underneath."

I crossed the room and stood beside Freddie. She slipped her hand in mine. "We can run away."

"Maybe when all this is done."

"Do you think it will work?"

"The voices said it might, but that it's dangerous." I nudged her with my elbow. "Either way, you should kiss me now in case I fail and die and we don't get another opportunity."

Freddie let go of my hand, wrapped her arm around my waist, and pulled me to her. "Nah. I'd rather save it for after."

The idea of Freddie wanting to kiss me should have dominated my every thought, but I couldn't stop staring at her sculpture. At the Valkyrie. In myths, a Valkyrie decided who would live and who would die. They traveled the battlefields and escorted their chosen to Valhalla. But that wasn't me. I wasn't going to choose who lived or died or who traveled to somewhere better. Everyone deserved to make that choice for themselves.

"We should get going," Freddie said after a moment. "Fadil's going to meet us there?"

I nodded. "Don't want to be late for the end of all things," I said.

Freddie and I walked to her car and took off. We had to drive to the past so that we could face the future.

# SIXTY

LIKE I SAID, the plan was simple. But simple doesn't always mean easy.

Step 1: Arrange to broadcast the miracle. I was going to do something that would change the world—something that could potentially end the world as we knew it—but I wanted to warn people first in order to keep the panic to a minimum. For that I needed someone who could broadcast my message. Mrs. Haimovitch gave me the card of the reporter she'd caught snooping around after the shooting. His name was Lou Johnson and he was a reporter for an Internet news site with a rabid following. Though he was initially hesitant to meet me, seeing as Mrs. Haimovitch had drugged him and showed him her colon the last time he'd come around, the promise of a live, exclusive miracle proved irresistible.

Step 2: Choose a location for the speech I was prepared to give and for the miracle that would follow. That part was easiest of all. It only seemed fitting that we end at the beginning.

Step 3: Show up. That proved to be the most difficult part of my plan. As Freddie and I neared our destination, fear began to gnaw at me. I believed I was making the right decision, but there were so many ways it could go wrong. What if the voices were right and I failed? I'd be dooming the entire world to die rather than simply those the voices would have left behind.

Freddie must have sensed my trepidation, because she took my hand and held it as we pulled into the Starbucks parking lot where Mama, Fadil, Naomi, and Javi were already waiting for us.

"You can do this, Elena," Freddie said. "You're the Miracle Girl. You're my Miracle Girl."

"I'm not a miracle," I said.

She smiled. "You are to me."

We parked the car and I walked alone to the patio to meet Lou Johnson while Freddie went to stand with the others. I'd already gone over the plan with them, so there was nothing left to discuss. They knew what I was going to do and had come only to offer their support.

Lou definitely had a face for television. Strong jaw,

perfect hair, bright smile, and a deep, soothing voice that might have lulled me to sleep if I hadn't been so nervous. While one of his assistants fitted me with a body mic, Lou explained that he would provide an introduction and then the rest was up to me. I didn't know if he honestly expected I was going to perform a miracle live for his viewers to see, but I doubted it mattered to him. I'd do what I'd promised or I'd fail spectacularly and expose myself as a fraud. Either way, it was certain to boost his website's hits. The only thing I was unsure of was whether it was possible to broadcast the miracle. Previous attempts to record me healing someone had failed. I hadn't told Lou that, though, because, for me, the speech I'd prepared was the important part, and whether the camera caught the miracle or not, when I was done the entire world would believe.

And then it was time. I stood on the Starbucks patio where, only a few weeks earlier, David Combs had tried to murder Winifred Petrine and had changed my life. A small crowd, which included Tori Thrash and Deputy Akers, had gathered outside to watch. My old manager, Kyle, stood with his face pressed to the glass. Mama, Fadil, Naomi, Freddie, and Javi waited for me behind the camera.

I didn't hear much of Lou Johnson's introduction before he nodded and turned the circus over to me.

This was the moment. This was the time. I'd made my choice, and all I could do now was see it through.

I stared straight ahead into the camera, smiled, and said, "Hello, my name is Elena Maria Mendoza, and I've come to end the world."

# SIXTY-ONE

"HELLO, MY NAME is Elena Maria Mendoza, and I've come to end the world.

"Some of you may already know who I am. You may have heard that I was born of a virgin or that I healed a young woman who was shot right here at Starbucks. You may have heard that I am a fraud, that my ability to perform miracles is a lie perpetrated by a lonely, mentally ill young woman desperate for attention. Or you may have no idea who I am at all. Either way, I'm about to tell you the truth, and when I'm done, you'll have a decision to make. One that will change the course of human history.

"It is true that my mother conceived me through the process of parthenogenesis. This is a fact, conclusively proven by Dr. Willard Milner, who went on to publish numerous peer-reviewed scientific papers about me and my mother. I'm not going to explain what parthenogenesis is. Google it yourself.

"It is also true that on September thirteenth, on the patio of this Starbucks, a young man named David Combs shot a young woman in the stomach, that I healed her, and that, as a result, a beam of light from the sky enveloped David Combs and caused him to vanish. At the same time, though I didn't know it, four other people around the world were also raptured.

"The apocalypse began at Starbucks, and I was the cause.

"Beginning when I was a young girl, I heard voices that spoke to me through inanimate objects. A stuffed Cthulhu doll, a tampon box, a My Little Pony named Snippity Snap. On September thirteenth, a voice from the siren in the Starbucks window told me I had the power to heal Freddie as I knelt on the pavement watching her bleed to death. I didn't believe the voices at first. Who would? But left with no other option than to watch a beautiful young woman die, I closed my eyes and attempted a miracle. That Freddie is alive today is proof that I succeeded.

"It wasn't until later that the voices warned me humanity was in danger—that we were facing extinction from an unknown threat to the world—and that I alone had the power to save us. I healed a cat with a damaged leg, my neighbor's hip, a little boy of cystic fibrosis, and many others. What I didn't know then was that each time I healed someone, it enabled the voices to rapture people from across the globe. I don't know where the voices come from or where those who have been taken go. The voices assured me they've gone to a better place. But once I realized the tradeoff, I began to doubt the mission I'd been given.

"See, the voices offered me a choice. Heal the sick and allow them to take people against their will or do nothing and doom humanity to death. The problem is that it's not my choice to make.

"I don't know how the world will end. I don't know if it will end. I do believe the voices are right that humanity is in danger. We make terrible choices. I've spent the last few weeks attempting to understand why David Combs tried to shoot my friend. I learned that he was bullied by his class-mates. That he was rejected by a girl he liked. That he was in love with a girl who didn't know he existed and that he had problems at home. I doubt I'll ever really understand why he did it. But I know he made the choice of his own free will. He could have chosen not to bring a gun to Starbucks that day. He could have chosen to ask to sit with us instead of trying to shoot Freddie. He could have asked for help in any of a thousand different ways. But he didn't.

"We make bad choices and we have to live with the

consequences of our actions. My neighbor, Mrs. Haimovitch, drove her daughter away because of a mistake, and it's a mistake she lives with every day. I have made more mistakes than I can possibly list. We kill each other and ignore the people around us who desperately need our help. We choose to pollute the planet and fight wars and to refuse to see each other as equals and deserving of respect. If and when our world ends, it won't be from a meteor or a viral outbreak or some other cosmic event; it will be us. We will be our own undoing. If we continue on the self-destructive path we're on, we will surely annihilate ourselves.

"But we can change. We can choose.

"We can choose to allow unseen forces to save us or we can choose to save ourselves. We can choose to be better, we can choose to fight. And we might lose—the world still might end—I can't promise it won't. Because, as a wise woman once told me, there is no light at the end of the tunnel. We are all stumbling through the dark, but we're not alone. You're not alone. We can walk together, and we can carry those who can't walk.

"Today, I'm giving you back the choice the voices attempted to steal from you. I'm going to do something the voices never intended. I'm going to perform a miracle, and when I'm done, the same lights that opened from the sky and raptured David Combs and so many others will appear all across the world. I will hold them open for as long as I'm able, and those who wish to leave may do so.

"I don't know what you're going to find on the other side. You may discover a better life. You may not. I won't blame you for going. The world is a mess, the fear feels inescapable sometimes, and I won't deny that starting over somewhere else is tempting. But you deserve to make that choice for yourself.

"I also don't know what will happen to those who stay. It's possible we'll all die in a matter of months. It's possible we'll destroy ourselves and each other. But it's also possible we'll choose to build a better world. To change course and thrive. The apocalypse started at Starbucks the moment I healed Winifred Petrine, and by doing this now I may be ending the world as we know it, but it is only one end, not *the* end. Not for those of us who stay and fight. Because we are the choice. We are the change."

# SIXTY-TWO

LEGO GANDALF HAD hinted that I had the ability to open the portals on my own when I'd asked if I could bring back Ava Sutter for Tori. The brass horse had confirmed it by showing me how to rapture Carmen Ballard, Harrison Bartlett, and the man watching Sofie and Conor.

I glanced away from the camera, over at where Mama, Fadil, Naomi, Freddie, and Javi stood watching me. I thought about Conor and Sofie and Mrs. Haimovitch. I drew strength from my love for them and their love for me—even from Javi—as I closed my eyes.

The crack in the darkness was easy to find now that I knew what to look for. When I'd opened it before, I'd only had to pry it apart enough to allow the light to take a couple of people, but this time I had to split it wide open without destroying the world, and hold it open long enough for those who wanted to escape to do so.

I wedged myself into the fissure, and as the light shot from the fracture and through me, I understood everything. I was an anomaly. My birth had created the tear. It had started small, barely a pinhole, but it had been enough for the voices to speak to me. And every time I healed someone, the voices slowly widened the rip between our worlds, allowing them to take more people as a result. It was like stretching an ear by slowly increasing the gauge of the plug, and the danger of what I was doing was that forcing the hole open too quickly could cause a rupture that might never seal and would consume us all.

So I worked carefully, pushing the fracture open until it was as wide as I could make it.

Beams of light shot from the sky and struck the ground on every continent, in every country and city and village. Thousands of them, tens of thousands—17,703 to be exact, some over a mile in circumference—all leading to somewhere. Better? Maybe. Different? Definitely.

I opened my eyes and wavered on my feet. Freddie and Mama rushed to my side to keep me from falling. Holding the portals open was taking every bit of my strength and concentration.

The small crowd outside of Starbucks had created a space

around a beam of light that had come down on the patio right where David Combs had vanished. The camera was no longer watching me. It was focused on the light. Tori Thrash pushed her way to the portal. She didn't look at me. She didn't look back. She walked into the light without hesitation and disappeared.

"I don't know how long I'll be able to keep them open," I said. "So make your choice. Stay or go. It's up to you."

# SIXTY-THREE

I STOOD BACK, watching the fallout from what I'd done, wondering what was going to happen next. I'd performed a miracle for all to see, but I suspected it would be my last.

Freddie slipped her hand into mine. "That was quite a speech," she said. "A little preachy though, don't you think?"

"Maybe."

We stood together in the parking lot and watched more people walk into the light. Kyle went, which didn't surprise me. I saw Javi eyeing it too, and I wasn't sure what he'd decide.

"So," Freddie said, "the world didn't end, and I think I'm ready for that kiss now."

"What if I'm not?"

"What if I don't give a fuck—"

But of course I was ready. I pulled Freddie to me and kissed her. The world dropped out from under me and we flew. I wrapped my arms around her and time contracted to encompass me and her and her lips on mine forever.

"Wow," Freddie said when I finally forced myself to pull away.

"I guess I had one miracle left in me after all."

"Don't flatter yourself, Mary."

# SIXTY-FOUR

I HELD THE portals open for a week. And though it grew more difficult with each passing day, I was determined to keep them open as long as I could to give those who were considering leaving the chance to make up their minds.

Opening the portals had thrown the world into chaos as broadcasts of my speech spread around the globe, translated into every language. Some nations, like North Korea, forbade its citizens from using the portals to escape. Others, plagued by overpopulation, encouraged it. But no one could force anyone else to choose.

"I can't find the bowls," Naomi called from kitchen.

Mrs. Haimovitch had announced she was holding her Sunday dinner on Saturday, and she'd invited me and Mama and the kids, Fadil and Naomi, and even Javi, though I'd tried to talk her out of it. We'd run out of dishes and I'd volunteered to fetch extras from our apartment, and Naomi had volunteered to help me.

"Cabinet over the sink," I said, coming from my room with a clean shirt for Conor, because of course he'd managed to spill soda on himself within the first ten minutes.

Naomi pulled out the bowls and set them on the counter by the plates she'd already found. "Do you think we need anything else?"

"Probably not," I said. I stood, looking at Naomi for a moment. She'd come with Fadil, and even though I'd told them the dinner was casual, she'd worn a pretty, short skirt and a sleeveless top.

"What?" Naomi asked. "Do I have something in my teeth?"

I shook my head. "You make Fadil happy," I said.

"Okay?"

I hadn't spent enough time alone with Naomi to know her well, and the truth was that I thought Fadil could do better, but it was his choice to make, not mine. "You know he's one of the good ones, right?"

Naomi leaned against the counter and folded her arms across her chest. "Is this some jealous thing?" she asked. "You tell me you'll break my nose if I hurt him or something?"

"I wouldn't have put it that way," I said. "It's just that he's special, and he really likes you. He even tried to get me to arrange for the two of you to accidentally run into each other, and then you did and I want to make sure you know he's not like other guys."

A smile crept across Naomi's lips. "It wasn't an accident."

"What wasn't?"

"Fadil running into me at the bookstore," she said. "I'd seen him there before, so I started going every Saturday hoping he'd notice me and talk to me." Naomi's smile morphed into a grin. "Don't tell him, though. He loves the idea that it was a chance encounter."

My opinion of Naomi rose immensely in that moment. Not only had she made their meeting happen, but she understood Fadil well enough to let him believe fate had brought them together.

"Are you going to leave?" I asked. "You'll break his heart if you do."

Naomi shrugged. "I don't know what's on the other side of those portals. And it's like you said, Fadil's one of the good ones. I'm not sure whether our relationship is going to last, but I think he's worth sticking around for to find out."

"I hope he's not your only reason for staying," I said. "I love Fadil, but making a decision like this because of a boy is kind of dumb."

"I've got other reasons for sticking around," she said. "My

grandfather's one, thanks to you. And I'm kind of hoping you and I can be friends."

As much as I wanted to keep Fadil to myself, I supposed there were worse people to share him with than Naomi Brewer. "Yeah," I said. "I think I'd like that."

We carried the dishes downstairs and I spotted Javi parking his car, so I handed my bowls off to Naomi, sent her inside, and walked over to meet him.

The joyful sounds of laughter and conversation echoed from within Mrs. Haimovitch's apartment, and Javi motioned at the door with his chin. "Sounds like a wild party going on."

"Mrs. Haimovitch's daughter and her grandchildren are here," I said. "Katie saw my speech and decided it was time to let go of the past."

A wide smile cut Javi's face. "So it's not the end of the world after all."

"Not today." We walked around the grassy edge of the parking lot, but I finally had to sit on the curb before I collapsed. "Are you going to go?" I asked Javi.

"Should I?"

"I don't know."

He seemed to think about it for a moment. Then he shook his head. "Nah. If there's no you on that other world, what's the point?"

I couldn't help laughing. "You know we're never getting back together though, right?"

"Never say never, Elena Mendoza."

"Never."

"Maybe?"

"Never, Javi. Not on this world or any other."

Javi sighed and nudged me with his shoulder. "Can't blame me for trying."

"Yeah," I said. "I really can."

Javi helped me up. "Come on, let's go join the others. I'm starving."

# SIXTY-FIVE

IT SURPRISED NO one that our wannabe dictatorial president left on the second day, despite making an impassioned speech urging all patriotic Americans to stay and promising he would do so himself. He slipped away in the middle of the night, along with his closest advisers, leaving the government in a state of disarray, though I had a feeling we were going to be better off for it.

I'm not sure how many left during the week I held the portals open. Some estimates put it at nearly a billion, others at over half the world's population. There were countless reasons to leave, and I couldn't blame anyone who made the decision to do so.

On the last day, I made an announcement that I would close the portals at sundown, and anyone who wanted to leave needed to do so by then. I asked Freddie and Fadil to take me to the beach, where we walked along the shore. One of the immense portals shone down into the ocean, and it looked like the sky was raining sunlight. We watched a boat full of people motoring toward it, and when they were near enough, twelve dove into the water and swam to another world.

"You could leave, you know," I said. "I would understand."

"Nah," Fadil said. "My parents don't want to go. They said the world is shit, but it's worth fighting for. Plus, I talked to Naomi about taking things slow and she's cool with it, so I've got that to look forward to."

I glanced at Freddie, who shrugged. "I'm not sure anything would be better there. I mean, don't you think we'd just drag our problems with us?"

"Maybe not."

"But probably," Fadil said.

Freddie took my hand and leaned into me. We'd spent a lot of time over the past week kissing, and I never wanted it to end.

"It's too easy to turn our backs on the shit we don't like," Freddie said. "Change doesn't happen because we hope for it; we have to work for it. And I kind of like working with you."

"Is that so?" I said with an impish grin.

"Sometimes."

"Well, I kind of like working with you, too."

Fadil made gagging noises, and I punched him in the arm.

We walked along a little farther. "Sean left," I said. "He came by the house to say good-bye to the kids, but they weren't there. Which turned out to be a good thing, because Mama punched him."

"Good riddance," Fadil said.

Freddie added, "That figures."

"Right?"

"Tori's parents left too," Freddie said. "Most of my friends did, actually."

"They might be the smart ones."

"I don't know," Fadil said. "I think we're going to be all right."

"That's because you have faith," I said.

But Fadil shook his head. "It's because I have you. Both of you now, I suppose."

When it became too difficult for me to walk, we sat in the sand. The sun was waning and I felt my strength ebbing with it. My grip on the portals was becoming tenuous.

"Do you think you made the right choice?" Freddie asked.

I'd spent much of the last week—the time not spent making out with Freddie—wondering the same thing. "I'm honestly not sure," I said. "But at least this way, the ones who left got to make that decision for themselves."

"What happens if the world ends?" Freddie said.

"Maybe it already has," I said, "and this is it. Now we have the opportunity to start over and try to do better this time around."

Fadil nodded. "For what it's worth, I think you did the right thing."

I hoped I had, but there was no way to truly know for sure.

"It's time," I said. Freddie and Fadil helped me stand, and I walked to the water's edge. I closed my eyes and returned to the rupture in the void. When I'd opened it, I'd also seen how to close it for good. And when I was done, I'd no longer be Miracle Girl. When I was done, we'd be on our own. I'd be nothing more than Elena Mendoza, and that would have to be enough.

"What do you think will happen after?" Freddie asked.

"I don't know," I said. "But we're about to find out."

# ACKNOWLEDGMENTS

EVERY BOOK HAS its own unique set of challenges, and I wouldn't have gotten through them without the help of so many amazing people.

I want to thank Amy Boggs for helping me shape this idea in its early stages, Michael Strother for seeing its potential, and Liesa Abrams for helping me bring Elena's story to life.

I'd like to thank my agent, Katie Shea Boutillier, for her fierce and tireless work on my behalf, even when it interrupted her maternity leave (sorry about that again!), as well as everyone at Donald Maass Literary Agency. It is an honor and a pleasure to work with so many dedicated folks.

This is my eighth book with Simon Pulse, but S&S feels more like a family to me than a publisher. I couldn't do any of this without their support. I'd like to thank Faye Bi for her extraordinary work getting me where I need to be, Adam

Smith for keeping my commas in line, Anthony Parisi, Mara Anastas, Mary Marotta, Mary Nubla, Jessica Smith, Sarah McCabe, Catherine Hayden, Lauren Hoffman, Chelsea Morgan, Michelle Leo, Sara Berko, Ian Reilly, Christina Pecorale and the sales team, Desiree Vecchio and the Simon & Schuster Audio team, and everyone I haven't had the opportunity to meet yet. Working with you all on every book is an adventure and a joy. Thank you.

Thank you to every teacher, librarian, and bookseller—the ones I've met and the ones I haven't—for being such amazing advocates. Not only for my books, but for all books.

As always, I owe so much to my family for their support. I wrote this book during a particularly dark time in my life, and they carried me when I couldn't walk.

This book would have collapsed if not for my best friend and first reader, Rachel Melcher. Her honesty helped me see my flaws, and her encouragement kept me from giving up.

I'd like to thank my brother and his husband, Syrus, for giving me a place to crash for the winter and for letting me pace their apartment and figure out the plot of this book.

Lastly, I'd like to thank you. All the readers who make this worthwhile. Thank you.

Turn the page for a look at another unforgettable
novel from Shaun David Hutchinson.

# DINO

I DON'T WANT TO BE HERE. SPENDING THE AFTERNOON collecting trash on the beach isn't how I wanted to spend one, or any, of my summer days. I could be sleeping or working at a job that pays me or reading or smack-talking some random kid while I kick his butt at *Paradox Legion* online. Instead, I'm here. At the beach. Picking up beer cans and candy wrappers and ignoring the occasional used condom because there's no way I'm touching that. Not even wearing gloves.

*Dear People:*
*If you have sex on the beach, throw away your own god-damn condoms.*
*Sincerely,*
*Sick of Picking Up Your Rubbers*

"Hey, Dino!"

I look up.

"Smile!" Rafi Merza snaps a picture of me with his phone, and I'm not fast enough to give him the finger.

"Jerk."

Rafi shrugs and wraps his arm around my waist and slaps a kiss on my cheek. His carefully cultivated stubble scrubs my skin. Everything about Rafi is intentional and precise. His thick black hair swooped up and back to give it the illusion of messiness, his pink tank top to highlight his thick arms, the board shorts he thinks make his ass look good. He's right; they do. It's showing off. If I looked like Rafi, I'd want to flaunt it too. Thankfully there's an underlying insecurity to his vanity that keeps it from slipping across the border into narcissism.

"You okay?"

"I'm fine," I say. "People need to worry about themselves." I point down the beach at Dafne and Jamal, who're poking at a gelatinous mass in the sand. "I hope they know jellyfish can still sting even when they're dead."

"They'll find out one way or another." Rafi has a hint of an accent that sounds vaguely British with weird New England undertones, which makes sense since his dad's from Boston and his mom's from Pakistan by way of London.

"And I'll keep my phone out just in case," I say.

"To call the paramedics?"

"To record them getting stung."

Rafi pulls away from me. "Sure, because there's nothing funnier than someone else's pain."

"They're playing with a jellyfish, not a live grenade."

He nudges me and I catch my reflection in his sunglasses. My enormous bobble head and long nose and I don't even know what the hell's going on with my hair. "No one dragged you out here—"

"You showed up at my house at dawn with coffee and doughnuts," I say. "You know I can't resist doughnuts."

Rafi tries to take my hand, but I shake free. "I get that today's difficult for you, Dino—"

"Please don't."

"I'm here for you." Rafi raises his shades, giving me the amber-eyed puppy dog stare that snared me from across an Apple store a year ago. "If you want, we can take off and go somewhere to talk."

Looking across the beach and then into Rafi's eyes makes the offer so tempting that I go so far as to open my mouth to say yes. But then I don't. "July Cooper is dead. Talking won't change it." I kick the wet sand, sending a clod flying toward the water. "Besides, we weren't even friends."

Rafi leans his forehead against mine. He's a little shorter than me, so I have to bend down a bit. "I'm your friend, right?"

"Of course you are."

"And so are they." He doesn't have to motion to them for me to know he's talking about everyone else who's out here with us on a summer day cleaning the beach. The kids from the community center: Kandis and Jamal and Charlie and Dafne and Leon. "They're your family."

"I've got a family," I say.

Rafi kisses me softly. His lips barely graze mine, and still I flinch from the public display, but if Rafi notices, he doesn't mention it. "That's the family you were born into. We're the family you chose."

There's a moment where I feel like Rafi expects me to say something or that there's something *he's* trying to say. It charges the air between us like we're the two poles of a Jacob's ladder. But either I imagined it or the moment passes, because Rafi steps away and starts walking down the shore, linking his first finger through mine and pulling me along with him.

The sun beats on us as we keep working to clean the beach. It's an impossible task but still worthwhile. My arms and legs are pink, and I have to stop to apply more sunscreen. I try to convince Rafi to put some on too, but he claims it defeats the purpose of summer. I'm kind of jealous of the way Rafi's skin turns a rich brown in the sun rather than a crispy red like mine.

"Don't forget about the party tonight," Rafi says as he rubs sunscreen into my back.

"What party?"

"It's not actually a party. The gang, pizza, pool, movies. Nothing too exciting."

My whole body tenses, and Rafi must feel it because he stops rubbing. "You don't have to come. I thought it'd be better than sitting home alone."

"The funeral's tomorrow, so I should probably—"

"I get it—"

"It's not that I don't want to see you—"

"Of course, of course."

This time there's no electricity in the silence. No expectation. Instead, it's a void. A chasm growing wider with each passing second. I know I should throw Rafi a line before the distance between us expands too far, but I don't know what to say.

"My offer stands," Rafi says.

I sigh heavily without meaning to. "If I change my mind about the party—"

"Not the party. The funeral. If you want me to go with you, I will."

"You don't have to."

"Have you ever seen me in my black suit?" he asks. "I look like James Bond. But, you know, browner."

I can't help laughing because it's impossible to tell whether Rafi's bragging or begging for compliments. "While the thought of you doing your best sexy secret agent impersonation is tempting, I think I need to go to the funeral alone."

Rafi squeezes my shoulders and says, "Yeah, okay," before finishing with the sunscreen. Funerals are awful, especially if you don't know the person who's died, but I can't help feeling like Rafi's disappointed.

"Come on," I say. "I probably need to get home soon." I pull Rafi the way he pulled me earlier, but instead of following, he digs his feet into the sand. His lips are turned down, and he's looking at the ground instead of at my face.

I covertly glance around to make sure no one's watching, and then I brush his cheek with my thumb and kiss him. "Fine. I'll consider coming tonight."

Rafi's face brightens immediately. He goes from pouty lips to dimples and smiles in under a second. "Really?"

"Maybe," I say.

"Maybe closer to yes or maybe closer to no?"

This time when I kiss him, I don't care if we've got an audience. "Maybe if you agree to go with me to Kennedy Space Center before the end of the summer, I'll think real hard about making an appearance."

Rafi turns up his nose. "But I went there in middle school, and it's *so* boring."

"Compromise is the price you pay for being my boyfriend."

"Fine." Rafi rolls his eyes dramatically. "But this relationship is getting pretty expensive."

"You're rich. You can afford it." I grab his hand. "Now, let's get out of here before I change my mind."

# DINO

I'M SITTING AT THE KITCHEN TABLE TRYING TO EAT DINNER when my mom stomps into the room and twirls. "Think this is okay for dinner with the Kangs tonight?" She's wearing a black dress with a fitted corset top that accentuates her curvy hips, black fishnet stockings, and combat boots, and she even straightened her platinum blond hair for the occasion. Both of her arms are covered in tattoos depicting scenes from her favorite comic books.

"Are you taking them to a club in the 1990s?"

"Smartass." My mom's basically goth Peter Pan, but I admire her devotion to the Church of Monochromism.

"Kidding. You look nice."

Mom smiles and kisses the top of my head. "What're you doing?"

I hold up my spoon. "Eating dinner."

"Cereal is not dinner."

"Then I'm eating a meal that's not dinner but will take the place of dinner tonight."

"You were supposed to get your dad's sense of humor and *my* sense of fashion, not the reverse."

I glance at my outfit. I'd showered and changed into a T-shirt and jean shorts when I got home from the beach. "Are you criticizing my style?"

Mom pats my cheek. "Kid, the way you dress isn't style in the same way that cereal isn't dinner."

"Ouch," I say. "This coming from the woman who believes that all clothes, shoes, and makeup should come in one and only one color."

"Hey! I have a blue dress up there." Mom taps her chin. "Somewhere." I'm hoping she's going to disappear the way she came, but she pulls out a chair and sits across from me. "How you holding up?"

"I'd be better if people would stop asking me that."

"July was your best friend."

"Was," I say. "But she's been dead to me for a year, so can you drop it?" My left fist starts trembling, and I have to drop my spoon because I didn't realize I was gripping it so tightly. These last few days it feels like everyone's waiting for me to melt down, and I'm starting to think they're not going to leave me alone until I do. But, no. I'm not going to give them the satisfaction of doing the thing they presume is inevitable. "I'm fine."

Mom watches me for a moment and then nods. "After . . . everything's done, I could use your help in the office. We've got Mr. Alire out there now, and Mrs. Lunievicz is being transported over tomorrow."

"I already have a summer job."

"Bussing tables at a diner isn't a job."

My eyebrows dip as I frown. "I spend a set amount of time at a place performing tasks dictated to me by a supervisor in exchange for an established wage." I pause and look up. "Sounds like the definition of a job to me."

Mom's hands explode with motion as she speaks. "You're wasting your talent!"

"It's my talent to waste."

"When it comes to preparing bodies, I'm good, and Dee's even better, but you could be van Gogh!" There are few things that get my mom's cold, black heart beating. Concrete Blonde popping up on shuffle, a sale on black boots, a new Anne Rice novel, and talking about my potential.

"Van Gogh was considered a failure and a madman who ultimately took his own life. I'd hardly call him an appropriate role model."

"Why can't you be more like your sister?" Mom says.

Speaking of perfect offspring, Delilah waltzes through

the kitchen door. She got my mom's hourglass figure and my dad's sunny disposition. She's the optimal genetic mix of our parents. I wish I could hate her for it but . . . Oh, who am I kidding? I totally hate her for it.

"Because then I wouldn't be me," I say to Mom, ignoring Dee for the moment. "And aren't you the one who drilled into us the importance of owning and loving who we are? Well this is me. I eat cereal for dinner, I dress like a slob, and I plan to waste my summer cleaning strangers' dirty tables."

Mom clenches her jaw as she slowly stands. She hugs Delilah and says, "I'm going to check on your father. We'll leave in an hour."

Dee nods. When Mom is gone, she strips off her white coat, tosses it over the back of the chair, and takes Mom's place at the table. "Do I want to know what that was about?"

It takes a few seconds for my body to relax and my muscles to unclench. "I'm wasting my potential, blah, blah, blah; I'm a disappointment, etcetera." I roll my eyes.

"You're not a disappointment." Dee frowns, but it's not a natural expression for her. My sister glided out of the birth canal on a rainbow, armed with an angelic smile that bestows blessings upon anyone fortunate enough to glimpse it. "You wanna talk?"

"I swear to God if one more person asks me if I'm okay or

if I need to talk or if I'm upset about July, I'm going to burn this house to the ground."

"Mental note," Dee says. "Hide the lighters."

"I was a Boy Scout; I don't need a lighter." I get up, dump the rest of my dinner down the drain, and rinse my bowl in the sink. I flip on the garbage disposal and use the grinding hum to re-center myself and come up with a way to steer the conversation away from my mental state. "You nervous about Mom and Dad meeting Theo's parents?" I ask when I return to my seat.

Delilah groans and scrubs her face with her hands. "The Kangs are awesome. It's our parents I'm worried about."

"Ten bucks Dad brings up skin slippage before the entrées."

"I'll murder him if he does." Dee's eyes narrow and her lips pucker. She doesn't get angry often, but I'm familiar with the signs. I consider warning Mom to keep the sharp knives away from my sister, but nah. If Dee stabs them, it'll be because they deserve it. "Do you remember what Dad told you the first time you asked him why people have to die?"

I frown, trying to recall it. "No."

She clears her throat and says, *"Death is as normal as diges-tion. People move through life the way food moves through our bodies. Their natural usefulness is extracted along the way to help enrich the world, and when they have nothing left to give, they're eliminated. Much like our bodies would clog up with excrement if we didn't defecate, the world would do the same if we didn't die.'*" Her impression of our father is scarily accurate.

I bust up laughing, which infects Dee, and once she gets started, it turns into a storm of snorting and donkey hee-haws that causes me to completely lose it until we must sound to Mom and Dad upstairs like we're torturing farm animals. I clutch my side as I stand to get a paper towel to dab the tears from my eyes.

"How did either of us turn out so normal?" Delilah asks. Her cheeks are flush with joy where I just look splotchy.

"Who says we did? You're a fusion of their weirdest parts, and I have no idea what I'm doing with my life."

Delilah reaches across the table and rests her hand on mine. "You'll figure it out, Dino. You always do." She smiles. "And if you don't want to work here, don't."

"It's DeLuca and *Son's*," I say.

"Names can be changed."

I sigh. "It's going to be weird not having you in the house once you're married."

"I won't be far," Delilah says. "We're planning to tell the parents at dinner, but Theo and I closed on a house last week that's only twenty minutes from here."

"Great," I say. "Now I'll never get rid of you."

"Probably not."

"So you're really marrying Theo, huh?" The Wedding has ruled our lives for the last six months. Not a day goes by when there isn't something that needs to be decided or tasted or fitted. But Theo's a cool guy, and he loves my sister, which proves that there really is someone for everyone, even over-achieving perfectionists who spend their days with the dead.

Delilah leans back in her chair. "That's what the invitations say."

"I thought they said you where marrying Thea?"

"Those were the old invitations."

"Thea's going to be disappointed."

"She'll move on." Dee glances at the time on the microwave. "And I should be doing the same. Can't show up to dinner smelling like corpses."

I fidget with my thumbs. "How do you know you're in love with Theo?"

Delilah freezes for a moment, narrows her eyes. "Is this about Rafi? Are you in love with him?"

I shake my head. "Just curious."

She relaxes, but there's a second where I think she's not going to answer. It was a stupid question anyway. But then she says, "You know how I used to keep that map on my wall with the thumbtacks in each place I wanted to visit?"

"Yeah?"

"When I couldn't sleep, I'd stare at the map and imagine

the adventures I'd go on. Backpacking through Bangkok, watching the stars from Iceland, eating noodles in Shanghai. But in those fantasies, I was alone."

"That's because you didn't have any friends."

Delilah slaps my arm. "I had friends!"

"Dad doesn't count."

"Jerk." Dee shakes her head at me. "Anyway. Theo and I had been dating for a couple of years, and I was in bed and couldn't sleep, so I started thinking about that map and the places I wanted to go. Only, this time I wasn't alone on my journeys. Theo was with me. He'd slipped into my life, and now I can't imagine my life without him."

"Gross." I mime puking onto the floor and even make the gagging sounds to go with it.

Delilah stands for real this time. "Love's only gross when you're not in it."

# DINO

PEOPLE, LIKE CATS, ARE OBSESSED WITH BOXES. CATS are content to squeeze their own furry asses into boxes clearly too small for them, whereas humans take sadistic pleasure in trying to shove one another into boxes. Slut boxes and Bitch boxes and Nerd boxes and Thug boxes. "He was such a nice" white boys often get to pick their own luxury boxes, unless they don't fit sexuality or gender norms, in which case they're crammed into Fag boxes and tossed out with the Trash boxes.

We claim this type of forced categorization provides us the ability to define our place in the world, and that, paradoxically, it's what's on the inside that truly counts. But once we stuff someone into a box, what's on the inside no longer matters. The boxes that are supposed to help us understand one another ultimately wedge us further apart. Even worse is that we rage against the artificial divisions the boxes create, claim that we're more complex and complicated than how we're defined by others, and then turn around and stuff the next person we meet into one and tape the lid shut.

And then, as if the indignity of life isn't enough, when a person dies, we cram what's left of them into one final box for eternity.

I thought I knew everything there was to know about July Cooper and that she'd known all there was to know about me. We'd spent more than half of our seventeen years on earth together, spreading the contents of who we were across Palm Shores, marveling at the complexities of one another. Then in one moment, I swept her up, crammed her into a box, closed it, and wrote "Ex–Best Friend" on the outside. And she did the same to me.

But boxes are meant to be unpacked. They're not intended to be filled and shut and stuffed into a dark corner to rot. If someone had asked me a month ago how I felt about July Cooper, I would have told them I didn't care, but now that she's gone, I want to unpack her. To unpack us and the myriad crap we stuffed into each other's boxes. I can't, though, and that's my fault. But I can see her one last time.

As soon as Mom and Dad and Dee leave to meet the Kangs for dinner, I walk across the lawn to the office and let myself into the prep room. I never go through the showroom unless I have no other choice.

Most people believe the preparation room is the creepiest part of a mortuary. The process of embalming bodies and readying them for burial sounds ghoulish to them, but that aspect of the business doesn't bother me. What I find grotesque is how people empty their wallets for caskets they're going to spend a couple hours looking at before burying them in the ground. It's not like they're burying fine art that's going to appreciate in value over time and that they can exhume in twenty years. They'd be better off digging a hole, throwing stacks of cash inside, and burying that instead.

The prep room is stainless steel and impeccably clean, which makes sense seeing as Dee was the last person to leave; her nightly cleaning ritual borders on obsessive. Two large sinks dominate one wall, with metal embalming tables at the stations, empty but ready for use; the other wall is covered with cabinets containing chemicals and tools of the trade; a small desk sits in the corner; and a large freezer takes up most of the space on the far side of the room. All of it lit by bright halogen bulbs instead of those flickering fluorescents that make even the living look dead.

See? Nothing creepy about the prep room, and it's cleaner than most restaurant kitchens.

I open the freezer door. There are two bodies inside.